INFERNO

By Troy Denning

INFERNO

TROY DENNING

DEL REY • NEW YORK

Star Wars®: Legacy of the Force: Inferno is a work of fiction. Names, places, and incidents either are products of the author's imagination or are used fictitiously.

A Del Rey Books Mass Market Original

Copyright © 2007 by Lucasfilm Ltd. & ® or ™ where indicated. All rights reserved. Used under authorization.

Round-Robin Interview © 2007 Lucasfilm Ltd. & ® or ™ where indicated.

Excerpt from *Star Wars®: Legacy of the Force: Fury* copyright © 2007 by Lucasfilm Ltd. & ® or ™ where indicated. All rights reserved. Used under authorization.

Published in the United States by Del Rey, an imprint of Random House, a division of Penguin Random House LLC, New York.

DEL REY and the HOUSE colophon are registered trademarks of Penguin Random House LLC.

This book contains an excerpt from *Star Wars®: Legacy of the Force: Fury* by Aaron Allston. This excerpt has been set for this edition only and may not reflect the final content of the published book.

ISBN 978-0-345-47755-2
Ebook ISBN 978-0-345-51053-2

Printed in the United States of America

starwars.com
randomhousebooks.com

For Jeffrey Olsen
Neighbor and friend

acknowledgments

Many people contributed to this book in ways large and small. I would like to thank them all, especially the following: Andria Hayday for her support, critiques, and many valuable suggestions; James Luceno, Leland Chee, Howard Roffman, Amy Gary, Pablo Hidalgo, and Keith Clayton for their fine contributions during our brainstorming sessions—initial and otherwise; Shelly Shapiro and Sue Rostoni for *everything,* from their remarkable patience to their insightful reviewing and editing to the wonderful ideas they put forth both inside and outside of the brainstorming sessions—and especially for being so great to work with; to my fellow writers, Aaron Allston and Karen Traviss, for all their hard work—coordinating stories *and* writing them—and their myriad other contributions to this book and the series; to Laura Jorstad for her attention to detail; to all the people at Lucasfilm and Del Rey who make being a writer so much fun; and, finally, to George Lucas for letting us take his galaxy in this exciting new direction.

THE STAR WARS LEGENDS NOVELS TIMELINE

BEFORE THE REPUBLIC
37,000-25,000 YEARS BEFORE
STAR WARS: A New Hope

c. 25,793 *YEARS BEFORE STAR WARS: A New Hope*

Dawn of the Jedi: Into the Void

OLD REPUBLIC
5000-67 YEARS BEFORE
STAR WARS: A New Hope

Lost Tribe of the Sith: The Collected
Stories

3954 *YEARS BEFORE STAR WARS: A New Hope*

The Old Republic: Revan

3650 *YEARS BEFORE STAR WARS: A New Hope*

The Old Republic: Deceived
Red Harvest
The Old Republic: Fatal Alliance
The Old Republic: Annihilation

1032 *YEARS BEFORE STAR WARS: A New Hope*

Knight Errant
Darth Bane: Path of Destruction
Darth Bane: Rule of Two
Darth Bane: Dynasty of Evil

RISE OF THE EMPIRE
67-0 YEARS BEFORE
STAR WARS: A New Hope

67 *YEARS BEFORE STAR WARS: A New Hope*

Darth Plagueis

33 *YEARS BEFORE STAR WARS: A New Hope*

Cloak of Deception
Darth Maul: Shadow Hunter
Maul: Lockdown

32 *YEARS BEFORE STAR WARS: A New Hope*

> **STAR WARS: EPISODE I**
> **THE PHANTOM MENACE**

Rogue Planet
Outbound Flight
The Approaching Storm

22 *YEARS BEFORE STAR WARS: A New Hope*

> **STAR WARS: EPISODE II**
> **ATTACK OF THE CLONES**

22-19 *YEARS BEFORE STAR WARS: A New Hope*

> **STAR WARS: THE CLONE**
> **WARS**

The Clone Wars: Wild Space
The Clone Wars: No Prisoners

Clone Wars Gambit
  Stealth
  Siege

Republic Commando
  Hard Contact
  Triple Zero
  True Colors
  Order 66

Shatterpoint
The Cestus Deception
MedStar I: Battle Surgeons
MedStar II: Jedi Healer
Jedi Trial
Yoda: Dark Rendezvous
Labyrinth of Evil

19 *YEARS BEFORE STAR WARS: A New Hope*

> **STAR WARS: EPISODE III**
> **REVENGE OF THE SITH**

Kenobi
Dark Lord: The Rise of Darth Vader
Imperial Commando 501st

Coruscant Nights
  Jedi Twilight
  Street of Shadows
  Patterns of Force
The Last Jedi

10 *YEARS BEFORE STAR WARS: A New Hope*

The Han Solo Trilogy
  The Paradise Snare
  The Hutt Gambit
  Rebel Dawn

The Adventures of Lando Calrissian
The Force Unleashed
The Han Solo Adventures
Death Troopers
The Force Unleashed II

REBELLION
0–5 YEARS AFTER
STAR WARS: A New Hope

Death Star
Shadow Games

0

STAR WARS: EPISODE IV
A NEW HOPE

Tales from the Mos Eisley Cantina
Tales from the Empire
Tales from the New Republic
Scoundrels
Allegiance
Choices of One
Honor Among Thieves
Galaxies: The Ruins of Dantooine
Splinter of the Mind's Eye
Razor's Edge

3 YEARS AFTER STAR WARS: A New Hope

STAR WARS: EPISODE V
THE EMPIRE STRIKES BACK

Tales of the Bounty Hunters
Shadows of the Empire

4 YEARS AFTER STAR WARS: A New Hope

STAR WARS: EPISODE VI
THE RETURN OF THE JEDI

Tales from Jabba's Palace

The Bounty Hunter Wars
  The Mandalorian Armor
  Slave Ship
  Hard Merchandise

The Truce at Bakura
Luke Skywalker and the Shadows of Mindor

NEW REPUBLIC
5–25 YEARS AFTER
STAR WARS: A New Hope

X-Wing
  Rogue Squadron
  Wedge's Gamble
  The Krytos Trap
  The Bacta War
  Wraith Squadron
  Iron Fist
  Solo Command

The Courtship of Princess Leia
Tatooine Ghost

The Thrawn Trilogy
  Heir to the Empire
  Dark Force Rising
  The Last Command

X-Wing: Isard's Revenge

The Jedi Academy Trilogy
  Jedi Search
  Dark Apprentice
  Champions of the Force

I, Jedi
Children of the Jedi
Darksaber
Planet of Twilight
X-Wing: Starfighters of Adumar
The Crystal Star

The Black Fleet Crisis Trilogy
  Before the Storm
  Shield of Lies
  Tyrant's Test

The New Rebellion

The Corellian Trilogy
  Ambush at Corellia
  Assault at Selonia
  Showdown at Centerpoint

The Hand of Thrawn Duology
  Specter of the Past
  Vision of the Future

Scourge
Survivor's Quest

THE STAR WARS LEGENDS NOVELS TIMELINE

NEW JEDI ORDER
25–40 YEARS AFTER
STAR WARS: A New Hope

The New Jedi Order
Vector Prime
Dark Tide I: Onslaught
Dark Tide II: Ruin
Agents of Chaos I: Hero's Trial
Agents of Chaos II: Jedi Eclipse
Balance Point
Edge of Victory I: Conquest
Edge of Victory II: Rebirth
Star by Star
Dark Journey
Enemy Lines I: Rebel Dream
Enemy Lines II: Rebel Stand
Traitor
Destiny's Way
Force Heretic I: Remnant
Force Heretic II: Refugee
Force Heretic III: Reunion
The Final Prophecy
The Unifying Force

35 YEARS AFTER STAR WARS: A New Hope

The Dark Nest Trilogy
The Joiner King
The Unseen Queen
The Swarm War

LEGACY
40+ YEARS AFTER
STAR WARS: A New Hope

Legacy of the Force
Betrayal
Bloodlines
Tempest
Exile
Sacrifice
Inferno
Fury
Revelation
Invincible

Crosscurrent
Riptide
Millennium Falcon

43 YEARS AFTER STAR WARS: A New Hope

Fate of the Jedi
Outcast
Omen
Abyss
Backlash
Allies
Vortex
Conviction
Ascension
Apocalypse

X-Wing: Mercy Kill

45 YEARS AFTER STAR WARS: A New Hope

Crucible

dramatis personae

Alema Rar; Jedi Knight (female Twi'lek)
Ben Skywalker; Junior GAG member (male human)
Han Solo; captain, *Millennium Falcon* (male human)
Jacen Solo; Sith Lord (male human)
Jae Juun; intelligence operative (male Sullustan)
Jagged Fel; bounty hunter (male human)
Jaina Solo; Jedi Knight (female human)
Leia Organa Solo; Jedi Knight (female human)
Luke Skywalker; Jedi Grand Master (male human)
Saba Sebatyne; Jedi Master (female Barabel)
Salle Serpa; GAG major (male human)
Tahiri Veila; Jedi Knight (female human)
Tarfang; master spy (male Ewok)
Tenel Ka; Hapan Queen Mother (female human)
Zekk; Jedi Knight (male human)

prologue

The scream and roar of combat began to reverberate through the empty grashal, and wisps of battle smoke materialized in the green beams of their helmet lamps. Jacen—now Darth Caedus, he reminded himself—continued to pull into the past, one glove clamped around the arm of Tahiri's pressure suit, the other anchored to the rim of a blaster-pitted gestation bin. The brown stains on the bin's exterior grew wet and red, and crouching forms started to manifest in the surrounding darkness.

As he drew more heavily on the Force, the sallow light of glow-lichen began to shine down through the thickening smoke, revealing the cloning lab in which Jacen's brother, Anakin, had died. Where there had been only barren vacuum a few moments before, now a pulsing jungle of white nutrient vines corkscrewed up from the gestation bins that lined the grashal floor. Streaks of color and darkness were flashing past in both directions, the air swirling with razor bugs and the floor shaking with grenade detonations.

"I hope I'm ready for this," Tahiri said. Over the suit comm, her voice sounded brittle and uncertain. "Maybe my first flow-walk shouldn't have been into the middle of a battle."

Jacen knew it was not the battle that made Tahiri nervous, but he saw no advantage in forcing her to admit it. "We'll be fine," he said. "We're ghosts here. Even if a Yuuzhan Vong sees us, he can't do us harm."

"It's *us* doing harm that worries me," Tahiri replied. "What if we change something we shouldn't—something that alters the present?"

"That's unlikely." Actually, Jacen should have said *impossible*. Any change they made in the past would be corrected by the Force, and the flow would return to its present course. But he did not explain that to Tahiri. He needed her to believe they were taking a small but terrible chance, risking temporal catastrophe to deal with her unresolved grief. "I won't let you do anything wrong. Just relax."

"*Unlikely* isn't very relaxing," Tahiri replied. "Not when you're talking about the fate of the galaxy."

"Trust me," Jacen said. "I've been flow-walking for years, and the galaxy hasn't come to an end yet."

"Not that we know of."

Tahiri turned toward the back of the grashal, where Anakin and the rest of the strike team were fighting through a breach in the wall. Their brown jumpsuits were blood-crusted and tattered, and their faces were haggard with fear and exhaustion—yet also tight with determination and resolve. This had been the objective of their mission, the cloning lab where the Yuuzhan Vong created the voxyn that had killed so many Jedi, and they would not leave until it was destroyed.

The Force began to hum with Tahiri's anger and sadness, and her hand drifted toward her lightsaber. Jacen could sense how she ached to do more than give Anakin the final kiss she had denied him at the time—how she longed to ignite her weapon and somehow prevent his approaching death.

A trio of thermal grenades detonated overhead, filling the dome with orange brilliance and spraying hot shrapnel in all directions. Nutrient vines fell in ropes of fire, and Yuuzhan Vong dropped to the floor in writhing heaps. Tahiri cringed and turned to dive for cover, but Jacen jerked her back. Shrapnel flew past without striking the pair, and flames licked at their pressure suits without melting anything.

"I *told* you we can't be harmed here," Jacen said.

"You also told me it was a coincidence we crossed paths on Anakin's anniversary day," Tahiri replied. "That doesn't mean I believe you."

Jacen frowned behind his visor. "You think I *arranged* to bump into you?"

"Come on, Jacen," Tahiri said. "I'm a smart girl."

Jacen hesitated, wondering how much she knew about what he had done a week earlier, whether she had linked their trip here to his aunt's murder on Kavan. It was foolish to think he could kill the wife of *Luke Skywalker* and avoid discovery indefinitely, yet he *had* to. Jacen had foreseen that the Confederation's boldness would soon put victory within the Alliance's grasp—but only if the Jedi did not interfere with his plans.

After a moment, Jacen said, "Okay, let's say I *did* arrange it. Why did you come?"

"Because I was tempted," Tahiri answered. "And I want to find out what you need from me."

"I don't need anything," Jacen lied. "I just thought this might help you move on."

"You expect me to believe that?"

"It's for Anakin, too," Jacen said. "I think my brother deserves this much . . . don't you?"

A guilty ripple rolled through the Force. "Not fair!" Tahiri protested. "And I still don't believe you."

Jacen raised the shoulders of his pressure suit in an awkward shrug. "Does that mean you don't want to go through with this?"

Tahiri sighed. "You know better than that."

"Then you have to trust my instructions," Jacen said. "You can't react to the past. The more you become a part of it, the more likely you are to be seen—and the more power it has to harm you."

"Okay, I understand." Over the suit comm, it was difficult to tell whether Tahiri's tone was resentful or embarrassed. "It won't happen again."

"Good."

Jacen turned back to the battle, where the momentary silence that had followed the grenade explosions had been shattered by screaming blaster bolts and droning razor bugs. In the back of the grashal, Anakin was just rising to his feet as the strike team took advantage of the enemy's disarray to overrun the cloning lab. When Jacen saw his own figure dodging through the battle, he remembered how sad he had been for his wounded brother, how wrong it had seemed for the war to take such a noble young life. It was like watching himself in a home holo, wondering how he could ever have been so naïve. Perhaps, once he united the galaxy, such idealism would no longer seem quite so foolish.

The boom of a longblaster sounded outside the grashal, then a trio of Jedi came rushing inside. The young Tahiri— then just fifteen—was in the lead. Her blond hair billowed behind her; the scars suffered during her imprisonment among the Yuuzhan Vong were still red on her forehead. She and the others had barely cleared the breach before a ball of yellow-orange fire followed them inside and exploded.

The shock wave hurled the Jedi in three different directions, but they quickly used the Force to bring their trajectories under control and come down safely. Young Tahiri tucked herself into a front roll and disappeared behind a gestation bin, then emerged from the other end returning to her feet. Anakin was already rushing to her side, his free hand cupped over his abdomen, his jaw clenched against the pain of his wound.

The voice of the older Tahiri came over the suit comm. "We need to move closer."

"Fine, but stay in contact with me or the current will carry you off." Still holding Tahiri's arm, Jacen started toward his brother and the young Tahiri. "And whatever you do, don't open your pressure suit. Our presences are still anchored in our own time, so you'll decompress."

"Thanks for the warning," Tahiri replied drily. "But I had kind of guessed."

Anakin and young Tahiri were now crouching together behind a gestation bin. Had his brother survived this battle, the pair would almost certainly have become lovers and then married. He sometimes wondered how that might have changed things, whether that extra bit of happiness and stability could somehow have kept the galaxy from spinning so wildly out of control.

As Jacen led the way around behind the pair, young Tahiri suddenly raised her arm and pointed across the aisle, toward a scorched bin overflowing with Yuuzhan Vong corpses. Next to the bin, the strike team's meter-high healer, Tekli, stood over the scaly bulk of Tesar Sebatyne. She was sprinkling stinksalts on the Barabel's forked tongue, trying to rouse him from his unconsciousness . . . and failing miserably.

Jacen continued to lead the way closer, moving very slowly and carefully. Flow-walkers tended to cause blurs around themselves both visually and in the Force, and the slower they moved, the less noticeable the effect would be.

As they approached, Anakin pointed toward Tekli and the wounded Barabel.

"Take him . . . and go," he said to young Tahiri. "You may need to cut a way out."

"*You?*" she responded. "I'm not going—"

"Do it!" Anakin snapped.

Her face fell, and even the older Tahiri began to radiate surprise and dismay into the Force.

Anakin's tone softened almost as soon as he had spoken. "You need . . . to help Tekli. I'll be along."

Even through a pressure suit's auditory sensors, Anakin's voice sounded weak and anguished, and it was clear that he had known even then he was about to die. A growing tightness began to form in Jacen's throat, and he was surprised at the effort of will required to make it go away. Jacen had loved his brother—and apparently still did—but he could not let his emotions draw him into the past. As he had warned Tahiri, any reaction at all would make them easier to see, and if the other strike team survivors suddenly started to recall a pair of blurry, pressure-suited apparitions at the battle, someone might realize he had flow-walked here with Tahiri—and that would make her useless to him.

By the time Jacen had quelled his emotions, Anakin had stood again. He was gently pushing young Tahiri across the aisle toward Tekli, who was kneeling astride Tesar's scaly bulk and trying to slap him awake. The Force grew heavy with older Tahiri's sorrow, but Jacen said nothing to her about the dangers of reacting to the past. He had known all along that she would not be able to control her emotions at this moment—he was *counting* on it—and he would just have to hope Tekli and the other survivors were too busy with the battle to notice any flow-walking apparitions.

"Tesar is not responding," Tekli said, looking across the aisle. "I cannot move him and work on him both."

Young Tahiri lowered her brow in doubt, clearly suspecting the Chadra-Fan of trying to draw her away from Anakin, but she could hardly refuse to help. Blinking back a tear, she stretched up to kiss Anakin—then caught herself and shook her head.

This was the moment when young Tahiri had pulled back, telling Anakin that if he wanted a kiss, he would have to come back for it. The Force seemed ready to break with the anguish of older Tahiri, who quickly stepped forward and pushed her younger self into Anakin's arms.

Young Tahiri's mouth fell open, but before she could cry out, Anakin leaned down and silenced her with a kiss. The surprise drained instantly from her posture, and they remained together, body pressed to body, for what seemed an eternity—even to Jacen, who often saw eternity in his visions.

Knowing by the sullen weight of the Force—and by his own breaking heart—that they were being drawn ever more deeply into the past, Jacen pulled the older Tahiri back to his side. If they were still there when the kiss ended, Tekli would certainly see them. In thirteen years or so— when Jacen and Tahiri returned to their own time—the Chadra-Fan would begin to recall seeing them here in their pressure suits. Once she reported her memory flashes to the Council, the Masters would realize that Jacen had flow-walked Tahiri back to the battle and begin to ask themselves why, and his plan would be ruined.

Jacen began to back them away, slowly releasing his hold on the past. The scream and roar of battle started to quiet, and the sallow light of the grashal's glow-lichens began to dim. Before long, all he could see were two forms locked in eternal embrace, their presences shining across time to illuminate the cold darkness. And then even that light faded.

A single heartbroken warble sounded over the suit comm, and Tahiri clasped the arm of Jacen's pressure suit.

"Did we have to leave?" she asked. "I wanted to see him after, to see if the kiss made his death any . . . any easier."

"I'm sorry. I couldn't let us be seen." Jacen no longer felt like Jacen inside. He was using his brother's death to manipulate Tahiri—to *corrupt* her—and it made him feel brutal and dirty. But what choice did he have? The Jedi were hunting Mara's killer with all their resources, and he needed a way to track their progress, to keep them under control while he saved the Alliance. "You were getting caught up in the past. We both were."

The strength left Tahiri's grasp, but she continued to hold his arm. "I know. It was just so . . ." She stopped and turned her faceplate toward Jacen, leaving him to stare at the anonymous reflection of his own helmet. "I thought the kiss would be enough. But it isn't, Jacen. I need—"

"Tahiri, no." It wasn't Jacen speaking now, but his new self, the one he had created when he killed Mara. "Your emotions—*my* emotions—make it too risky. We can't go back."

"I know, Jacen." Tahiri turned her back on him and started for the exit. "I just wish we didn't have to leave it that way. I wish I could be sure he died knowing how much I loved him."

Darth Caedus smiled sadly inside his helmet.

"I'm sure he knew." Caedus started after her. This was what it meant to be Sith: to use friends without hesitation, to sacrifice family for destiny, to live with a stained soul. "I mean, you *did* tell him, didn't you?"

Tenel Ka sensed the hole in the Force the instant she entered the bedchamber. It was lurking in the black depths of the corner farthest from the entrance, a void so subtle she recognized it only by the surrounding stillness. She moved quickly through the doorway, her spine tingling with a ripple of danger sense so delicate it made her blood race.

Before her lady-in-waiting could enter the room behind her, she looked back over her shoulder and called, "That will be all, Lady Aros. Ask DeDeToo to lock down the nursery."

"*Lock* it down, Majesty?" Aros stopped at the threshold, a slender silhouette still holding the evening gown Tenel Ka had just removed. "Is there something I need to—"

"Just a precaution," Tenel Ka interrupted. Her robe was still hanging inside her refresher suite, so she was standing in her underclothes. "I know our embassy should be secure, but this *is* Coruscant."

"Of course . . ." Aros dipped her chin. "The terrorists. This rach warren of a planet is absolutely teeming with them."

"Let's not be too disparaging, shall we?" Tenel Ka chided. She casually reached down and unfastened the thigh holster where she carried her lightsaber. "We *did* have to call on Colonel Solo to dispose of a few raches of our own recently."

"I didn't mean anything negative about the colonel," Aros said, practically cooing the reference to Jacen. After his recent heroics defending Tenel Ka against the traitors trying to usurp her throne, he had become something of a sex symbol to half the women in the Hapes Consortium . . . Tenel Ka included. "Quite the opposite. If not for Colonel Solo, I'm *sure* Coruscant would have sunk into anarchy by now."

"No doubt," Tenel Ka said, casually shifting her grasp on the holster so that she held her lightsaber by its hilt. "Now if you'll excuse me, I believe I can turn down my own sheets tonight."

Aros acknowledged the order with a bow and withdrew into the anteroom. Tenel Ka used her elbow to depress a tap pad on the wall. Half a dozen wall sconces glimmered to life, revealing a chamber as ridiculously opulent as the rest of the embassy's Royal Wing. There were three separate seating areas, a life-sized HoloNet transceiver, and a huge hamogoni wood desk stocked with stacks of flimsiplast bearing the Hapan Royal Crest. On the far side of the chamber, a dreamsilk canopy shimmered above a float-rest bed large enough to sleep Tenel Ka and her ten closest friends.

Despite the two sconces flanking it, the room's farthest corner—the one near her refresher suite—remained ominously dark. Tenel Ka could not sense any sort of optical field keeping it that way, but then again, the only thing she *could* sense was . . . well, nothing. She reached out with the Force to make certain Aros was not eavesdropping from the other side of the door, then ignited her lightsaber and took a few steps toward the corner.

"You would be wise to show yourself," Tenel Ka said. "I have no patience for voyeurs . . . as you should well know by now."

"I'm a slow learner." The darkness melted away, revealing a tall, shadow-eyed figure with a melancholy echo of his father's famous lopsided grin. He was dressed in black GAG utilities and smelled faintly of hyperdrive fuel, as though he had come to her straight from a space hangar. "And I don't usually get caught. My camouflage powers must be slipping."

"No, Jacen. I am just growing better at sensing your presence." Tenel Ka deactivated her lightsaber and tossed it on the bed, then smiled warmly and opened her arms to him. "I was hoping you would find time to call."

Jacen cocked his brow, then let his gaze slide down her body. "So I see."

"Well?" Tenel Ka asked. "Are you just going to stand there gawking? Or are you going to do something about it?"

Jacen chuckled, then stepped out of the corner and crossed to her. His Force presence remained undetectable—he was so accustomed to concealing himself that he did so even around Tenel Ka—but she could tell by the shine in his eyes how happy he was to see her. She slipped a hand behind his neck and drew his mouth to hers.

Jacen obliged, but his kiss was warm rather than hot, and she could tell that tonight his heart was not entirely hers. She stepped back, embarrassed to realize how insensitive she was being.

"Forgive me if I seem too joyful," she said, able to perceive now the sadness that tinged his hard eyes, the grief that tainted his clenched jaw. "Tomorrow is Mara's funeral. *Of course* you have other things on your mind."

Jacen's snort was so gentle that Tenel Ka almost did not hear it.

"It's okay." He took her hand, but the softness had vanished from his face, leaving in its place only the stoic, unreadable mask that he had worn since his escape from the Yuuzhan Vong. "I wasn't thinking about Mara."

Tenel Ka eyed him doubtfully.

"Well, not exclusively," Jacen admitted. "I'm happy to see you, too."

"Thank you, but I'm not offended," Tenel Ka said. "Our thoughts *should* be on your aunt tonight. Have you found her killer yet?"

Jacen's face flickered with emotion—whether it was anger or resentment was impossible to say—and something like guilt flashed through the Force so quickly that Tenel Ka was still trying to identify it when Jacen closed down again.

"We're still working on that." Jacen's tone was defensive, and his gaze slid away in . . . could that be shame? "We don't have many leads, and I don't like the direction they're going."

"That is very cryptic," Tenel Ka observed. "Can you—"

"Not yet," Jacen said, shaking his head. "It's still early in the investigation, and I don't want to taint anyone's reputation."

Tenel Ka frowned at the implication. "You think it was someone *inside* the GA?"

Jacen flashed a mock scowl. "Did I *say* that?"

"Yes." Tenel Ka looped her hand through the elbow of his black utilities and changed the subject. "But it was thoughtless of me to ask about the investigation, especially with the funeral tomorrow. I hope you'll—"

"Don't apologize." Jacen detached himself and moved to the nearest couch, then sat on the arm. "The truth is, I *haven't* been doing very much to find her killer. The Alliance has higher priorities at the moment."

"The war?"

Jacen nodded. "I'm sure you're receiving the military's briefing holos."

"Of course." In fact, the holos had been arriving twice a day for nearly a week now, along with urgent requests for

Hapan reinforcements, which Tenel Ka could not provide. "Don't tell me that Admiral Niathal has prevailed on you to talk me out of my last fleet?"

Instead of answering, Jacen slipped over the couch arm onto a cushion, then sat staring into the flame tube that was the focal point of the seating area.

"I see," Tenel Ka said, astonished that Jacen would agree to even attempt such a thing. He knew as well as she did that granting the Alliance request would place both their daughter and her throne in profound danger. "There is nothing to send, Jacen. As it is, the Home Fleet is barely enough to secure the Consortium from my own nobles."

"You still need to hear this." Jacen continued to stare into the swirling tongues of blue inside the flame tube. "You're aware that Corellia and Bothawui are moving against Kuat, right?"

Tenel Ka nodded. "While the Hutts and Commenor make preparations to attack Balmorra." She retrieved her dressing gown from inside the refresher, then added, "I *do* watch those holos they keep sending me."

"Sorry—just making sure," Jacen said. "But what the briefings don't say—what they *can't* say—is that after the battle at Balmorra, the Confederation is going to mass its fleets at Kuat. Whoever wins there wins the war."

"Military planners always think the next big space battle will end the war." Tenel Ka slipped the dressing gown over her shoulders and returned to the seating area. "They're usually wrong."

"This doesn't come from the planners," Jacen said. "I've *seen* it . . . in the Force."

"Oh." Tenel Ka dropped into a chair adjacent to Jacen's, stunned by the implications of what she had just heard. If Jacen's Force-vision was accurate—and she knew enough about his Force powers to think it would be—the Confederation would soon have a massive force in position to threaten Coruscant herself. "I see why you are worried."

"*Worried* might be an understatement," Jacen replied. "So would *terrified*. The Alliance just doesn't have the strength to stop them yet."

"*Yet?*" Tenel Ka asked. "Are you telling me that Thrackan Sal-Solo wasn't the only one building secret fleets?"

Jacen shook his head. "Sorry. I'm talking about the Wookiees. Kashyyyk is certain to assign their assault fleet to our command, and that will tip the balance back in the Alliance's favor."

"I doubt the Confederation is going to wait *that* long," Tenel Ka said, almost bitterly. Alliance holochannels were filled with impatient speculation about the endless debate on Kashyyyk, with the commentary ranging from simple impatience to accusations of cowardice. "Are you telling me the public reports are misdirection?"

"Not a bad idea, but no," Jacen said. "I'm telling you that our agents assure us it's a matter of *when*, not if."

"In this instance, when *is* if," Tenel Ka said. "Wookiees are very stubborn. By the time they finish their deliberations, the Confederation will be storming Coruscant."

"I hope you're wrong." Jacen tore his eyes from the flame tube, then met Tenel Ka's gaze. For once, she could sense his emotions through the Force, could feel how frightened and worried he truly was. "But I just don't know."

"I see," Tenel Ka said, finally starting to realize what Jacen was trying to tell her. "And you didn't come to ask for the Home Fleet?"

Jacen shook his head. "Not really."

"I was afraid of that." Tenel Ka sank back in her chair, calling on the Force to keep her heart rate under control, her thoughts focused. "So you only came to warn me that the Galactic Alliance is about to collapse."

"Well, that's not the *only* reason." Jacen grinned and cocked an eyebrow.

Tenel Ka groaned. "This is no time for jokes, Jacen. Your timing is worse than when we were teenagers."

"Okay, then I could use some advice instead," Jacen said, accepting the rebuff as gracefully as he had when they were younger. "Have any?"

Tenel Ka's answer was immediate. "The Jedi could do something. Perhaps they could launch a StealthX raid, or perhaps Master Skywalker could speak to—"

"I asked for advice, not wishful thinking." Jacen's voice was suddenly sharp. "The Jedi won't lift a finger to help us. They're practically traitors themselves."

"Jacen, that's not true," Tenel Ka said, refusing to be intimidated. "The Jedi have supported the Galactic Alliance since its inception, and Master Skywalker is on the same side you are. If the Alliance is to be saved, you two must put aside your differences and work together."

A flash of fear flickered through Jacen's eyes, then he looked away, reminding Tenel Ka of some petulant courtier refusing to acknowledge a rebuke.

"And if we can't?" he asked.

"Can you stop the enemy's advance *without* the Jedi?"

Jacen shook his head. "Not at the moment—and maybe not *with* them."

"Then what choice is there?" Tenel Ka made the question a command. "The Jedi Council is unhappy about your coup, but the Masters will not stand idle while the Alliance falls—especially not if you grant concessions."

Jacen fell silent a moment, then turned to face Tenel Ka. "It's more complicated than that. Luke hasn't been himself since Mara died." His dark brows arched in concern. "He barely talks to anyone, and he's drawn in on himself so far he's practically cut off from the Force."

"Surely you don't expect him to remain unaffected by his wife's death?"

"It's more than grief," Jacen said. "You heard about Lumiya?"

"I heard that he truly killed her this time." Tenel Ka's answer was cautious, for the 'Net had been full of reports linking Lumiya's death to Mara's—until the Jedi Council had issued a terse statement asserting that Lumiya's demise involved other matters. "It's hard to believe the timing was purely coincidental."

"It wasn't," Jacen said. "I'm afraid it was a vengeance killing."

"A vengeance killing?" Tenel Ka shook her head in disbelief. "Even if Master Skywalker would do such a thing, it doesn't make sense. The Jedi Council itself said that Lumiya had nothing to do with Mara's death."

"Luke didn't discover that until after he killed Lumiya— and *that's* when he began to draw in on himself." Jacen leaned forward, propping his elbows on his knees and staring at the polished larmalstone between his boots. "I think he's having a crisis of confidence, Tenel Ka. I think he's stopped trusting himself . . . *and* the Force."

Tenel Ka frowned. She had the feeling that Jacen was forcing his emotions; that he was merely *trying* to be concerned while secretly relishing his uncle's mistake. And who could blame him? Master Skywalker *had* accused Jacen of some fairly terrible things lately—such as collaborating with a Sith and staging an illegal coup—so it would only be natural to gloat when his denouncer did something even worse.

After a moment, she said, "Perhaps you're right, Jacen. That would explain why Master Sebatyne turned me away when I tried to call on your uncle."

"Luke wouldn't see *you*?" Jacen was incredulous. "Then matters are worse than I thought. He can't be up to his duties."

"That is more than understandable." While it saddened Tenel Ka to think of Master Skywalker's pain—and Ben's—she shared Jacen's alarm. *Now* was a disastrous time for the Alliance to be without its Jedi. "But Master Skywalker is not the only member of the Jedi Council. You can still ask for their help."

"I can *try*," Jacen countered. "But I've already reached out to individual Masters."

"And?"

"They're all against me." Jacen spoke matter-of-factly, merely reporting the truth as he saw it. "They think I'm trying to take advantage of the situation. Until I have Luke's support, I can talk myself breathless. The Jedi are not going to cooperate."

Tenel Ka felt a sudden deflation as she realized just how correct Jacen was. It only made sense for the Masters to close ranks at a time like this, and the growing gulf of suspicion and ill will between Master Skywalker and Jacen was hardly a secret. *Of course* they would be suspicious of any attempt to press the Jedi into service—especially while their leader remained incapacitated.

"I see." Tenel Ka rose and stood staring into the flame tube. "Perhaps if I talked to the Council—"

"And convince them *you're* part of my plan?" Jacen stood behind her. "The Council is blinded by their suspicions. They refuse to see that I'm only doing what is best for the Alliance. Anything you say will be viewed as repayment for my help against Lady AlGray and the Corellians."

Tenel Ka nodded. "You're right, of course." The true nature of their relationship remained a closely guarded secret, and only they knew that Jacen was the father of her daughter. But he *had* saved her throne, and Jedi Masters were not fools. Even if they believed she was sincere, they would suspect her judgment of being influenced by gratitude. She shook her head in despair and turned to Jacen. "What are you going to do?"

"We've given Admiral Bwua'tu command of the First and Sixth fleets, so maybe he can do something brilliant to

stop the Corellians and Bothans before they reach Kuat."
Jacen tightened his lips, then said, "But honestly, our best
hope is still the Wookiees—and that's almost no hope at
all."

Tenel Ka nodded. "The briefing holo mentioned that
they have rebuffed all attempts to hurry things."

"They have." He looked away for a long time, then finally met her gaze again. "If we can't stop the Confederation, what happens to you?"

Tenel Ka answered immediately, for it was a question to
which she had been giving much thought lately. "I'll continue to hold my throne until the rebels consolidate their
victory and turn their attention to Hapes. I'll put up a hard
fight at first, to see if I can force a peace negotiation—but I
won't subject my people to an invasion I have no hope of
stopping."

"I know you'll do the best thing for *Hapes,*" Jacen said,
sounding slightly amused. "I was asking about you and Allana."

"About us?" Tenel Ka was surprised by the question, for
the answer was as obvious as it was painful. "You must
know the answer to that already."

The color drained from Jacen's face. "What about hiding? I could ask the Fallanassi to take you in."

Tenel Ka smiled sadly. "That will work for a time,
Jacen—perhaps even until the Confederation grows tired
of looking for us. But no invader can rule Hapes without
Hapan blood on the throne, and whoever Confederation
installs as their puppet *won't* tire. The pretender will be too
frightened of me or Allana trying to return, and she'll keep
looking until we're dead."

Jacen's shoulders slumped, and he dropped back onto
the couch and cradled his head. "Then we have no choice."

"About what?" Tenel Ka asked, alarmed by the desperation in his voice. "Jacen, if you are considering using something like Alpha Red—"

"We don't have anything like that—at least nothing that wouldn't kill us, too." He took his head out of his hands and looked up. "What I mean, Tenel Ka, is that you have to give me the Home Fleet."

Tenel Ka felt her jaw drop. "Jacen, you *know* what will happen—"

"It will take even Hapan nobles time to organize a rebellion," he said. "And the Alliance only needs your fleet until the Wookiees commit."

Tenel Ka shook her head. "Jacen, I can't risk a rebellion."

"You can—and you *must*." He rose and took her by the arm. "You said yourself that any pretender to your throne would never stop looking for you."

"*I* don't matter," Tenel Ka said. Jacen was squeezing her arm so hard it hurt, but she didn't want to appear frightened or angry by trying to pull free. "I won't put my subjects through another civil war."

"I don't care about your subjects. I care about you and Allana." Jacen pulled her closer. "And *I* won't take chances with your lives."

"The decision isn't yours to make." Tenel Ka wondered how much of the conversation Jacen had planned before coming here—if he had deliberately linked her fate and Allana's to the Alliance's in a bid to talk her out of her last fleet. "I must look after my subjects first, my family second."

"Then *look* after your subjects," he insisted. "The Confederation isn't interested in a unity government. What do you think they'll do with the galaxy if they win the war?"

Jacen *had* thought this conversation out in advance, Tenel Ka realized, and it made her heart sink to see just how carefully. The Confederation would redraw the galactic map, probably with the Hutts or the Corellians claiming control of Hapes. She glared down at Jacen's hand and did not look away until he removed it.

"I'm not wrong about this," he said, stepping back. "The Confederation will do what barbarians always do—divide the spoils."

Tenel Ka nodded, but moved away from the seating area and stood looking at the wall. He would sense her feelings through the Force, but at least she would not debase her throne by allowing him to see tears in the eyes of the Queen Mother.

"You're right, of course."

"I'm sorry, Tenel Ka," Jacen said, starting toward her. "But if you don't give me the fleet, what do you think the Corellians are going to do to the Consortium? Or the Hutts?"

Tenel Ka held her hand out behind her, signaling him to stay away. Jacen was right—she had no choice but to give him the fleet. But she had been queen long enough to know that even when there was no choice, there was opportunity.

"I will give you the fleet, Jacen."

Jacen stopped two steps behind her. "Thank you, Tenel Ka," he said, having the good grace to sound grateful. "You're saving the—"

"Not yet, Jacen," Tenel Ka interrupted. "There is one condition."

"Very well," he said. "I'm hardly in a position to bargain."

"That's right—you aren't." Tenel Ka blinked her eyes dry, then drew herself up and turned to face Jacen. "You must make peace with Master Skywalker."

A shadow fell over Jacen's face. "There's no need to worry about the Jedi," he said. "They won't be interfering anymore—you can be sure of that."

"I am not worried about interference," Tenel Ka said. "You need their *cooperation*."

Jacen took a step back, as though he had been pushed.

"I'm not sure I can make that happen. It takes two to make peace, and Luke—"

"*Peace*, Jacen. That is my condition." Tenel Ka took him by the arm and started him toward the door. "And may I suggest you start by addressing your uncle as *Master* Skywalker?"

two

Five stories below lay the Morning Court of the new Jedi Temple, a large circular atrium carpeted in living sturdimoss and surrounded by curving walls of mirrored transparisteel. This morning the roof membrane was retracted, and the enclosure was packed with Alliance dignitaries dressed in somber shades of gray and black. On the far side of the crowd, several rows of Jedi Knights in white robes knelt before a large pyre. Atop the pyre lay a lithe female body wrapped in white gauze, hands folded across her chest, red hair cascading over the logs beneath her.

The distance was too great to observe the dead woman's face, but Leia knew that no matter how well the mortician had plied his art, there would be lingering hints of outrage and anxiety, of hostility and fear. Mara Jade Skywalker would have died angry, and she would have died worrying about Ben and Luke.

Han stopped beside Leia and peered through the transparisteel wall. "I don't like it. How come she didn't return to the Force?"

"That doesn't always happen," Leia explained. "Tresina Lobi didn't return to the Force."

"Because her body was evidence. She wanted Luke to see her wounds, so he'd know Lumiya was after Ben."

"I'm not sure it works that way." As Leia spoke, Saba Sebatyne and a group of brown-robed Jedi Masters emerged from a door on the far side of the Morning Court.

"But it *might*," Han insisted. "Maybe Mara's trying to tell us—"

"*Han*," Leia interrupted. "I'm sure the Masters have already considered that possibility, and it looks like we're running late."

She pointed across the courtyard to Saba and the other Masters, who were escorting Luke and Ben toward the head of the funeral pyre. Both Skywalkers wore gray robes with raised hoods, but father and son could not have looked more dissimilar. With squared shoulders and the heavy gait of a soldier, Ben managed to seem both angry and in control, as though his mother's funeral had brought his adolescent energies into perilous focus. In contrast, Luke had stooped shoulders and an erratic gait that made him look as though it required all his strength just to be there.

Leia reached out in the Force to let him know they had arrived, but Luke's presence was so drawn in on itself that it was almost undetectable—and it shrank even more when she tried to touch him.

A terrible ache filled Leia's chest. "We should have been here, Han. Maybe he would have held up better if I had—"

"We're here *now*." Han took her elbow. "And being here when it happened wouldn't have changed anything. It's hard to comfort someone from a cell inside a secret GAG detention center."

Leia chuffed out her breath, then said, "I know."

She allowed Han to guide her down the corridor, both irked and saddened to be reminded of the detention warrant their own son had issued against them. Jacen had turned so terribly dark that she often found herself wondering why she had failed to see it coming—why she *still* couldn't name the thing that had changed him. Had it been his captivity among the Yuuzhan Vong? Or had he lost his way during his five-year sojourn among the stars?

It hardly mattered. Leia had not recognized the moment when she could have reached out to save him. Her son had simply slipped into darkness one day when she wasn't looking, and now, she feared, it was already too late to pull him back.

They rounded a bend in the corridor and came to a turbo-lift station. Han touched a pad requesting descent to the courtyard level. Nothing happened.

Han struck the pad again, this time with a bent knuckle, and the status light still refused to turn green. He sighed in exasperation.

"Great." He started down the corridor to look for another lift. "You're giving the eulogy, and we can't even get a—"

"Wait." Leia grabbed his arm and pulled him back. Her spine was tingling with danger sense. "I think we're being watched."

"Of *course* we're being watched." Han hitched a thumb at the Morning Court, more or less aiming at the dignitaries on the near side of the enclosure. "Have you *seen* who's out there? Every apprentice in the Temple must be monitoring security holos."

"Which is why I am surprised you and Princess Leia decided to come, Captain Solo." The voice was crisp, deep, and behind them. "But I should have known by now not to doubt the colonel. He *said* you would come."

Leia turned to find a shaved-head lieutenant leading a small squad of black-uniformed soldiers around the bend. It took a moment to recognize who they were, for she couldn't believe even Jacen would set a trap for his own parents at his aunt's funeral. Yet here Leia was, looking at half a dozen GAG troopers who clearly thought they were going to arrest her and Han.

Han scowled. "How'd you get in here? This is Jedi territory."

"And the Jedi serve the Alliance." The lieutenant stopped five meters away, his troopers spreading across the corridor behind him, and glowered in Leia's direction. "At least they're *supposed* to."

"You're making a big mistake, Lieutenant," Leia said, putting some ice into her voice. She and Han had taken elaborate precautions to avoid detection *outside* the Temple, but sending troopers inside was an inconceivable affront, one that Luke would never tolerate—were he not consumed by grief. "The Jedi Council won't view this intrusion lightly. You *might* save your career by leaving now."

"The Jedi Council will do what the colonel tells them to—just as *I* do." The lieutenant snapped a finger, and the troopers leveled a line of T-21 repeating blasters at the Solos. "Now come along quietly. We don't want to disturb Master Skywalker's funeral any more than you do. It would be disrespectful."

"Yes, it would." Leia put the strength of the Force behind her words, at the same time waving two fingers to keep the captain from focusing on the suggestive timbre of her voice. "That's why my son gave us safe passage."

The lieutenant furrowed his brow, then said, "There must be a mistake." He motioned his squad to lower their weapons. "The colonel gave them safe passage."

The troopers continued to aim at the Solos, and the corporal beside him snapped, "Sirrr! She's doing that Jedi thing to you."

The lieutenant's gaze flickered away for a second, then returned clear and focused. "Try that again and we open fire," he warned. "I'm not weak-minded, you know."

"No?" Han asked. "Then how come you're taking orders from my son?"

The lieutenant's face reddened. "Colonel Solo is a great patriot, perhaps even the savior of the . . . arrrgggh!"

His voice broke into a scream of alarm as Leia Force-hurled him into the troopers behind him, knocking half the squad off its feet and sending the rest stumbling for balance. She snatched her lightsaber off her belt and started down the corridor in the opposite direction.

Han was already three steps ahead, tugging his blaster pistol from its holster with one hand and reaching back for her with the other.

"There's got to be another lift up ahead. If we hurry, we can still get you there in time to deliver the—"

"Are you *crazy*?" Leia was touched by his devotion, but the last thing she wanted to do was cause a firefight at Mara's funeral—as appropriate as that might seem. "We *can't* go out there."

"We *have* to," Han said. "Why do you think Jacen is trying to catch us now, instead of after the service? If he was going to grab us, wouldn't it have been easier when we were all broken up and not paying attention?"

Leia nearly stopped running. "He doesn't want us to see Luke!"

"That's my bet," Han said. "He must be afraid we'll buck up the competition or something."

Han's suggestion made perfect sense. Immediately following Jacen's coup, several Masters on the Jedi Council had publicly condemned the act—condemnations that had no doubt cost Jacen and Admiral Niathal some crucial early support. But since Mara's death, the entire Council had remained silent, too occupied with Jedi concerns to intrude on Alliance politics, and that silence could only come as a welcome relief to the new Chiefs of State.

Before Leia could agree with Han aloud, they rounded a bend and found a line of black-uniformed figures stretched across the corridor. There was barely time to recognize them as a second squad of GAG troopers before three *poopf*s sounded and the air was suddenly blurred by flying webs.

Leia waved a hand, using the Force to sweep two of the shock nets into the wall. The third sailed past along the far side of the corridor, crackling with energy and trailing tart whiffs of adhesive.

Han dropped to his belly and began to lay suppression fire, and a trooper collapsed in stun-bolt-induced spasms. Leia extended her hand and, when the next *poopf* sounded from the firing line, used the Force to hurl the shock net back toward the trooper. He tumbled over backward, gurgling and convulsing as the charged mesh tightened.

Boots began to pound down the corridor behind them, the first squad of troopers rushing to close the trap.

"This time, Jacen's gone too far," Han growled, still firing down the corridor at the second squad. "We're gonna have to do something about that kid."

"Let's get out of this first, okay?"

"Good idea. What's your plan?"

Leia didn't really have one, but she ignited her lightsaber and charged anyway. "Follow me!"

The four troopers remaining in the second squad threw their net launchers aside and pulled their blaster rifles, but Leia was on them before they could open fire. She took one man out with a roundhouse kick to the head and sent another cartwheeling into the wall with a spinning crescent—then found herself looking down the barrel of an E-11 blaster rifle. When she raised her gaze, it was to see a young recruit only two or three years older than her son Anakin had been when he died.

The boy's pupils widened, and Leia knew he was going to blast her. She brought her lightsaber up beneath his arms, slashing them off at the elbows, then spun away feeling sick and sad. This was not right, fighting on the day of Mara's funeral, drawing blood inside the Jedi Temple, maiming her own son's troopers.

The second squad's last trooper was already on the floor in convulsions, his utilities still crackling with residual energy from Han's stun bolts. Outside in the Morning Court, Leia glimpsed a few Masters frowning in their direction, no doubt sensing through the Force what the enclosure's mirrored transparisteel prevented the rest of the audience from seeing. Luke seemed oblivious to the disturbance, but Ben's attention was fixed on the Masters, and Leia knew he, too, would soon feel what was happening.

Han ran up beside her and slipped a concussion grenade off the utility belt of the screaming boy whose arms Leia had just amputated, then grabbed her by the elbow.

"Not your fault," he said, steering her down the corridor. "That's on Jacen."

Leia started to say that it didn't matter whose fault it was, but her reply was cut short as the first squad of troopers caught up and loosed a flurry of blaster bolts. She spun around and began to back down the corridor after Han, batting screaming dashes of color back toward their attackers. Unfortunately, the lieutenant and his men had learned from the mistakes of the other squad and were hugging the inner curve of the corridor, using the transparisteel wall for cover and taking care never to present a clean target.

A bolt ricocheted off the wall above their heads and left a smoking furrow in the transparisteel.

"Hey, those bolts are full power!" Han complained. He thumbed the activator switch on the grenade he had taken, then turned to face the troopers. "All right, if you want to play dirty—"

Leia caught his arm. "No, Han. We can't do that—not here, not today."

She thumbed the switch back to its inert position, then took the grenade from Han's hand and tossed it at their pursuers, using the Force to guide it into their midst.

The blasterfire fell instantly silent. Cries of *grenade!* and *cover!* filled the corridor as the lieutenant and his troopers hurled themselves out of sight.

Leia took Han's hand and sprinted down the corridor to the next intersection. When she turned *away* from the Morning Court, Han looked over and stopped running.

"Wrong way!" He tugged her in the opposite direction, back toward the funeral. "You're never going to make it in time—"

"I know, Han." Leia remained where she was, using the Force to anchor herself to the floor. "But our presence has already caused too much of a disturbance. We can't turn Mara's funeral into a blaster battle."

"We're not the ones to blame!" Han objected. "*Jacen* sent the goons."

"And what does that change?" Leia asked. "If we go out there, they'll still follow and try to arrest us, and *then* where will we be?"

Han's face fell as he contemplated the alternatives—surrender nicely and be hauled off to a GAG prison, or start a firefight in the middle of Mara's funeral. Either way, they would not be doing Luke—or Ben—any good. He stopped pulling.

"Nowhere," he said. "Looks like Jacen wins again."

"For today," Leia said. She started down the corridor in her original direction, pulling Han after her toward the Temple exit. "But you're right, Han. It's time for us to do something about that kid."

three

Saba Sebatyne had been living among humans for well over a standard decade, and still there was so much she did not know about them. She didn't understand why Master Skywalker seemed so lost right now, why he had stopped talking to his friends and turned all his attention inward. Surely he knew Mara wouldn't want that? That she would expect him to stay focused and guide the Jedi through this time of crisis?

But he just stood staring at the funeral pyre, as though he couldn't quite believe it was *his* mate up there, as though he expected her to awaken at any moment and climb down to stand beside him. Perhaps he was only trying to understand why Mara had failed to return her body to the Force, wondering—like so many other Masters—whether it still held some clue to the killer's identity that had been missed during the autopsy. Or he could be worried that something in Mara's past had interfered, that she had done something as the Emperor's Hand so terrible that the Force could not take her back.

Saba only knew that she did *not* know; that Master Skywalker had been wounded in some way she could never understand and had lost himself. And she feared that if he did not return to himself soon, something terrible would happen. She could feel that much in the Force.

Saba felt the weight of someone's attention and turned to find Corran Horn's green eyes fixed on her back. He was standing about three meters away, discussing something with Kyp and Kenth Hamner while Cilghal, Kyle Katarn, and the rest of the Masters remained with Master Skywalker and Ben. When he noticed Saba looking, he gave a little head-jerk, summoning her over.

Saba nodded, but glanced back to make certain the dignitaries filling the courtyard weren't growing too impatient with the delay. Tenel Ka was in the front row, kneeling in meditation alongside Tesar, Lowbacca, Tahiri, and most of the other Jedi Knights—except Jaina and Zekk, who had been ordered to continue their pursuit of Alema Rar. In chairs behind the Jedi Knights, Admiral Niathal and her entire High Command sat bolt upright, too disciplined to fidget no matter how late the ceremony was running. Behind them sat most of the Senate and the secretaries of every major department, putting their time to good use by chatting with one another in solemn whispers. The only person of note whom Saba did *not* see was the man who should have been in the vacant chair to Admiral Niathal's right, the co-leader of the coup government—Jacen Solo.

Satisfied that the distinguished audience members were not on the verge of departing, Saba excused herself to Ben and a barely cognizant Master Skywalker, then joined Corran and the others. Kyp Durron still wore his dark brown hair long and shaggy, but at least he was cleanly shaven for the occasion. Kenth Hamner, who looked old enough to be Kyp's father, appeared as carefully groomed and dignified as ever.

"*What?*" Saba demanded. "Can you not see how all this waiting is affecting Master Skywalker? When are we going to start?"

Corran and Kyp shot each other a nervous glance, then

Kenth said, "We'll start as soon as you are ready, Master Sebatyne."

Saba flicked her tongue between her lips, trying to figure out why they would be waiting on her. "*This* one?"

"That's right," Corran said. He cast a glance over her shoulder toward Ben and Master Skywalker, then lowered his voice to a barely audible whisper. "You felt that disturbance on the upper access level a few moments ago?"

"Yes," Saba replied. "What was it? A newz crew trying to sneak holoz of the funeral?"

"Not exactly," Kyp said, also speaking softly. "It was a GAG squad."

Saba's jaw fell. "A GAG squad? *Inside* the Temple?"

"I'm afraid so," Kenth replied. "They tried to arrest the Solos."

Saba thumped her tail against the slatstones, pondering, then finally shook her head in bewilderment. "Only a squad? That is not enough."

"Not even close," Kyp agreed. "But we'll talk about that later. The pursuit has already moved outside the Temple, and we have other things to worry about right now."

Saba nodded. "Of course. This one will inform Master Skywalker."

As she started to turn away, Corran reached for her arm—then seemed to remember what could happen when one grabbed a Barabel and quickly drew his hand back. Saba sissed in relief—she would have been embarrassed to find herself biting his wrist in front of so many dignitaries— and cocked her brow.

"Do you think it's wise to involve Master Skywalker?" Corran asked. "He has enough on his mind right now."

"This one thinkz he does not have *enough* on his mind," Saba replied. "Mara would not want him turned inward like this."

"No, but she *would* understand," Kenth said. "Humans need to grieve, Saba. We need to let him have this funeral."

"It's the only way he'll get better," Corran added.

Saba riffled her scales and looked away. There was that word again, *grieve*. She did not understand what good it was—why humans found it so necessary to swim in sorrow when their loved ones died. Was it not enough to hold them in one's heart, to honor their memories in how one lived one's own days? It was as though humans could not trust their minds to keep lost ones alive; as though they believed that a person was gone just because her life had come to an end.

Saba returned her gaze to Corran and the others. "We cannot let the intrusion go unpunished," she said. "Jacen is already swinging us like a tail."

"We won't," Kyp assured her. "We'll do something right after the funeral."

Saba nodded. "Good. But somehow this one does not think you told her about the intrusion just to ask her *not* to tell Master Skywalker."

Corran shook his head. "Not really," he said. "You see, Princess Leia was supposed to give the eulogy."

"Ah. Now this one understands why Jacen didn't come."

"Jacen didn't know," Kenth said. "But that's not really the problem."

"Of course not." Saba had seen enough human funerals to know there was always a speech, that it was an important part of drawing out the tears that the service was to unleash. She glanced at the crowd of dignitaries, then back to Master Skywalker and Ben. "Now how are we to give Master Skywalker his grieving?"

Corran and Kenth exchanged glances, then Kenth said, "We were hoping you would speak."

"This one?" Saba began to siss—then recalled that humans did not like humor at their funerals and bit her tongue. "You are serious?"

Kenth nodded. "You were Mara's friend," he said. "If

anyone understands what she meant to Luke and the rest of us, it's you."

"But this one is not even human," Saba said. "She doesn't understand *grieving*."

"That's okay," Kyp said. He locked gazes with her in a silent challenge. "We'll understand if you're afraid. I can always fill in instead."

"This one is not afraid!" Saba knew he was manipulating her, but she also knew he was right—refusing would not be worthy of Mara's memory. "She just doesn't know what to say."

Kyp nodded sympathetically. "So does that mean you want *me* to do it?"

"No!" The last thing Mara would have wanted was Kyp speaking at her funeral. While he had been fairly supportive of Master Skywalker's leadership of late, there had been a time when that was not so—and Mara had been a woman with a long memory. "This one will do it." She turned to Kenth. "What does she say?"

"Just speak from your heart." Kenth gave her a gentle Force nudge toward the speaker's lectern. "You'll do fine."

Saba swallowed hard, then returned to Master Skywalker's side and spoke into his ear. "Leia and Han were delayed," she said. "This one will start."

Luke's gaze rose to the top of the pyre and locked on Mara's face, and he said nothing. The shadows beneath his hood were almost deep enough to hide the red bags beneath his eyes, but even drawn in on himself, his Force aura beamed anguish.

Ben leaned out from behind Luke and nodded. "That's good," he said. "Mom would like that."

A stream of warmth flooded Saba's heart, and her anxiety about speaking in front of so many dignitaries vanished. She turned toward the audience and straightened her robes, then stepped up to the lectern. A silver hovermike rose to float before her throat, but she deactivated it with a flick of her talon and returned it to its charging socket. When she spoke about Mara, she would not need a voice projector to make herself heard.

The courtyard quickly fell silent. Saba took a moment to make eye contact with Tenel Ka, Admiral Niathal, and many of the other dignitaries in the audience. Then, using the Force to carry her voice to the farthest edges of the courtyard, she began.

"We have come to this sacred place to say farewell to our dear friend, to a fierce warrior and a noble dispenser of justice. Mara Jade Skywalker was one of the brightest starz of the Jedi Order, and we will miss her."

Saba shifted her gaze to the Jedi Knights kneeling in the front row of the audience. "Her light has been taken from the galaxy, but it has not been extinguished. It lives on in us, in the times we shared the hunt, in the lessons she taught us as a Master." She turned and spoke directly to Master Skywalker and Ben. "It lives in the love and counsel she gave as a mate, in the sacrifices she made as a mother. As long as our hearts beat, her light lives inside us."

Master Skywalker finally tore his gaze from the pyre. Though his expression was not exactly peaceful, there was at least a hint of gratitude in his eyes, and she could tell that her words were reaching him. It was harder to tell whether she was being any comfort to Ben. His attention was fixed on the slatstones beneath his feet, his brow furrowed in concentration, his Force aura swirling with pain and confusion and a rage that Mara would have found very frightening.

As Saba contemplated what she might say to quell that rage, a low murmur arose from the audience, starting from the back of the courtyard and rippling slowly forward, growing louder and more animated as it drew closer. Saba turned back to the listeners, wondering if her words could be generating that much excitement, and found the entire audience craning their necks to look back toward the entrance.

Striding up the central aisle was a black-clad figure in knee-high boots, with a long shimmersilk cloak rippling from his broad shoulders. His face was somber and his eyes sunken in shadow, his bearing brusque. Once it grew reasonably apparent that every eye in the audience was on him, he raised a black-gloved hand in a gesture that was half apology and half greeting.

"Excuse my tardiness," Jacen Solo said. "I was detained by urgent matters of state. I'm sure everyone understands."

A general drone of agreement rose from the audience, though Jacen could feel Saba's ire through the Force. He pretended not to notice her indignation and continued down the aisle, taking care to keep his presence hidden from the Force so no one would sense how nervous he felt. The Masters still had no idea he was Mara's killer, but he was all too aware how easily the slightest slip on his part could change that.

Still, there was no question of missing the funeral. His absence would have drawn too many comments and started too many people thinking—and it would have been a clear signal to Tenel Ka that he had no intention of reconciling with Luke. So Jacen had to be here, and he had to make it look like he wanted peace with the man whose wife he had killed just a week earlier.

When Jacen reached the front of the crowd, he ignored the seat that had been reserved for him beside Admiral Niathal. He continued instead to where the Jedi Knights were kneeling, then bowed to Tenel Ka.

"Thank you for coming, Queen Mother," he said, trying to make it appear that they had not yet seen each other since her arrival on Coruscant. "In these times, I know your journey couldn't have been an easy one."

"Master Skywalker was an extraordinary Jedi and an

uncommon friend." Tenel Ka's gray eyes betrayed nothing as she spoke. "We would have endured worse to be here."

"I'm sure your presence is a great comfort to Ben and . . ." Jacen paused, then finished, "*Master* Skywalker."

Tenel Ka dipped her head in an almost imperceptible nod. "We can only hope so."

Jacen excused himself with a polite click of his boot heels, then continued forward to stand at Luke's side. The Force boiled with the outrage of the Masters, but Jacen pretended not to notice. Mara's funeral was the perfect opportunity to raise the public's perception of his standing among the Jedi—to plant the idea in the minds of hundreds of dignitaries that he was his uncle's equal—and he could not afford to pass that by. As for his promise to Tenel Ka—well, as long as he made it *look* like he was trying to reconcile with Luke, he would still have her fleet.

When Luke remained oblivious to Jacen's presence, Kenth Hamner stepped forward and spoke in a voice of fatherly reproach.

"Jacen, you *know* you're not a Master." Kenth gestured toward the Jedi Knights kneeling in the front row. "Your place is with the other Jedi Knights . . . should you care to assume it, *Jedi* Solo."

"I think that's where we misunderstand each other, Master Hamner." Jacen pulled his dark cloak aside, revealing the empty lightsaber snap on his utility belt. "I'm not here as a Jedi."

"You're still standing in the wrong place," Kyle Katarn said, joining them. "This is a *Jedi* funeral."

"A funeral I'm attending as family." Jacen spoke in a deliberately reasonable voice, trying to create the impression that it was the Masters who were causing the disturbance. "I'm only here to comfort my cousin and uncle."

"To *comfort* them?" Kyp Durron came forward. "You expect us to believe that?"

"It *is* the truth," Jacen said gently.

Kyp ignored the objection and took Jacen by the arm—then Luke surprised them both by raising a hand.

"Wait." Beneath the grief, there was an odd note of urgency to Luke's voice. "Jacen is welcome to stand with Ben and me."

Kyp's jaw dropped. "But Master Skywalker, Jacen is just using the funeral to—"

"It's fine." Luke gestured for Kyp—and Kenth and Kyle—to resume their places. "I *want* Jacen here."

Kyp scowled, but joined Kenth and Kyle in obeying.

Jacen watched them retreat, feeling as confused as they looked, until Luke turned and extended his hand.

"Thank you for coming, Jacen."

"Mara was a great Jedi and a loving aunt." As Jacen clasped arms, he took extra care to hide his feelings from the Force. It was hard to imagine his uncle having the strength to probe for guilty emotions right now, but the galaxy was littered with the body parts of those who had underestimated the strength of Luke Skywalker. "I would never have missed the chance to show my respect for her."

"I'm glad. It's time we healed this rift between us." Luke returned his gaze to Mara's body. "I think that must be what she's trying to tell us."

"*Tell* us?" Jacen echoed.

He looked to the top of the pyre and decided Luke must be losing touch with reality. Mara lay as dead as before, neither her lips nor anything else moving; there was no sound coming from anywhere near the vicinity of the body.

Then he noticed that Mara's white-swaddled form was starting to grow translucent and glow with Force energy. Saba sissed in astonishment and several other Masters sighed in relief, but Jacen nearly choked on his shock. If Mara was trying to tell anyone *anything*, it had nothing to do with reconciliation—and everything to do with exposing her killer.

Luke clasped Jacen's shoulder. "She waited until we were together," he said. "I think there's a message in that, don't you?"

"Uh, yes . . . of course." To Jacen's amazement, there was no hint of deception or cynicism in his uncle's voice or presence. Luke had clearly drawn the wrong conclusion about what Mara was trying to tell him—perhaps because she had died while keeping her activities secret from him— and Jacen was more than ready to embrace his good fortune. "I think that must be *exactly* what Mara is telling us. We can't save the Alliance without working together."

"Good point," Luke said. "I'll try to remember that this time."

"And so will I." Jacen sneaked a glance in Tenel Ka's direction and was rewarded with a tiny nod, barely perceptible but distinctly approving. "I promise."

Luke dipped his head in agreement, or perhaps even gratitude, and Jacen found himself struggling to keep his relief—his *exhilaration*—from spilling into the Force. He was going to have his fleet, and with it would come the strength to lure the Confederation into a trap and smash it, to unite the galaxy in justice and peace.

As Jacen fought to control his emotions, Luke turned toward the lectern where Saba Sebatyne stood watching them, studying Jacen but looking somewhere beyond him—or perhaps it was deeper *into* him, as though she were seeing not Jacen's public face, but his inner one, that of Darth Caedus.

"Saba?" Luke called softly.

There was a new vitality to his voice, a note of renewed confidence that Jacen might have found alarming, but which Caedus knew would last only as long as their "reconciliation."

"Saaaba?"

Saba's gaze finally swung back to Luke. "Yes?"

Luke gestured at the audience. "Maybe you should continue." He glanced at Mara's luminous body, which had already grown so transparent that the back wall of the courtyard could be seen through it. "I'd like to finish before Mara is completely gone."

"Yes, please forgive this one," she said. "She was . . . distracted."

Saba turned toward the courtyard again, but did not return immediately to her speech. Instead, she studied the audience for a moment, ruffling her scales, then glancing from them to Luke to Jacen and finally back to the courtyard. Jacen could feel her struggling with a decision, fighting to swallow her outrage at how he was taking advantage of Luke's grief, and he realized she was about to make this a very unpleasant funeral for him.

"Surely," Saba began, "this one speakz for everyone here when she sayz how glad she is Colonel Solo could spare a few minutes to honor his noble aunt."

The opening was enough of a shock to tear most eyes in the audience from Mara's rapidly vanishing form. A chorus of confused murmurs and indignant gasps arose from the audience, but Jacen maintained an expressionless face and continued to gaze politely at the lectern. Whatever Saba said, it was not going to make Tenel Ka change her mind.

Jacen even found himself wondering whether it might be possible to keep his promise to Tenel Ka, to truly reconcile with Luke and work together to save the Alliance—but of course that was impossible. Sooner or later, someone would discover the identity of Mara's killer, and the Jedi had to be either firmly under Caedus's control by then—or eliminated.

After a moment, Saba continued. "And it iz good that Colonel Solo arrives at this point in our remembrances, because the greatest gift Mara Jade Skywalker left us is the lesson of her life—a life that began under the darkest of shadowz." She half turned to face Jacen, Luke, and Ben. "As a young child, Mara was taken from her parentz and shaped into pure spy and assassin, and her keeper set her to doing terrible thingz when she was barely old enough for the hunt. She did them because she believed they were right, because she believed in the dream of a single galaxy with one justice, a galaxy bound in peace by a single fist.

"That fist belonged to Emperor Palpatine, and his dream was one filled with darkness." Now Saba locked gazes with Jacen, her face-scales ruffling in rebuke. "It meant the deathz of billionz and the enslavement of trillionz, the end of freedom and the silencing of dissent. It brought fear to those it claimed to protect and misery to those it pretended to serve.

"As Mara's missionz carried her farther afield, she began to see the evil in her master'z dream. For a time, she tried to carry on, telling herself that evil was necessary to bring peace, that some must suffer before all could live in harmony."

When Jacen still had not looked away, Saba finally broke gazes and turned back to the audience. "We all know how *that* ended."

A chorus of soft chuckles rolled through the courtyard, and Jacen could feel in the Force that the audience's mood was shifting, that even some of his supporters were growing more thoughtful. He allowed himself to glare at the Barabel darkly—nothing threatening, but with enough indignation to express the proper outrage at such a comparison.

Saba ignored him, of course. "After the Emperor died, there were those who would not relinquish his dark dream, who attempted to keep the Empire alive and even restore Palpatine's clones to power. Mara was not one of them. After the Emperor'z death, she wandered the galaxy for many years searching for a new life, and she began to see more clearly what she had been, the evil *she* had done. Then fate placed her life in the handz of a man she had once considered an enemy—a man whom she still felt compelled to kill—and during their difficult journey together, she began to understand that there was another way, a way filled with freedom and love and trust.

"Mara once told this one that all it took to lift the Emperor'z veil from her eyes was a long walk in the forest with this man." Saba extended her arm toward Luke. "That after she had come to know Luke Skywalker, it was easy to step into the light."

Tears welled in the eyes of both Luke and Ben. Ben at least had the pride to turn away and wipe his face, but Luke merely let his tears flow, his gaze never straying from the top of the pyre as Mara's body paled from a radiant ghost to a shimmering blur of light.

When it had finally vanished altogether, Luke closed his eyes and let out a soft breath, then laid an arm over Ben's shoulder. "She's with the Force now, son," he whispered. "She'll be with us always."

"Yeah, Dad." Ben's voice did not even come close to cracking, and Jacen was proud of him for that. "I know."

Jacen reached over to give Luke's shoulder a comforting squeeze—then felt the weight of Saba's gaze and looked up to find her glaring at him, her eyes filled with anger and sorrow and warning.

"And *that* is the lesson of Mara's life," the Barabel said. "If we wish to live in goodness, all we need do iz open our heartz. If we wish to bring justice and peace to the galaxy, all we need do is step into the light."

Jacen lowered his hand and returned Saba's glare with a tight smile. The embarrassment she had caused him here did not matter. He had won Tenel Ka's fleet, and now he would have the strength to lay a trap and crush the Confederation—and once he had done *that,* the public would not care what Saba or any Master thought of him. They would realize that it was Caedus, not the Jedi, who was the true guardian of the Alliance.

Saba slipped out from behind the podium and—making

a point of ignoring Jacen—bowed to Luke and Ben, then stepped to the foot of the empty pyre. Instead of setting the wood ablaze, as she would have done had there still been a body, she simply faced the other Masters, and together they began the traditional recitation of the Jedi Code.

THERE IS NO EMOTION; THERE IS PEACE.
THERE IS NO IGNORANCE; THERE IS KNOWLEDGE.
THERE IS NO PASSION; THERE IS SERENITY.
THERE IS NO DEATH; THERE IS THE FORCE.

As soon as they had finished the recitation, Jacen left Luke's side and went straight for Saba.

"A touching eulogy, Master Sebatyne." He kept his voice angry, but not quite menacing. "Very instructive. I'll remember it for a *very* long time."

"Good," Saba replied evenly. "This one only hopes you come to understand it, as well."

A series of gasps and titters betrayed the eavesdroppers in the front rows of the audience, and Jacen realized he was in danger of looking weak. He dropped all pretense of civility and glared at Saba in open hostility.

"Your humor has always been a mystery to me, Master Sebatyne," he said. "It's a wonder I haven't taken offense before this."

"And I hope you'll forgive us now." Luke stepped to Jacen's side, then said, "None of us are quite ourselves today. Please don't let that stop you from joining Ben and me after the ceremony. I meant what I said about healing the rift between us."

"That *would* be best for everyone," Jacen said. His gaze slid toward Ben and lingered there. "We must think of the future."

Ben only shrugged and looked away.

The hostility was painful, though hardly surprising. Jacen had known when he killed Mara that he was sacrific-

ing his cousin's devotion—but that should not have occurred until *after* Ben learned the identity of her killer. So
either the boy was taking his mother's death harder than
Jacen realized, or he suspected the truth and was telling no
one.

Caedus wondered whether it would prove necessary to
kill Ben to protect the secret of Mara's death a few days
longer. Jacen hoped not; he still saw potential in his young
cousin, and a part of him believed it might be possible to
make a proper apprentice of him yet.

Deciding that it was best to let Ben mourn in private—
for now—Jacen assumed a grave air and turned back to
Luke. "I'm afraid I can't join you today, Master Skywalker," he said. "I'm due topside earliest."

Luke's brow fell in confusion. "Maneuvers?"

"No, I'm accompanying the Fourth Fleet into action."
Jacen cast an accusatory glance toward Kenth, Kyle, and
the other Masters. "I'm surprised the Council didn't tell
you. I *requested* Jedi StealthXs."

Luke frowned at Saba, who could only nod and say, "We
didn't think you should be disturbed."

The irritation in Luke's eyes changed to comprehension.
His face clouded with something that might have been
shame, then he frowned at Saba and the other Masters.

"You can fill me in later."

It was Kenth Hamner who answered. "We'll be happy
to." He glanced in Jacen's direction and added, "There are
a *lot* of things you need to know."

Luke narrowed his eyes, but turned to Jacen. "I
understand—duty calls. But I hope you'll think about what
happened here today."

"I will be thinking about it," Jacen said. "You can be
sure of that."

"Good. May the Force be with you."

"And with you."

Jacen turned and strode down the aisle, driving his boot

heels into the sturdimoss and using the Force to gently move people aside. Luke watched him go in equal parts hope and dread. If anything remained of the gentle-hearted boy he remembered from the Jedi academy on Yavin 4, he could no longer find it. Jacen was swaddled in a darkness deeper than any he had felt in recent memory—perhaps since the days of Darth Vader and the Emperor—and it was not at all clear that he could be drawn back into the light. Yet Luke had to try—if not for Jacen, then for Leia and even the Alliance . . . but most of all for himself. After the mistake he had made with Lumiya—after his erroneous vengeance killing of her—he could not bear the thought of making such an error with his own nephew. If there was still a way to reach Jacen, he had to try.

Kenth Hamner stepped to the lectern and thanked everyone for helping the Jedi celebrate the life of Mara Jade Skywalker. He reminded them to keep her example in mind during the difficult days to come and invited them to the remembrance feast being laid out in the Hall of Peace. As the crowd rose to leave, Luke turned toward the courtyard's rear exit, motioning for Ben, Saba, and the rest of the Masters to follow.

The last thing he wanted to do right now was focus on the Order. With only an aching void where there used to be Mara, Luke felt like the victim of a heart amputation, everything inside burning in grief, his thoughts whirling with memories of Mara's death . . . that sudden awful pulling on their Force-bond, as though she were falling into a star, then trying to reach out and draw her to safety, but the bond just snapping and leaving him broken and lost and hurting.

But with Jacen making his first tentative attempts to assert control over the Jedi, the Order needed Luke now more than ever, and as Mara had returned her body to the Force he had realized that she expected him to be strong, to pull himself together and prevent Jacen from using her death to destroy anything else.

Once the group was inside the fern-filled lobby that had served as the funeral's staging area, Luke turned to Saba.

"Was that really necessary?" he demanded. "We're not going to bring Jacen back into the fold by antagonizing him in public."

"We are not going to bring Jacen back at all," Saba said. "Jacen is beyond saving."

"That's not your call," Luke said. "Mara held on to her body for a reason. She was trying to tell us that if we want to save the Alliance, we have to work *with* him, not against him."

"I don't think so," Kyp said, shaking his head. "Saba's right. Jacen was just using Mara's funeral to make himself look more important to the Order."

"Don't you think I know that?" Luke asked. "It still gives us an opening—and it will be better for the Alliance, for the Jedi, and for the galaxy if we guide Jacen rather than fight him."

"No, Dad, it *won't*," Ben said. "In fact, I don't think Mom meant the message for you at all—if there even was a message."

"Of course there was a message," Luke said, growing confused. "Why else would your mother wait until *Jacen* arrived to return her body to the Force?"

Ben shrugged and avoided Luke's eyes. "I don't know, but I don't think she was telling us to trust Jacen."

Luke scowled. "Ben, what aren't you telling me?"

Ben shook his head. "Nothing."

If Ben was lying, Luke couldn't feel it in the Force. He considered trying to wait the boy out, but anyone who had witnessed as many GAG interrogations as Ben had would hardly fall for such rudimentary tactics. Instead, he gave up and turned to Corran Horn.

"Is *anyone* going to tell me what's going on?"

Corran glanced at Kyp, who turned to Kyle, who pursed his lips and looked away, apparently as he debated whether Luke was strong enough to hear the truth.

Luke turned to Kenth. "You said you had a lot to tell me," he reminded. "Start telling."

"We didn't want to upset you during the funeral," Kenth replied. "But a unit of GAG troopers tried to arrest Han and Leia. That's why they didn't make the funeral."

"They let GAG catch sight of them?" Luke was incredulous. "The *Solos*?"

"It happened inside the Temple," Kenth explained. "Less than an hour ago."

This time, Luke was stunned. "A GAG squad, in here?"

"On level six," Kyp said. "The Solos were coming in from the Ministry of Justice mezzanine."

"Why didn't anyone tell me about this?"

Even as Luke demanded this, he could see by the troubled expressions on the faces of the Masters that they had doubts about whether they should have told him *now*—and he had only himself to blame. Given the way he had drawn in on himself, what were they to think? Awash in doubt—about himself, about the Force, even about the Order itself—he had shut himself off from everyone except Ben. And he had been playing straight into his nephew's hands, practically inviting Jacen to step in and take control of the Order.

When no one answered his question, Luke said, "Forget I asked. Where are they now?"

All eyes turned to Corran, who was monitoring the Temple security channels over an ear comm.

"We don't know," he said. "They escaped into Fellowship Plaza, and Leia's been Force-flashing the security cams."

"Not the Solos," Luke said. "I mean the GAG squad."

Corran frowned. "They're gone, chasing Han and Leia."

"Can we be sure?" Luke asked. "If we don't know where Han and Leia are—"

"How do we know the GAG unit iz still chasing them?" Saba finished. "You think the arrest attempt was a diversion?"

"I think it's a possibility," Luke said. "The way I've been hiding from responsibilities—"

"You haven't been hiding from anything," Kenth said. "Your grief is more than understandable."

"Thanks," Luke said. "But the fact is, I've left us vulnerable. With everyone focused on finding Mara's killer and worrying about me, there'll never be a better time to cripple the Jedi."

"Then we'd better find that unit fast," Kyp said. He turned toward a turbolift on the far side of the lobby. "If we don't hurry, there'll be a whole battalion—"

"It's okay," Corran said, catching Kyp by the arm. "Temple security spotted them. They're outside, escorting Jacen across Fellowship Plaza."

Saba gnashed her fangs in confusion—or perhaps it was disappointment. "Jacen changed his mind about seizing the Temple?"

Corran shrugged. "Who knows? We have reports of a lot of heavy hoversleds moving away from the Temple—but that doesn't mean they were carrying GAG troopers."

A sudden silence fell over the gathering, and the Masters stood looking at one another in a fragile blend of relief and trepidation. Luke could sense how worried they all were that they had just come very close to letting Jacen take control of the Temple—or worse.

It was Ben who broke the silence. "So what are we going to do about it? We can't let him get away with trying to arrest us."

Luke looked down in surprise. "*We*, Ben? I thought you wanted Jacen to be your Master."

Ben's cheeks reddened with embarrassment. "I might

have made a mistake," he said. "I'm entitled. I'm fourteen."

In another time, on another day, Luke might have laughed. Instead, he said, "You don't have to be fourteen to make mistakes. I've been making plenty."

"If you say so," Ben said, shrugging. "And that's not an answer to my question. You're not going to let him get away with this, are you?"

Luke thought for a moment, then said, "Actually, I think we will."

"*What?*" The question came from three Masters at once, and Saba added in all sincerity, "This is a poor time for jokes, Master Skywalker. We have serious troubles."

Luke nodded. "That's true—and so is what I said to Jacen about working together. *Somebody's* got to take the first step."

"Right into a trap," Ben muttered.

"Maybe—but Jacen isn't the only one who knows how to set a trap," Luke said. He laid his hand on Ben's shoulder and, feeling more confident than he had since before Mara's death, started toward the remembrance feast. "And it might be nice to surprise *him* for change."

four

Even from an altitude of a thousand meters, the Jedi academy on Ossus looked enormous. Spread across a verdant bench-land between a lush mountainside and a gloom-filled rift valley, its tidy sweeps of green turf were surrounded by burgeoning plots of foliage and connected by snaking ribbons of gray paving stone. To Jaina's surprise, there were no tiny dots dodging among the glistening spires and elegant halls; if not for the Force presences she could detect inside the buildings, she would have thought the place deserted.

Perhaps the Solusars had called a week of meditation out of respect for Mara's funeral. They would have regretted not being there as much as Jaina did, and the children would need ritual to help them deal with the loss of such an important Jedi Master.

Jaina only wished that she and Zekk and Jag could have afforded the time to join the meditation. She was hurting in a way she had not hurt since the war with the Yuuzhan Vong, when she had lost Anakin and Chewbacca and a hundred other dear comrades. It was taking all her strength to just let the grief come and not retreat into herself as she had during the war.

Jagged Fel's crisp voice sounded over the intercom of the

StarDrive Dactyl that the Alema-hunting team was flying this week. "Sense anything?"

"Negative," Zekk answered from several meters behind Jaina. He was seated on the opposite side of the fuselage, staring through an observation blister similar to Jaina's. "Maybe we shouldn't put so much faith in vector readings. We don't know anything about that new ship she's in . . . and why would she come *here*?"

"Because she's Alema Rar," Jaina responded. "And if we waste time trying to figure out why she does *anything*, we're crazier than she is."

Jag chuckled—as he usually did whenever Jaina disagreed with Zekk—then said, "To a degree. Does that mean you sense something?"

"Give me a chance," Jaina replied. "We just got here."

"We need time to attune ourselves to the local currents," Zekk explained. "It's not like that new ship of hers is a dark side beacon. It was just giving off a little aura before."

"So you're saying we need to make a second pass?" Jag asked.

"And probably a third and a seventh," Jaina answered. "It might take some effort to find her, but I'd bet my shirt that Alema is here."

Jag said, "I accept!" at the same time Zekk said, "Okay!"

Jaina frowned, confused by their enthusiasm. *"What?"*

"Your bet." Zekk leered across the fuselage. "I accepted."

"Hey, I was first!" As usual, it was impossible to tell from Jag's tone whether he was joking, but Jaina thought he probably was. The only gambling she had ever seen him do involved starfighters and slim chances of survival. "The bet is with *me*."

"Ha, ha—very funny," Jaina said. "What part of *not interested* don't you two understand?"

Jaina did not bother to keep the irritation out of her

voice. She had grown weary of the competition between Jag and Zekk even before Mara was killed, and now it just made her angry. Besides, there wasn't even supposed to be a competition. Zekk had claimed way back on Terephon that he was over her. And when Jag had reappeared, he had been so angry over her actions during the Dark Nest crisis that a romance had seemed out of the question.

Of course, *that* blissful state had lasted about as long as a soap bubble in an open air lock. As soon as the two men realized someone else was hoping for a place in the family holo, they had begun to knock heads like two bull rontos. Jaina had finally grown so sick of it that, after Mara's death, she had told them *both* to leave her alone.

The entrance to the academy hangar suddenly passed by beneath the Dactyl, then Jaina's observation blister filled with sky as Jag rolled the ship on its side and began to swing around for another pass. The Dactyl was a lot less maneuverable than the YT-2400 they had been using as a mother ship until a few days ago, but Jag insisted on changing vessels frequently, believing it would make it more difficult for Alema to spot them coming. At least this one had a private berth for everyone *and* room for StealthXs.

Once Jag had brought the vessel around, he swung away from the academy proper and began to fly low and slow along the adjacent mountainside. Jaina started to suggest that the rift valley would be a more likely hiding place— then remembered how long Jag had been hunting Alema and remained quiet. Half crippled as the Twi'lek was, she was unlikely to hide her vessel anyplace that involved scaling two thousand meters of valley wall.

"This may be our last pass," Jag said over the comm. "Academy flight control is starting to ask questions."

"The flyover is making them nervous," Zekk guessed. "Tell them we're doing a security sweep."

"I did," Jag said. "And flight control command asked what was wrong with *their* security."

Jaina chuckled. "Tell her we're bird-watching."

Jag was silent a moment, then reported, "Command says good luck. We'll see some magnificent gokobs in the tree-tops."

Jaina and Zekk laughed simultaneously.

"What's so funny?" Jag asked.

"You'll see," Jaina said. Gokobs were hairless rodents that spent most of their time rummaging for food around the academy kitchens—friendly, but reviled for their habit of spraying a foul mist when startled. "But if you *do* come across anything big and bright in the treetops, *don't* go down to take a look."

"Not a gokob?" Jag asked.

"Not a gokob," Zekk confirmed. "There are some pretty big tree frogs on Ossus. They've been known to bring down Tee-sixty-five trainers."

"Their tongues are that strong?" Jag gasped.

"That sticky," Jaina corrected. "If you get a big bunch of 'em dangling from your hull, you lose a lot of lift."

The Dactyl continued along the mountainside for an-other half a kilometer before Jaina noticed a faint depres-sion in the forest canopy, about a kilometer upslope. There was no dark side energy in the Force to suggest they had found Alema's strange ship, but the indentation was about the correct size and shape.

"Mark," she said.

"Marked," Jag said, acknowledging that he had re-corded their exact location in the navigation system. "Did you sense something?"

"Sort of." Jaina explained what she had seen, then said, "It's probably nothing—"

"But we should check it out," Zekk said, finishing her thought, "if we don't find something else first."

Jag fell silent, and a distinct chill radiated through the

Force from the direction of the flight deck. Although the Joiner bond between Jaina and Zekk was long dissolved, like any good pair of mission partners they seemed to read each other's thoughts on occasion—and Jag's aversion to Killiks was still so strong that he was creeped out by any hint of thought-sharing. If she needed to discourage his advances, Jaina decided, all she'd have to do was rub forearms with Zekk.

Of course, then *Zekk* might get the wrong idea . . .

They completed the sweep without finding any other hints of Alema or her strange ship, then returned to the depression Jaina had noticed. The trees this low on the mountainside were primarily majestic kingwoods, with tall straight trunks and spreading crowns of giant heart-shaped leaves. Almost all the boughs within the circle appeared more barren than those outside it, and there were several gaps where huge limbs had snapped off and fallen away.

Through the gaps, Jaina could catch glimpses of yellow-white splinters and sharp crooks where branches had been only partially broken, then pushed back into place. These branches tended to sag a little, creating the small bowl-shaped depression that had first drawn her attention.

"Something definitely came down here," Jaina observed.

"And not very fast," Zekk agreed. "This was a descent, not an impact."

"So we've found it?" Jag asked.

"Maybe," Zekk said.

Jaina grabbed her electrobinoculars and, using the light-gathering function, peered down into the forest. For the most part she saw only leaves and branches, but when she *did* glimpse the ground, all she found was undergrowth and dead leaves. At the same time, she was reaching out through the Force, searching for even the tiniest hint of dark side energy. There was none. In fact, the entire area was remarkably still, almost devoid of any sort of Force presence at all.

She lowered her electrobinoculars, then turned to find Zekk's dark eyes staring across the fuselage at her, looking as surprised as worried.

"Do you feel that?" he asked. "I mean, did you *not* feel that?"

Jaina nodded. "It's hiding from us."

"So it's down there?" Jag sounded confused. "You're sure?"

"Something's down there," Jaina said. "And it doesn't want to be found. It's hiding its presence in the Force."

"The *ship* is hiding its presence?" Jag asked. "Can ships *do* that?"

"This one can," Jaina answered.

Zekk unbuckled his crash webbing. "Hold us steady. I'll drop through the belly hatch and disable the ship."

Instead of doing as Zekk suggested, Jag swung away from the hiding place and resumed their search pattern.

"Uh, Jag, maybe you didn't hear me?" Zekk asked. "I said I'd disable Alema's ship."

"I heard you," Jag said. "But I want to leave it alone. There's too much about this vessel we don't know, and if it can warn Alema that it's been found, she'll disappear before we have a chance to catch her."

"Good," Jaina said. "The sooner we chase her off, the better. Whatever she's doing here, I don't want her doing it around these young ones."

"What makes you think you'll chase her off?" Jag countered. "This is *Alema Rar*. If she gave up that easily, she would never have survived Tenupe."

"He's got a point," Zekk said. "We'd probably just set her off. We could get a lot of kids killed for no reason."

Jaina sighed, knowing they were right. They had picked up Alema's trail this last time only after hearing about the turmoil she had created at Roqoo Depot, a supply base on the fringes of the Hapan Consortium. Apparently, a freighter captain had made the mistake of remarking on her deformities, and she had responded by inflicting wounds similar to her own—not only on the captain, but on his entire crew, as well. The survivors had been unable to remember much of anything about the fight or their assailant, but Zekk had managed to locate a security holo confirming that Alema had been the attacker.

Jag seemed to interpret Jaina's hesitation as disagreement. "We won't get another chance like this," he said. "If we let Alema get away, who will she target next? Your father? Your mother?"

"My brother?" Jaina suggested hopefully. When Jag and Zekk responded with only nervous silence, she rolled her eyes and said, "Never mind—we couldn't get that lucky."

"Then we're decided," Jag said. It wasn't quite an order—though, as formal leader of their team, he could have made it one—just verification that they had reached a consensus. "We'll try to trap Alema and end it here."

"As long as we don't put the younglings at risk," Jaina said. "If there's a choice—"

"We have to let her go," Jag agreed. "But she won't give us that choice—not Alema Rar."

He swung around the mountain, placing its bulk between their Dactyl and the academy.

"Zekk, take your StealthX and sit on top of that ship." Now Jag's tone made clear he *was* issuing an order. "If Jaina and I don't locate her, maybe we can flush her into an ambush."

Zekk made no move to start aft. "*You* sit on the ship." His voice was civil but firm. "I'll go with Jaina. I know the academy a lot better than you do."

"And I know *Alema*." Jag's tone assumed a sharp edge. "Besides, I'm the commander of this mission, so you'll do as—"

"I'll *do* what makes sense," Zekk bristled. "I'm a Jedi Knight, not some brainbolted soldier who—"

"Boys!" Jaina was disgusted with both of them. It was as

though they hadn't been listening when she explained how Mara's death had opened her eyes, how she needed to focus on being a good Jedi right now. "Whatever you're *really* arguing about, I know it's not me. You wouldn't do that—not right now."

Zekk's face flushed with shame, and Jag bled embarrassment into the Force.

"Maybe Jaina should sit on the vessel," Jag suggested. "She's the better pilot anyway, and you and I will be just as effective on the ground."

"No, you and Jaina wandering around the academy might make sense to Alema," Zekk said, starting aft. "You and I won't. If she sees the two of us here together, the first thing she'll do is start looking for Jaina."

"You're right, of course," Jag said. "Thank you."

"Don't mention it."

Zekk disappeared through the hatch into the aft cargo hold, and a few minutes later Jaina felt him open himself to the battle-meld that Jedi used to communicate while flying StealthXs. The Dactyl gave a little shudder as the rear cargo doors slid open, altering its atmospheric flight profile. She turned back to her observation blister and, a moment later, saw Zekk's StealthX dropping away behind them.

Jaina sent him a good-hunting wish through the Force, then unbuckled her crash webbing and went aft to close the cargo door and prepare the Dactyl for landing. By the time she had finished, Jag was already flying through the hollowed-out cliff face that served as the entrance to the academy's main hangar.

A hint of danger sense tickled Jaina between the shoulder blades, and she went forward to join Jag on the flight deck.

"Everything okay?" she asked.

"Of course." Jag was sitting in the pilot's seat in textbook posture, his back straight, both eyes forward, and both hands on the steering yoke. He slipped the ungainly Dactyl into the berthing area outlined by the green lights on the floor, and did not look over until the vessel had settled onto its landing struts. "Why do you ask?"

Jaina peered through the forward viewport. "Something feels wrong."

Jag frowned, driving the scar on his brow downward like a lightning bolt. "Wrong how?"

Jaina only shrugged and continued to study the hangar floor. Like the rest of the academy, it was strangely deserted, packed with transports, skiffs, and trainers, but—save for a few droids going about their tasks in near darkness— devoid of the maintenance activity that usually kept such places bustling. Jaina stretched her Force-awareness to the far corners of the hangar and found no sentient presences in the vast cavern at all.

Finally, she said, "Just empty. Have you ever seen a hangar this quiet?"

"Not an active one." Jag unbuckled his crash webbing, then stood and attached his blaster holster to his belt. "Do you think Alema could already have done something?"

Anything was possible, of course. But Jaina had seen no overt signs of violence, and she just didn't see how a single Force-user—even one as crazy as Alema—could take control of the entire Jedi academy.

Her musings were interrupted by the crackle of the cockpit speaker.

"How long are you going to stay down there looking for gokobs?" asked a throaty female voice. "I'd like to hear what you found on your security sweep."

Jag cocked a questioning brow in Jaina's direction.

"I guess there's only one way to find out." She leaned down and opened a channel to reply. "Sorry, command. We'll be right up."

"Very well," answered the flight control commander—a

Duros woman named Orame. "Just watch out for the gokobs—the smell up here is bad enough."

"Will do." Jaina closed the channel, then frowned in confusion. "What is it with her and gokobs today?"

"What *are* gokobs?" Jag asked.

"I'll explain on the way." Jaina turned to leave the flight deck.

By the time they had left the Dactyl and reached the lift that would take them to the flight control bunker, Jag had heard more about gokobs than anyone would enjoy knowing.

"So Orame is telling us to watch out for overfriendly vermin?" Jag asked.

"Basically." Jaina snapped the lightsaber off her belt and stepped into the lift, then motioned for Jag to follow. "Coming?"

"Of course." He flicked the safety off his blaster, then asked, "Stun or kill?"

"Let's stick with stun until we know what's going on," Jaina replied. "If it's Alema, we can always switch it back to kill and blast her after she's already down."

Jag glanced at her from the corner of his eye. "You're joking, right?"

Jaina shook her head. "Not if she's done anything to the young ones." She placed her thumb over a pad on the control panel. "Ready?"

Jag nodded, and a few moments later, the turbolift delivered them to the flight control level. Jaina didn't sense anyone lurking in the corridor—but if Alema was out there, she wouldn't. She left the turbolift in a diving roll and came up with her lightsaber ready to ignite.

She found only Jag facing her, holding his blaster with both hands and looking slightly amused.

"Gokobs?" he asked.

"Very funny."

Jaina led the way down the corridor to the flight control

bunker. She could sense the usual dozen Force presences inside, all calm and seemingly focused on the task at hand. Still, she kept her lightsaber ready as the door hissed aside to reveal a huge holodisplay ringed by individual control stations. Floating above the display was an image of the planet Ossus and its moons, along with numerical designators for dozens of artificial satellites.

A tall Duros woman—the flight control commander, Orame—motioned to Jaina from the other side of the holodisplay. "Come in. There's something I need to—"

Jaina's spine nettled with danger sense, and she sprang into a high, arcing Force flip that carried her into the heart of the planetary hologram. Several of the flight controllers cried out in alarm and sprang to their feet, their hands rising from their laps holding blaster pistols they hadn't had time to draw. Jaina ignited her lightsaber and batted half a dozen stun bolts back at the men who had fired them, then came down next to Orame.

"Jaina, no!" Orame cried. "You don't understand!"

"I understand—" Jaina paused to return a stun bolt into the chest of a "flight controller." "—that they're shooting at me!"

On the opposite side of the holodisplay, two men fell convulsing, their tunics smoking where Jag's stun bolts had struck them from behind. Jaina Force-jerked the feet from beneath one of her attackers, then pointed at another and Force-hurled him across two control stations into the last man holding a weapon.

She pointed the tip of her lightsaber at this last pair of attackers, then ordered, "Don't move."

They fell motionless, as did everyone else in the chamber except Jag, who secured the door behind him and set about collecting weapons. Keeping her lightsaber ignited to emphasize the peril any resisters would face, Jaina helped by using the Force to slide blasters away from a few semiconscious attackers.

Without looking away from the men—whoever they were—Jaina tipped her head toward Orame and asked, "Gokobs?"

"You might say that," she replied. "I was *trying* to tell you the situation stinks, but they're friendly."

"Don't seem very friendly," Jag said. He was pressing a knee into the back of one of the men he had stunned, binding the fellow's hands while making certain his prisoner could not attack. "Friendlies don't fire blasters at you."

A deep voice spoke from several meters to the right, almost behind Jaina. "They were stun bolts—and Jedi Solo *did* make a rather alarming entrance."

Jaina looked toward the voice and found a tall human ducking through the doorway from Orame's private office. He had a long face with sunken eyes and a blade-like nose, and he was wearing the black uniform of a GAG major. He stopped a pace outside the office and spread his hands, palms out, to show he was unarmed.

"Now I would appreciate it if you would allow my men to resume their duties."

Jaina continued to hold her lightsaber at middle guard. "I don't think so." She cocked her head toward Orame. "Why don't you tell me what's going on here?"

Orame waved a blue, long-fingered hand toward the major. "Allow me to present Major Serpa," she said. "Apparently, he's here to protect us."

Serpa spread a smile that made ice seem warm. "You never know what those terrorists might attack next."

A dark storm boiled through Jaina's veins, and she very nearly didn't stop herself from Force-hurling the smug major through the nearest durasteel wall. "Jacen is holding the academy *hostage*?"

Serpa continued to smirk in her direction. "There's no need to look at it that way." He held his hand out toward her lightsaber. "But it would be wise to surrender your weapons before there are any more . . . misunderstand-ings."

"Not going to happen," Jaina said. "But I *will* give you an hour to take your men and clear out of here."

Serpa's smile vanished. "I'm afraid that isn't going to hap-pen, either. The colonel entrusted the safety of this facility and everyone in it to my battalion, and I *won't* abandon that duty—no matter who gets caught in the crossfire."

Jag's eyes narrowed with the same outrage that Jaina found herself struggling to contain. He started toward Serpa, circling the holodisplay opposite Jaina so their quarry would be trapped, saying nothing.

Serpa merely watched him come, his Force presence be-traying more excitement than fear, and Jaina suddenly real-ized why her brother had chosen the major for this particular duty.

"Hold on, Jag," she said. "I don't think the major is right in the head."

Serpa's eyes darkened, and he turned to Jaina with an air of disappointment. "That would depend on how one de-fines *right,* but if you mean to suggest I'd *enjoy* destroying this facility rather than risk having it fall into, um, *un-friendly* hands . . ."

He extended his arm toward the man Jag had been bind-ing. A hold-out blaster slid out of his sleeve into his hand, and he fired one bolt into the man's face. Orame and sev-eral GAG troopers cried out in shock. Serpa merely looked back to Jaina and smiled.

"You're absolutely right," he said. "I'm happy to kill *anyone.*"

Jag glared at Serpa like a bug that needed crushing, but Jaina deactivated her lightsaber and motioned for Jag to lower his blaster. She could tell by the eagerness in Serpa's Force aura that he was fully prepared to order the acade-my's destruction—actually *hoping* they'd give him an ex-cuse to do so.

"I can't believe what my brother has come to," Jaina said, "calling on the likes of you."

"You know what they say . . . desperate times and all that." Serpa cocked his arm, and the hold-out blaster vanished into his sleeve. "Now perhaps you'd care to surrender your weapons?"

"Not really," Jaina said, resigning herself to working with the sociopath to capture Alema. "And I doubt you'd want us to, if you knew why we're here."

Serpa frowned. "I'll decide that."

"Fine," Jag said. "Do you know who Alema Rar is?"

"Of course—a Jedi Knight gone bad." Serpa smirked again. "Imagine that."

"It happens," Jaina said, fuming. "And she's here somewhere. We don't know what she's up to, but you can bet it's no good."

Serpa scowled in suspicion. "How long?"

"Probably since last night," Jag said. "We're working off a set of vector plots that go all the way back to the Hapes Consortium, so we're fairly sure—"

"She came from the *Consortium*?" Orame interrupted. "*Where* in the Consortium?"

"On the Terephon side, just outside the Transitory Mists," Jaina answered. "A place called Roqoo Depot. Why?"

Orame lowered the corners of her thin-lipped mouth. "I wonder if Roqoo Depot is between here and Kavan?"

Jaina had a sinking feeling. She didn't know Hapan astrometry well enough to know the answer, but she had heard that Kavan was where Mara's body had been found.

"I'd be very interested in the answer to that question," Jaina said.

Before Serpa could object, Orame tapped a string of commands into a control console. The image above the flight control holopad shifted to a map of the Hapan Consortium. Roqoo Depot's approximate location was noted on the fringes of the map, on the side closest to Ossus. A few dozen light-years away, in the same system as Hapes, the planet Kavan sat at the far end of a hyperdrive route running straight past Roqoo Depot.

"A straight shot!" Jaina gasped.

"From what the astrometry files say, yes," Orame replied. "And if Alema Rar was at Roqoo Depot—"

"It's too big a coincidence," Jaina agreed. "If she didn't do it, she was involved."

"You can't jump to that conclusion yet," Jag warned. "Remember, Alema didn't chop up that freighter crew until *after* Mara died. Would she really have drawn attention to herself like that so soon after the murder?"

Jaina gave him a *don't-be-stupid* look and said nothing.

"Okay." Jag sighed. "We can assume she knows something."

"At the least," Jaina said. Growing more worried about the young ones by the moment, she turned to Serpa. "*Now* do you want us to surrender our weapons?"

"Actually, yes," Serpa replied. "Your little play was very convincing, but Alema Rar isn't on Ossus. My team has been in control of the flight room—"

"Would you have seen her come down in a StealthX?" Jaina asked.

She didn't bother explaining that Alema had been flying something else, a vessel they didn't quite understand but that nevertheless seemed to be as elusive as a StealthX.

Serpa considered this a moment, then removed a comlink from his sleeve pocket and opened a channel. "Captain Tong, give me a status check on all stations. Note anything out of the ordinary—anything at all."

"As you wish, sir," a clear female voice responded. "I'll report back in a few moments."

Instead of clicking off and waiting for a paging chirp, Serpa held out his arm and stared at the comlink, smiling and nodding to himself each time a station reported everything normal. Jaina saw that she and Jag were going to have to be very careful how they dealt with the major, lest they prompt him to do something rash.

As Serpa continued to listen to the reports, Jaina lowered her voice to a whisper and asked Orame, "What about the instructors? Why didn't they try to stop him?"

Orame shook her head. "The only Jedi here are the Masters Solusar and half a dozen new Jedi Knights stuck on patrol duty," she said. "Everyone else went to the funeral on Coruscant."

"Imagine that," Serpa said, looking up from his comlink. "Stripping the academy of its Jedi when terrorists are running rampant across the galaxy. It's fortunate we arrived when we did."

Orame's blue face darkened to purple. "The *only* reason your shuttle reached the ground in one piece was because you declared an emergency and requested medical assistance."

"Bombardment seemed rather extreme, under the circumstances," Serpa said amiably. "After all, the Jedi and the Galactic Alliance Guard *are* on the same side."

"At least we're supposed to be." Though Jaina wasn't really surprised by the depth of Jacen's treachery, she *was* stinging from it. He had been such a gentle spirit as a teenager—such a caring brother—that she could never have imagined what he would become as an adult, how he would wound her and the entire Jedi Order. "Frankly, I'm beginning to have my doubts."

"You see?" Serpa asked. "That's why the colonel sent me—to make sure we all *stay* friends."

"I've never cared for Jacen's idea of friendship," Jag said. "What did you find out about Alema?"

"You know what I found out." Serpa flashed him a sly grin. "That wherever she is, it's not here."

"You can't know that," Jaina said. "Just because none of your security stations reported anything unusual—"

"We have a *lot* of security stations," Serpa interrupted. "I can tell you how many gokobs are sneaking potams from the kitchens."

"Alema is no gokob," Jaina said. "She could walk right past one of your guards and he wouldn't remember seeing her."

"My guards wouldn't remember seeing her." Serpa mimicked the monotone voice often used by targets of a Force suggestion—then rolled his eyes. "*Pleeeaase*! Colonel Solo has inured us to your Jedi mind tricks."

"This is no trick," Jag said. "Alema Rar has the ability to wipe the memory of seeing her from even *Jedi* minds. It would be no challenge at all to deceive the witless sculags in your command."

"Witless sculags?" Serpa appeared to consider the term for a moment, then nodded and extended his hand toward Jaina. "You're probably right. I'm afraid I'll have to take your weapons and comlinks now—my *sculags* might mistake you for the enemy and get themselves killed."

"Not going to happen," Jaina said. She nodded Jag toward the door, then started around the big holodisplay herself. "We're going hunting for Alema Rar. Tell your people to stay out of our way."

"Sorry—that won't work for me," Serpa said from behind them. "As I said before, I'm not going to place this facility at risk by allowing unauthorized personnel to walk around with weapons—no matter *who* gets caught in the crossfire."

No prickle of danger sense ran down Jaina's spine, but there was something cold in Serpa's voice that made her stop and turn. "I hope you're not threatening the young ones."

"I'm merely pointing out the danger *you'll* be placing them in," Serpa said evenly. "The rules have been established for the safety of everyone. I really must insist on hav-

ing your comlinks and weapons . . . if you intend to stay on
academy grounds."

Jaina frowned. "*If* we intend to stay?" She hadn't really
expected that Serpa would let them depart, but—compared
with the young ones—she and Jag were relatively worthless
hostages. "You'd let us leave?"

"Colonel Solo does want this operation conducted under
the strictest secrecy, but—" Serpa waved a hand at the battered squad of troopers still struggling to pick themselves
up off the floor. "—does it look like I could stop you? If
you want to leave Masters Tionne and Solusar here with
only a handful of inexperienced Jedi Knights to, um, *coordinate* between my battalion of sculags and all those Jedi
young ones . . . well, I'm enough of a realist to realize the
choice is entirely yours."

Jaina felt suddenly sick to her stomach. Serpa wasn't exactly threatening the young ones, but he *was* pointing out
how much danger they would be in if the situation between
Jacen and the Jedi continued to deteriorate. Eight Jedi—
especially when six of them were inexperienced—would
not be enough to protect hundreds of children from an entire GAG battalion.

Jag arrived at the exit and reached for the control panel
to unlock the door he had secured earlier.

Jaina motioned for him to stop. "Jag, hold on." She
could not believe her brother would actually order Serpa to
harm the academy students—but Jacen had done many
things lately that she could not believe. "I think we'd better
turn over our weapons."

Jag scowled as though she were as unbalanced as Serpa.
"Why in the six novas would we do *that*?"

"Same reason Masters Tionne and Solusar did." As
Jaina explained, she was reaching out to Zekk in the Force,
opening a battle-meld and urging him to forget about
Alema, stay hidden, and wait until he was needed. "Because we can't destroy an entire GAG battalion without

getting a lot of kids killed, and because matters aren't that desperate yet."

Serpa smiled. "I thought you might see it my way."

"You can be very persuasive." Jaina opened her lightsaber and removed the focusing crystal. "I'm sure that's why my brother entrusted you with this mission."

"One of many reasons." Serpa came around the holodisplay and accepted her lightsaber and blaster pistol, then turned to face Jag. "Fel?"

Jag removed the power packs from his blaster and vibroknife, then returned to Jaina's side and held the weapons just out of Serpa's reach.

"I want to continue our search," Jag said. "Whether you and your men realize it or not, Alema Rar *is* here."

"By all means." Serpa waited until Jag placed the weapons in his hands, then said, "And if you find her, let me know. I'll send someone to pick up the pieces."

five

A sudden compulsion to hide welled up inside Alema's chest. Worried that her pursuers had found her after all, she peered over the top of the study carrel where she was working. In the front lobby, she saw only the same two GAG troopers who had been guarding the library when she arrived. They were leaning against the front desk, talking softly and gazing into each other's eyes. A faint voice droned over the woman's comlink, but either the orders did not concern her or Alema's Force suggestion had fallen on ground more fertile than she had realized.

The compulsion to hide became an entreaty to wait, then a premonition of trouble, and Alema realized the sensations were coming from outside herself. Someone was projecting those feelings so powerfully they had overspilled a battle-meld and rippled out for just anyone to sense. Probably the academy's GAG "protectors" were giving Jaina and her two lust-toads more trouble than they had Alema, and that was a relief. The trio had been hounding Alema's trail since Roqoo Depot, and she had known it would only be a matter of time before they caught up and began to snoop around the academy.

Alema stretched her Force-awareness toward the guards,

then focused her attention on the drone coming from the woman's comlink.

". . . and her escort searching academy grounds." The voice was male and assertive, no doubt that of the mission commander. "Don't interfere, but don't let them . . . the hostages."

Hostages?

Stunned to hear the term actually being used over a comm channel, Alema dropped back into her seat. She had known all along that the GAG troops were there to prevent the academy from being used to foment resistance to Jacen's coup, but she had never suspected he would actually be foolish enough to take the young ones *hostage*. It was a bold move—but also a rash one, far more likely to provoke Luke than to contain him.

Alema did not understand how Jacen could have made such a mistake. Until now, his stratagems had been nothing short of brilliant. He had won over the population of Coruscant and much of the rest of the Alliance with his tough-on-terrorists approach, and he had used his popularity to take personal control of nearly half the galaxy. So why had he made such a terrible blunder *now*? Why had he suddenly grown arrogant enough to believe he could threaten the Jedi Order and succeed?

The answer, of course, was Lumiya. Jacen had not blundered until his mentor was killed, then—within days of her death—he had overreached himself. Obviously, the colonel still needed guidance . . . and Lumiya had clearly foreseen that he would. Why else would she have allowed Alema to follow her to her asteroid hideout? Lumiya had wanted to make sure that if she were gone, Alema would have the resources to carry on in her place.

Alema linked her datapad to the archives computer she had been accessing, then downloaded the limited data she had found regarding the vessel she had inherited from Lumiya. According to Jedi histories, Ship—it refused to reveal

its name, so Alema just called it Ship—was an ancient meditation sphere, a sort of thinking starship that had at one
time been used by Jedi and Sith alike. From what little the
records had revealed, the meditation sphere was a sort of
Force-augmented control vessel, designed to amplify a commander's battle meditation abilities while also concealing
his or her location from the enemy.

The datapad displayed a message announcing that it had
completed the download. Alema deactivated the datalink
and erased her access trail on the main computer, then
tucked the datapad into its pouch on her utility belt and
started toward the exit. The two guards were so taken with
each other that they failed to notice her until she had
passed the front desk and was halfway across the lobby.

"What the kark?" the male gasped. "Where'd *you* come
from?"

The woman was quicker to recover from her surprise.
"Halt!" she ordered. "Move those hands a centimeter, and
I blast you."

Alema turned to find a big Merr-Sonn power blaster
pointed in her direction. She raised her hand anyway, and
the guard pulled the trigger.

The weapon issued a single soft *click,* and now it was the
female's turn to gasp, "What the *kark*?"

"There's nothing to be concerned about." Alema waved
her hand, then pulled a pair of power cells from her robe
pocket. "You gave these to us for safekeeping."

The woman scowled in suspicion. "Why would I—"

"You remember." Alema addressed herself to the man,
who—as usual—was weaker-minded than his prospective
mate. "We're a friend of Jacen's."

"It's okay, Tiz," the man said. "You remember. She's a
friend of the colonel's."

Tiz's scowl melted away, and she holstered her blaster.
"That's right." She smiled at the man. "I remember now."

"Good."

Alema would have Force-tossed the power cells into Tiz's head for letting a male make up her mind for her, but it was important to keep her visit to the library a secret. If Jaina and her lust-toads learned that she had come to Ossus to use the Jedi library, they would find a way to identify the records she had accessed, and then they would know as much about Ship as she did. Alema used the Force to float the power cells back to the lobby desk, at the same time backing toward the exit.

"You two have fun," Alema suggested. "The colonel won't mind."

By the time she was out the door, the pair were pulling at each other's utilities. Confident that her slippery Force presence would rob their minds of any memory of her visit, she worked her way through the academy gardens into the forest where Ship was waiting. The hike up to its hiding place wasn't particularly difficult, even with Alema's damaged foot and useless arm. But it *was* an unpleasant reminder of the time she had spent injured and marooned on Tenupe, of all that had been taken from her; every step into the night was a burning reminder of her duty to the Balance and her obligation to set matters even between her and Leia Solo.

As Alema approached the ravine where Ship had concealed itself, the strong-willed vessel rose into view without waiting for a summons. It was fantastically hideous, a bloated orb with a web of raised veins pulsing over an amber-colored hull that could be opaque or transparent depending on its mood. It held its four wings folded flat against the sides of its round belly, and as it spun to face her, it looked to Alema like a giant, disembodied brain—a very *old* giant disembodied brain.

Ancient, Ship corrected. A two-meter section of hull melted into a ramp and extruded itself toward the bank where Alema was standing. *And brainy enough to feel when the enemy is watching.*

The reproach in Ship's thoughts was unmistakable, but Alema merely smirked and strolled up the ramp at her own relaxed pace. They had nothing to fear from *these* enemies, at least not at the moment. Wisely or unwisely, Jacen had given them something more important to worry about than Alema Rar.

Ship was doubtful, but it waited until Alema was kneeling inside, then sealed itself up and awaited a destination.

"Kanz sector," Alema said aloud. "We assume you remember the coordinates of Lumiya's asteroid."

Ship remained in the ravine, and the smoldering flame that seemed embedded in its bulkheads grew brighter and redder. It would serve as the Broken One's transport because it had nothing better to do, but it had no intention of taking her to Kanz sector. Lumiya would not have wanted Alema rifling through her home.

"Are you *certain*?" As Alema spoke, she was using the Force to push sideways against Ship's resolve, trying not so much to challenge its decision as to merely shift its perspective. It was the same technique she had employed as the Dark Nest's Night Herald, one that she had used many times to control UnuThul and his nest. "Lumiya *wanted* us to continue her work with Jacen."

Ship recoiled angrily from her mind-touch. It had served Masters more powerful than she could imagine. Did she really think it would not feel a simple thought veer? It was insulted beyond expression.

Despite the protests, Alema could feel the vessel slowly yielding to her will. And why shouldn't it? At its core, Ship was still a machine, and that meant it had been designed to serve. All Alema need do was prove herself capable of commanding it. She pushed harder against its resolve, this time forsaking subtlety for sheer power.

"You *remember*," she said. "Lumiya *invited* us to her asteroid."

Ship struggled to hold firm, recalling that Lumiya had

not actually invited the Broken One to her asteroid. Alema had *followed* her there.

"That doesn't change facts," Alema insisted. "Lumiya *asked* for our help."

Lumiya hadn't asked—the Broken One had volunteered.

"And Lumiya *accepted*," Alema pointed out. She was careful to continue her pattern of stressing important action words; that was a key part of the technique. "She *assigned* us to keep watch on Mara."

Ship knew what she was doing, but it was not a sentient being, and it did not have the strength to resist the pressure she was bringing to bear. What the Broken One said was true, Ship realized at last. Lumiya had *sent* her to watch Mara.

"Because Lumiya *trusted* us," Alema said. "Because she was *counting* on us to continue *helping* Jacen . . . like we did at Roqoo Depot."

When you reconfigured that freighter crew? Ship asked.

"So the Jedi would *know* we were near when Mara died," Alema clarified. "So they would suspect *us* instead of Jacen."

To ensure his success, Ship added. *To ensure that the Sith would rise again.*

"Yes," Alema agreed. "We promise. The Sith *will rule* again."

In the next instant Alema found herself pressed against the rear bulkhead as Ship accelerated skyward. A sense of frustration flooded the Force as one of her pursuers—Zekk, judging by the labored purity of his presence—alerted his fellows to her escape. Jaina's reaction was not discernible, but the fact that no one launched a shadow bomb or a proton torpedo at Ship told Alema all she needed to know. For now, her hunters had more pressing matters on their minds.

The journey to the Kanz sector was as uneventful as it was unnerving. Ship seemed to take a special delight in tax-

ing her composure, flying most of the way with a hull so
transparent that Alema felt as though she were traveling
across the galaxy in a bubble. For a spacefaring species like
the Duros or Gands, the illusion might have produced feelings of exhilaration and awe—but not so for Alema. Twi'leks
were cave dwellers by nature, born to the snug comfort of
total darkness and tight spaces. By the time Ship entered
the unnamed system and a silver nugget of rock appeared
in the vacuum ahead, every instinct in her body was screaming for her to close her eyes, to slam shut all perception of
the brutal, sickening vastness of the galaxy.

Alema ignored those instincts, forcing herself to watch
calmly as the nugget swelled to a tumbling stone, then to a
dust-caked boulder glinting in the light of the distant sun.
Ship was testing her, searching for any indication that she
was too weak to make good on her promise, and Alema refused to provide one. She knew that Ship could see in her
thoughts how terrifying she found the void, but she also
knew that it could sense the resolve with which she faced
that terror, her utter willingness to sacrifice *anything* to restore the Balance between her and Leia.

When the asteroid had grown so large that nothing else
could be seen ahead, Ship swung around to its dark side
and made a breakneck hangar approach. Sensing that it
was still trying to rattle her, Alema resigned herself to the
possibility of a fiery death as the price of flying such a fine
vessel, then watched in stoic silence as murky crags swelled
into looming cliffs. At the last possible moment, a camou-
flaged blast door slid open, and Ship shot into the hideaway's cramped hangar, decelerating so hard that Alema
had to Force-anchor herself in place to keep from being
hurled into the forward bulkhead.

Ship stopped almost a meter from the far wall and extruded three landing struts, then settled onto the hangar
floor, hissing, creaking, and groaning as though it were the

Millennium Falcon. Alema allowed herself an enormous smirk of victory.

"Satisfied?" she asked.

Ship let out a final disgruntled rumble, then, once the hangar had repressurized, shaped a door and ramp for her.

"Wait for us here," Alema said, rising. "You may as well top off your fuel and tend to your maintenance needs. This may take a few hours."

Ship seemed amused by that, and Alema had the distinct impression that it expected her to be here much longer than a few hours—*forever*, probably.

"In that case," Alema said, descending the ramp, "if we fail to return within a hundred years, consider yourself released."

If Ship made any reply, it was lost to the dark side aura that began to rise around her as she set foot on the permacrete floor. The energy was so thick it was almost tangible, a cold cloud of gloom that trailed up her thighs like lovers' fingers. She shuddered with what she thought were pleasant memories—until the shuddering continued and an icy knot of danger sense began to form between her shoulder blades.

Traps.

Of course there were traps. This *was* a Sith hideaway, was it not? Alema opened herself to the Force and felt a sharp sense of peril from the far wall of the hangar, where two dozen coolant drums stood stacked in a triangle seven meters high. The smart thing would have been to climb back aboard Ship and flee before one of those drums exploded. Instead, Alema started across the hangar at a sprint.

Ship's surprise was exceeded only by its alarm. It seemed less concerned about Alema than about her orders. If she wanted to get herself killed, that was fine with Ship—but she couldn't expect it to—

Stay. Alema put the weight of the Force behind her thought-command. *My turn to test* your *nerve.*

Ship withdrew its presence in a huff, leaving Alema free to concentrate on the problem of the coolant drums. The knot between her shoulder blades was growing colder and tighter by the second, and of course the danger seemed to be emanating from the bottom of the stack. Without breaking stride, she made a clutching motion with her hand, and the middle barrel slid out of line.

As Alema floated the drum across the hangar to meet her, the rest of the stack crashed down in a cacophony of sloshing liquid and ringing metal. Several barrels burst, pouring hundreds of liters of viscous blue fluid onto the floor and filling the air with the caustic sweetness of hyperdrive coolant.

Alema already had her lightsaber in hand. Ignoring the burning pain that the fumes brought to her eyes, she ignited the blade and slashed the top off the drum in front of her.

What she found inside was a barrelful of baradium with a proton grenade detonator—enough explosive power to shatter the asteroid into hundreds of pieces. A thick harness of multicolored wires ran from the detonator to a digital timer currently displaying the number 10 and counting down by seconds. Next to the display was a red disarming switch.

Rejecting the switch as much too obvious for Lumiya, Alema deactivated her lightsaber and dropped it, then frantically began to sort through the wire harness with her one good hand. By the time she found a single gray disarming wire, the display read 3. She started to pull it—then recalled how Lumiya had nearly killed them aboard the *Anakin Solo* by mistaking a proximity sensor feed for a safety delay. She released the gray and grabbed the most orange of the three orange wires. When no warning chill raced down her spine, she held her breath and jerked the wire free.

The timer reached 0. Nothing exploded.

Alema felt her one lekku uncurl in relief. She recovered her lightsaber and, coughing violently from the hyperdrive fumes, turned to Ship with her brow cocked in triumph.

Ship seemed unimpressed. There were a hundred ways to die in Lumiya's sanctuary. Certainly one of the most foolish was standing in a cloud of coolant fumes to gloat.

The vessel had a point, Alema had to admit. She crossed the hangar to the hatch that led into Lumiya's chambers, then began to work her way past the gauntlet of traps that had once protected the privacy of the Dark Lady of the Sith. First there was the flechette spray behind the false control pad at the entrance. Then came the air lock with the reversed controls and the poison "decontamination shower," followed by a clever Force illusion of Lumiya herself that somehow transferred the damage of any attack directed at *it* back to the assailant. Alema *really* wanted to learn how that was done—once the throbbing inside her skull subsided enough for her to concentrate.

Finally, Alema found herself standing inside the foyer of Lumiya's suite of chambers, her lekku prickling in anticipation of the wonders she would soon discover. Each of Lumiya's traps had whetted her appetite for Sith technology, and each time she had defeated one, her expectations had risen. Whatever Lumiya had been trying to guard, it was obviously very important—and valuable. Alema began to have visions of a Sith megaweapon, something that might be able to bring the Galactic Alliance to heel with a single demonstration. Or maybe it was something more subtle, such as an artifact that allowed one to read an enemy's thoughts from afar. Maybe she would find both—or a whole cache of strange new Sith technology. All those traps had been designed to protect *something*.

Alema started by focusing on her Force-awareness, looking for any cold places or disturbances that might suggest a nexus of dark side energy—then quickly gave it up as hopeless. The whole asteroid was suffused with the dark side, so much so that she almost felt as though she were snug in the Dark Nest again, surrounded by the familiar presences of her fellow Gorog. It was a bittersweet sensation, one that threatened to undermine her safety by lulling her into a false sense of security.

Alema advanced to a careful reconnaissance of the quarters. With a handful of beige sleeping chambers, a keet-paneled study, a vaulted dining room, and a sunken conversation parlor, the suite was comfortable enough. But it was hardly grand or opulent, far from the kind of place that one would expect someone of Lumiya's power and resources to call home. There was no artwork or memorabilia to make it feel inhabited, though the full-length mirrors on every wall did hint at Lumiya's vanity.

Somehow, the mirrors always seemed to reflect Alema at the best possible angle, concealing her disfigurements and accentuating her still-svelte figure. She was enormously pleased—but that did not prevent her from cautiously checking behind each one to make certain it did not conceal a safe or hidden doors.

Unfortunately, she discovered no secret chambers behind the mirrors, or anywhere else in the suite. The only hint of a secure room was an ancient synthwood door tucked in back of an old-fashioned kitchen. The infrared ovens and particle beam cooktops were too clean to have been used anytime recently, but the door was the only locked portal she had found in the entire suite.

Alema checked for each kind of trap she had encountered so far, then for all the others she had been trained to identify. Finding none, she opened herself to the Force and ran her hand over the door's surface, alert for the faintest prickle of danger sense.

She felt nothing. Whatever trap Lumiya had placed on

this door, Alema could not find it. And that could only mean one thing: this was where the Sith treasures were hidden.

Alema stepped back, taking a moment to calm her pounding heart and consider how to attack the problem. There was no question of leaving the door unopened. To restore the Balance between her and Leia, she had to turn Jacen into what Leia hated most—another Emperor. To turn Jacen into another Emperor, she had to be able to control him, to stop him from doing foolish things like taking the Jedi academy hostage. And to control Jacen, she needed leverage—leverage such as the Sith artifacts hidden behind that door.

After a few minutes of calming exercises, Alema's heart finally stopped pounding. She felt confident that she had considered the problem from every angle, and still she could not figure out how the door might be trapped. Her only resource was her knowledge of Lumiya.

The Dark Lady of the Sith had been a sophisticated and subtle woman, someone who planned in layers and took great pride in reading her prey. She would expect anyone who had made it this deep into her inner sanctum to be as cunning and complex as she was, and her trap would be designed with that type of person in mind. What she would *not* expect was an intruder who acted like a common thug, who took the easiest, most direct route to what she wanted.

Alema took a small concussion grenade off her utility belt, then used a dab of synthglue to affix it to the door over the lock. She retreated into the adjacent room and used the Force to activate the trigger. There came a silver flash and an earsplitting bang, and a cloud of black smoke rolled into the dining room.

Once the smoke had cleared, Alema braved a shower of fire-suppression foam to return to the kitchen. The door in back was hanging twisted and half open. In her excitement,

Alema barely remembered to check for more traps, but she still didn't find any—sprung or otherwise. She activated a glow rod and peered through the charred doorway into an old food storage closet.

The shelves were lined with cybernetic supplies—tools, fluids, replacement parts—all the equipment Lumiya might need to maintain her mechanical half. As far as Alema could tell, the little room did not contain a single Sith arti-fact.

Completely forgetting her own safety now, she slipped past the door. An overhead glow panel activated automati-cally, filling the chamber with soft white light. Along one wall, she found a huge stockpile of powdered mixes for the protein and vitamin drinks that had served Lumiya's half-cyborg body as food. On a low shelf on the opposite wall, she found a few power cells and extra strands for the Dark Lady's lightwhip.

"Spare parts?" Alema felt herself swelling up with anger, the frustration and fear of the search stoking the fire inside. *"Protein drink?"*

She swept half a dozen powdered protein canisters off a shelf, then kicked out in the opposite direction and sent fly-ing a carton of sharpened Kaiburr Crystals. *That* felt so good that she ignited her lightsaber, then caused a sour-smelling cascade of hydraulic fluid by slashing open an en-tire row of plastoid jars.

"We want artifacts!" Alema swung again, cutting the supports from beneath a high shelf. "We want Sith trea-sure!"

A cybernetic arm came crashing down on her, battering her about the head and shoulders. She shrugged it off and started to bring her lightsaber around to hack the offend-ing part into so much chaff—then noticed a finger-length datachip holder lying in the hydraulic fluid near the open end of the arm's hollinium casing.

"Well . . . what have we here?" Alema deactivated her

lightsaber and retrieved the datachip holder. "Could *you* be the reason Lumiya kept this door locked?"

She stared at the fiberplast case as though waiting for an answer—which, in a sense, she was. After a moment, she began to perceive a faint ripple in the Force, the barest hint of the last emotion she had expected to encounter: hope, perhaps even comfort.

"Interesting," Alema said. "What *are* you?"

This time she did not wait for an answer—despite what Ship believed, she was not *that* broken. Instead, she looked for more datachips, first searching through the other cybernetic supplies, then the Kaiburr Crystals she had scattered across the floor and the other cartons of lightwhip parts. She ended by emptying every canister of vitamin drink and powdered protein into the growing mess on the floor.

There were no more datachips to be found, though Alema did discover over a million credits in generic chits hidden inside some of the protein canisters. She left the currency on the floor with everything else she did not want; *credits* she could get anytime, and stealing them was always so much more fun.

Convinced there was nothing else to discover in the food closet, Alema returned to Lumiya's study and inserted the chip into a datapad. She expected to encounter a request for a password or some other form of security; instead, a hooded head appeared on the display and instantly began to speak.

"Our apologies for the brevity of your journey." The speaker's face remained hidden in the shadows beneath his hood, but the voice was male—and full of dark power. "Had we foreseen the speed of the invaders' advance, we would have sent a more sizable escort. Should you survive and care to reach us on your own, the navigation string attached to this message will guide you . . . *once.*"

The figure appeared to lean away from the light, and the display went dark. Alema extracted the datachip, then sat back to consider. She had been taught as a young Jedi that only two Sith existed at any one time: the dark side drive for personal power always prevented them from establishing a larger Order. But Lumiya had once hinted—in the missile hold of the *Anakin Solo,* as she made preparations that might involve sacrificing herself to kill Luke Skywalker— that there *were* more than two Sith, and that their plan for the galaxy did not necessarily involve Lumiya's survival. The figure in the message certainly supported this idea; at the least, he seemed to be part of a larger group.

Alema returned the datachip to its holder and started for the hangar. Clearly, she had set her sights too low. She did not need Sith *artifacts* to guide Jacen to success.

What she needed were the Sith themselves.

six

To the starboard side of the observation bubble hung a crescent of smog-shrouded world, its planetary defense shields dappled with gold overload circles, its legendary defense platforms reduced to flickering twinkles of flame. Balmorra was lost. Jacen was certain of that. But the Confederation would pay dearly for victory here, provided that the pilots of the Fourth Fleet lived up to their fearless reputation—and provided that he could finally bring his battle meditation into play.

When Jacen closed his eyes, he could see the Hutt armada—a motley swarm of vessels ranging from heavy marauders to fast corvettes—attacking Balmorra. He could see a flotilla of Commenorian Star Destroyers performing a screening action to keep the Alliance at bay. What Jacen could *not* see was the readiness of his crews: whether they were eager for a fight, whether their commanders were alert or distracted . . . whether they were loyal to the new government or considered it an illegal regime.

Jacen turned his attention to the Fourth's new flagship, *Peacebringer,* then pictured Admiral Ratobo's noseless face, the big eyes and huge bald head. The image darkened to gray-blue, and a pair of pensive creases climbed the Bith's high brow. For a moment, Jacen sensed Ratobo's distaste for the battle they would soon be fighting—and his anger at the politicians for allowing it to become necessary.

Then the image began to fade, the face became scaly and reptilian, and for the thousandth time Jacen found his thoughts returning to Mara's funeral—to the lecture Saba Sebatyne had hurled at him. Who was *she* to chastise *him*? Who was *any* Jedi to criticize *Darth Caedus*? At least *he* was fighting to save the Alliance. All the Jedi ever did was dither and debate and balk at the necessities of this dirty war.

But Jacen knew the lecture was not the real problem. Saba's eulogy might mean that she knew how Mara had died. And what if Luke's words of reconciliation had been even more of a ploy than his own? Tahiri claimed the Jedi were still investigating Mara's death, but what if the Masters were deliberately misinforming her? Or what if *she* was misleading him, acting as a double agent?

That was why Darth Caedus had "secured" the academy. The Masters would be reluctant to move against him while the students were under his control. When they tried to free the students, he would know they were coming for him. And even if the Masters did *not* know he had killed Mara, the maneuver would draw resources away from the investigation. It would buy him time—perhaps enough time to win this war.

Of course, Jacen would have some explaining to do when Tenel Ka learned of the takeover, but he wasn't worried that it would affect her decision to lend him the Home Fleet. She would understand when he explained that he was only protecting the interests of the Alliance *and* the Jedi. Tenel Ka was the one person in this galaxy he would always be able to count on; she had proven that already.

The voice of a female comm officer came over the intercom. "Colonel Solo, holo for you on GAG channel bacta-two."

Caedus scowled. The entire bridge crew had clear instructions never to disturb him when he was inside his observation bubble. "Not *now*, Ensign."

"I'm sorry, sir, but it's *top urgent* priority," the comm officer said. "And it's *Lieutenant* Krova, sir."

"Not anymore," Caedus retorted, deliberately allowing his frustration over the failed battle meditation to creep into his voice. "What part of *never disturb*—"

"It's Ben Skywalker, sir." Krova's voice was cracking with anxiety, but she pressed on. "He said to tell you he knows who killed his mother."

Caedus's heart suddenly felt like a cold, still stone. "He does? That's . . . wonderful news." He touched a pad on his armrest, and his heavy meditation chair slowly spun toward the tiny HoloNet transceiver tucked next to the bubble entrance. "Very well, *Lieutenant*. Transfer the signal."

"Thank you, sir," Krova said, obviously relieved that she had retained her rank. "And, sir?"

"Yes, Lieutenant?"

"When you catch the dung-worm who killed her, don't go easy," she said. "Do a Habuur on him."

"A *Habuur*?" Caedus echoed. Ailyn Habuur had died under his interrogation during the early stages of the war, when it had still looked like it might be possible to avoid a major conflict. He had not learned until later that she was the daughter of Boba Fett, the famous bounty hunter who had delivered his father to Jabba the Hutt frozen in carbonite. "Thank you for the suggestion, Lieutenant. I'll keep it in mind."

He tapped the control pad on his armrest, and a moment later Ben's shoulders and head appeared over the projector pad. It was the first Caedus had seen of his younger cousin since Mara's funeral, and the boy was holding up better than expected. Rather than red and puffy, his eyes were sunken, dark, and angry, and his hard expression suggested that sympathy was the last thing he wanted from anyone.

It all pointed to how wrong Lumiya had been about him, to what a fine apprentice Ben still might make.

Deciding to forgo the sympathetic act he had planned, Caedus put on a slightly distracted expression, then said, "This will have to be quick, Ben. We're about to counter-attack."

"It will be." There was a sharpness in Ben's voice, and his brow was knitted in anger. "I only have one question."

"Very well." Caedus changed to a slightly bewildered tone; he knew what was coming, and he had a plan to handle it. "Go ahead."

Ben narrowed his eyes. "Did you kill Mom?"

Caedus shot his brow up as though shocked, and it was not entirely an act: he *was* surprised at how directly Ben had put the question.

"Did I *what*?" Caedus sank back in his chair and shook his head in feigned bewilderment. "You think *I* killed Mara? Why?"

"You were *there*," Ben stated flatly. "In the Consortium."

"A *lot* of people were there." Caedus's reply was cautious; he had expected Ben to do this in person, where the boy would have a better chance of reading his reactions—and be able to seek his vengeance immediately. "Are you going to accuse us *all* in the hope that someone confesses?"

"I don't have to," Ben replied. "You're *already* confessing."

Caedus frowned. The "assured accusation" was a common interrogation tactic, so he doubted his cousin knew anything for certain. But Caedus *did* wonder more than ever why Ben was doing this over the HoloNet. Maybe the boy just wanted to avoid getting himself killed by keeping a few hundred light-years between his temper and its object. Or maybe Ben wanted to make it more difficult to detect any lies *he* told. Caedus began to ponder who else might be listening to this conversation. Was Saba Sebatyne sitting just outside holo range, telling Ben what to say?

When Caedus failed to ask the expected question—*how* was he confessing—Ben supplied the answer anyway. "You're *acting* like you did it."

Caedus decided he had to take the bait. If he didn't, Ben—and whoever might be sitting there beside him—would decide he already knew what Ben was talking about. "Okay, Ben. *How* am I acting like I did it?"

"By trying to keep Dad and the Masters off-balance," Ben explained. "You don't want them to find out it was you."

"If you're talking about trying to arrest my parents at the Jedi Temple, that was strictly a protective measure," Caedus said. "Captain Shevu had reports of Bothans smuggling a proton bomb onto the planet, and my mother and father *are* known terrorists. With most of our Jedi Masters at the funeral—"

"I suppose there's another bomb on Ossus?" Ben asked, cutting him off.

"Not that I know of." Caedus wasn't terribly surprised that Major Serpa had been unable to keep the operation secret. Jedi had many ways to communicate across the stars—some that could never be jammed. "And I intend to keep it that way. The GAG battalion I placed on Ossus is strictly a security measure."

"Come *on,* Jacen. You took the Academy *hostage.* You're just trying to keep the Order from coming after you!"

"I'm trying to protect the students," Caedus insisted calmly. "Your father isn't himself right now, and the Council has been handling your mother's death very foolishly. If I can land an entire *battalion* on Ossus, what do you think the Bothans could do?"

"*Bothans* wouldn't have our clearance codes," Ben

countered. "And nobody would make the mistake of thinking they're on our side."

Seeing that Ben was not being persuaded, Caedus decided to change tactics. He sighed wearily, then said, "I should have known better than to try fooling you, Ben. The truth is that our office—and by that I mean the joint Chiefs of State—has been hurt badly by the lack of support from the Jedi Council."

Ben wrinkled his brow. "So you killed Mom?"

"No, Ben—that was someone else," Caedus said. He had no way to determine whether Saba or any of the other Masters were listening in, but he actually hoped they *were*. His explanation was entirely reasonable, and it just might be enough to convince suspicious minds that he had nothing to do with Mara's death. "But I *have* been trying to take advantage of the situation. The Alliance needs a united front right now, and with your father so consumed by his grief . . . well, I've been trying to consolidate power in the Chiefs' office."

Ben looked more bewildered than ever. "You're trying to take over the Jedi Order?"

Caedus shook his head. "*Neutralize* it," he said. "Perhaps Saba and the other Masters will think twice about what they say in public if they remember that the safety of the Order's younglings is in my hands."

To his credit, Ben wasn't foolish enough to say that Jacen would never harm the academy students. "What about all that stuff you said at the funeral about trying to get along better with the Jedi?"

"That would be nice, but I haven't been able to talk with your father since the funeral," Caedus said. "Frankly, I think he's been avoiding me. What else am I to do?"

"Well, taking over the academy doesn't seem like a very good idea," Ben said. "You're just going to make people mad."

"I'm sorry about that," Caedus said. "But it's for the good of the Alliance."

"The good of the *Alliance*?" The disbelief in Ben's voice was reflected in his eyes. "Right—just like killing Mom."

Caedus exhaled in frustration. "Your interrogation technique is excellent, Ben." The conversation was hardly going as he had planned—and perhaps it was time to change that. "But no matter how long you continue to assert the suspicion, I won't confess to what Ca—" He stopped abruptly. "To what someone *else* did."

The "slip" worked exactly as planned. Ben's eyes widened in excitement, then quickly narrowed.

"To what *who* did?" he demanded.

Caedus looked Ben straight in the eye, holding the gaze just long enough to make sure it looked like an act. "Ben, if I knew who killed Mara," he said, "don't you think they'd be dead by now?"

"That depends on how useful they were," Ben replied.

Caedus winced, but only on the outside. Inside, he was smiling. Ben had gone from accusing him of Mara's murder to demanding that he reveal the name of the guilty party. As he had foreseen, Ben was more interested in vengeance than justice—all Caedus need do was point him toward a plausible target.

"Ben, I don't *know* anything."

"But you have suspicions," Ben surmised.

Caedus let a moment of silence hang between their images, then finally nodded. "What I have isn't *proof,*" he said. "It just tells us where to look."

Ben sneered. "Since when do you need *proof*? Suspicion has always been good enough for GAG."

"The circumstances aren't ordinary. This time, we're going to need proof—and plenty of it. You'll see." Caedus looked to his armrest and made a show of fumbling with the controls, then assumed a tone that was both hurt and slightly bitter. "I'm only playing this for you to prove that

I'm not the one who killed your mother. You can't act on it, Ben. We have to do this right—for the sake of the Alliance."

Ben's expression changed to equal parts impatience and curiosity. "Sure. I just want to know who killed Mom."

"All right." Caedus poised a finger over the transfer pad, then looked back to Ben. "I have your word as a Jedi?"

"Yeah," Ben said, "as a Jedi."

Caedus nodded. "Good."

He dropped his finger. The familiar voice of Cal Omas began to crackle from his transceiver speakers—and, he assumed by Ben's shocked expression, from those at the other end of the channel.

"I *do* have allies on the Jedi Council," Omas was saying, "and Luke is one of them. But he's not going to intervene. He doesn't believe it's proper for Jedi to insert themselves into domestic politics."

There was just enough static to make it sound like the statement had been captured during an eavesdropping operation—and to hide the electronic glitches that invariably arose when someone's words were digitally rearranged.

"No, I'm *saying* we need Skywalker out of the way," Omas's voice continued. "Then my friends will be free to act on their own authority and reinstate me."

Omas's voice paused again.

"This was captured via parabolic dish," Caedus said, explaining the reason they had only one side of the conversation. "The comlink he was using belonged to the lieutenant in charge of guarding him. We didn't have it tapped at the time."

Ben nodded his understanding, and Omas's voice continued, "Are you crazy? We can't do that to Luke Skywalker—even if we knew someone who *could*. Just redirect his attention."

Omas paused again, and Caedus could see that the anger

and hatred Ben had been holding barely under control was quickly rising to the surface.

"Look," Omas said, "I really don't want to know *how* you plan to do it—just make it happen."

The recording had barely clicked to an end before Ben's voice was blaring from the transceiver. "Who was he talking to? Fett?"

"We don't know yet." Caedus had to bite back a smile at the idea of siccing Ben on Fett—except that he still hoped to make an apprentice of Ben, and he was fairly certain Fett would not come out at the worse end of that fight. "It's one more reason to be patient. Sooner or later, Omas is going to have to pay up—and when he does, the credits will lead us straight to your mother's murderer."

"I know who my mother's murderer is," Ben retorted. "And before he dies, he's going to tell me who his weapon was."

Caedus forced a look of alarm. "Ben, you gave me your word. Acting on that information would be very bad for the Alliance—we have to prove what Omas did publicly. We can't have people thinking we just assassinated him."

"Don't worry," Ben said. "I'll *get* proof."

"Ben, you have to stand down on this." Caedus made his voice stern. "That's an order."

"With all due respect, sir, you can shove that order down the nearest black hole." Ben's arm appeared in the holo, as though he were reaching for the transceiver controls. "*You're* the one who turned me into a killer."

The hologram dissolved into static, leaving Caedus to the starlit darkness of his observation bubble. He touched the controls on his armrest, spinning himself back toward the impending counterattack, then smiled and opened a channel to the comm officer.

"Lieutenant Krova?"

"Yes, Colonel?"

"Perhaps you should send a top urgent message to the unit guarding former Chief of State Omas." Caedus paused, injecting the proper note of concern into his voice. "Lieutenant Skywalker seems to think there's going to be an assassination attempt."

seven

This high in the wroshyrs, the limbs were barely wide enough to walk on, while low-hanging clouds slicked every surface with cool dew. Wookiees had no trouble clinging to the narrow pathways and tiny spectator platforms that ringed Council Rock, but for beings without claws—beings such as Han and Leia—the going was slow, dangerous, and nerve racking.

Han stopped at a fork in the limb. One branch descended toward a fog-shrouded porch, and the other snaked toward a spectator platform already sagging beneath the weight of too many Wookiees. Glimpses of sheer black cliff—Council Rock—were starting to show through the dancing wall of leaves ahead.

Their guide, a lanky young Wookiee with bronze fur and shades of Chewbacca in his expression, stopped three paces down the descending branch, then looked over his shoulder and rumbled a question.

"Doing . . . fine," Han panted. "Don't worry about us."

"Though I *do* see why you insisted on leaving Threepio with the *Falcon*." Leia came up beside Han and draped a hand over his shoulder, hanging on while she pretended to rest—but, Han suspected, actually checking to see how steady he was. "This is quite a hike, Waroo."

"Twelve hours is a hike," Han complained. "Four days is a kriffing expedition. I don't see why we couldn't have taken a cloud car—at least as far as Thikkiiana City."

Waroo—more properly Lumpawaroo, Chewbacca's son—groaned a long explanation.

"Yeah, so we could've gotten back in the *Falcon* and flown to Thikkiiana City, and then *that's* where we would've been starting."

Waroo let out a very Chewie-like grunt of disgust and, shaking his head, started down the branch again.

"You know it doesn't work that way," Leia said. "The walk is part of the tradition."

"No wonder they're so slow to decide anything," Han complained. "It takes half a year just to collect everyone."

"Including *us*," Leia pointed out. She nudged Han after their guide. "Hurry up. Waroo said they were close to making a decision."

"Right. Any month now."

Han extended his arms for balance and started down the slippery branch, careful to place each foot dead in the center and trying to stay loose in the knees so Waroo did not accidentally bounce him off. With Leia right behind him and ready to reach out with the Force at a millisecond's notice, he had no fear of actually falling, but there was more than one way to die up here. At his age, embarrassment could be a real killer.

As they drew closer to the crowded porch, Han began to hear Wookiee voices booming from the entrance to the council circle. They were speaking in Xaczik—the difficult Wartaki Island dialect they had used to fool their Imperial slave masters three wars ago—so Han could not quite catch what the delegates were saying. But it *did* sound like the council was close to agreement. The current speaker was roaring speech rather than groaning it, and the exclamations threatening to drown him out were clearly being made in enthusiasm rather than dispute.

"Uh-oh," Han said. "Sounds like we're arriving just in time."

"So maybe they *are* going to commit to Jacen sometime this month," Leia said, rubbing Han's nose in his own sarcasm. "I *said* their fleet was making ready."

"Okay, I believe you," Han said. "*Now* the Wookiees are in a hurry. Who knew?"

Waroo reached the porch and began to push through the crowd, rumbling apologies and groaning explanations—he might be the son of the mighty Chewbacca, but he was young and still a hundred kilograms too light to bellow and demand. Nevertheless, the mob slowly parted, glancing down at Han and Leia in surprise and growling conjecture about what *they* might be doing there.

Finally, Han and his companions drew near enough to the front of the porch to see a pair of huge guards standing beneath an archway of bent wroshyr boughs. Behind them, a set of black stone stairs led up to the summit of Council Rock, a slender column of volcanic basalt that rose almost as high as the wroshyr trees themselves. In front of the guards hung a pair of lashed-log gates, closed to indicate that the Rock Council was in session and could not be disturbed.

Standing on the bottom rail of the right-hand gate, clinging to the top rail so they could peer up the stone stairs, were a pair of short, all-too-familiar figures. One was furry and black with a white stripe running diagonally across his back, while the other was bald, jug-eared, and a little too pear-shaped for a Sullustan.

"Great," Han grumbled. "What are those two doing here?"

"Eavesdropping, it looks like," Leia said quietly. "Even if your speech works, Jacen may not be as surprised as we'd like when the Wookiees withhold their support."

Sensing the commotion behind them, the two figures glanced over their shoulders—then dropped their jaws and jumped off the gate.

"Princess Leia!" The Sullustan stepped forward and bowed formally, then turned to Han and offered his hand. "Captain Solo! What an unexpected pleasure!"

"Yeah, same here, Juun." Han allowed the Sullustan to take his hand and pump his arm. "Small galaxy, huh?"

"It's a pleasure to see you again, Jae," Leia said, addressing the Sullustan by his first name. "I assume you're here monitoring the situation for Admiral Bwua'tu?"

Juun shook his head. "For Supreme Commander Niathal herself," he said. "Since the Dark Nest crisis, we've been climbing the intelligence ranks steadily."

The black-furred Ewok jabbered something sharp at Juun, then turned to glare up at Leia.

"No sense worrying about it, Tarfang," Han said, taking a guess at the nature of the Ewok's complaint. "You two aren't exactly undercover here. I'll bet Confederation Intelligence already knows who you work for."

Tarfang ignored Han and chittered something else. This time, both Han and Leia had to look to Juun for a translation.

"Tarfang says you're both traitors—and I'm afraid he's right." Juun's expression grew concerned. "This is Alliance territory, you know. You two really shouldn't be here."

"Sure we should," Han said. He stepped past the two Alliance spies and addressed himself to the Wookiee guards. "Open up, fellas. I've got something important to say to the council."

The two guards looked to Waroo, who assured them that the delegates would want to hear what Han and Leia Solo had to report—then reminded them that Han had earned a life debt from his father because he could not bear to see a Wookiee enslaved. The two guards nodded to each other, then started to open the gate—until Tarfang leapt on it and began chattering so ferociously that both recoiled in shock.

"He says you *can't* admit them into the council," Juun translated. "They're enemy agents."

The two guards furrowed their brows at this, and several Wookiees in the crowd groaned the opinion that "Little Killer" was correct. The Solos were known Corellian sympathizers. It just would not do to let them address the Rock Council while carrying weapons.

"Forget it," Han said. "I'm not giving up my blaster."

The guards each drew a pair of scythe-like ryyk blades and folded the weapons across their chests.

Leia grasped Han above the elbow. "Han—"

"All right, all right." He unbuckled his blaster belt and handed it to Waroo for safekeeping. "The sacrifices I make to keep you out of trouble."

Leia did the same with her lightsaber and hold-out blaster, and again the guards started to open the gate. This time it was Juun who stepped forward.

"You *do* know that if you open that gate, you'll be in violation of the Anti-Sedition Provision of the Galactic Loyalty Act. Allowing any terrorist sympathizer to address a public forum is punishable by incarceration in a MaxSec Orbital Facility for a term of up to twenty standard years— or until the insurrection ends, whichever is longer."

The Wookiees looked at each other—then shrugged and continued to open the gate . . . until Tarfang jumped onto the top rail and loosed a string of invective that made even Han shudder.

"Tarfang says they're traitors," Juun translated. "And if you raise that gate for them, so are you."

When Juun said nothing more, Tarfang looked back at him expectantly.

"Are you *sure* you want to say that to a pair of Wookiees?"

Tarfang spat back something affirmative.

Juun sighed and, as Tarfang returned his glare to the two guards, said, "He says if you *act* like traitors, then he'll *treat* you like traitors."

A chorus of astonished mutters rustled through the crowd, and the two guards looked bewildered—a little nervous, too, but mostly just bewildered.

Juun took advantage of the confusion to turn to Han and Leia. "It really would be best if you just left," he said, "before duty compels me to do something I truly don't want to."

"Do your worst—just remember who wrote the book on dirty tricks." Without awaiting the Sullustan's reply, Han turned back to the guards. "Are you going to open this thing or do I have to do it myself?"

It was Han's bad luck that the two Wookiees had finally reached their threshold of tolerance. They stepped forward together, one brandishing his blades at Han, the other launching Tarfang off the gate with a swift kick to the midsection. Someone in back growled the suggestion they ask Old Tojjelnoot what they should do.

"Old Tojjelnoot?" Leia asked.

"*Old* means he's the council leader," Han explained. "Hope he's not still sore about Tojjevvuk."

"Oh," Leia said. "*Those* Tojjes."

Han nodded. "Afraid so."

Several more voices from the crowd moaned agreement with the first, and one of the guards finally turned to climb the stairs.

"Great," Han said. "Just when you think things aren't complicated enough."

The Tojj clan had spent decades trying to kill Chewbacca in retribution for the death of Tojjevvuk in a fight over Chewbacca's wife-to-be, Mallatobuck. Waroo started to moan an assurance that the council would not allow Tojjelnoot to decide the matter on the basis of an old clan feud—

then let out an enormous roar of surprise as a blaster bolt zinged past his head.

Han and Leia spun around simultaneously—both reaching for weapons they no longer had—and found themselves staring down the barrel of a huge Merr-Sonn Flash 4 blaster pistol.

"*Tarfang!*" Juun cried. "Put that away!"

Tarfang babbled a long string of something that definitely included a refusal, then made the mistake of training the weapon on Han.

Leia's hand flashed up, and the blaster flew from Tarfang's hand and vanished over the side of the porch. She extended her arm, and in the next instant the little Ewok was flying into her grasp, screeching in rage and clawing at the air with all fours.

"*Enough!*" Leia yelled. She flicked her wrist, spinning Tarfang upside down and leaving him to hang in the air before her. "You may have the death mark on nine planets, but that doesn't matter to—"

"Put him down." Juun's voice was unusually forceful. "*Now.*"

Han looked over to find the Sullustan pointing his own blaster pistol in Leia's direction. "Juun, what the blazes are you doing?"

Juun's eyes did not veer from Leia. "I tried to do this the nice way, but you wouldn't listen." His voice remained hard, his face unapologetic. "And Tarfang is my partner. I can't let *anyone* do that to him."

"Do *what*?" Han demanded, stepping to the Sullustan's side. "Tarfang shot first."

He lashed out to snatch Juun's blaster—then felt a huge furry hand clamp down on his arm and lift him off his feet. A deep Wookiee voice rumbled an order in his ear. He found himself nose-to-snout with a silver-furred male much larger than Chewie had been.

"Okay, take it easy," Han said. "It's not like I was going to *kill* anyone."

The Wookiee glanced at Leia and growled another command. Han snuck a peek in Waroo's direction and found that the crowd had closed in around him, completely separating the Solos from their weapons—and their only ally.

"Uh, honey," Han said. "Maybe you should put the nice Ewok down now."

"Fine."

Leia lowered her hand and allowed Tarfang to crash on his head. The Ewok sprang up immediately and started toward her—then bounced off the legs of a big blond female who scowled and wagged her finger at him.

The silver-furred male rowwled at Han, advising him to come along quietly.

"Are you *kidding*?" Han demanded. "You're arresting us?"

The blond female growled an apologetic explanation, pointing out that he and Leia *were* the subjects of a Galactic Alliance arrest warrant, and they *had* just assaulted two duly authorized officers of the Alliance.

"I don't care if they *are* Alliance officers," Han objected. "They're the ones who assaulted *us*—"

The male asked his question again, this time roaring it so loudly that Han's eardrums ached.

"Okay, okay!" Han glanced over at Leia and received a resigned nod, then sighed and spread his hands. "No need to get all violent. We'll come quietly."

eight

A turbolaser strike blossomed against the *Anakin Solo*'s shields, and space beyond the observation bubble flared into sapphire brilliance. The blast-tinting darkened against the glare, leaving Caedus momentarily blind—though hardly unaware. He could still sense the doubt threatening to engulf the entire Fourth Fleet, and he could feel the Force shuddering at the sudden detonation of the frigate *Zoli*. He could even perceive the fury of Admiral Ratobo, who had twice interrupted his meditations to demand authorization to break off.

By any sensible military standard, Caedus should have granted the authorization as soon as the Commenorians opened fire with long-range turbolasers. The tactical planners had not expected the new technology when they proposed a frontal assault, and now the Fourth would be exposed to a barrage during its entire approach. At the same time, the fleet would be unable to return fire until it reached standard range, since even the largest Star Destroyers could not energize long-range batteries and still have enough power to maneuver and maintain shields.

But Caedus could not break off now. The future was such a tangle of possibility that he could flow-walk only a short time forward—to the *next* battle, the one at Kuat that he had foreseen—before the path vanished into a miasma of uncertainty. Even with Tenel Ka's Home Fleet under way to join them at Kuat, the Alliance simply was not strong enough to guarantee victory. To triumph *there,* Caedus needed to extract a heavy price *here.* He had to make the attackers pay so dearly for Balmorra that the Hutt and Commenorian fleets would be reduced to mere skeletons.

And the Force seemed to be suggesting that Caedus had made the right decision. His meditations had touched on a growing sense of expectation, a subtle feeling that the battle would soon turn in the Alliance's favor. Caedus had no idea what might be causing that sense of expectation—he even wondered whether he might be imagining it—but he had to trust it. The alternative was simply not acceptable. If the Confederation won at Kuat, it would be in good position to drive on Coruscant herself.

The blast-tinting finally faded and restored Caedus's view. The battle ahead was a vast web of light and energy flashing against the pearly disk of a smog-cloaked Balmorra, with clusters of blue dots—the efflux nozzles of the Fourth Fleet—accelerating through a storm of blossoming color toward the dark specks of Commenorian capital ships.

Save for damaged vessels trailing smoke plumes as they plunged down Balmorra's gravity well, the Hutt fleet was too distant to be seen by the naked eye. But Caedus could tell by the smug satisfaction he sensed in the Hutt commanders, and by the utter desperation of the defenders, that the landing had already begun. This much he *had* foreseen; there had never been any question of saving Balmorra, only of how much he could make the rebels pay for taking it.

The blue dots ahead narrowed to ovals as the Fourth Fleet began to turn. For a moment, Caedus thought the fleet was simply maneuvering, approaching on the oblique in order to present their flanks to the enemy and relieve their forward shields. But when the ovals continued to narrow and began to sprout blunt blue tails, he knew that he was wrong, that the "Fearless Fourth" was breaking off.

Caedus had Lieutenant Krova open an audio channel to the *Peacebringer* and was quickly put through to Admiral Ratobo. Despite his irritation, Caedus spoke in a deliberately calm tone.

"You appear to have decided I'm an idiot."

"That's not a mistake I would make, Colonel." Beneath the resolve in Ratobo's voice, there was a note of resignation; clearly, he realized that by disobeying Caedus's orders, he was sacrificing not only his career, but possibly his life as well. "However, your lack of tactical training is telling. There's no question of winning the battle now."

"Winning *battles* is your concern, Admiral," Caedus said. "Winning the *war* is mine."

"And fribbling away the Fourth Fleet will accomplish that?"

"Making the Commenorians *pay* for Balmorra will accomplish that," Caedus said. "As will trapping the Hutts dirtside."

"*Assuming* we break through, and *assuming* we have enough strength left to exploit," Ratobo retorted. "Those are big assumptions right now."

"I have great faith in you, Admiral."

"Faith is a poor substitute for tactical advantage." Ratobo was speaking with the boldness of the condemned. "What if long-range turbolasers aren't the only technology Confederation spies have stolen? What if they have our missile deactivation transmitters? Comm wave descramblers? Transponder friend codes?"

"Have you seen any evidence of that?" Caedus asked.

"Not yet," Ratobo admitted. "But if they do have other stolen technology, they won't use it until it's too late for us to withdraw."

"If they *had* any other stolen technology, they wouldn't

have tipped their hand by using the long-range turbolasers in the first place," Caedus countered. "We'll reevaluate when and if the situation calls for it. Until then, proceed as planned."

Ratobo could not have missed the note of authority that Caedus had put into his voice, but the Bith was not ready to yield. "With all due respect, Colonel, perhaps it would be wise to consult with Supreme Commander Niathal. She *is* the one who's vested with military authority."

Caedus's first reaction was anger, but that quickly changed to respect as he recalled that the admiral believed he was sacrificing a lifelong career by speaking so candidly. Ratobo was resisting Caedus's orders not out of ego, but because he believed it was his *duty* to object to what appeared to him a disastrous course of action.

"I find your candor refreshing—misguided, but refreshing." As Caedus spoke, he focused his attention on the blue ion tail belonging to the *Peacebringer* and quickly began to develop a clear picture of the Star Destroyer's combat situation. "So perhaps I'll *show* you why I'm here instead of Admiral Niathal. Do you see that flight of hostiles preparing to target your bridge?"

There was a moment of silence while Ratobo had the ship's defense data copied to his display. Caedus took the time to concentrate on the Commenorian pilots, simultaneously following their progress and pushing his Force-awareness forward into the next few seconds.

"Yes." Ratobo sounded slightly surprised. "I see them."

It took an instant for the fate of the Commenorians to grow clear, then Caedus said, "No need to close your blast shutters. They're not going to make it."

"You're *sure*?" Ratobo's voice was openly skeptical. "Their approach lane looks—"

The sentence came to a halt as the Commenorian pilots had their presences abruptly returned to the Force. Caedus could not tell whether they had been the victims of a well-trained cannon crew or one of the *Peacebringer*'s defensive cluster bombs or just a random combat accident—only that their lives had been snuffed out in the time it took to register the thought.

An astonished gasp came over the comm channel. "Amazing!"

"I have good reason for my orders," Caedus said, driving home his point, "even if it doesn't always appear that way."

"Of course." Ratobo sounded chastened, if not quite convinced. "And that *good reason*—it has its basis in the Force?"

"It does." Caedus saw no need to mention the vague nature of his feelings—or the possibility that they might be no more than wishful thinking. "I can't foresee the outcome of continuing to press the attack, Admiral, but I *can* tell you that if we don't make the Confederation pay dearly for Balmorra, they're going to make *us* pay dearly at Kuat."

Ratobo fell silent for a moment, then said, "Very well. I'll resume our attack immediately."

"Thank you, Admiral." As Caedus replied, he suddenly grew aware of something else in the *Peacebringer*'s future—something it would not avoid. "I'm glad you trust me."

"I wouldn't say that, Colonel," Ratobo replied. "But I find I no longer have a legitimate basis for challenging your orders. If you don't choose to court-martial me after the battle, I'll be submitting my—"

"A resignation really won't be necessary, Admiral," Caedus said. "Just carry on—and quickly."

Caedus closed the channel and watched impatiently as the Fourth's ion tails slowly changed back to ovals. The feeling of expectation in the Force had grown stronger, but so had the doubt he sensed among the Fourth's crew members. Their beloved fleet was being thrown against the enemy with no hope of saving Balmorra, and it was making them resentful and angry.

Caedus strengthened his battle meditation until he

started to touch individual beings, then tried to imbue his Force presence with confidence and calm. The fleet reflected back only confusion and fear—perhaps because Caedus himself did not understand exactly what he expected to happen.

An aura of cold loss drew the focus of Caedus's battle meditation back to the *Peacebringer*. Giving up on his attempt to improve morale, he touched a pad on the armrest of his chair.

"Transfer fleet flag to the *Trucemaker*," he said. "Inform Admiral Darklighter he is now in command."

"You're relieving Admiral Ratobo?" Krova asked, clearly astonished.

"Not exactly."

As Caedus spoke, a dozen crimson bolts converged in the distance outside his observation bubble, and he felt the familiar Force shudder of thousands of lives ending in a millisecond.

"Oh!" Krova gasped. "Transferring flag now."

It was hardly the smooth transition Caedus had hoped for, and he had to endure several seconds of shock and despair as the Fourth reacted to the loss of its beloved commander. He monitored the comm channels until Gavin Darklighter—newly transferred from the Fifth after his promotion to rear admiral—issued a string of orders and immediately refocused the fleet on the job of destroying the Commenorian defenders.

Within seconds, the Fourth's entire starfighter screen began to stream away from the fleet, rushing to swarm the Commenorian capital ships. The maneuver was as bold as it was unconventional, designed to force the enemy Star Destroyers to divert power from their long-range turbolasers to their shields.

But it also left the Fourth vulnerable to the Commenorian starfighters, basically transforming the battle into a game of high-stakes shock-ball, with daredevil pilots keeping score in capital ships killed. It was exactly the kind of innovative, desperate tactic that just might save Balmorra . . . and cost the Fourth so many vessels that it would lack the strength to fight at Kuat.

Caedus touched a control pad on his armrest. "Open a channel to Admiral Darklighter. Urgent priority."

Krova acknowledged the order, then reported, "Admiral Darklighter will be available in a moment, Colonel."

"A *moment*?" Caedus fumed. "Did you tell his aide—"

"Of course," Krova interrupted. "She said he was aware of the priority."

Caedus scowled. "Did she?" He focused his attention on the *Trucemaker*. "Very well. Thank you, Lieutenant."

It took only a few moments to pick out Gavin Darklighter, a still, confident presence amid a swirling mass of worried subordinates. Caedus charged his own presence with the irritation he felt at being put off, then began to press down on the admiral through the Force.

Darklighter seemed more irritated than intimidated, and the comm speaker remained silent.

Caedus was about to press harder when the Commenorian turbolasers suddenly fell dark. The tiny specks of their capital ships began to drift across Balmorra's pearly face, tails of blue efflux flickering at their sterns. Rather than gamble with Darklighter—and hope their starfighter complement would be as efficient as the well-trained wings of the Alliance—the Commenorians were retreating.

Caedus found the retreat doubly surprising. First, it would allow the Fourth Fleet within turbolaser range of the Hutt landing force. Second, he had not sensed it coming. The maneuver had been one of those rare pivotal moves that even the Force could not anticipate, the kind that made fools of tactical planners and Force diviners alike. It was a humbling reminder that battle meditation was not infallible; Caedus could be surprised just like any commander—and the results would be doubly disastrous if he made the mistake of believing otherwise.

Darklighter's presence became tinged with smugness, then his voice came over the comm speaker. "Yes, Colonel?"

Caedus released the pressure he had been applying—and swallowed the irritation he still felt at being put off.

"I just wanted to congratulate you on a brilliant tactic," he said. "It took even me by surprise."

"Thank you, sir." Darklighter paused, then asked, "Are you telling me you sent an urgent priority summons to *congratulate* me?"

"Let's just say I'm happy with your performance." Caedus kept his tone light; it had occurred to him that this might be the source of the expectation he had been sensing in the Force: Darklighter's ascension to command might be the change that was going to turn the tide for the Alliance. "How did you know the Commenorians would retreat?"

"Let's just say I'm happy with their choice." Darklighter's tone was not quite as light as Caedus's had been. "Will that be all, Colonel? I need to keep an eye on those hotshot squadron leaders."

"Yes, thank you." Caedus started to close the channel, then decided he couldn't afford to alienate Darklighter. "And, Gavin?"

"Yes, *Colonel*?"

"I apologize for any, um, *pressure* you may have felt regarding your decision."

"Don't worry about it, Colonel," Darklighter said. "You're still young. You'll learn."

He closed the channel and was gone before Caedus could react to the condescension. Clearly, Darklighter—and probably many of the other senior officers who had fought alongside the legendary Han and Leia Solo against the Empire—disapproved of what Caedus was doing to save the Galactic Alliance. Eventually, the officers' feelings would become known outside military circles, and then his mother—or some other traitor—would reach out to them in an attempt to arrange a countercoup.

Caedus made a note to add all senior military officers to GAG's watch-list. It would not do to grow lax now that he was in charge. Even *he* could be surprised—wasn't that what Admiral Darklighter had just taught him?

And Caedus was even more surprised when, an instant later, the Force blossomed with Jedi presences. He felt dozens of them—perhaps as many as a hundred—all somewhere nearby, all strong and clear and resolute. His battle meditation vanished in an eruption of fear and anger, and he Force-leapt from his chair, doing a reverse flip over the seat back, his head passing so close beneath the upper bulkhead that his hair brushed durasteel.

Caedus came down three meters inside his day cabin, his lightsaber in hand and ignited, his gaze fixed on the still-secure hatch on the wall opposite. There were no Jedi inside the day cabin with him. Nor could he sense any coming through the corridor, creeping through the ventilation ducts overhead, or crawling through the mechanical tunnels beneath the deck.

But that didn't mean they weren't coming for him. If Caedus could hide his presence in the Force, so could the Masters—as Mara had demonstrated when she nearly killed him on Kavan.

A raspy voice sounded from Caedus's left. "Has some furniture offended you?"

"Quiet!" Caedus glanced toward the voice and saw SD-XX, his Tendrando Arms security droid, stepping out of the hidden security station where he kept himself stowed. "They're *here*."

"Who?" The droid's photoreceptors darkened as he switched scanning protocols. With thin armor and blue photoreceptors set in a black, skull-like face, he resembled a scaled-down version of a YVH battle droid. "I detect no living beings within thirty meters."

"No?"

Caedus frowned. The presences of the Jedi were stronger than ever, distinct enough now that he could recognize many of them—Saba Sebatyne, Kyp Durron, Corran Horn, most of the Masters, along with Tesar, Lowbacca, and more Jedi Knights than he could name. Yet when he tried to get a sense of their location, they seemed to be everywhere and nowhere, as if they were inside his head—just as they might feel during a Jedi battle-meld.

The Jedi weren't *hunting* him, he realized. They were reaching out to the *Anakin Solo,* inviting him to join their meld. As confused as he was relieved, Caedus deactivated his lightsaber.

"Stand down, Double-Ex," he said. "They're not here."

SD-XX regarded Caedus with a cocked head. "Isn't that what I just said? Perhaps it's time you had yourself degaussed, Colonel. Your circuits are ghost-firing."

"I *said* stand down." Caedus hung the lightsaber back on his belt. "My circuits are fine."

SD-XX continued to scrutinize him. "I'll be the judge of that."

Caedus pointed toward the droid's hidden security station. "Go. That's an order."

SD-XX's voice changed from merely domineering to menacing. "Acknowledged."

The droid stalked to his compartment in utter silence and vanished back into the wall. Caedus returned to his bubble, but made no attempt to resume his battle meditation. The technique—at least as Lumiya had taught it to him—was Sith, and he did not want to risk using it while what felt like half the Jedi Order was attempting to draw him into a meld.

Instead, Caedus unmasked his presence and opened himself to their meld. It was full of half-familiar feelings, of purpose and commitment and hope, of inclusion and fellowship and warmth—none of it directed at him, of course. He was surprised how lonely the exclusion made him feel, and how much he missed the companionship of family and friends. He had thought himself above such sentimental trivialities. But of course, he was not, and never would be.

The Sith way was one of deep sacrifice, and only now was Caedus coming to understand that he had not sacrificed the ability to love—only the ability to be loved in return. Time after time, he would be forced to betray his family and friends for the good of the galaxy, and time after time they would hate him for it. Yet he could never shrink from making those sacrifices. To do so was to sow the seeds of selfishness within himself, and down that path lay the greed and power lust that had corrupted Palpatine—and so many Sith before him.

So Caedus would continue to do what was necessary. At the moment, that meant accepting the revulsion, malice, and even pity that flooded the meld as the Jedi detected his presence. He returned their feelings with nothing more than curiosity.

Once the meld had adjusted to his arrival, Caedus began to get a clearer picture of the Jedi purpose. They were here with what seemed to be a whole wing of StealthXs—over seventy craft, if the techs had managed to put all of them into action—and they seemed ready to fight. To his relief, the mental images he kept glimpsing were the sterns of *Imperial*-class Star Destroyers and Empire-era cruisers.

The Jedi were targeting Commenorian capital ships.

Caedus could not quite keep a smug feeling of triumph from seeping into the meld. The occupation of the academy was working even better than expected. He projected his pleasure into the meld, simultaneously welcoming the Jedi to the battle and inviting them to open fire.

The only response was stony displeasure, and no shadow bombs erupted in the sterns of the Commenorian capital ships. A sense of expectation filled the meld—the same sense of expectation he had been experiencing since the battle opened—and he had the sinking feeling that he finally understood its meaning.

Caedus punched a control pad on his armrest. "Open a channel to Admiral Darklighter, urgent priority. And *don't* let his aide put you off this time. It's important."

Krova acknowledged the order, leaving Caedus to pound his armrest in frustration. *Anyone* could be surprised. He had learned that from Darklighter, and *still* he had advanced straight into a trap. Now the Fourth Fleet was committed to a costly attack that only the Jedi could turn into success, and Caedus had no doubt they would demand a very steep price indeed for their cooperation.

Darklighter's voice came over the speaker a moment later. "Yes, Colonel?" In the background, Caedus could hear the rumble of discharging turbolaser batteries and the crackle of shields dissipating excess energy. "We're pretty busy right now, so I hope this isn't another message of congratulations."

"It isn't," Caedus replied. "I wanted—I *needed*—to advise you that—"

"That help is on the way," interrupted a familiar voice behind Caedus. "Be ready to exploit."

"Is that who I *think* it is?" Darklighter gasped.

"Yes," Luke's voice replied. "Carry on, Gavin."

Caedus was already spinning his meditation chair around, but the motor was far too slow for his comfort. As soon as he had a clear path into his day cabin, he dived over the armrest and rolled to his feet, lightsaber in hand. Luke stood about a meter away, dressed in a StealthX flight suit and staring at the weapon in Caedus's grasp with a bemused, slightly sad scowl.

"Is it still that bad between us?" he asked.

"You tell *me*." Caedus continued to hold the lightsaber. "It wasn't the Force urging me to press the attack, it was you."

"And you think that was a setup?" Luke asked.

"I *know* it was." Caedus allowed a bit of animosity to creep into his voice. "You tricked me into committing the Fourth Fleet to a dangerous attack, and only *you* can keep it from turning into a disaster. What is it you want in return?"

Instead of looking smug, Luke's face fell. "Nothing, Jacen. We didn't set you up." He reached into the battlemeld and urged the Jedi to attack. "I just wanted you to know we *could* have."

Caedus didn't know whether Luke was ordering the Jedi to attack the Commenorians—or him. Then the Force shuddered with the stunned anguish of thousands of beings perishing in a surprise attack, and Caedus half expected to feel the *Anakin Solo* bucking and twisting beneath his feet.

But the deck remained reassuringly steady, and no damage sirens sounded, and Caedus finally began to understand that the Jedi threat had been an empty one. Their trick had been little more than a halfhearted attempt to intimidate him, to remind him they possessed both the courage and the means to destroy him—and the Alliance. But the very fact that they had warned instead of acting betrayed their bluff. As long as GAG controlled the academy grounds, they would never risk an assassination or treason. They were too frightened of his ruthlessness—of his brutality.

Caedus returned his lightsaber to his belt, then gestured to the small tactical holodisplay in the corner of his day cabin. "Shall we see how the battle is progressing?"

"Be my guest," Luke responded. As Caedus crossed the cabin, Luke turned to watch, but did not follow. "I think you'll be impressed, Jacen."

When Caedus activated the holodisplay, he *was* impressed. Most of the identifier codes for the Commenorian capital ships were blinking in distress, their colors ranging from amber—for battle-impaired—to deep red for totally crippled. And Gavin Darklighter was taking full advantage. The forward elements of the Fourth Fleet were already moving through the enemy lines. Knowing that they stood no chance against Alliance Star Destroyers, the Hutt marauders and corvettes abandoned their landing force and started to withdraw.

As the battle continued to unfold, Luke kept his distance from Caedus, watching the holodisplay from over near the observation bubble. Caedus was just as happy to have the extra space between them; he remained suspicious of Luke's presence and was glad for the reaction time.

After a minute, the Fourth reached turbolaser range and opened fire, targeting not the Hutts' fleeing capital ships but the assault shuttles still dropping toward Balmorra's surface.

Caedus punched a comm pad on the holodisplay's console. "Open a channel to Admiral Darklighter—"

"Urgent priority," Krova finished. "Right away, Colonel."

A moment later, Darklighter asked, "What is it, Colonel?"

"Redirect your fire and pursue," Caedus ordered. "Our first priority is the destruction of the Hutt fleet, not the landing force."

"With all due respect, Colonel," Darklighter said in a tone completely devoid of it, "we can't abandon the Balmorrans to a Hutt occupation, and it's a lot easier to destroy those shuttles now than to fight their passengers dirtside."

"The Balmorrans will have to handle the occupation themselves," Caedus said. "I want those capital ships *destroyed*—better to trap the Hutts on one world than let them occupy a dozen."

Darklighter remained silent, and over the comm channel Caedus could almost feel him struggling with his decision.

"That's an *order,* Admiral," Caedus said. "I know it seems wrong, but we're not going to defeat the Confederation by blowing up shuttles. We need to kill the big ships."

Darklighter remained silent a moment longer, then sighed. "Very well, Colonel. Redirecting fire and pursuing."

Caedus watched as the Fourth Fleet accelerated after the Hutt capital ships and began to hammer their sterns. When the first marauder designator turned red and faded into destruction, Luke's voice sounded from where he had remained standing.

"You *planned* this. You sacrificed a whole planet—"

"I *foresaw* it," Caedus interrupted, turning back to his uncle. "All I did was take advantage . . . of . . ."

He let the sentence trail off as he realized Luke was no longer standing there. Caedus frowned and extended his Force-awareness first to his entire day cabin, then to the entire *Anakin Solo.* He felt no sign of his uncle's presence anywhere.

"Luke?"

SD-XX emerged from his security station and ran his electronic gaze around the perimeter of the cabin, then reported, "There's no one here, Colonel."

"What about Luke Skywalker?" Caedus asked. "I was just talking to him."

SD-XX fixed his blue photoreceptors on Caedus's face. "You were talking," he said. "But there was no one here. I assumed your circuits were misfiring again."

Caedus considered this, wondering whether his anxiety over being discovered might be making him imagine things. Then he remembered that Gavin Darklighter had not only spoken to Luke, but also reacted to his instructions.

"No, he was here." Caedus opened himself to the battle-meld again and felt his uncle among the other Jedi, his presence filled with sadness and disapproval . . . and admonition. "I don't know how, but he *was* here."

nine

The target sat alone in his study, turned toward a transparisteel wall where the twinkling spires of the Senate District skytowers poked through a blanket of night clouds. An aura of bitterness and regret made the room feel chill and heavy in the Force, but Ben could not be sure whether the feelings were his own or Omas's. Sitting slumped in his big chair, with disheveled hair and purple bags hanging low beneath his eyes, the disgraced chief certainly did not *look* like a man who was plotting a return to power.

Still, appearances could be deceiving, and Cal Omas had not held the Galactic Alliance together for so long by being naïve or principled. During the Dark Nest crisis, when the Jedi had angered him by insisting that the Chiss come to a fair settlement with the Killiks, he had been more than willing to use false bargains, political manipulation, and even unwarranted imprisonment to undermine the power of the Jedi Order. It wasn't much of a stretch to think he had sanctioned the killing of Ben's mother—or to expect Ben to *believe* he had.

Ben turned his attention to the big Tendrando Arms Guardian standing next to the Chief's desk. With gray laminanium armor, thick weapons-packed arms, and a stern downturned vocabulator opening, it was basically a VIP version of the same Defender Droid that had served as Ben's companion and protector during his childhood. Assuming this droid had the same internal design as his Nanna, he visualized the circuit breaker hidden beneath the neck armor and used the Force to trip it.

The Guardian's photoreceptors dimmed for an instant; then there was a *click* as the breaker reset itself. The droid's blocky head swiveled toward the entrance alcove where Ben stood watching.

"Blast!" Ben flipped the circuit breaker again—then heard another *click*. Clearly, *that* particular design flaw had been corrected. "Double blast!"

The Guardian raised an arm and swung it toward the entry alcove where Ben was lurking.

"Do not be alarmed!" the droid said. A stream of tiny flechettes began to fly from its fingertips. "Armed intruder. Take evasive action."

It was speaking to Omas, but Ben was already diving. He landed in a forward roll and pulled a gauss ball—the equivalent of a stun grenade for droids—off his equipment harness and came up flinging. The ball splatted into the Guardian's chest plate and flattened into a crackling mass of energy.

Instead of turning into the buzz-zombie Ben expected, the droid began to stagger about blindly, flailing its arms and spraying a line of energy bolts through the ceiling. Clearly, its mag-shielding had been upgraded beyond even military standards. *Blast and double blast!* So far *everything* was going wrong on this operation. Ben somersaulted toward the droid. It changed directions and crashed into a credenza along the adjacent wall, opposite Omas's fancy desk.

Ben ignited his lightsaber then rolled to his feet, Force-sprang to the droid's side, and swung at its cannon arm. The laminanium was so strong that his first strike cut only halfway through. The Guardian spun toward him, its other arm coming around like a club, its fingers spraying flechettes in random directions.

Ben stepped after the cannon arm and swung again, using the Force to guide his blow. He felt his lightsaber sink into the same cut as before and slice through, then turned toward the other arm and attacked the flechette-spraying hand at the wrist.

The hand clunked to the floor, but the forearm caught him in the head and knocked him into the wall. Ben slid to the floor with his skull ringing and ears spinning, but still conscious and alert—more or less. He deactivated the blade and grabbed the bottom edge of the droid's chest plate, then pulled himself up and jammed the hilt of his weapon against its armpit.

Confused though it was by the gauss ball, the droid recognized its vulnerability and tried to pivot away. Ben held tight and reignited his lightsaber. The blade shot through the thick torso like a gamma ray, scrambling the processing core and burying Ben beneath an avalanche of armor as the ruined Guardian slumped down on top of him.

Was *anything* going to go right?

Ben used the Force to throw the Guardian off, then came up staring straight down the emitter nozzle of a Merr-Sonn Power 5 blaster pistol. To his great relief, the next thing he saw was not a flash of death-dealing energy, but Chief Omas's puzzled face frowning over the barrel of the weapon.

"Ben?"

Ben flicked his hand and sent the blaster flying.

The chief watched it clatter into the wall, the confusion in his face changing to sorrow. Ben sensed no hint of comprehension or remorse in the Force to suggest that Omas felt any guilt over the death of his mother.

"Ah, Ben." Omas stepped slowly back, holding his hands in plain view and sadly shaking his head. "I'm sorry it has to be you. This is a nasty business for someone so young."

Taking care to keep his lightsaber between himself and Omas, Ben rose to his feet. "You know why I'm here?"

Omas dropped his head in acknowledgment. "I'm only surprised Jacen has taken this long."

"Jacen didn't send me," Ben said. He was fairly certain that Omas *didn't* understand why he was there—not really. "I came on my own."

Omas looked doubtful. "What point is there in lying, Ben? I'm going to be dead in a few minutes."

Ben didn't deny it, couldn't bring himself to give the man false hope. "Probably." He pointed across Omas's wroshyr-wood desk to a bank of control buttons near the far edge. "Which one of those lowers the interior blast doors?"

Omas cocked a graying brow, now growing curious. "So I have a few minutes longer?" Without awaiting permission, he leaned across the desk toward the buttons. "You'll still have to be fast, Ben. For a Jedi, you haven't been very stealthy."

"Tell me about it." Sensing no hint of deception in Omas's Force aura, Ben didn't stop the chief from pressing the buttons. "But only the interior doors. Leave the viewing wall open."

Omas cast a knowing glance at his viewing wall—Ben's best escape route, now that he had caused such a tumult—then touched a button. A pair of blast doors slid down to seal the study exits. He turned back toward Ben.

"Now, what can I do to make this easier?" Omas gestured toward a flechette-pocked cabinet, where a stream of sweet-smelling spirits was leaking from beneath closed doors. "Something to drink?"

Ben frowned. "You mean . . . intoxicants?"

Omas's eyes brightened with amusement. "Worried that you're too young, Ben? That it's against the law?" He snorted in laughter, his tone brittle and close to hysterics. "Imagine that, me trying to corrupt my assassin. Perhaps Jacen can charge me with *that,* too."

"That's not what I meant." Ben didn't know why he felt so much on the defensive here—perhaps because he was fairly certain that Omas did *not* deserve what was about to happen to him; that he was about to become collateral damage in a war so secret, even Jacen didn't know about it. "But you go ahead. We've got a couple of minutes before Coruscant Security arrives."

The look Omas shot Ben was more judgmental than shocked. "You mean you took out the whole detail guarding me?"

"Not *dead.*"

Considering what he was about to do to Omas—what he *had* to do—Ben didn't know why he cared what his target thought of him, but he did. He deactivated his lightsaber, then pulled an empty cylinder off his equipment harness and tossed it to the Chief.

Omas was so badly shaken that he shied away from the cylinder. It bounced off the transparisteel wall and clanged to the floor without detonating or emitting anything noxious.

Ben rolled his eyes. "It's an empty coma-gas canister."

Omas exhaled in relief, then turned back to the cabinet. "That's good, Ben. I thought you had become . . . well, like Jacen." He selected an unshattered bottle, took down a single glass, and poured for himself. "But before you do this, there's something you need to know."

Omas opened his cloak and turned back to Ben, revealing a small scanner clipped to his tunic vest. Across the display ran a single line, rising and falling in the familiar pattern of a human heartbeat.

"You're death-trapped?" Ben asked.

Omas nodded. "A venerable tradition for deposed Chiefs. You'll have to make sure I die slowly, or . . ." He cast a meaningful glance at the ceiling, suggesting it would come crashing down amid a torrent of flame and shock wave. Then he nodded toward the transparisteel viewing wall beside him. "And you can't go out that way, either. It's rigged to a thermal detonator."

"*Great.*" Ben sighed. This operation was getting more complicated every second—and not because he had to find a new escape route. That was easy, compared with killing someone who was being so kind to him. "Thanks, I guess."

"Sorry, Ben. I had hoped it would be Jacen standing there."

Ben shook his head. "Jacen's too smart for that."

Omas shrugged. "Everyone makes mistakes," he said. "I certainly made my share."

As Omas spoke, a pair of armored hovercars flew slowly past the viewing wall and began to circle back around. Omas watched them out of the corner of his eye, then pressed a button on his desk. A blast curtain descended over the transparisteel viewing wall, shielding the study from outside scrutiny.

"It looks like we're running out of time," Omas said. He tipped up his glass and drained the contents, then set it on his desk and stepped toward Ben, spreading his arms. "I'm sure you know better than I where to strike. Don't worry if it's painful—I've done enough to deserve that. Just give yourself plenty of time to escape. I don't want to leave this life with your death on my conscience."

Ben used the Force to stop Omas from approaching. The fear and sadness in the Chief's presence suggested that he was telling the truth—he truly did want to make this easy—and *that* was what made it so difficult for Ben to follow through on his plan.

"Ben." Omas was hanging in midstep, still caught in Ben's Force grasp. "Coruscant Security has to be in the tower by now, and they won't care *who* you are, only that someone attacked me."

"I can't do it," Ben said. He pulled a recording rod from his tunic pocket. "Not until you know *why*."

"Ben, I already know—"

"No, Chief," Ben said. "You really don't."

Ben activated the recording rod, then watched Omas's eyes widen as he heard his own voice speaking, saying *they* needed to redirect Luke Skywalker's attention so his friends on the Jedi Council would be free to reinstate him—that he really didn't need to know how some mysterious *you* planned to make it happen.

As the recording came to an end, any doubt lingering about the chief's complicity in the death of his mother vanished. A politician as practiced as Omas might have been able to fake the expression of horror that came to his face, but he would not have been able to feign the shock he was pouring into the Force—or the outrage and despair.

The muffled *thump* of a door-breaking charge sounded from the front of the apartment, and Omas's gaze finally shifted from the recording rod to Ben's face.

"You think *I* had your mother killed?"

"Actually, I don't." Ben tucked the rod into his belt, then released his Force grasp on Omas. "And I never really did."

Omas frowned. "But the recording. Surely, you must have—"

"I imagine it happened like this," Ben said. "One of your guards started to become friendly when there was no one around, and eventually he confided that he was sympathetic to your cause."

"*She*," Omas corrected. "Lieutenant Jonat."

Ben nodded. Jonat was actually a GAG sergeant, one of Captain Girdun's favorite undercover operatives. "Then one day she lets you use her comlink—just so you can let your family know you're alive and well."

It was Omas's turn to nod. "I was suspicious, of course,

but I thought Jacen was only trying to see who I would call—and I *was* desperate to talk to my daughter one more time before—well, before Jacen sent someone like you."

"So you accepted Jonat's offer."

"And used it for exactly the purpose it had been offered," Omas said. "I *did* say some of the things you heard—"

"But not in that context," Ben surmised.

"I was only trying to keep up Elya's hopes," Omas said. "But I never asked her or anyone else to distract your father—especially by killing Mara."

"I know you didn't," Ben said. "Because I'm fairly certain the killer was Jacen."

Omas's jaw dropped. *"Jacen?"*

"He was close by when it happened," Ben explained. "And Mom knew he was working with Lumiya."

"The *Sith* Lumiya?" Omas staggered back, bracing his hand on his desk as though he might fall, and suddenly he began to look hopeful. "You have proof of this?"

"Not yet," Ben said, shaking his head. "To tell the truth, that's sort of the reason I'm here."

Omas frowned. "I don't see how I can help. I'm not aware of anything incriminating."

"Of course not," Ben said. "Jacen is too careful for that."

Muffled bootsteps began to sound through the blast doors, growing louder as they drew nearer the study. A new plan was formulating inside Ben's mind, but he knew he had no time to work out the details. He pointed to the health scanner on Omas's chest.

"Can you take that off?"

Omas frowned, a hint of suspicion coming to his eyes. "Why would I want to?"

Ben sighed. "Jacen is the one who gave me the recording," he explained. "And to find evidence, I need to get close to him again."

Omas's eyes lit in comprehension—then suddenly grew darker and more penetrating. "You're not going after evidence, Ben."

"Of course I am," Ben said. Through the blast door, he could hear muffled voices shouting orders—through *both* blast doors. "But it's not going to be easy—"

"You want to kill Jacen." Omas made it a statement, not a question. "And to get close enough, you have to convince him you can be trusted."

Ben nodded. "That's right. So we have to fake your death."

"That's not why you came here." Omas's gaze remained dark and piercing, almost maniacal. "Jacen would see through that kind of deception in a heartbeat."

"Not if we do it right. I can fool him."

Ben couldn't afford to lose Omas's trust right now, not with Coruscant Security breathing down his neck—but even more importantly, Ben couldn't bear admitting that he *had* become exactly what the chief had feared, a cold-blooded killer, a younger version of Jacen himself.

But Omas wasn't buying. His gaze flashed to the blaster pistol that Ben had Force-hurled against the wall earlier, and just then a security officer's voice began to rumble through the door, informing Chief Omas's assailants that they were completely surrounded.

Omas's eyes flashed to the blast door. "Hurry!" As he yelled, he threw himself to the floor and amazed Ben by coming up with the discarded blaster pistol. "He's going to kill me!"

The Chief started to fire in Ben's direction, his aim not quite true, but close enough that Ben had to ignite his lightsaber and deflect the bolts.

"Wait!" Ben yelled at Omas. "You don't understand!"

The sonorous *boom* of a door-breaker charge thumped from the alcove through which Ben had entered the study.

The detonation wasn't powerful enough to blow the blast door off its hinges, but it *did* draw Ben's gaze away from his attacker for just an instant.

And in that instant Omas was on his feet, charging and firing as he came, yelling for help. Ben retreated, using his lightsaber to bat the Chief's bolts aside, and quickly found himself backed against the wall.

Another charge—this one louder—sounded from the other side of the blast door. Omas kept coming, charging right at Ben, firing not at chest height for a kill-shot, but at his abdomen.

Ben sidestepped, sliding along the wall and still yelling at the Chief to stop, and he didn't understand what Omas was doing until a third *boom*—a huge one—shook the blast door. The Chief hurled himself forward—not at Ben, but at the wall beside him, where the blade of Ben's lightsaber hung at gut level.

Ben thumbed off the blade and saw Omas crash into the wall beside him, then the awful stench of scorched meat filled his nostrils, and he knew he had been too slow. The Chief slid to the floor beside him, a terrible wound smoking just below his rib cage, stretching from the midline of his torso to his flank. He tossed his blaster pistol aside, then looked up at Ben through eyes filled with pain.

"There was no other . . ." Omas stopped, coughing blood and smoke, then continued. "The only way to get to him."

Another detonation—this one an earsplitting *bang*—sounded from the direction of the blast door, and wisps of smoke began to drift out of the alcove.

Omas looked toward the sound. "Go, Ben," he said. "And forgive me."

"Forgive *you*?" Ben dropped to his knees, glancing at Omas's wound just long enough to know that the Chief had achieved exactly what he wished—a wound certain to be fatal, but not for thirty or forty seconds more. "I'm the one who—"

The rest of the sentence was lost to a thunderous *crack* that left Ben's ears ringing, then the whole study shook as the blast door finally came apart and crashed against the wall and floor. Knowing what would come next, Ben rose and pressed himself to the wall next to the alcove. When the expected pair of hand-sized spheres came sailing through the smoke, he caught hold of them in the Force and sent them hurling back through the alcove into the hallway outside.

The silver-white flashes of detonating stun grenades lit the smoke near the alcove, and Ben felt the presences of perhaps a dozen security officers quake with shock, fear, and confusion. Keeping his lightsaber ignited, he stepped into the alcove and half ran, half leapt over the cockeyed blast door, past a dozen beings stumbling around the hallway outside, holding their helmets and groaning.

Stopping to help them was out of the question. Omas was only going to last another ten or fifteen seconds, and it would have taken Ben that long simply to make the dazed security officers understand that they were in danger. He raced down the hallway that led out of the apartment, feeling as guilty and ashamed as he had expected to at this point in the operation—though not quite for the reasons he had imagined.

The backup team ambushed him at the foyer, foolishly yelling at him to surrender instead of opening fire. Ben simply leapt into a series of evasive Force flips, batting their blaster bolts aside and coming down in the apartment's main entrance.

Rather than flee down the corridor to safety, Ben further astonished the security officers by stopping and spinning around. He batted aside a couple of more bolts, then switched to a one-handed grip and waved them after him.

"Come on!" he yelled. "I was too late—the whole place is about to blow!"

The confused officers looked from him into the apartment's smoky interior, then back to their officer.

The officer lowered his blaster rifle and started after Ben, yelling, "Let's go—he's a Jedi, isn't he?"

ten

The Confederation fleets were drifting slowly across the ultradef wall display, a cloud of ion-blue needles burning bright against the star-spangled velvet of space. After a moment, a corona of spacedocks emerged from the edge of the screen, glittering orange-silver in the light of the Kuati sun. Lines of energy too brilliant to have color began to stab out from the leading elements of the advance, sometimes touching the twinkling speck of a spacedock and changing it to a fading spray of sparkles.

Luke watched conscientiously—though not quite attentively—from the head of the ready room where he and his Jedi pilots were awaiting the call to their StealthXs. The battle would hinge on the mission they would soon be launching, and he knew his thoughts should have been on what he could do to ensure success—and on the many young Jedi Knights who would not be returning. But his mind kept drifting back to his son.

This war had forced Ben to grow up so fast that it was easy to think of him as an adult, yet Luke knew better. He had sensed enough guilt and self-loathing in Ben to know that his son held himself responsible for Mara's death. Like so many children who lost parents, he seemed to believe deep down that he must have done something terrible to make her leave.

And those were the kind of thoughts that could lead a young Jedi to the dark side. Luke had seen it happen before—in Kyp Durron, temporarily, and more permanently in Alema Rar—and he would not allow it to happen to Ben.

Luke extended himself toward Coruscant, hoping to find his son and remind him that he still had one living parent—and that *both* his parents still loved him very much. But Ben was hiding from the Force again—one more thing Jacen should not have taught him so early—and Luke felt nothing in return except the anonymous mass of life that called the planet home. Not for the first time, he had the sense that he was failing his son in some way he did not quite understand.

Soon, Luke thought, promising himself as much as Ben. *After this battle, the war will be over, and then we'll have the time we need to figure things out.*

The Confederation fleets reached the center of the wall display. Immediately they sent out swarms of scout ships, trying to locate the Alliance vessels that their sensor operators couldn't separate clearly from the myriad spacedocks orbiting Kuat. The Alliance—following a strategy laid out by the First Fleet's new vice admiral, Nek Bwua'tu—reacted by swarming the scouts with thousands of pre-positioned starfighters.

The Confederation lost its scouts without locating more than a handful of enemy vessels, but its tactical planners—drawing heavily on Bothan talent, no doubt—had gathered enough information to estimate their opposition's strength. The Confederation began to advance more aggressively, concentrating its fire to clear a lane through the spacedocks.

The wall display shifted scales, and clouds of glittering flotsam filled the screen. Streaks of blazing energy flashed across the image in both directions, sometimes striking the ghostly double bars of a spacedock and blasting it into confetti. The Confederation fleets appeared along one edge of the display and began to penetrate the debris field, a thousand durasteel slivers riding long dashes of blue efflux.

Luke faced his Jedi, who had all turned their flowform chairs toward the battle display. Some were lounging comfortably with one arm propped on their squad tables. Others sat nervously on the edge of their seats. Despite the caf dispensers and snack platters in the center of each table, only Tahiri Veila had a dish or drinking vessel in front of her. Berthing the StealthX wing aboard the *Anakin Solo* might have been a military necessity, but that didn't mean the Jedi had to accept Jacen's hospitality.

"Exactly as Bwua'tu predicted," Luke said. To the alarm of the Alliance's senior tactical planners, the admiral had insisted that the Confederation would attack where the Kuati spacedocks were densest and thickest. "They're gambling on catching us out of position."

"How does Bwua'tu *do* that?" asked Kyp Durron, who was seated at the head of the Shadow Saber squadron. "He must be Force-sensitive."

"Better," Saba answered. She was seated beside him, at the head of the Night Blades' table. "He is *prey*-sensitive."

Corran Horn asked, "Prey-sensitive?"

"He knowz how his prey thinkz," Saba explained. "More, he knowz how they think *we* think."

"Which is?" Corran asked.

"Rigid and unimaginative," Kenth Hamner said. He was on the other side of Kyp, sitting at the head of the Dark Sword squadron. "Isn't that how rebels always see their enemies?"

"With good reason," Luke said, recalling when *he* had been one of the rebels. Had matters really been as simple as they had seemed then, an uncomplicated fight between good and evil? It was hard to believe now, when it was just as easy to see evil in the side he was fighting *for* as the one he was fighting against. "But let's talk about *this* battle. Is everybody clear on how it's supposed to develop?"

"What is there to be confused about?" Saba's tone was polite but uninterested, a reflection of the general lack of enthusiasm on the Jedi Council for this mission. "Once the Fourth Fleet has our prey fully engaged among the dockz, the Hapan Home Fleet leaves Ronay'z sensor shadow and surprises the Confederation from behind."

"Trapping them among the docks so the Seventh and Fifth fleets can open fire from the flanks," Kyp added. "Assuming, of course, the Bothans don't notice the Alliance has them surrounded *before* then."

"Bwua'tu says no," Luke said. He had to remind himself that Kyp was always this blunt—that he was merely expressing his own skepticism and not deliberately trying to sow doubt in anyone's mind. "The Confederation commanders won't believe we could have predicted *where* they would attack, so they won't be looking for an ambush."

"If you'll think about it a moment, you'll see they really *can't*," Kenth said, clearly appealing to Kyp to be reasonable. "The Confederation has already lost most of their scout craft, and we can all see what it's like trying to get a sensor picture in there."

"And their admirals *aren't* going to send starfighters on recon missions." Corran sounded a bit desperate, like a used-vehicle salesman eager to focus attention on an airspeeder's sleek body instead of its worn-out hoverpads. "They barely have enough to screen their advance as it is."

"Right," Luke said, adding his voice to the sales effort. "So the Confederation *is* going to be trapped, just as Bwua'tu planned. Now, our objectives—"

"Are as clear as Vorsian crystal," Kyp said. "We take a little pleasure flight through the middle of the Bothan fleet and unload all our shadow bombs on those nice new cruisers of theirs."

When Kyp stopped there, Luke turned to Corran. "Then?"

"Then we rendezvous with the *Megador* and—"

"Hangar fifty-one," Saba interrupted, turning a big Barabel eye on the pilots of her squadron. "That is very important."

"Right," Corran said. "We go to Hangar Fifty-one and rearm, then come *back* through the Corellian fleet."

"Targeting capital ships only," Luke reminded, grateful to Corran and Kenth for helping him return the conversation to the *how* of their mission. "Don't waste your shadow bombs on anything smaller."

"And we *keep* going back and forth," Kenth said. "Until the Confederation fleet finally collapses on itself like a canister full of vacuum."

"And the Alliance wins the war in one big battle," Kyp said, not sounding exactly enthused about the prospect. "Does it bother anyone else that we're delivering the galaxy to Jacen on an aurodium platter?"

Someone unfamiliar with the Jedi Order might have interpreted the uneasy silence that greeted Kyp's question as a rebuke—or at least a sign of polite disagreement. But Luke knew better. Had anyone—at least a Master—felt differently than Kyp, he or she would have said so. The fact that everyone remained quiet meant that they *agreed* with Kyp but were reluctant to upset Luke.

"The sooner this war is over," Luke said, "the sooner Jacen and Admiral Niathal will resign as co-Chiefs and hold the elections they promised."

"Jacen has made a lot of promises," Kyp replied. "But he only keeps the convenient ones. The last I heard, Zekk was still reporting a GAG battalion camped at the Jedi academy on Ossus."

A murmur of agreement rustled through the ready room—and the swiftness with which the squadron leaders silenced it made Luke realize that, with the exception of

Kyp Durron, the Masters were trying to protect his feelings. They didn't want him to know just how disappointed the Jedi Knights—perhaps the entire Order—were in him for agreeing to support this attack while Jacen continued to hold the academy hostage.

"There's no denying that we have problems with Jacen," Luke said. "But we're here for the *Alliance,* not Jacen. Let's win this war. We'll deal with Jacen if he doesn't resign."

"You mean *when* he doesn't resign," Kyp corrected. "We'd better go into this with our eyes open, Master Skywalker."

Of all the Masters on the Jedi Council, only Saba turned to scowl at Kyp—and Luke knew she did so only because she felt Kyp had spoken too boldly. He was surprised to realize how hard the Masters were trying to protect his feelings, but he knew he shouldn't have been. He'd won the Council's support for Jedi involvement at Balmorra the week before only by arguing that it was the best way to make Jacen see he had more to gain by working *with* the Jedi than against them.

When GAG had remained at the academy after the battle—supposedly only until enough Jedi Knights were free from other duties to provide "proper" security—the entire Jedi Order had been outraged. And when Luke had suggested to the Council that they fly their StealthXs at Kuat anyway, he had not sensed any support at all, only consent. He saw now that it had been a mistake not to insist that the Masters express their own views so they could reach a decision together . . . especially when even *he* questioned the clarity of his judgment right now.

Fortunately, it was never too late to correct a mistake. Luke fixed his gaze on Corran, then said, "I appreciate everyone's concern for my feelings, but that's not what I need. It's not what the *Order* needs."

Corran managed to appear both guilty and confused. "I'm not sure I understand, Master Skywalker."

"You think this mission is a mistake," Luke said.

Corran's eyes lit in understanding, and now the other Masters began to look guilty. "I don't like it," he admitted. "Jacen is playing us."

"Probably—but what should we *do* about it?" Luke asked. "Change sides and support the insurrection?"

Corran flushed. "Nobody's suggesting that, Master Skywalker."

Knowing he had to involve all of the Masters in the consensus, Luke shifted his gaze to Kyp. "Maybe we should arrest Jacen for . . . well, I'm not exactly sure what *law* he's violated—or how we could prove it," he said. "But I'm serious. Should we go up to the bridge and arrest him on general suspicion?"

Kyp dropped his gaze. "Probably not a good idea," he admitted. "The Alliance can't stand any more chaos at the moment."

Luke turned to Kenth next. "We *could* do nothing and see how the battle comes out. At least then we'd know we're not doing the *wrong* thing."

Kenth considered the suggestion for a moment, then shook his head. "The galaxy's future is hanging on this—we've got to do *something*." He looked at the other Masters. "Given the choice between a despot and utter lawlessness, I think we have to go with the despot. For now."

"That's what I've been thinking, too," Luke said. He turned to Saba. "But when do we decide Jacen has gone too far? Where do we draw the line?"

"You are asking this one?" Saba flattened her cheek scales in the Barabel equivalent of embarrassment. "Jacen is of the brood of *your* brood."

"And he is the son of *your* apprentice," Luke countered. "You're as responsible for this decision as I am."

"Leia has already turned away from him," Saba pointed

out. "Unless Military Intelligence was mistaken about her business on Kashyyyk."

"Leia isn't a Jedi Master," Luke reminded her. "*You* are."

Saba raised her dorsal spikes and studied Luke for a long time. Nobody wanted to be the one to suggest that the Jedi take arms against Jacen, but they all knew the time was coming . . . and that when it did, they would probably be taking arms against the government of the Galactic Alliance itself.

Finally, Saba half turned in her chair, looking away. "*You* are the longfang, Master Skywalker. We draw the line where you say to draw it."

It wasn't an answer that Luke particularly wanted, but it was the one he'd been expecting. Nothing would have pleased him more than being able to turn leadership of the Order over to someone else while he devoted himself to finding Mara's killer and helping Ben come to terms with his grief. But he didn't have the luxury right now. Jacen had made that much clear, at least.

Luke waited until each of the Jedi Masters and Knights had signaled their assent, then nodded.

"Thank you. We won't let Jacen push us much farther, I promise." He returned his attention to the wall display, where the image had disintegrated into a glittering blizzard of flotsam webbed by bolts of turbolaser fire. "In the meantime, we have a mission to complete—and it doesn't look like it will be long before we're called to it."

As Luke spoke, he grew aware of Cilghal's presence rushing across the corridor from the direction of the infirmary. An instant later, the hatch in the back of the room hissed open, and the Mon Calamari healer slipped into the room. Her bulbous eyes were bulging even more than usual, and her skin had gone gray and dry with shock.

"Switch to HNE!" she cried. "Chief Omas has been murdered—and they're saying Ben was there!"

eleven

Caedus knew now that the path he had chosen—the path of the Sith—was the right one. Despite the bewildering snarl of glitter and light flashing beyond his observation bubble, he could sense through the Force that the battle was all but won. As soon as Admiral Bwua'tu brought the Hapan Home Fleet out of hiding, the traitors' doom would be sealed.

The Corellians were carrying the brunt of the fighting, of course, throwing their battle cruisers and assault frigates against the Star Destroyers of the Fourth Fleet. But Jacen could sense that the Bothans were having trouble, too: the ambushes and minefields they kept encountering were making it impossible for their light cruisers and corvettes to flank the Alliance defenders. And the Commenorians and Hutts weren't even factors. The few vessels they had been able to contribute after the Battle of Balmorra were being relegated to rear defense, along with the flotillas from the Confederation's minor partners.

So Caedus did not understand what Bwua'tu was waiting for, why he had not yet asked for the Hapan Home Fleet. Surely, the admiral could see that everything was going according to plan; all he need do was make this one request and the Alliance would be saved. Caedus only hoped that it had not been a mistake to trust the Bothan. He had been the one who insisted—on Gavin Darklighter's recommendation—that Bwua'tu be given command of the battle, and he had sensed no deception when the vice admiral assured him that his vow of *krevi* demanded that he remain loyal to the Alliance.

But with Bothans, one could never be sure. For all Caedus knew, the *krevi* might have been a cultural fiction that Bothans maintained to take advantage of situations like this.

Caedus turned to the little tactical display near the entrance to his observation bubble, then fixed his gaze on the transponder code of the *Welmo Darb*. Although the Star Destroyer was hardly the largest in the First Fleet, Bwua'tu had selected it as his new flagship so that he would have the option of putting his heaviest firepower in the forefront without risking his command structure. Caedus didn't sense anything amiss aboard the *Darb*, only a calm Bothan presence pondering options while the vessel's harried crew struggled to defend their ship.

Caedus touched a pad on the arm of his meditation chair, then asked, "Is the *Darb* reporting a sensor malfunction? Or data-streaming problems?"

A moment later, the voice of Lieutenant Krova—his personal communications officer—came over the speaker. "They're reporting all systems optimal, Colonel. I could ask them to confirm."

"No," Caedus said quickly. "I wouldn't want Bwua'tu to think I'm impatient."

"The vice admiral is a perceptive being, Colonel Solo," Krova replied. "I'm sure he knows."

Caedus was in too good a mood to be irritated by her sarcasm—at least until his comlink chimed with a special two-tone alert assigned to one of the few people for whom he always needed to make time. He flipped open the device and opened the channel.

"Shouldn't you be in the ready room?"

"I'm in the refresher," Tahiri replied. "And we're not launching anytime soon. Master Skywalker is on his way up to see you."

"What for?"

Tahiri paused, then asked, "When can we go back again?"

"That depends on how long you take to answer my question," Caedus replied. Since their return to the voxyn cloning lab on *Baanu Rass,* they had already flow-walked back to two more time-locations to visit Anakin, and each time Caedus had managed to end the trip leaving Tahiri desperate for more. "I'm very busy right now, as I'm sure you realize."

"This isn't healthy for me," Tahiri said, ignoring his warning. "You can't keep pulling us back before I'm ready."

"Then pick our destination more carefully," Caedus said. "Something that isn't so emotionally charged for you."

"Fine," Tahiri said. "HNE just reported Omas's assassination, and Master Skywalker's as mad as a yanskac on ice. You'd better be ready."

Caedus's insides went cold with dread. Apparently, the HoloNet had decided to ignore the security hold he had placed on the story, and Ben's involvement alone would be enough to bring Luke to the bridge ready to fight a rancor. But he couldn't help fearing there was more to the visit— that his uncle had finally, somehow, discovered the identity of Mara's killer.

Caedus closed the comlink without signing off, then refocused his Force-awareness on the *Anakin Solo*'s bridge. Luke's presence was already close, ascending a nearby turbolift, and the Force was rolling and crashing with his anger.

Caedus touched the comm pad again. "Inform Bridge

Security that Master Skywalker is on his way to my day cabin."

"Master Skywalker?" Krova was silent for a moment while she checked the security monitors, then said, "Of course. What are their instructions?"

Caedus thought for a moment, considering the possibility of trying to delay Luke while he prepared himself, then realized that would only look suspicious.

"Tell them to stay out of his way." Caedus did not bother asking for a summary of recent events in the Jedi area of the *Anakin Solo*. Even had Luke not bothered to disable the monitoring equipment, the only thing the security officers would have seen was what the Jedi wanted them to. "And see that we're not disturbed. I think we're going to need some privacy."

By the time Caedus had instructed SD-XX to secure the cabin against eavesdropping—physical or otherwise—and hidden the droid safely inside its security closet, Luke was marching into the cabin. In his high boots and black StealthX flight suit, he resembled a GAG trooper—at least until he hammered a slap-pad to close the door and started across the floor.

Caedus was glad to see Luke's lightsaber still hanging from its belt clip, but he took the precaution of slipping toward his desk, where he would have access to a dozen weapons and traps he had prepared in anticipation of just such a confrontation.

Luke jabbed a finger in Caedus's direction. "Now I understand why you've been avoiding me." His tone was even and soft, but there was no mistaking the wrath in his Force aura. "And this time, you've finally crossed the line."

"What are you talking about?" Caedus asked, pretending ignorance. If the news of Omas's death was just breaking on the HoloNet, an *innocent* Jacen wouldn't logically have heard about it in the middle of his battle meditation. "I'm sorry I haven't been available to console you, Uncle

Luke, but I've been kind of busy trying to save the Alliance."

Luke narrowed his eyes and stopped in the center of the cabin. "I'd sooner cry on a Hutt's shoulder than yours. I think you know that."

"I suppose family *should* be honest with each other." The sadness in Caedus's voice was genuine. He had always regretted losing his uncle's respect and love—just another of the many sacrifices he was making to bring peace to the galaxy. "But Admiral Bwua'tu will be calling for the Hapan fleet soon. We can work this out—whatever it is—*after* the battle."

Luke shook his head. "I don't think so."

Caedus exhaled in exasperation. "Is this about the academy?" He sneaked a glance toward his observation bubble, where a halo of battle light could be seen flashing around his chair, broken only by the thick triangular pedestal on which it rested. "I told you, I'm not going to leave one of the Alliance's most valuable assets unprotected—"

"Don't play stupid," Luke snapped. "This isn't about the academy. It's about Ben."

"Ben?" Caedus stopped at the corner of his desk, feigning shock. "Did something happen to him?"

"You tell me," Luke said. "You're the one who sent him."

"Sent him *where*? I've hardly spoken to Ben since the funeral."

In the next instant, Caedus found himself flying across the cabin toward his observation bubble. Luke had not gestured, had not flinched, had not even shifted his gaze; he had simply grabbed Caedus in the Force and hurled him five meters into his chair.

"Don't lie." Luke started across the cabin. "I'm getting tired of it."

Caedus sprang out of the chair . . . or *attempted* to. Instead, he found himself struggling against an invisible weight. He felt as if he were accelerating to lightspeed with a faulty inertial compensator.

"Luke, you've gone mad." Caedus reached for the controls on the arm of his chair and discovered he couldn't even do that much. "You can't *do* this. I know you're having trouble dealing with Mara's death, but—"

"This has nothing to do with Mara," Luke said. "And you're lucky it doesn't. If she were here—if she had *known* what you were using Ben for—there'd be pieces of you scattered along the entire length of the Hydian Way."

The irony of the statement was far from lost on Caedus, but he was too astonished—and too frightened—to take any pleasure in it. While it was true that Luke had taken him by surprise, it was equally true that he had done so with no visible effort—and that he was *continuing* to hold him with no apparent exertion.

Keenly aware that all that stood between him and a quick death was Luke Skywalker's much-strained sense of decency, Caedus let a little of his very real fear seep into the Force, just enough to seem properly alarmed.

"Does this have something to do with Cal Omas?" he asked. "Tell me Ben didn't do anything foolish!"

Luke's eyes grew narrow and cold. "Tell *me* what makes you think he might have."

"Of course," Caedus said. "Ben learned of a conversation that made it look as though Omas had something to do with Mara's death."

"That's ridiculous," Luke said. "Chief Omas would never have done something like that."

"Never *have*?" Caedus echoed. "You mean Ben . . . you mean Omas is dead?"

Luke looked at him without answering.

Caedus would have shaken his head, save that it was still being held motionless with the Force. Had it been Mara's death instead of Omas's that Luke had just heard about,

Caedus knew he would already be dead. Another reminder that *anyone* could be surprised.

"I tried to tell Ben the same thing, but he's so full of anger." He locked gazes with Luke. "I'm afraid he's going to become its servant, if one of us doesn't reach him soon."

Luke nodded, then sat on the corner of Caedus's desk. "*How* did Ben find out about this conversation?"

Caedus forced himself not to look away. "I wish I knew."

"*You* told him." When Luke's expression did not change, Caedus realized that his uncle had been expecting the lie, that he had already worked matters out for himself. "It's just so convenient for you, isn't it? You let something slip in an innocent conversation and point Ben like a missile."

"That's not what happened." The denial was strictly for form; Caedus knew Luke wouldn't believe it. "But even if it were, *now* is hardly the time to discuss it. We're a Squib's hair from victory. After we crush the Confederation, I'll be—"

Krova's voice came over the comm speaker. "I'm sorry to interrupt, Colonel Solo, but Admiral Bwua'tu is ready for the Hapans."

Caedus felt a knot unwind inside. *Finally.*

"Tell Admiral Bwua'tu the Hapans will be coming shortly." Caedus had retained personal control of the Hapan Home Fleet, determined to prevent any risk to Tenel Ka or Allana by not using it until victory was certain. He waited until Krova had acknowledged the order and closed the channel, then turned to his uncle. "I've told you all I know about Omas's death, and I need to transmit that order myself. The Queen Mother insisted I take personal responsibility for committing her fleet."

Luke raised his brow. "You think you're dismissing me?"

"I *know* I am." Caedus put an angry edge in his voice; he

might be trapped in a humiliating position right now, but he was still the leader of the Galactic Alliance—and Luke was still its servant. "If you like, we'll open an inquiry into Omas's death *after* we've saved the Alliance."

Luke glared at Caedus for a long moment, then finally slipped off the desk. "Is that a promise?"

"It is."

"Then I'll take it for what it's worth," Luke said. Leaving Caedus Force-pinned in his chair, he started toward the door. "I'll show myself out."

Caedus knew he would be freed as soon as Luke turned his concentration to something other than Force-pinning him—but that might take minutes, and Caedus needed to send in the Home Fleet *now*. Besides, he was the Chief of State of the Galactic Alliance, and he could not allow anyone, even Luke Skywalker, to humiliate him and simply leave. He had to assert *some* sort of authority.

"Luke," Caedus called. "Aren't you forgetting something?"

Luke stopped at the door and looked back, the rage in his face now softening to what looked like remorse. "You're right. I should warn you that you'll have to crush the Confederation without StealthXs. The Jedi can support you no longer."

"What?" Caedus was so shocked that he tried to rise—and found himself as unable to move as before. "You can't desert *now*. We can end this war!"

"We could destroy the Confederation fleets and kill a lot of rebels," Luke admitted. "But I don't think you *can* end this war, Jacen. I don't think you even know what it's about."

"That's absurd." Caedus did not understand how a man who had been fighting wars for forty years could be so foolish. "After their fleets are destroyed, Corellia and Both-awui will have to accept our terms, and once *they've* surrendered, the rest of the Confederation will have no choice but to come racing to rejoin the Alliance."

Luke shook his head and reached for the touch pad beside the door. "There's always a choice, Jacen."

"And if you go through with this one, you'll regret it." Caedus could not understand why Luke wanted to desert him just when they were on the brink of saving the Alliance, but he did know how to prevent it. "Have you forgotten the academy?"

The door opened. Instead of stepping through, Luke faced Caedus and spoke in a very calm voice. "I'm *sure* you're not threatening the younglings."

He pointed at the base of Jacen's meditation chair and made a tapping motion with his finger. The pedestal gave a loud *whumpf,* and the seat dropped a quarter meter.

"Because you really *don't* want to see me angry." Luke made the tapping motion again. The pedestal emitted a metallic shriek, and the seat dropped another quarter meter. "And I think you're smart enough to know that."

Luke tapped a last time, and the pedestal collapsed with a low loud *crump,* depositing Caedus on the floor with his feet sticking out in front of him like a child.

"But if you want to try me, go ahead and make that threat."

Luke lowered his hand, and the weight vanished from Caedus's chest. He could have leapt up to attack—had he been that foolish—but Sith were not slaves to their emotions. Avenging his humiliation could wait until after he had saved the Alliance.

So, remaining on the floor where Luke had deposited him, Caedus simply touched the comm pad on his armrest. "Lieutenant, do we have an open channel to Prince Isolder yet?"

"Actually," replied a deep Hapan voice, "you're speaking to him now, Colonel Solo."

"My apologies." Caedus looked across the day cabin to

lock gazes with Luke. "Are you ready to commence your attack?"

"I am," Isolder said.

Luke lowered his gaze and shook his head.

"Then please proceed," Caedus said. "And may the Force be with you."

"May it be with all of us," Isolder replied. "If this plan doesn't work, we're going to need it."

The channel closed with a *pop*.

Moving very slowly so his uncle would not misinterpret his actions as an attack, Caedus stood.

"I know you too well," he said to Luke. "You're not going to abandon the Alliance."

"There is no Alliance." Luke turned to leave. "It died with Cal Omas."

"For you, maybe." Caedus couldn't understand why his uncle was so focused on Omas's death; it was one among millions, and even if Caedus *had* put the idea in Ben's head, he hadn't actually ordered the assassination. "But you *are* going to support this attack; I'm quite certain the Senate would frown on turning the security of the Jedi academy over to an order of deserters."

Luke's hand brushed the hilt of his lightsaber, and Caedus thought for a moment that the fight he had been anticipating since Mara's death—anticipating, dreading, and wanting—was finally going to come. He stepped away from the observation bubble, giving himself some maneuvering room in case Luke came at him in a tumbling pass.

But Luke seemed to realize that attacking Caedus aboard his own Star Destroyer—even if he was fortunate enough to kill him—would only put the academy and the rest of his Jedi in an even more precarious position. He moved his hand away from his lightsaber and put it out to stop the door behind him from sliding shut.

"Okay, Jacen," he said. "If that's how you want to play this, we will."

"It's not how I *want* anything," Caedus said. "But if that's what it takes to win this war, I'll do it."

Luke studied Caedus for a moment, then seemed to surrender to circumstances. "I don't know why that surprises me, but it does." His voice was weary and sad. "It looks like I should be getting back to my StealthX."

"It looks like you should," Caedus agreed. "And may the Force be with you out there."

Luke snorted, half in disgust and half in humor. "Thanks, I guess." He stepped through the door and started across the anteroom, his disappointment hanging in the Force as heavy as fog on Dagobah. "Good-bye, Jacen."

It did not escape Caedus that Luke had departed without returning the traditional kind wishes, but that was probably too much to ask of someone who had just been brought to task. Caedus waited until his uncle had passed out of sight, then closed the door and turned to find SD-XX standing at his back.

"That went well," the droid said. "For a time, it appeared you would have to kill him, too."

Jacen frowned. *"Too?"* He hadn't told the droid about Mara. Hadn't told *anyone*. "What do you mean by *that*?"

"In addition to his wife, of course," SD-XX explained. "You've been letting secrets slip in your sleep."

Caedus thought of Tenel Ka and went empty inside. The only time he slept well anymore was in her company.

"What do I say?" he asked. "Is it clear?"

SD-XX leaned forward, pushing his skeletal face close to Caedus's. "So you *did* kill her." Droids weren't supposed to have *smug* in their repertoire of voice inflections, but SD-XX managed to sound fairly close. "I wasn't sure."

"What do I *say*?" Jacen shouted.

SD-XX remained faceplate-to-nose with Jacen. "You never actually admit anything," he said. "It's just a lot of talk about necessary sacrifices and making the galaxy safe for children like your daughter."

"My *daughter*." Caedus's heart sank; he was putting Allana at risk in his *sleep*. "Do I ever call her by name?"

SD-XX cocked his head sideways, no doubt focusing his photomicrometer on Jacen's pupil so he could gauge the degree of shock his answer caused.

"You call her by a lot of names," SD-XX said. "Jaina, Danni, Anni, Allaya—"

"Enough!" Caedus ordered. He would have liked to send the droid back to Tendrando to have an owner-exception entered into its probe programming, but that wasn't really an option. Lando had made clear where his loyalties lay—by abetting Han and Leia Solo in their efforts to avoid capture. "Return to your monitoring duties. Let me know if crew members start gossiping about trouble between Luke and me."

SD-XX reluctantly pulled his face away from Caedus's. "Allana?"

"I'm about to have you converted to torpedo parts," Caedus warned.

"You don't have to threaten." SD-XX started toward his security closet. "*I'm* not the one mumbling secrets during shutdowns."

Caedus started back across his day cabin worrying about how preoccupied Tenel Ka had seemed the morning of Mara's funeral, wondering whether she had been hearing things in his sleep that made her suspect him of the killing. At the time, he had attributed her withdrawal to common sorrow, but now he couldn't help wondering. Was she even at this moment pondering whether to reveal what she had heard to Luke and the Council Masters?

Probably not, Caedus decided. Had Tenel Ka heard anything incriminating, she would never have seemed preoccupied or aloof. She would have taken great care to make sure that she appeared perfectly normal, and the first he would have known about her suspicions was when she stuck a lightsaber against his back and started to interrogate him.

At least that was what he hoped.

By the time he reached the observation bubble, the battle had erupted into a curtain of light and flame that was stretched all the way across space. The *Anakin Solo* was pouring fire into the conflagration from all four of its long-range turbolaser batteries, causing the decks to shudder and the illumination to dim and flicker. Every couple of seconds, a tiny dash would emerge from the firestorm and swell into a crimson streak of energy in the blink of an eye, then blossom into a boiling wall of death against the ship's shields.

Any attempt to make visual sense of the firestorm was hopeless, but the sight of so much unleashed energy filled Caedus with awe and pride. *He* had arranged this, marshaled the death-dealing power and lured the enemy into its path, and it made him feel like a . . . well, not quite like a deity, but like a man standing at the brink of destiny. This victory would place the galaxy in his grasp—and once he had the galaxy, peace would be within his reach.

Krova's voice came over the comm. "The Jedi are ready to launch, Colonel."

"*All* of them?" Caedus asked. "Master Skywalker, too?"

There was a brief silence while Krova consulted the hangar chief, then she said, "Master Skywalker is the one making the report."

"That was quick," Caedus said, raising his brow. "Are the Hapans in position?"

"Opening fire now," Krova reported. "But Admiral Bwua'tu's plan doesn't call for the StealthXs to attack until the Bothans turn to meet the Hapans. He feels the added element of confusion will—"

"I'm *aware* of the battle plan, Lieutenant." Caedus focused his Force-awareness deep inside the *Anakin Solo*'s belly, where he felt a snarl of angry Jedi presences. Deciding it would be better to have them dodging missiles and turbolaser volleys than sitting idle and stewing about his authority, he said, "And Master Skywalker is aware of the plan, as well. Let him launch."

Krova acknowledged the order, and a moment later Caedus felt the Jedi moving away from the *Anakin Solo*. Realizing it would soon be time for him to coordinate their attack with Admiral Bwua'tu, Caedus grabbed his meditation chair in the Force and discovered that he could not turn it back toward the battle. No matter how hard he exerted himself, it would not budge.

Krova reported that the Hapans had sealed the Confederation's escape route and were now fully engaged.

Caedus gave up on the chair—he couldn't see anything useful through the bubble anyway—and dropped into the seat facing away from the battle. Instead of leaving his legs stretched out in front of him as they had been before, he drew his knees up to his chest and felt no less foolish.

Krova reported that the Bothans were turning to engage the Hapan Home Fleet. The First and Seventh fleets began to press the flanks, trying to squeeze them into a crossfire, and the Confederation fought desperately to hold position, dealing as much death as they suffered. Caedus closed his eyes and did his best to grasp the battle in all its complexity, nudging a task force commander forward here, warning off a Star Destroyer captain there, always keeping track of the Jedi StealthXs creeping along the edges of the fight toward the Bothan fleet.

Finally, Krova patched Bwua'tu's gravelly voice through directly to Caedus. "Congratulations, Colonel. The time has come to end this war. Send in the StealthXs, please."

"My pleasure," Caedus replied. "And, Admiral?"

"Yes?"

"Thank you for your loyalty."

"That's nothing to thank me for, sir," Bwua'tu replied. "A *krevi* can't be broken, no matter who takes command."

"All the same, I'm glad to have you on our side."

As Caedus spoke, he reached out to the Jedi, urging them to attack. They responded with a wave of anger even greater than what he had sensed in the hangar, and their presences began to grow noticeably weaker as their StealthXs accelerated away at full power.

To Caedus's alarm, the Jedi presences *continued* to grow weaker, entirely bypassing the Bothans and shooting out through the Hapan Home Fleet toward the fringes of the Kuat system. Finally, they vanished altogether.

A moment later, Bwua'tu's voice came over the comm. "Where are those StealthXs, Colonel? If the Bothan core doesn't start collapsing soon, this is going to turn into the longest, bloodiest battle since the Yuuzhan Vong took Coruscant."

Caedus was too shocked, too angry, to answer immediately. The Jedi *had* deserted him—worse, they had betrayed him, deliberately misled him without regard for what it would do to the Alliance.

"Colonel?" Bwua'tu demanded. "I can't press the attack until the Jedi strike."

"What happens if you do?" Caedus asked. "Press the attack without the Jedi, I mean?"

Bwua'tu was silent for only a moment. "We lost our StealthXs?"

"My questions first, Admiral," Caedus said sharply. "Can we do this without them?"

This time, it didn't take even a moment for Bwua'tu to answer. "It's *possible*," he said. "But I wouldn't want to try it. We've lost our big advantage—and if we lose here, we lose everything."

"I see."

If Caedus ordered Bwua'tu to press the attack anyway, he would be gambling with the lives of Tenel Ka and Allana—and growing up in the Solo household, he had learned enough about high-stakes gambling to know that only a fool risks everything without a big edge.

"Then I'm afraid we can no longer press the attack, Admiral." Caedus went cold inside. "The Jedi have betrayed us."

twelve

Despite a brisk wind, and the lush tang of wroshyr pollen it carried, the musky smell of so many Wookiees gathered for so long in such a small place was . . . overpowering. Not sickening, but certainly dizzying. As Leia followed Han through the jungle of roaring fur that was the Rock Council, it took an act of will just to continue breathing. She did not bother trying to remain steady on her feet. The way she and Han were being bounced around by shifting hips and flying elbows, that was a lost cause.

A particularly large elbow, descending from a ferocious cheer, crashed down on Leia's shoulder and drove her to her knees. She didn't cry out—Saba had broken her of that particular urge by rapping her on the head until she learned to accept pain silently—but it didn't prevent the elbow's owner from scowling down to see what kind of critter he had just smashed.

"No harm." Leia rose and rotated her arm. "See? It still works."

The Wookiee, a lanky male with graying fur, narrowed a pair of silvery eyes and growled something in a dialect Leia might have understood, had she been able to hear it over the howls of approval rolling across Council Rock. She chided herself silently, thinking she had allowed her concentration to slip. The Solos' furlough from their week-long stay in jail was not exactly authorized; without a Force mask suggesting they actually belonged here, Leia worried that it would only be a matter of moments before they were seized and returned to their cell.

"There's no need for concern," she said, waving her hand between them. Wookiees were rarely weak-minded, but she had nothing to lose by trying. "We've come to hear the—"

"No problem," Han interrupted, addressing himself to the Wookiee. "It was an accident."

He grabbed Leia by the hand and softly hissed, "He's just apologizing." He pulled her between a pair of furry torsos, then added, "And cut out the Force stuff already. That isn't allowed here."

"*We're* not allowed here," Leia said, squeezing to his side. "We're supposed to be in jail, remember?"

Han shook his head. "We're supposed to be in jail when Waroo gets back from lunch," he said. "Didn't you hear him?"

Leia frowned. "I *thought* I had," she said. "Didn't he say, *You'd better be here when I get back*?"

"That's *exactly* what he said—not *You'd better* still *be here* or *You'd better not go anywhere* or *Don't use the Force to open that lock while I'm gone.*" Han shook his head, then added, "Sometimes I wonder how you ever made it as a diplomat."

"He *let* us escape?" Leia asked. "I thought Wookiees had an honor code."

"They do," Han said. "And only Wookiees understand it."

They finally reached the center of Council Rock, emerging from the crowd at the foot of a natural basalt dais standing half again as tall as a man. Atop the pedestal, a dome-muzzled male paced back and forth, roaring at the crowd and waving a meter-long mandible lined with hooked fangs. Leia could make out enough of what the Wookiee was saying to realize he was evoking memories of the galaxy's fractured response to the Yuuzhan Vong, assuring his fellow delegates that they were making the best decision for Kashyyyk *and* the Alliance.

"Han, I think the debate's over," Leia said, using a Force whisper to project her voice into his ear. "That's not an argument he's making, it's a pep talk."

"Then we'll just have to start a new debate."

"What about Waroo?" Leia was reading Han's lips as much as she was hearing him. "Wookiee debates take forever, and he'll be in more trouble than *we* are if we're not there when his relief comes."

"So he won't *ask* for relief. Why do you think they picked Waroo to guard us in the first place?" Han turned toward Leia and stepped in close. "Besides, we'll be back in jail before you know it. This won't take long."

Leia scowled. "*What* won't take long?"

Han jerked a thumb at the Wookiee on the Council Rock. "You see that tyrossum jaw he's holding?"

"How could anyone miss it?"

"If I want the floor, I've got to take it from him." Han reached into Leia's pocket and pulled her hold-out blaster—among the weapons Lumpawaroo had left conveniently unguarded when he went to lunch—then hid it between them as he changed the setting to stun. "*Without* using any weapons."

Leia put her hand over the blaster. "Then what's *this* for?"

"If I cheat, they have to stop this debate to decide whether I've violated the Rock Council rules," Han said. "And then they'll have to settle on a fitting punishment. The whole thing should take about a month if I can get 'em good and stirred up."

"Han, I'm not sure that's really a solution," Leia said. The more she heard about the idea, the less she liked it.

"From what Waroo said, the battle at Kuat is going to last a lot longer than a month."

Han shrugged. "You got a better idea?"

"In all likelihood." Leia slipped off her outer robe and unclipped her lightsaber, then pushed them both into Han's arms. "Hold these."

Han's eyes widened. "Leia, you can't do—"

His warning was lost to the general din as Leia Force-sprang onto the top of the rock. She landed beside the dome-muzzled Wookiee a couple of meters away—and still almost caught a face full of fangs as he swung the tyrossum jaw in a sweeping, cheer-rousing arc. Leia saved herself—or at least her good looks—by cartwheeling to the forward edge of the platform.

By the time she returned to her feet, the tumult was quieting to a confused murmur, and the speaker was cocking his head with an expression that seemed equal parts confusion and apology. His face fur was dappled with gray flecks and his fangs were rounded with age, yet he still looked like he could lift a landspeeder as easily as he could a human woman who stood barely as high as his waist.

Leia pointed at the huge jawbone he held. "If you can't be careful with that thing," she said, "maybe it would better if I held on to it."

The Wookiee grew even more bewildered, pushing his head forward as though he didn't quite believe what he was hearing. The rest of the Rock Council caught Leia's meaning instantly and erupted into peals of booming laughter. At the foot of the rock, Han shielded his eyes as though he couldn't bear to watch what was about to happen—but he was peeking between his fingers, and the tip of Leia's hold-out blaster was poking out of the robe folded over his arm.

Leia shrugged off Han's lack of confidence as simple overprotectiveness and stepped toward the Wookiee. "You heard me. Hand it over."

Finally seeming to realize that he was being challenged,

the Wookiee raised the jawbone over his head—about a meter out of Leia's reach—then shook his head and taunted her with a fang-filled grin. Another peal of laughter rumbled across Council Rock, and a handful of voices began to yowl warnings not to let Han's bedmate do to him what Han's shipmate had done to his son.

Leia glanced down at Han. "*This* is old Tojjelnoot?"

Han pulled his hand away from his eyes and nodded. "Who'd you *think* would be closing the council?"

"Great." Leia looked back to old Tojjelnoot, who was now eyeing her like something he intended to eat at his next meal. "All I have to do is take that jawbone from him, and then I get to talk?"

"For as long as you hold on to it," Han answered. "Just don't kill him. The last thing we need right now is a bunch of Tojjes following us all over the galaxy."

"No promises." Leia winked. "He's big."

A hint of uncertainty flashed through Tojjelnoot's eyes. Leia raced straight at him, and he finally seemed to realize she really did intend to bowl him over. He snorted in contempt and raised his free hand to slap her aside.

Leia dived under the blow, then planted her hands a meter in front of him and launched herself into a handspring. Both heels hit square in his stomach.

Tojjelnoot would probably have fallen even without the Force, but Saba had drilled into Leia the folly of taking unnecessary chances in any combat. She waited until her legs had extended fully, then added just enough power to be certain the Wookiee would go down.

Tojjelnoot dropped to his seat gasping, groaning, and clutching at his stomach. Leia pushed into a forward roll, then pirouetted around and retrieved the jawbone from where it had clattered to the floor.

Wookiee voices immediately began to boom both approval and accusations of Force-cheating. Leia allowed the tumult to continue for a moment, then used the Force to project her voice over the uproar.

"I wasn't supposed to use the Force?" she asked, feigning ignorance. "Is it against the rules?"

The roaring grew more unified as the entire council assured her that using the Force was *completely* against the rules. The Talking Bone had to be taken without the use of claw, weapon, or fang, and the Force was clearly a weapon. Tojjelnoot stopped groaning long enough to add that Force use was *totally* forbidden on Council Rock—Han should have told her that.

Leia put on an expression of contrition and faced Tojjelnoot, who was still struggling to sit upright. She offered the jawbone to him.

"I wouldn't want to cheat," she said. "Shall we go again?"

Tojjelnoot's eyes flashed with alarm and anger—then began to twinkle with appreciation as Leia used the Force to gently pull him to his feet so he wouldn't appear quite so defeated. He turned to Han and grunted that Han should have explained the rules before bringing his mate here, then motioned for Leia to keep the jawbone and slipped off the rock.

"Thank you—that's very generous." She turned her attention back to the rest of the council. "And when someone else wants to take the floor, I promise not to use the Force on them, either."

This drew a chorus of approving guffaws. Leia waited for quiet, then continued in a deliberately soft voice.

"You all know me," she began. "You all know who my son is, and I daresay you all know of the trouble between him and my husband and me."

A murmur of sympathetic agreement rumbled through the crowd.

"It is a sad sign of our times that many families are divided like mine, separated not by selfish interests or conflicting loyalties or even necessity, but by deeply held principles. I know Jacen holds *his* principles even more deeply than Han and I hold ours, even more deeply than his own life, because that's what it would take to make him fire on the *Falcon*."

The incident could hardly be news to the council, since it had been reported throughout the Alliance as proof of the colonel's uncompromising dedication to duty. But among the family-oriented Wookiees, it remained enough of a controversy to draw a chorus of snorts and snarls.

"But holding principles deeply doesn't make a being right—and it doesn't make what he's *doing* right." The snorts began to grow indignant, but Leia pressed on, knowing she had to make her point quick and hard before someone grew angry enough to challenge her. "And that's what I'm here to talk to you about.

"Jacen Solo, my son, has seized power in an immoral coup—"

The floor erupted into a deafening storm of objections. Unable to make herself heard without using the Force, she banged the heavy jawbone down on the dais—and only felt more ignored.

After the uproar had continued for more than a minute, Tojjelnoot hopped up and politely held out his hand for the jawbone. Seeing that the thing was doing her no good anyway, Leia passed it over. He went to the edge of the rock and slammed the flat side into the shoulder of the nearest Wookiee, roaring for him to respect the bone, then repeated the process twice more.

Finally, the tumult began to subside. Tojjelnoot boomed something in Xaczik that instantly silenced the crowd . . . and made Han wince.

Leia knelt at the edge of the rock. "What did he say?"

"Uh, I'm not sure, exactly," Han said sheepishly. "Do I *look* like a Wookiee?"

"Only in the morning," Leia said. "And don't dodge my question."

"Okay, okay," Han said. "He threatened to let you use the Force on the rock—said nobody would shut you up then, judging by the speeches you used to make as Chief of State."

Leia was still trying to decide whether to be offended or grateful when Tojjelnoot appeared at her side, holding out the jawbone. She accepted with an ingratiating smile and returned to the center of the rock.

Leia had barely started to speak again before a nasal Sullustan voice rose from somewhere deep in the crowd.

"Stop! Don't listen . . . that woman. It's *illegal*!"

Leia glanced down at Han, but saw that sending him to silence Juun would be hopeless. Even if he could find the Sullustan in the middle of that jungle of fur out there, it would take several minutes to reach him. She decided to try the Wookiee approach and simply shout down her heckler.

"As I was saying, Colonel Jacen Solo and Admiral Cha Niathal have seized power in an immoral and illegal coup—"

"It was perfectly legal!" Juun yelled from about twenty meters back. "Under an amendment to the Emergency Measures Act, GAG has the authority to detain heads of state, politicians, and any other individuals believed to present a risk to the security of the Galactic Alliance."

"It *was* illegal," Leia insisted. "I'd bet my lightsaber that Jacen is the one who tabled the amendment in the first place, and that makes his actions a scheme to seize the power of the executive through means other than a legal election, and *that* is a gross violation of the constitution of the Galactic Alliance."

Leia's argument caused even Juun to fall silent in contemplation, but she knew by the tide of indecision rolling through the Force that she could not talk the Wookiees out of helping Jacen by arguing legalities. She had to find a way to convince them of the utter *wrongness* of his actions, to stir their moral outrage.

"But let's talk about what Jacen has done even with the authority he *has* legally," Leia continued. "By GAG's own figures, there are less than ten thousand terrorists operating on Coruscant. Yet he's imprisoned over a million Coruscanti residents—for what? Sympathizing with their homeworld? The crime of being *descended* from Corellian parents? Looking crosswise at the GAG troopers standing guard in their apartment hallways?"

This drew a few thoughtful grunts, and Leia began to think she was making progress.

"And what about the Bothans?" she pressed. "Was it any coincidence that the True Victory Party's entire membership on Coruscant turned up dead? No wonder Bothawui entered the war on Corellia's side."

"You can't prove Colonel Solo had anything to do with that!" Juun objected. He seemed to be about five meters closer, but remained hidden in all that Wookiee fur. "And you can't blame—"

A fierce Wookiee voice barked at Juun to be quiet, and another growled that if he wanted to talk, he had to climb up on the Council Rock and steal the Talking Bone like anyone else.

"Thank you." Leia was starting to think she just might convince the Wookiees to change their minds about supporting Jacen—and if she could do *that,* then maybe the Jedi could broker a peace that would prevent the conflagration above Kuat from spreading any farther. "I've already reminded you that Jacen fired on the *Falcon* during the recent Hapan crisis. What I *didn't* tell you—what GAG has been very good at keeping out of the holonews—is that at the time we were rescuing several Jedi and other Alliance personnel who had been left adrift during the battle, including his own sister, Jaina Solo, and his cousin and apprentice, Ben Skywalker. Jacen *knew* this, and still he fired on—"

The council broke into roaring peals of disbelief and outrage. But what prevented Leia from continuing was the waist-high ball of black fur that came clambering onto the rock, spitting and sputtering and pointing at the Talking Bone.

Leia stared down at Tarfang in disbelief. "You've got to be kidding," she said. "You're *challenging* me?"

The Ewok nodded and jabbered something nasty. The Wookiees nearest the rock cringed and looked away.

Leia glanced down at Han. "What's with them?"

"Tarfang's got a nasty reputation," Han said. "Look, you've already made your point. Maybe you should just give him—"

"You think he can take me?" Leia turned back to Tarfang, who was standing with his hands on his hips glaring at her. "*That* little rugger?"

Leia's insult came to an abrupt end as Tarfang flew at her head, all flailing claws and gnashing teeth. She dropped to her side and rolled, bringing her leg up behind him and catching him in the small of the back with a form-perfect roundhouse kick.

The blow launched the Ewok off the far end of rock, where he vanished into a mass of astonished fur-faces. Leia returned to her feet and started to step over to see what had happened to him—then heard a snarl of rage coming from somewhere down around the knees of several nearby Wookiees. As they scrambled to get out of the way, Leia looked over at Han.

"I can't believe I have to do this," she said. "Brawling with an Ewok?"

"You could always let him have the bone." Han glanced over at where Tarfang had disappeared, then added, "Watch it!"

The Ewok came sailing back onto the rock as though he

had been fired from a missile launcher. Leia pivoted away, presenting her flank and lifting the jawbone out of reach. She saw Tarfang purse his lips and realized something disgusting was about to come flying her way.

Leia tried to duck, but was too slow and caught a spray of blood and broken teeth full in the face. Her vision went instantly red and blurry, and then the Ewok was on her, slamming his brow into her temple, clamping his tiny hands around her throat, slamming his little knees into her ribs and chest.

Leia heard Han yelling, *"Hey! No claws!"* then felt herself going down and barely managed to toss the bone aside so she didn't land on top of it. Tarfang immediately switched tactics, releasing his choke hold to slam her skull against the stone instead.

Leia's head exploded into stars, and when she felt it being pulled up for another blow, she began to realize the Ewok intended to do more than just steal the Talking Bone. She drove her elbow up into his stomach, putting the Force behind it, then felt hair ripping out as Tarfang tumbled away.

To her astonishment, there was no roaring for her or against her, no one complaining she had used the Force; even Han was quiet. The entire Rock Council had fallen silent, and the Force was charged with surprise and curiosity. Leia sprang to her feet. Half expecting her crazed opponent to come flying at her with claw and fang, she turned to find the Talking Bone lying unclaimed between them. Tarfang was scowling at the crowd, looking every bit as confused as Leia.

Keeping one eye on the Ewok, Leia extended her Force-awareness over the entire expanse of Council Rock—and quickly realized why everyone had fallen silent.

"Luke?" she gasped. "What are you doing here?"

"The same thing you are." Luke's voice came from the

fringe of the crowd, near the entrance. "I came to address the Rock Council."

A triangular furrow appeared in the crowd as the Wookiees stepped aside to let him pass. A few moments later, Leia saw her brother for the first time since her glimpse at Mara's funeral. His eyes were bloodshot and sunken with exhaustion, and his complexion was the color of durasteel. But his jaw was set and his shoulders square, and he was leading Saba Sebatyne and the other Council Masters toward the Council Rock with a strong, purposeful gait.

Leia knelt at the edge of the platform and offered her hand. When he allowed her to pull him up, she asked quietly, "Luke, how *are* you?"

He smiled and squeezed her shoulder, then admitted, "I've been better." He gestured at the tyrossum jaw lying on the rock. "Do you mind?"

Leia shook her head. "Be my guest."

Luke turned to Tarfang. "How about you?"

The Ewok picked up the jawbone and dragged it over. He glared up at Leia, then dropped the bone at Luke's feet and jabbered something that sounded vaguely like "She's *your* problem now."

"Thank you."

Luke picked up the Talking Bone, then waited politely for Leia and Tarfang to yield the platform. Leia gave Han a summoning nod, then dropped off the stone next to Saba.

"Master Seb . . ." Leia's throat went dry, and she had to pause to wet it. "Master Sebatyne, it's good to see you again."

Saba shook her head. "It will be good to go on the hunt together again," she said. "But this is *not* a good day for anyone, Jedi Solo—especially not for you."

Before Leia could ask what Saba meant, Luke began to address the Rock Council in a voice as sad as it was weary.

"I'm sure the Rock Council has heard of the assassination of Cal Omas," he said. "And of my son Ben's involvement in it."

A murmur of acknowledgment rustled through the Rock Council, and Leia began to have a terrible feeling that she knew what was coming next.

"What you probably don't know is that Jacen Solo arranged it." The Rock Council received this news in utter, stunned silence, and Luke pressed on. "Therefore, the Jedi Council has voted to begin active opposition to his continued leadership of the Galactic Alliance, and we have come to Kashyyyk to ask the Wookiees to join us."

thirteen

Ben found his cousin on the bridge of the *Anakin Solo,* a gaunt black-clad figure silhouetted by flashing fans of turbo-laser fire, staring out the Tactical Salon viewport as though he could actually make sense of the conflagration he had ignited. It occurred to Ben that he was finally seeing Jacen in his true form: a stain on the galaxy, a shadow spreading fire across the stars. He pushed that recognition from his mind as quickly as it had come. If Ben wanted to get close enough to kill his cousin, he had to keep his thoughts pure, to actually *believe* in the dark dream again. Jacen would see through anything less—Omas had been right about that much, at least.

A dozen analysts were bustling around the holodisplay of the battle in the center of the Tactical Salon, and several glanced in Ben's direction. Their eyes flashed sometimes with sympathy and sometimes with scorn, but no one seemed surprised to see him, and no one offered a nod of greeting. Even Jacen's administrative aide—the cheeky Jenet, Orlopp—was careful to ignore Ben and continue clicking his datapad.

Clearly, Jacen was determined to make Ben lick decks before taking him back. It was a good sign. Were Jacen planning a bad end for Ben, he would have tried to put him at ease. But it rankled nonetheless, and only the memory of that last happy afternoon with his mother gave him the strength to reach for the contrition and embarrassment he would need to fool Jacen.

Ben was still trying to summon the feelings when his head began to prickle beneath the pressure of someone's careful inspection. At first, he was confused about where the scrutiny came from, since the tactical staff continued to ignore him and his cousin's eyes had not strayed from the unrelenting battle beyond the viewport. Then a small Force tug summoned Ben forward, and he realized Jacen had been studying him with a faculty other than sight.

"I must say, you Skywalkers continue to surprise me." Jacen's gaze shifted so that he was looking at Ben's reflection in the viewport. "Did you come all the way out here to gloat? Or are you just here to slip away with the fleet's bacta supply?"

"I'm sorry about Dad." Ben started forward, circling wide around the holodisplay to avoid interfering with the analysts. Jacen's back was still turned to him, but he knew better than to think he stood any chance of killing his cousin now. He would have to be patient, win Jacen's trust again, and then strike. "I didn't think he'd blame you for Omas."

"That's the trouble. You *didn't* think—not at all." Jacen turned and faced Ben. "You killed a former *Chief of State* of the Galactic Alliance. Technically, he was *still* the Chief. The Senate hadn't even had a chance to begin a formal inquiry."

Ben stopped in front of Jacen and shrugged. "He killed Mom," he said, forcing himself to believe in the lie. "I'll stand trial if you want."

Jacen shook his head. "There *can't* be a trial. It would look like GAG sent you."

The outrage, Ben knew, was feigned. He had done exactly as Jacen had hoped he would—though a lot less smoothly. If his cousin was angry about anything, it was about how badly he had botched the operation. Still, he did his best to believe Jacen's act, so that his Force presence would feel properly chastened.

"As far as the public is concerned," Jacen continued, "you were trying to *save* him—just like the holonews is saying. Is that clear?"

Ben nodded. "Yes, sir, if that's what you want."

"What I *want* is to throw you in a detention cell and weld the door shut. But that's not the best thing for the Alliance, so count yourself lucky." Jacen ran his gaze over Ben's black GAG uniform, then said, "Now tell me why you risked your life to fly out here through the middle of a battle—and what you're doing in uniform."

"I'm reporting for duty," Ben said simply.

"After what you accused me of?" Jacen's brow shot up in carefully rehearsed disbelief, and it grew apparent that he had received Ben in the Tactical Salon for more than the satisfaction of public groveling. He wanted witnesses to hear a Skywalker say he hadn't murdered Mara. "Does this mean you *don't* think I had anything to do with your mother's death?"

"*Omas* is the one I killed," Ben answered. He could probably have hidden an outright lie from Jacen, but he found himself reluctant to actually *speak* the words, as though that might somehow absolve Jacen of the crime. "There's your answer."

All too confident in his ability to manipulate Ben, Jacen didn't even hesitate to accept it. "I suppose so. I only wish that undid the damage."

Motioning for Ben to follow, he led the way into the commander's office at the back of the salon. Though the cabin contained both a desk and a small conference table with several chairs, Jacen did not go to either. He simply closed the door and opaqued the transparisteel privacy partition, then turned so fast that Ben began to fear his cousin knew exactly why he had returned.

"Who else did you share your suspicions with?" Jacen demanded. "Your father?"

Ben shook his head. "I didn't talk about it with anyone."

"You're lying." Jacen stepped closer. "Why else would he have deserted me when he did?"

"I didn't say *anything*." Ben found himself retreating toward a corner and stopped. It would not do to get himself trapped. "I didn't have proof, and I didn't think anybody would listen to me."

"He wanted to wound me, Ben." Jacen continued to advance, coming so close that Ben could feel his breath as he spoke. "To wound the *Alliance*. Why would he do that, unless you had convinced him that I had killed your mother?"

"I d-don't know." Actually, his father had explained over a secure comm channel that Omas's assassination was the final outrage in a whole series that had sent him nova, but the angry gleam in Jacen's eye suggested there was no use telling him he had brought this on *himself*. "It wasn't because of anything *I* told him. Honest."

Jacen stopped so close that their toes touched, and he began to stare through Ben to somewhere about a light-year beyond Kuat, his Force aura crackling with anger.

"Look," Ben said, allowing his hand to drop toward his lightsaber, "if I *had* told Dad that I thought you killed Mom, he would have done a lot more than desert. One of you would be *dead* now."

The comment seemed to draw Jacen back into the cabin. His gaze dropped to the hand hovering above Ben's lightsaber, then a glimmer of astonishment came to his eyes. He stepped away.

"You may have a point," he said, smiling faintly. "But that doesn't mean I should take you back. I don't know that I can trust you anymore."

Ben nodded; he had been expecting this. "Trust is in short supply these days. So what? You need me."

Jacen cocked his brow and said nothing.

"With Dad and the Jedi gone, I'm good for your image," he said. "And I'm a pretty decent assassin."

"Not *that* decent." Jacen turned away, presenting his back to Ben, then sighed wearily. "Tell me this, Ben—what am I to do about your father?"

"About his desertion?" As much as Ben ached to plant his lightsaber between Jacen's shoulders at that moment, his cousin's "mistake"—turning his back to him—seemed just a little too deliberate. He moved his hand away from the weapon, then asked, "What *can* you do?"

Jacen made a *tsk*ing sound and continued to stare at the blank wall. "How quickly you forget, Ben. Wasn't taking the academy hostage one of the, um, *items* that convinced you I was acting guilty?"

Ben's heart dropped so fast his knees almost buckled. Until now, he had never imagined Jacen would actually *harm* the students—but a couple of weeks earlier, he couldn't have imagined Jacen working with Lumiya, either. Or killing his mother. Ben covered his alarm by recalling his reaction to Lumiya's voice coming from Jacen's GAG office, then pulled that same confusion over his mind like a cloak.

"I guess that's right . . . ," he said slowly. "But I don't think those students are going to replace Dad and the rest of the Jedi. Most of them haven't even built their first lightsaber."

Jacen spun around. "*Replace* isn't really what I was thinking."

"It wasn't?" Ben pretended to struggle with Jacen's meaning for a moment, then allowed his face to fall. "Oh."

"What do you think?" Jacen asked, watching him intently. "Does your father care about his students enough to return to duty for them?"

Ben knew he was being tested—that Jacen was checking to see whether his loyalty was to the Jedi or to him. But Ben also knew by the gleam he had seen in Jacen's eye earlier that his cousin was quite capable of carrying out the threat, and the thought of having the blood of young ones on his hands was too much for Ben. If he condoned something like that, even to avenge his mother, he would never be able to step back into the light—which could be exactly what Jacen intended. His head began to ache.

"Well," Ben began cautiously, "the trouble with threatening the students is that nobody will believe you'd do it. So you're going to have to kill a few to show you're serious."

Jacen nodded. "Go on."

"But if you do *that*, the first thing the Jedi will do next is come after you," Ben finished. "The Masters were already talking about arresting you when you'd only put the academy under protective custody."

"*Were* they?" Jacen sounded interested but disappointed, and Ben had the distinct feeling he had been measured and found lacking. "They should have been grateful, don't you agree?"

"Masters aren't idiots, Jacen," Ben said. "They called your bluff, and you've got nowhere to go. If you make good on your threat, you're just adding enemies. But if you *don't*, you're wasting GAG resources protecting the academy while they run around causing you trouble."

"Interesting point." Jacen's tone had turned bitter. "I imagine you're about to tell me I should withdraw soon."

"At least then the Jedi would have to protect the academy themselves." Ben could see by the way Jacen's eyes hardened that he was not reestablishing trust—quite the opposite. "But if I were you, I'd just stick to my first plan."

Jacen scowled. "What plan would that be?"

Ben rolled his eyes. "Come on. You're always telling me to think ten steps ahead, and right now that means thinking about where the Alliance is going to get its Jedi *after* the war. Seems to me the academy is full of potential, just waiting for you to shape it in your own image."

Jacen actually smiled. "So you *were* paying attention."

"Some of the time," Ben said. "But Dad's desertion is going to throw a real hydrospanner in your plans, isn't it?"

"Eventually," Jacen admitted. "But so far, your father is content to do exactly as you suggest—allow *me* to guard the academy while he stirs up trouble."

"Then we'd better move first," Ben said, sensing an opportunity to demonstrate his loyalty to Jacen. "I'll handle it, if you like."

Jacen glanced at his chrono, then asked, "*We*, Ben?"

"If you'll take me back," Ben said. "I'm sorry for what I said, but everything was so confusing—"

"That's no excuse, Ben," Jacen said. "Any apprentice of mine needs to be the master of his emotions, not a slave to them."

"I know." Ben thought he was doing a fairly good job of that now, forcing himself to appear humble when what he really wanted was to drop a thermal detonator at Jacen's feet. "You taught me better than that."

"I'm glad you recognize that," Jacen said. "But I'm not sending you to the academy to kill the Solusars and Jaina, if that's what you mean by moving first."

Ben scowled. "You don't think that will make Dad think twice?"

"It might—but if you can't handle an old man like Omas, how are you going to eliminate two Jedi Masters and Jaina?" Jacen shook his head to indicate that Ben *wasn't*, then checked his chrono again and started toward the door. "I'm due at a staff meeting."

"What about me?" Ben asked. He could not sense anything in Jacen but distrust and disappointment. "Do I still have a place here?"

Jacen did not even hesitate as he reached for the control

panel. "I don't know, Ben. I haven't seen any reason to take you back."

Ben grew hollow and cold inside, not because Jacen was turning him down, but because he was asking for more—something that only Ben could give him.

"Whatever you decide, there's something you should know." Ben told himself it really didn't matter *whom* he betrayed right now, because Jacen wasn't going to live long enough to make use of the information. "Dad told me to meet him on Kashyyyk."

Jacen's hand dropped without touching the control panel. "Kashyyyk?" He sounded surprised—just not surprised enough to be hearing the information for the first time. "So he intends to join your aunt and uncle in asking the Wookiees to stay out of this."

Ben shook his head. "He's a lot madder than that." Suddenly he felt very dirty inside—even dirtier than he had after he assassinated Gejjen. "I think he wants them to help throw you out of office."

This time Ben did get the reaction he was hoping for—first confusion, then shock, then total red-faced anger. "He wants the Wookiees to move on *Coruscant*?"

Ben shrugged. "He didn't say, exactly—just that it's time to put someone else in charge."

"Someone *else*?" Jacen punched the wall so hard that it triggered the opaque control, and the bustling Tactical Salon slowly appeared on the other side of the wall. "No one else can *do* this. No one else is willing to make the necessary sacrifices."

"*I* am," Ben said, sensing that he was finally starting to make some progress. "I just *did*."

If Jacen heard Ben, he didn't acknowledge it. His gaze was fixed on the tactical display outside, and he had that blank look he got when he was seeing something in the Force. After a moment, Jacen opened the door and went to stand at the holodisplay, shouldering aside a Duros lieutenant and a Mon Calamari commander.

Ben followed and heard Jacen muttering to himself, saying the *Confederation* needed more members, that they couldn't stand the attrition any better than the Alliance could. From what Ben could see, that was hardly news to anyone. The Battle of Kuat had been raging for over a week now, and both sides were losing several capital ships a day and suffering casualties ten thousand at a time. The holodisplay showed more derelict vessels than it did functional, and rescue beacons were glittering so thick they looked like electronic snow.

Jacen turned to his aide, Orlopp. "Get me the latest report on the readiness of the Wookiee fleet."

"I *am* monitoring the situation—as ordered." Orlopp pulled at the nose whiskers on his slender Jenet snout, then continued, "Military Intelligence hasn't heard anything from our agents since the Solos escaped from jail, but the last report indicated that the Wookiees had just started lighting their reactor cores. We won't be seeing their fleet for some time, I'm afraid."

"That may be a blessing," Jacen said. "Prepare orders sending the Fifth Fleet to Kashyyyk. Tell Admiral Atoko that the *Anakin Solo* will be joining him there—and open a channel to Admiral Bwua'tu. I need to discuss a change of strategy with him."

"You're going after Dad and the Jedi?" Ben gasped.

"No—*we're* going to Kashyyyk to hunt down a band of traitors and deserters." Jacen waved Ben to his side, then added, "Welcome back, Lieutenant Skywalker. You're going to help me make an example of these people."

fourteen

Be ready. It was not an actual voice Jaina kept hearing in her dreams, not even words, but she recognized that this message came from Ben. He was terrified for her and the others, and he felt somehow responsible for . . . what? And suddenly her dream had her aboard her parents' beloved *Falcon* at Hapes, turbolaser strikes slamming the old girl like a Nkllonian boulder storm, air whistling out through a breach in the central access core, Zekk lying wounded on the deck. Next to Zekk stood Ben, his face slack with horror and an ignited lightsaber droning in his hand, the children murmuring in confusion and pouring fear into the Force, her father telling her to take the kids and . . . the *kids*?

There hadn't been any kids aboard when Ben wounded Zekk. Yet Jaina heard them whispering just beyond the bulkhead, sounding frightened and confused and resentful, and she could feel them in the Force, reaching out to her, seeking direction and reassurance, and then her dream had her someplace where there really *were* kids, back in the dormitory on Yavin 4, where she and Jacen and Zekk had been students at her uncle Luke's Jedi academy.

All of you, be ready.

Ben still had no voice, but Jaina knew it was him, which

seemed very strange since he hadn't even been born yet. Luke and Mara would not be married for another . . . Mara was dead. That fact came crashing down on Jaina like a falling star, and now she realized that her dream had her in the wrong academy, that she was actually sleeping in the dormitory at the Jedi academy on Ossus. Her brother had sent a battalion of Blackboots to secure the students—to hold them hostage, actually—and she and Jag and Zekk had been forced to call off their hunt for Alema Rar to stay here and help watch over the students.

For a little over two weeks now, Jaina had been living with a group of the academy's youngest students, acting as a dorm parent while Jag helped supervise the teenagers. Zekk continued to hide in the surrounding forest, a deadly surprise against the day it actually became necessary to defend the young ones against Jacen's troopers. For the most part, it had been easy to believe that day would never come. The GAG commander, Major Serpa, was only mildly unbalanced, and as long as the academy remained orderly and under his control, he was content to leave the children to Jaina and the other adults and concentrate his efforts on planetary security. The Solusars had even begun to hold classes again.

But it felt far too early for the morning lessons, and the young ones in Jaina's charge didn't usually try to sneak off to class without disturbing her sleep. Just the opposite. Usually, she was the one who had to get *them* out of bed, begging and threatening and enticing until she had all twenty children at the refectory table playing with their breakfast.

So why were they out in the hallway *now*, whispering and trying to slip past her door without rousing her?

Jaina snapped awake—and found that her eyes remained closed. She sat up and discovered that her body was still lying in bed. She tried to roll onto the floor, then just to lift a leg. Her body remained fast asleep, and a dream-like quality began to creep in around the edges of her thoughts again.

Coma gas.

A long male face with sunken eyes and a blade-thin nose drifted across Jaina's mind, and she began to understand what Ben was trying to tell her. Even deranged Major Serpa would need a reason to gas her; her brother had to have ordered him to do something bad, and he needed to keep her out of the way.

Jaina grabbed hold of that realization, held on tight to keep from sinking back into sleep, used it to pull herself back toward wakefulness. Jacen was going to hurt the young ones; she *had* to fight through the gas and stop Serpa.

Jaina began by expanding her Force-awareness, anchoring herself to the reality of the dorm master's room where she was staying, locating first the desk, then the closet and refresher, the opaqued viewport and the door across from it. Just outside the door, she sensed a jittery male kneeling down near the floor. He seemed to be concentrating hard, his presence filled with worry and dark intent.

He was the one spraying coma gas into her room.

Jaina grabbed him in the Force, then hurled him against the far side of the corridor, slammed him into the wall twice, and pulled him back into the door. She felt him slip into unconsciousness and would have followed, save for the young ones reaching out to her, silently pleading with her to wake up. She found the door controls and used the Force to depress the slap-pad, then felt a welcome rush of air as the door *whoosh*ed open.

For several seconds, Jaina could do nothing but listen to the hoarse whispers of the GAG troopers as they cursed and threatened their prisoners. Frightened as they were, the young ones seemed to be doing a superb job of making their captors' jobs difficult, shuffling their feet noisily and forcing the troopers to repeat their instructions over and over again. Still, the sounds were fading rapidly as the children were herded out the far door into the Ossan night.

Jaina filled her lungs with clean air perhaps a hundred times before her head finally began to clear. She opened her eyes to the dim illumination of the corridor's night-light spilling through the open door. After a moment, she rolled off the bed and saw a GAG trooper sprawled across the threshold, a small canister with a slender delivery hose lying on the floor next to him.

Jaina crawled toward him, rapidly growing more alert as the effort of moving began to circulate her blood and carry the toxins out of her brain. Despite a queasy stomach and throbbing head, by the time she reached the door she was strong enough to stand. She dragged the trooper into the room and gave him a lungful of his own coma gas, then took his comlink and slipped into her clothes. She would have taken his blaster, too, except he wasn't carrying one.

A muffled voice called down the corridor, "Got 'em all, Delpho. Time to go."

Jaina lowered her voice into the male range and, buckling her belt around her robe, grunted an acknowledgment.

"Delpho?"

Jaina cursed under her breath, then reached into one of her robe's inner pockets and withdrew her only weapon, a spoon that she had laboriously sharpened into a knife over the last few days.

"Delpho?" The voice sounded closer now, as though the speaker was entering the corridor. "Report!"

Jaina stepped through the door, simultaneously dropping to a crouch and hurling her knife down the corridor. A trio of bolts flashed out of the dark lounge and ricocheted off the doorjamb. She used the Force to guide her weapon toward the voice, then heard the officer scream and crash to the floor.

A second passed. When no more fire came, Jaina retrieved her boots and started down the hall. The dormitories on Ossus were small one-story structures with only twenty-five habitation cells per building, so she had no trouble hearing the wounded man groaning and thrashing against the lounge floor. All the doors she passed were open, and she didn't feel any children hiding inside. In several of the rooms, activated lights revealed overturned beds and lockers emptied on the floor. In one, a string of red spatter marks ran up the far wall.

By the time she reached the lounge, Jaina was convinced the dorm had been emptied of young ones. The only presences she felt were her own and the two GAG troopers she had disabled. She knelt beside the one she had wounded and quickly realized she would not be getting any answers from him. Her knife had caught him square in the throat, and he was suffering a slow, gurgling death. She pulled a hypo from the medpac on his belt.

"A quiet good-bye is more than you deserve," she said. "But Uncle Luke keeps telling me I shouldn't hold a grudge."

As her words registered, the man's eyes widened, and he clutched at Jaina's arm, silently begging her to save him.

"Sorry." She placed the tip of the hypo to his arm and injected the painkiller. "I've got kids to look after."

Jaina took the time to pull on her boots and crush the dying man's comlink beneath her heel, then stuck his blaster and spare power packs into her belt and went to the viewport. Outside, young ones ranging from Jaina's five-year-old Woodoos to Jag's fifteen-year-old Wampas were being herded toward the central exercise pavilion, where Major Serpa stood under bright lights with a squad of bodyguards.

She saw no sign of the Solusars, who had—like Jaina—been acting as dorm parents. She reached out in the Force and sensed them in their own dorms, feeling angry and worried, probably kneeling at a viewport just as she was.

She felt Zekk creeping through the jungle behind the complex. Jag seemed to be moving toward Jaina.

As each squad of troopers arrived with their young ones, Serpa meticulously directed their placement. It soon grew apparent that he was arranging them in a circle around the pavilion, alternating groups of taller children with groups of shorter ones, being careful to keep them segregated by a line of guards.

Once everyone had arrived and been directed to a location, the major returned to the pavilion and studied his work thoughtfully. After two full minutes, he left again and switched three groups, so that he had the Wampas flanked by a group of ten- to twelve-year-old Banthas on one side, and thirteen- to fourteen-year-old Veermoks on the other.

Jaina watched all this impatiently, trying not to read any meaning into the major's actions. The man was clearly unbalanced—an impression that had only grown in their dealings since their first meeting in flight control command. She and the Solusars had been debating whether Jacen had put Serpa in charge to keep the Jedi off-balance, or to have a ready patsy when he ordered retaliation against the academy's young ones. Knowing her brother, he had probably done it for both reasons.

Serpa returned to the pavilion and studied the assembly for another minute or so, then nodded approvingly.

"Much better." He spoke loudly, clearly intending to make himself audible to anyone eavesdropping from the dormitories. "This will give me a central focus, a place to begin."

The Force rippled with anger and alarm, but Jaina and the other Jedi dorm parents were too disciplined to show themselves before they knew Jacen's game. Serpa pointed to a slender Codru-Ji female standing in the front rank of the Wampas, then to a frightened-looking boy in the second rank of Woodoos.

"Her and him."

A pair of troopers left the pavilion and stood by the young ones, taking them by the arm. Serpa turned his attention to the Banthas and Veermoks next, selecting a female human from the first and a Rodian male from the second. He continued in this manner until he had chosen a child from each age group.

Once Serpa had made his selections, he had the young ones escorted onto the pavilion one at a time, carefully arranging them in a circle around him, alternating between male and female, human and nonhuman, and tall and short.

By the time he had finished his strange ritual, Tionne Solusar was striding across the courtyard, her silver hair flying and her brow lowered in anger.

"You had better have a good reason for this, Major," Tionne said, stepping onto the pavilion. She was saying this, Jaina knew, more to assure the children she was in control than because she expected any reasonable explanation. "And for the trooper who died trying to gas me in my sleep."

Serpa looked at her over the young ones separating them. "You *killed* him?" He shook his head in disapproval. "That doesn't seem very fair, does it? He was only trying to keep you out of the way."

Tionne stepped through the circle of children and stopped so close to Serpa that, from Jaina's perspective, it almost looked like she intended to kiss him. "Out of the way of *what*?"

"Nothing to be concerned about," Serpa said. "Unless you Jedi fear truth as much as you do battle."

Tionne dipped her head, no doubt frowning and feigning confusion. With GAG suppressing all normal modes of communication to and from the academy, any admission that she already knew about the Jedi desertion at Kuat would expose their secret means of remaining in contact with the outside galaxy—namely Zekk.

After a moment, Tionne replied, "Fear has no control over Jedi—and neither does anger, which is a good thing for you right now."

Serpa's brow shot up. "Are you *threatening* me, Master Solusar?"

"I'm making a suggestion for your own good," she replied. "Return these children to their beds immediately, and your unfortunate timing will be forgiven."

Serpa studied Tionne for a moment, then nodded—more to himself than to her. "That's a threat." He turned back to his captive audience. "It might even frighten me, if I hadn't heard how Luke Skywalker and his bunch of cowards ran at the Battle of Kuat."

The Force crackled with the outrage and disbelief of the young ones—who hadn't heard about the Jedi desertion—but even the little Woodoos were too disciplined to betray their feelings outwardly.

"Address your remarks to me," Tionne said, using the Force to spin Serpa back toward her. "Whatever you *think* you know about what . . ."

Tionne let her sentence trail off as Serpa came around holding his blaster. She extended her hand, trying to Force-slap the weapon aside. But he was too quick. A single bolt flashed between them, and Tionne's leg buckled. She dropped to a knee, shuddering surprise and pain into the Force.

To the credit of Kam Solusar, the unprovoked attack on his unarmed wife did not draw him into the open. He remained in hiding, pouring rage and bloodlust into the Force, but heeding the same rules he and the other adults had been drilling into the young ones all week—take only focused action; never *react*, only *act*.

Jaina, however, had seen enough—especially when some of the Woodoos couldn't help crying out in fear. She backed away from the viewport . . . then came within a finger twitch of blasting the shadow she glimpsed coming through the back door.

"Watch it!" Jag hissed, raising his hands. "Don't you know better than to point a live blaster at your commanding officer?"

"I know better than a lot of things." Jaina lowered the stolen blaster. "What are you doing sneaking up on me, anyway?"

"You're a Jedi," Jag replied. "How can *anyone* sneak up on you?"

"People have been managing." Jaina waved a hand vaguely in the direction of the two troopers she had left lying in the lounge and corridor. "And I'm a little distracted by what Serpa's doing out there. He just blasted Tionne's knee apart."

Jag nodded as though he had been expecting this. "He's trying to draw you out. There's a sniper team on your roof, probably other places, too."

"How did they get past Vis'l and Loli?" Jaina asked. Vis'l and Loli were two of the young Jedi Knights who had been on guard duty when Serpa tricked flight control into granting permission to land his battalion at the academy. "I can't imagine those two missing a sniper team."

"It's easy to miss things when you're dead," Jag explained solemnly.

A cold lump formed in Jaina's stomach. Vis'l and Loli were as young as Jedi Knights came, still in their teens and just back from their final training mission with their Masters.

"How?" she asked.

"Snipers, I think," Jag replied. "I found them behind different dorms, both with scorch holes in the sides of their heads. It looked like they'd been lured outside and blasted simultaneously. My guess is that Serpa is after *all* of you."

Jaina shook her head. "If he wanted us dead, a thermal

detonator would be a lot more effective," she said. "Why bother putting us under with *coma gas?*"

"Because he knows Jedi," Jag said. "It's pretty hard for an assassin to sneak up on you guys in your sleep. Your danger sense kicks in and wakes you."

"Something like that," Jaina admitted, thinking of her dream of Ben. "I still don't see why he thinks coma gas is better."

"Because then it looks like he's only trying to keep you out of the way," Jag said. "You'll misinterpret his intentions, and *then* he can kill you."

Jaina glanced back toward the viewport, recalling Serpa's time-consuming preparations and provocative insults, then nodded.

"Okay, so maybe he's as smart as he is crazy." She slipped past Jag and started through the door. "The first thing we need to do is take out those snipers—*quietly.*"

"Don't forget *quickly,*" Jag said. "Serpa doesn't strike me as the patient type."

As they slipped through the refectory toward the dormitory's back door, Jaina was reaching out to Kam and the other adult Jedi, sharing the wariness she felt for Serpa's tactics. It probably wasn't necessary. Even without knowing about the snipers on the roofs, it was fairly obvious that Serpa was trying to draw them out. But the extra warning might prevent someone from reacting rashly to the major's next provocation.

At the back door of the dormitory, Jaina paused to peer into the night for a moment. It was too dark to see anyone lurking in the hedges across from them, but she could feel two presences hiding in the shrubs off to the right, behind the adjacent building.

"It's times like this when I really miss my lightsaber," she whispered. "Did you notice the two over by the wodobo bushes?"

"The two what?" Jag asked.

"That's what I was afraid of." Jaina passed her borrowed blaster to Jag. "Cover me—but don't shoot unless *they* do."

Jag scowled. "Jaina, if those are snipers, they've got longblasters. A blaster pistol isn't going to be much help—"

"Just make lots of noise," Jaina said. "And trust me."

She used the Force to snap a branch behind the two ambushers, then slipped through the door and sprinted across the little yard into the hedge. When the snipers did not open fire, she decided her distraction had worked and circled behind them, moving through the underbrush in absolute silence. She found the pair lying prone under the arcing fronds of their wodobo bush, the spotter keeping watch toward the snapped branch while the sharpshooter continued to train his weapon on Jaina's dormitory. Both men wore body armor and helmets with full-face nightvision visors.

Had Jaina been as skilled as her uncle, there might have been a way to incapacitate the pair without killing them. As it was, if she wanted to be quiet, she had to be deadly. She dropped a knee into the small of the sharpshooter's back, then, as he started to twist around, grabbed his chin and helmet and snapped his neck with a violent twist. The spotter spun toward the sound—and caught a Force-enhanced knife-hand strike across the gullet.

The trooper went down gurgling and clutching at his throat. Thankfully, it was too dark to see the face behind his visor. Jaina repeated her neck-snapping maneuver, turning a slow death into a quick one.

Her guilty feelings were forgotten when a single blaster bolt sang out from the other side of the dormitories and a chorus of children cried out in terror. The Force trembled beneath Tionne's anguish, and suddenly Jaina felt her struggling to bear her pain in silence.

Jaina reached out to Kam and the other Jedi, pouring wariness into the Force, trying to urge them to ignore the bait—and failing to get through. Their fear for Tionne was all-consuming, and their attention felt entirely focused on whatever was happening on the pavilion.

The screech of another blaster bolt sounded from the courtyard. This time Tionne could not help howling in pain. Kam's rage boiled over, and Jaina sensed him losing control. Then she felt the anger of Ozlo and Jerga—two young Mon Calamari Jedi Knights—harden into resolve, and she knew Serpa was winning.

By the time Jaina had grabbed the sharpshooter's long-blaster and stepped out of the wodobo bush, Jag had already clambered onto a porch railing and was pulling himself up over the eaves. She chose a faster route, taking two running steps before launching herself halfway up the roof in a Force leap.

Her landing was hardly quiet, but there was no need to worry about betraying her presence. Her boots had barely hit the tiles before the sniper team Jag had warned her about earlier opened fire into the courtyard, revealing the silhouettes of two men crouching at the far end of the roof ridge.

Jaina crossed the roof in two Force bounds and came down between the two troopers. Before they could turn, she had pressed the muzzle of her longblaster against the sharpshooter's helmet and planted one boot in the middle of his spotter's back.

The spotter was the first to react, trying to twist around to bring his repeating blaster to bear. Jaina pulled the trigger of her longblaster, burning a hole through the sharp-shooter's head before he could move, then slapped the weapon's hot barrel across the spotter's face and sent him sliding down the roof. He disappeared over the edge, and the sickening crackle that followed left no doubt about his fate.

Jaina turned her attention to the courtyard below and was horrified to see Kam Solusar on the ground, three columns of smoke rising from his motionless body. Ozlo and Jerga were in even worse shape, their long Mon Calamari heads cratered with blaster pocks.

Jag scrambled up behind Jaina, then grabbed her arm and pulled her down. "Are you *trying* to get blasted?"

Jaina dropped behind the roof ridge and finally saw what had drawn Kam and the others into the open. Tionne lay curled at Serpa's feet, the lower parts of a leg and an arm lying a meter from their smoking stumps.

The little Woodoos were crying. The rest of the young ones were flooding the Force with shock and fear, but outwardly they remained composed and submissive. They were waiting for Tionne—or someone—to speak the word that would activate the escape plan that Jaina and the other adults had been drilling into them for the past couple of weeks.

Serpa's voice came over the comlink in Jaina's belt. "Do we have them all?"

A long chain of sick-sounding troopers answered. "K. Solusar down . . . Ozlo down . . . Jerga down . . . Vis'l and Loli already down . . . Alfi down in his cell . . . Hedda down in her dorm . . ."

"That's everyone," Jaina whispered.

Jag nodded and eased the second longblaster out of the hands of the dead sharpshooter. "Except us and—"

"What about that Solo smooka?" Serpa demanded over the comlink. "And Fel?"

When no answer came, another voice—barely audible—sounded from the helmet of the sharpshooter lying beside Jaina. "Ralpe?"

"That would be *our* guy," Jaina said, turning to Jag. "Did you get a fix on the other snipers?"

"Of course," Jag said.

The second voice sounded from inside the dead sharpshooter's helmet again. "Ralpe?"

"He's *dead,* you Gungan." Serpa addressed Jaina directly. "Well, Jedi Solo, I see that you're as big a coward as your uncle."

Jaina would have blasted him dead right then, had she not known that the bolt might pass through his body and strike the trembling Bantha girl behind him.

Serpa pressed his blaster to Tionne's head. "Are you just going to *hide* while I kill a Jedi Master?"

"Ignore him." Tionne raised the stump of her arm and gestured, turning Serpa's blaster aside. "Look after—"

A GAG trooper fired over the children shielding Serpa, and Tionne cried out as another ten centimeters was burned from the stump she had used to gesture.

"It's time we gave that braintick what he's asking for." Jaina sprang over the ridge of the roof and started to slide down the other side. "Cover me!"

Jag was already firing, pumping bright crimson bolts across the courtyard toward the sniper with the best angle of attack. Jaina fired at the closest team, trusting her aim to the Force, then barrel-rolling, firing again, and dropping off the roof into the courtyard.

A pair of fiery blossoms exploded against the wall behind her. She dived into a somersault and came up shooting again, saw a longblaster and one arm fly up behind a roof ridge and disappear, then found herself pivoting sideways as a trio of bolts droned past so close that she felt heat welts rising on her cheeks.

Jaina *really* missed her lightsaber.

Jag's longblaster sounded behind her, and *that* attacker fell silent. Jaina turned her attention to the young ones, who remained in their groups, craning their necks to watch her—and still awaiting their orders.

"Enough!" she yelled. "We've had—"

The courtyard exploded into a riot of astonished screams and stray blaster bolts as the young ones turned on their guards, using the Force to hurl the troopers into one another and jerk the weapons from their hands.

Jaina dropped to a knee and spun back toward the dormitories, but all that remained of the sniper teams were a handful of smoking tiles and a few bloody hands clinging weakly to the roof ridges. She signaled Jag to continue covering her, then began to push her way through the angry mob of students, who were using their budding Force talents to beleaguer—and in some cases, injure—the astonished GAG troopers who had *thought* they were in charge of the academy.

Of course, the young Jedi were suffering casualties, too. Everywhere Jaina looked, there were young ones lying on the ground with smoke rising from their blaster wounds. In some cases, groups of unarmed ten-, twelve-, or fourteen-year-olds were fighting hand-to-hand with an armored GAG trooper. She did what she could to help—a quick Force-nudge here, a well-placed strike with the butt of her longblaster there. But her focus remained on the one who had instigated the carnage, Major Serpa.

Jaina found him on the exercise pavilion. His bodyguards were lying on the floor, either dead or dying from an assortment of blaster wounds or well-placed slashes from makeshift weapons like her sharpened spoon. To her dismay, Serpa remained alive, holding the red-haired Bantha girl—Vekki, Jaina recalled—in a choke hold, the muzzle of his blaster pressed against her temple for extra insurance.

"You call *me* a coward?" Jaina asked. Hoping to distract him enough to pull the blaster away from the girl's head, she continued to advance on Serpa . . . then stopped when Zekk reached out to her from the other side of the pavilion, urging patience. "While *you* hide behind children?"

Serpa shrugged. "It's different. They're *Jedi* children."

"I'm sure the judges will take that into account at your trial." Jaina glimpsed Zekk's tall figure stepping into the light on the far side of the pavilion, but she was careful to keep her gaze locked on Serpa. "Assuming you *make* it to trial. Surrender now, and I'll be sure you do."

Serpa snorted. "There isn't going to be any trial." He swung his blaster toward Jaina. "I'm just following orders—*your* brother's—"

Before Serpa could pull the trigger, Zekk's lightsaber snapped to life and came down on the major's weapon arm, severing it at the elbow.

Serpa's attention remained oddly fixed on Jaina, as though he could not at first understand why she was not dead, or how she had managed to cut off his arm without moving. Finally, he seemed to hear the lightsaber droning behind him, and his jaw dropped in disbelief. He whirled around, swinging Vekki with him—apparently oblivious to his pain.

"Where did *you* come from?" he demanded.

Zekk lashed out so fast that even Jaina did not see the attack, only Serpa's remaining arm swinging away from Vekki's neck and his body whirling to the floor.

"From now on," Zekk said, "we'll be asking the questions."

fifteen

How ironic it seemed to Jacen that he should confront his betrayers here, in the home system of a species famed for its honor—how sad that he must battle his own blood above Kashyyyk, where loyalty counted for more than life itself. Even after all that had happened, he still loved his family—still *cherished* them. It was their courage that had instilled in him the strength to do what he must soon do, their example that had taught him to serve above all else. He only wished there were some way to bring them back, so all of the Solos and Skywalkers could be on the same side again, fighting not each other, but the injustice that always seemed about to tear the galaxy apart.

But there *was* no way. Even were Jacen to convince them of their mistake, he could not absolve them of what they had done, could not pardon their treason against the Alliance. That was the burden and the fate of Darth Caedus, to deliver justice wherever it was deserved, and he dared not shirk his duty. Sith Lords could not turn a blind eye to the crimes of their own relatives. Down that path lay corruption and selfishness—the belief that he was the master of the galaxy and not its servant.

A squadron of new Owool Interceptors appeared in the bridge viewport, still so distant that only the curving stripes of their paired efflux tails were visible against Kashyyyk's emerald face. The pride of an innovative new shipyard named KashyCorp, the Owools had been designed to serve the Galactic Alliance as heavy starfighters. Like the Wookiees who piloted them, they were tough, fast, and ferocious.

"What a dismal showing," Ben said. He was standing with Caedus and Commander Twizzl on the primary flight deck, watching fifty-odd crewbeings calmly coordinate the *Anakin Solo*'s combat preparations. "If those Owools are all they have ready, there won't *be* a fight. Even Wookiees aren't that crazy."

"Wookiees are resolute, not crazy," Caedus replied. Ben had been trying to talk him out of attacking Kashyyyk since the *Anakin Solo*'s escape from the Battle of Kuat. It made Caedus worry that his young cousin lacked the ruthlessness to carry out his plea of vengeance—that Lumiya might have been right about the boy being too weak to be a Sith apprentice. "And they *will* fight, Ben. Never confuse hope with expectation."

"I wasn't," Ben insisted. "But we need the Kashyyyk fleet, Jacen. If there's any way to take it without a fight—"

"There isn't," Caedus interrupted. "And I'd like you to call me Colonel, not Jacen."

Ben looked surprised, but not hurt. "Okay, *Colonel*."

"Thank you." Caedus's appreciation was sincere. He didn't mind Ben calling him by his first name, but it was starting to feel wrong to be addressed by his old moniker. Jacen Solo was gone. "And I didn't say we wouldn't give the Wookiees a chance to avoid a fight—only that they won't take it."

"They certainly don't seem inclined," Commander Twizzl said from Caedus's other side. "Those Owools are threatening to open fire if we don't stop and explain ourselves."

Caedus glanced at the tactical holodisplay and smiled.

With the entire Fifth Fleet spread across space behind the *Anakin Solo*, the Owools were outnumbered two-to-one by capital ships alone.

"You *do* have to respect their courage," he said. "Very well, Commander. Tell them we'll respect their orders."

"You intend to comply?" Twizzl asked, surprised.

"Of course," Caedus said. "Bring the *Anakin Solo* to a dead stop and have Admiral Atoko form the fleet around us."

Twizzl frowned. "Sir, Lieutenant Skywalker has a point. If we move now, we may capture their assault fleet intact. It's still trying to free itself of the tenders, and their orbital guard is no match for the Fifth Fleet."

"Commander, I hope you're not advocating an unprovoked attack on a current member world of the Galactic Alliance," Caedus said. "As far as we know, all the Wookiees have done is *listen* to the Jedi deserters. They haven't betrayed us yet."

"So you're *not* going to attack?" Ben sounded more confused than he did relieved. "Then why did we pull the Fifth Fleet out of the Core?"

"To give the Wookiees an *opportunity* to do the right thing." Caedus turned to Twizzl, who was looking increasingly perplexed and unhappy. "You have your orders, Commander. Tell the Owools we've come for the prisoners, and we'll depart as soon as we have them."

Twizzl's eyes hardened in disapproval, but he nodded and stepped over to his communications officer's station.

Ben wasn't so easily persuaded. "This is only going to make things worse, Ja—er, Colonel. They're *not* going to turn Uncle Han and Aunt Leia over to you."

"Of course not—they're Wookiees," Caedus said. "They're too stubborn. But when they refuse, we'll have justification to proceed."

"*After* their fleet is deployed." Ben's tone was growing more desperate, but he was hiding his presence from the

Force—a sign that he was finally gathering himself to strike. "We'll never capture it then. They'll fight until the last vessel is slagged."

"True." Caedus knew that if Ben tried to kill him now, the youth would be acting for noble reasons, trying to save thousands of lives by ending one. Reasons didn't matter, though; actions did. The mere attempt would be the catalyst that moved Ben to the next stage. "But we didn't come here to capture the Kashyyyk fleet."

Ben contemplated this a moment, then asked, "You're serious about taking the prisoners back?"

"Of course not," Caedus said. "We're here because *this* is what's going to keep the Confederation from capturing Kuat and moving on to Coruscant."

Ben fell silent again, staring out the bridge viewport, where the Owools had swelled into gleaming dots with sickle-shaped bows. Finally, he gave up and shook his head.

"I don't get it."

"Good." Caedus stepped over to join Twizzl at the communications station, presenting his back to Ben—and inviting the youth to take his vengeance. "Neither will the Confederation."

When no attack came, Caedus began to wonder if he had misjudged his young cousin. Ben still believed him to be Mara's killer—that was obvious by how carefully he kept his feelings masked—so why wouldn't he attack? He certainly had the courage, or he would never have come back to Caedus in the first place. Nor could it be moral qualms. Ben might have been able to assassinate Dur Gejjen and convince himself he was still acting ethically, but not so with Cal Omas. He had killed the former chief simply to provide a cover when he returned to the *Anakin Solo*, and *that* required the heart of an assassin. Mara would have been proud.

So why didn't he act?

Two steps later, Caedus found himself next to Twizzl behind the communications officer, listening to the voice of the Wookiee squadron commander and feeling betrayed by his cousin's failure.

The comm officer—a Bith female with ebony eyes as large as Caedus's palms—was listening to a translation in a comlink earpiece.

"Colonel Solo, they're saying they don't have any—"

"It's not necessary to translate. I've understood Shyriiwook since I was five." Caedus leaned over her shoulder and keyed the mike. "We're here for Han and Leia Solo and the Jedi deserters. If you're having trouble with the Jedi deserters, we're prepared to assist. That's why we brought a fleet."

The squadron leader rumbled a denial, claiming the Solos had escaped, and the Jedi had not even come to Kashyyyk.

"Wookiees shouldn't lie. It's not in your genetic code."

Caedus glanced at Ben. Perhaps the youth hadn't attacked yet because he had been sent to lead the *Anakin Solo* into a Jedi ambush. But when Ben nodded and confirmed that he had been instructed to rendezvous at Kashyyyk, Caedus thought of his Allana and how much she meant to him. With Mara dead, would Luke *ever* send Ben on such a dangerous mission?

Caedus turned back to the microphone. "Our information is solid," he said. "If you're saying the Solos are no longer your prisoners, then Kashyyyk has betrayed the Alliance, or the Jedi are holding the planet hostage. Either way, we'll be forced to attack."

The Wookiee replied that he would check with his superiors, and the channel fell silent. As Caedus and the others waited for a reply, the *Anakin Solo* continued to decelerate. The Fifth Fleet began to form up around her, deploying starfighter pickets and positioning its aging Star Destroyers with overlapping fields of fire. The Owool squadron continued to approach, swelling from sickle-nosed dots into fork-prowed wedges.

Finally, the Wookiee's voice came over the speaker again, insisting the colonel had been misinformed. No Solos were being held on Kashyyyk, and they had no problem with any Jedi deserters.

"That's what I like about you Wookiees," Caedus replied. "You never hide where you stand."

He had barely deactivated the mike before Twizzl began to issue orders, preparing to resume the advance.

"That won't be necessary, Commander," Caedus said. "The planet is already within range of the *Anakin Solo*'s long-range turbolasers, is it not?"

Twizzl's bushy brows dropped so low that they nearly covered his eyes. "Of course, but the Kashyyyk fleet is—"

"Unimportant." Caedus faced Twizzl, presenting his back to Ben again. If the order he was about to give did not prompt his cousin to attack, then nothing would. "Have the long-range batteries open fire."

Twizzl's face went slack with confusion. "On the Owools?"

"On the *planet*." As Caedus spoke, he was careful to keep his hand away from his lightsaber. He wanted to give his cousin every chance to attack; if Ben did not strike soon, he would have to be eliminated as unworthy. "Have them direct their fire to the same target area; the objective is to create a firestorm."

Caedus's command was greeted by utter silence, and he could feel the Force reverberating with the shock of the officers and crew who had overheard the command. Only Ben failed to seem surprised—though perhaps it was because he was still hiding his presence from the Force. Jacen continued to face Twizzl, giving the youth plenty of time to strike.

After a couple of moments, Twizzl finally seemed able to respond. "You want to *burn* the wroshyrs?"

"Precisely," Caedus said. "The entire world-forest if we can."

Twizzl's expression changed from stunned to condemning. "But that's . . . that's just *madness*. It won't accomplish anything!"

"That's not your conclusion to reach, Commander," Caedus replied. Giving the order wasn't easy—in fact, it made him feel sick. As a child, he had both loved and respected Chewbacca, and the last thing he wanted to do was burn the homeworld of his friend and protector. But the Wookiees had brought this disaster on themselves by betraying the Galactic Alliance. "However, just this once, I *will* explain myself to you."

"I'd appreciate that, Colonel." Twizzl's tone suggested that the explanation would need to be a good one, if Caedus expected him to obey. "Thank you."

"Very well. You were at the Battle of Kuat, so you *know* how evenly matched our militaries are."

Twizzl nodded. "The Confederation will have to break off soon," he said. "They can't match the Alliance in a war of attrition."

"And *we* can't afford one," Caedus countered. "We're already too weak to defend all the worlds under our protection, and the Confederation knows it. So you're wrong—they're *not* going to withdraw. They're going to keep fighting and hope *we'll* withdraw, which we can't do. It would leave a clear lane all the way to Coruscant."

"So we're in a stalemate," Ben said, disappointing Caedus by stepping toward him—not to attack, but to join the conversation. "How's burning Kashyyyk going to change that?"

Unable to hide his frustration, Caedus whirled on the boy. "*Think*, Ben. What do we *both* need to break the stalemate? What are we losing here and the Confederation gaining?"

Ben recoiled from the venom in Caedus's voice, but he answered quickly. "Allies."

"Correct." Caedus placed his hand on Ben's shoulder, but he was so angry he had to stop himself from drawing back and striking the youth. "And if the Confederation hopes to make an ally of the Wookiees, what must they do?"

Twizzl's eyes lit with angry comprehension. "Come to Kashyyyk's defense."

"Which means they have to abandon their drive on Coruscant," Ben finished. "And burning the forests is going to provoke a lot more public outrage than just capturing the Kashyyyk assault fleet. If the Confederation *doesn't* help the Wookiees, they're going to have trouble recruiting more worlds. It'll look like they don't care about anyone but themselves."

"Right again," Caedus said.

"But who'll want to join *us*?" Twizzl demanded. "We're going to look like monsters."

Caedus smiled. "*Exactly*, Commander. Worlds will tremble at the thought of deserting us. If we're willing to burn the Kashyyyk forest as punishment, who knows what we might do to *them*?"

Twizzl's mouth dropped in horror, and he stared at Caedus without saying anything.

"I have grown weary of waiting, Commander," Caedus said. "Will you relay my order now, or do I need to appoint a new commander?"

The threat was enough to shake Twizzl out of his daze. "That won't be necessary, Colonel. I see no military reason to disregard your orders—your rationale seems as sound as it does chilling."

Caedus dipped his chin in mock gratitude. "I'm glad you approve, Commander."

The blood drained from Twizzl's face, and he turned to relay the order.

Caedus glanced over and found Ben's expression as unreadable as his Force presence. The order to burn Kashyyyk had to be eating the boy up inside, but even *that* wasn't enough to make him strike. Caedus returned to the tactical holodisplay and didn't bother giving Ben another chance. If setting the wroshyrs ablaze didn't make the boy act, nothing would.

"This will make the Wookiees go nova," Ben said, sticking as close to Caedus as he had years earlier, when he was just a child starting to overcome his fear of the Force. "Where do you want me?"

"At my side will be fine."

It was a struggle for Caedus to keep the sadness out of his voice; it pained him to think of what he would soon have to do, but there was no avoiding it. Even if Ben didn't have the courage to strike today, one day he would—and under less controlled circumstances.

"I'll need you close when the fighting starts," Caedus said. "We'll have to keep an eye out for StealthXs."

"Yeah," Ben said. "The plasma will really splash the shields when the *Anakin Solo* opens fire."

The viewport tinting dimmed as four ribbons of brilliance flashed from the tip of the *Anakin Solo*'s bow and streaked toward the dark ovoid of the planet's night side. A wave of shock and fear rippled through the Force from the direction of the Owool squadron, then quickly changed to confusion as the Wookiees realized the attack had not been directed at them. When the turbolaser bolts burned through Kashyyyk's atmosphere and blossomed into a pinpoint of scarlet flame, the confusion changed to disbelief.

The batteries flashed again, striking in the same place and enlarging the pinpoint to a flickering red speck. The disbelief changed to rage, then—as the turbolasers flashed a third time—to seething resolve. Caedus saw the Owools dip their prows toward the *Anakin Solo*'s bow, then lost sight of them when the turbolasers fired again.

Twizzl stepped to the holodisplay, dutifully placing himself at Caedus's side—opposite Ben—despite the fear and revulsion he was radiating into the Force.

"Assessment is estimating a forest fire half a kilometer square and growing," he reported. "I've instructed them to change target areas every time they reach a self-perpetuating threshold."

"Well done," Caedus replied. "We don't want the Wookiees undoing our hard work."

"Maybe it would be smart to target a city or two," Ben said. "That way we can keep their fire-suppression teams busy trying to save populated areas."

Twizzl's jaw fell, and he looked past Caedus at Ben with a look of loathing and incredulity, as though he could not quite believe the thoughts that sprouted in teenage minds.

"*Excellent* idea, Lieutenant." Caedus turned to Twizzl. "Pass it along to fire control, Commander."

"As you wish." Twizzl started to turn away—then stopped, scowled at the tactical display, and looked to an ensign standing on the opposite side of the holopad. "What happened to the Owools?"

"I think they got in the way of a turbolaser strike, sir," sang the ensign, a waist-high Bimm female with floppy ears and blond fur. "They were there before the last strike, then they were just . . . gone."

Caedus's heart rose into his throat. He could still feel the Wookiees' rage burning in the Force. "That's not what happened," he said. "They're still there. I sense them coming."

Twizzl returned to Caedus's side and slapped the activation switch of a shipwide comm. "Incoming starfighters! Arm the cluster bombs and activate the auto cannons, all ship-defense systems fire at will!"

The Bimm aide laid her ears out flat. "I don't understand. Do Owools have stealth—"

"No," Caedus interrupted. "They're riding the stripe."

The Bimm looked more confused than ever. "Riding the—"

"Using our own turbolaser strikes for cover," Ben explained. "It's an old Jedi trick. The flash-static prevents our sensors from locating them, and since our own fighters have to keep clear of the firing lane—"

"Only Jedi can fly like that," Twizzl interrupted, having finished with his shipwide alert. "If we're facing Jedi—"

"We're *not*." Just to be certain, Caedus concentrated his Force-awareness on the presences of the Owool pilots. "Unless one of those Wookiees is . . ."

Caedus let the thought trail off and began to concentrate on individual pilots, searching for one in particular, one he would certainly recognize . . . and then he found it, a Force-sensitive presence he had known since childhood.

"Of course!"

Caedus's exclamation of recognition was reflected by an explosion of rage and bewilderment in the Force, and he could almost hear Lowbacca roaring in the cockpit of his Owool, demanding to know how his old classmate could betray their friendship so terribly.

And, for a moment, Caedus became Jacen once again, filled with sorrow for what he had become, yet still knowing how necessary it all was. It was the only way to bring order to a galaxy that fed on strife and war, the only way to create a home where his daughter and the daughters of all his allies and enemies would one day be able to grow up in peace and security.

Jacen opened himself to the Force and reached out to Lowie, inviting his old friend to join a battle-meld of a different sort—one filled with regret and apology. Lowie responded, again wanting to know *why*, again trying to impress on Jacen that he did not have to do this, that perhaps they could still find a way to be friends . . .

That was when Jacen located his old classmate in the Force and felt him coming up under the *Anakin Solo*'s bow.

He also felt the presences of non-Jedi Wookiee pilots blinking out as the Star Destroyer's cluster bombs and auto cannons did their work. And for an instant he sensed the weight of a shadow bomb in Lowbacca's Force grasp.

Sorry, Jacen thought, and then he was Caedus again, breaking the meld so he could turn to warn Twizzl. "It's Lowbacca, coming up—"

Caedus did not feel what came next, not really. He simply realized a bolt of danger sense was sizzling down his spine and whirled away from the holodisplay, then felt the heat of a lightsaber brush across his ribs as Ben's blade snapped to life and buried itself in the torso of Commander Twizzl.

Suddenly the air was filled with the stench of scorched flesh—both Caedus's and Twizzl's—and Ben was gasping in shock and guilt and *still* attacking despite it all, slicing Twizzl's torso half off as he swung his blade back toward Caedus, stepping in close to be certain of the kill.

It might have been Lowbacca's shadow bomb or Caedus's own swift reflexes that saved his life. He doubted that either he or anyone else would ever know. The *Anakin Solo* simply bucked beneath his feet, then he saw Ben's lightsaber sweep past his face and slammed down hard and found himself lying on the deck with everyone else. His vision narrowed and his ears rang. How terribly he had underestimated his young cousin! How patiently Ben had bided his time, willing to sacrifice Kashyyyk's forest, Commander Twizzl, even his own life—all to make certain he killed Caedus.

Maybe there was hope for the boy after all.

With no time to snatch his own weapon off his belt, Caedus lashed out, loosing a bolt of Force lightning that sent Ben tumbling across the floor in a smoking, convulsing heap. He summoned the boy's lightsaber to hand, then sprang to his feet amid the wreckage that—until a moment ago—had been the *Anakin Solo*'s flight deck. Corpses lay strewn everywhere, especially toward the front of the cabin where Lowbacca's shadow bomb had breached the viewport—or so he assumed from the crushed body parts lying at the base of the lowered blast curtain.

Caedus stepped over to Ben. The youth was already starting to recover from the Force lightning, straightening his curled limbs and taking short gasps of air. Ignoring the Bimm ensign who reached out for help, Caedus squatted next to his young cousin and nodded in approval.

"Not bad." He had to use the Force to make himself heard over the blaring damage alarms and the screams of the wounded. "Artfully done, even."

Ben's eyes rolled toward Caedus, filled with anger and hate. "Just . . . finish it."

"*Finish* it?" Caedus deactivated the lightsaber and tucked it into his belt, then used the Force to pull the boy to his feet. "Ben, we're just getting started."

sixteen

The smoke in Military Hangar 15 hung gray and gritty, seeping between floor panels and door seams, billowing through the entrance every time the barrier field was lowered. Wookiees with singed fur and patches of blistered flesh were loping back and forth, rushing to ready the Jedi StealthXs before the hangar went up in flames. Leia was alarmed by how quickly the conflagration was spreading across Rwookrrorro, but she was hardly surprised. Even in a damp climate like Kashyyyk, fires of a certain size were self-feeding monsters, drying the surrounding forest so they could devour it. And Jacen was making sure every fire reached the necessary size.

"Burning the wroshyrs is bad enough," Han said, stepping off the *Falcon*'s ramp beside her. "But targeting the cities?" He stifled a cough. "We should have dropped that kid out the medcenter window the day he was born."

The bitterness in Han's voice made Leia's heart ache. "Han, please." Her eyes began to water, but she convinced herself it was the smoke to blame. "You don't mean that."

"Oh, no?" Han retorted. "Look around, sweetheart. These beings used to respect me."

Leia didn't bother doing as he suggested. It was impossible to miss the furtive looks being cast their way, or—for a

Jedi—not to feel the mix of anger and pity permeating the Force.

"I'm certain they'll forgive you for not doing a better job with Jacen," C-3PO said, clunking down the boarding ramp behind them. "Wookiees tend to be very understanding about difficult children."

"It's been a long time since Jacen was a child, Threepio." Leia peered into the smoke, searching for her brother, and said to Han, "And if we *had* dropped him out a window, the galaxy would belong to the Yuuzhan Vong right now. Whatever Jacen has become, he was a hero once. Jacen Solo saved the galaxy."

"Yeah? Well, there *is* no Jacen Solo now." Han started across the hangar floor toward a quiet corner, where Luke and the Council Masters were barely visible through the smoke, gathered in a tight group plotting strategy. "Jacen Solo is dead. My son wouldn't do this."

"Where have I heard that before?" Leia started after him, shaking her head at his customary hyperbole. "Let me think. We were on the *Falcon,* inbound toward Corellia, and we'd just learned what he'd done to Ailyn . . ."

Leia stopped in her tracks, letting the sentence trail off. Han wasn't exaggerating, she realized. He was *right*. After what had happened to Jacen as a prisoner of the Yuuzhan Vong, their son might have been capable of torturing Ailyn Habuur to death. But he would never have been capable of setting an entire planet ablaze, not the compassionate child who used to sneak pets into his room in the Jedi academy on Yavin 4—and certainly not the Jedi Knight who had shown the galaxy how to make peace with a species that didn't even have a word for it.

That Jacen *was* dead. Leia felt it now as clearly as she had when Anakin died, a terrible ripping deep inside that left an aching hole in her heart. But this time the ripping had come slowly, and she hadn't recognized what was happening. She hadn't believed she was losing Jacen, not really, until her lungs were burning with smoke from the fires he had set and her stomach was queasy from the smell of singed fur and scorched hide . . . until she heard Han say the words.

Jacen Solo is dead.

It only took about seven steps for Han to realize Leia wasn't following. "Ah, stang," he said, marching back. "Don't be mad. I didn't mean it like *that*."

Leia tried to answer, but all that came out was a garbled croak.

Han frowned. "What's wrong? I haven't seen you look like this since . . ." His jaw dropped, and suddenly he looked as crestfallen as Leia felt. "What is it? Has something happened to Jaina?"

"No," Leia managed. She wanted to wail, to tear at her hair and sink into catalepsy, but she could not. Her grief seemed trapped inside, a fuming reservoir of rage and pain that would keep burning her up until it finally exploded. "Jaina's . . . she's fine. It's Jacen."

"Jacen?" Han's scowl returned, then he glanced heavenward as if to suggest that he knew his greatest disappointment was still up there. "I don't get it. Are you saying Lowie *got* him?"

Leia shook her head. "No, Han. I'm saying you're right. There's nothing left to get."

Han looked more confused than ever, but before she could explain, her brother arrived with Saba and the other Masters and came straight to her side.

"Leia, what is it?" he asked. "I felt—"

"It's about Jacen," Han said, answering for her. "I said something stupid."

"Han, you're not listening." Leia still felt like she had a hole in her heart—or maybe it was an abscess—but she was starting to recover; after all, she had been through this before. "It *wasn't* stupid. You were right."

Luke looked to Han. "About what?"

An expression of chagrin came over Han's face, and he didn't answer.

"If Captain Solo is having trouble remembering, perhaps I can help," C-3PO volunteered. "He said—"

"I *said* Jacen is dead," Han said, cutting off the droid. He put an arm around Leia's shoulders and pulled her to his side. "Sorry, sweetheart. I thought you'd figured that out by now."

There was a lot of bitterness in his voice, but it was directed at the monster who had taken Jacen's place, and that was how Leia knew he was hurting as much as she was.

Luke didn't seem to find either of the Solos' tones reassuring. His lips tightened in the way they always did when he steeled himself to make a difficult statement, and he made a point of meeting Han's gaze.

"I'm sorry, but you're not in a good frame of mind to fight." He glanced at Leia, then added, "Either of you."

Han's jaw dropped, his expression changing from disbelief to anger to determination. "Just try to stop us," he said. "Jacen's our son, and that makes him *our* problem."

"Master Skywalker is right, Han," Kyp said. "You're too angry to fight. If you could feel yourself in the Force—"

"I don't need the Force to tell me how angry I am," Han said. "And I've got a kriffing good reason."

And then they fell to arguing, Han insisting that nobody was going after Jacen without him, Luke and the Masters using the weakest of all weapons against his stubbornness—logic—to argue otherwise. Leia did not join in. While she knew her brother and the others were right, she also knew it would be easier to hit escape velocity off a black hole than to fight Han on this.

Besides, Leia was too burdened by her sorrow, by the knowledge that it had finally come to this—Han ready to kill their own son, and she ready to help him. Was *that* the limit of a mother's love? Torture and murder were not enough to turn parents against their child, but burning a planet *was*? She thought back to her last conversation with her sister-in-law, when Mara had asked whether she thought Jacen could be corrupted by Lumiya, and she wondered what had prompted the question. Had Mara sensed then what Han and Leia knew now, or had the coup finally been enough to make her doubt Jacen?

And then it hit her. Maybe Mara wasn't the only Jacen supporter who had started to question her own judgment. If an illegal coup was enough to raise doubts in Mara's mind, how would setting fire to Kashyyyk affect Tenel Ka? Had the colonel finally made a calamitous mistake? The kind that could change the destiny of a galaxy?

By the time Leia returned her attention to the argument, Tahiri had arrived to join in. With purple circles under her eyes and her StealthX flight suit hanging off her as though it were two sizes too large, she looked anything but rested, and Leia worried that Jacen's transformation was taking a toll on her, too. The two of them had grown fairly close after Anakin's death—drawn together, she thought, by their love of him and their common experiences as captives of the Yuuzhan Vong.

". . . even if the *Falcon* did have stealth technology," Tahiri was telling Han, "in your mind frame, it's a suicide run."

"I *know*," Han shot back. "I've made lots of 'em."

"Han, they're right." Leia took his arm and squeezed hard, interrupting his rant long enough to make her point. "Getting ourselves killed isn't going to stop Jacen—*or* help Kashyyyk."

Han scowled down at her. "Yeah, so?"

"So I don't know about you, but I'm not big on mean-ingless death," she said. "I'd rather do something that actually has a chance of saving some of these wroshyrs."

"Like *what*?" To Leia's surprise, it was Tahiri who asked

this. "If you think you can fool us by saying one thing and doing another, try again."

"Jedi Veila!" Saba admonished. "Princess Leia would do no such thing. She is a Jedi Knight, the same as you."

"She's also married to Han Solo," Tahiri retorted. "And that's been one of his favorite tactics since before *you* were hatched. I want to know what she's got in mind."

"Not that." Leia kept her attention focused on Han. "We're not ready for the scrap heap yet, flyboy. What do you say we do something useful?"

Han's arm finally began to relax. "You've got a plan? You're not just saying that?"

Leia smiled. "It's a real beauty." She started to pull him back toward the *Falcon*. "Trust me."

"This *can't* be the place."

Alema was staring out through a transparent band of Ship's hull, studying a dusty wreck of a spaceport. Half the berth space was occupied by rusting transports, and the other half was so saturated with spilled service fluids that the slightest spark might send the whole place up in a toxic fireball. A mixed-species ground crew of slovenly technicians was squatting outside the portmaster's office, rolling fist-sized knucklebones and making a point of ignoring her.

"You made a mistake," she said to Ship.

Ship did not think so. *This* was where the navigation string had led. If the Broken One had not wanted to go to Korriban, the mistake was hers.

"*This* is Korriban?"

Alema was horrified . . . and confused. Every Jedi student read about Korriban and its dark past—especially the Valley of the Dark Lords, where the spirits of ancient Sith Masters were said to still linger. But there was no mention of it being a modern Sith stronghold. In fact, Luke seemed mostly to want to ignore the place, banning all navigation data regarding it from Jedi computers and asking the Galactic Alliance to do the same.

Looking out at the dilapidated spaceport, Alema could not imagine why he'd bothered. Even if the planet *was* a nexus of dark side power, it was hardly going to tempt anyone. From what she had seen as they landed, the village that surrounded the spaceport was even more of a ruin.

"Are you sure this was the only population center?" Alema asked. "There can't be Sith *here*."

Ship had detected no other concentration of habitations anywhere on the planet. It was not lost on Alema that it said nothing about the Sith. Recalling how devoid of luxury Lumiya's habitat had been, she closed her eyes, clearing her mind of the prejudice of appearance, and started to meditate.

It didn't take long before she began to feel the cold pall that hung over the planet, a miasma of dark side energy that felt as ancient as it was strong. If there *were* any Sith here, it would be hard to separate their Force auras from that of the planet itself. And that made it the perfect place to hide.

Alema went to the spot where Ship usually extruded a boarding ramp for her. "We have come all this way," she said, assuming a casual tone. "It will not hurt us to have a look."

The hull remained solid, and Ship seemed to feel vaguely insulted that she thought it could be fooled so easily.

"We are not trying to *fool* you," Alema said, using the Force to push sideways against Ship's desire to keep her aboard. "We only wish to ask the ground crew where we are, to prove you made a navigation mistake."

Ship had *not* made a mistake. It knew what the Broken One really intended to ask the crew, but it was not going to fight her. Perhaps the Force would grant its wish and let her get herself killed. A section of the hull melted open and shaped itself into a ramp.

A bit unsettled by the uncustomary ease with which she had won the argument, Alema descended the ramp and crossed the grime-slickened floor to the ground crew. They looked more shabby than tough, with holes in their overalls; gaunt faces suggested they were not eating well. The Bothan's fur was matted close to his body, the Barabel's scales were too caked with mold to lie flat, and the human's skin was pocked with red sores.

Alema stopped at the edge of their game and watched them play. When the Bothan cursed and passed the bones to the Barabel, she cocked her hip and placed her good hand on it.

"Hello, boys. We know you're busy, but maybe you can help a girl out."

The Bothan and the human looked her up and down in a way that no male had since before Tenupe. Alema was so flattered that, when the Barabel took advantage of their distraction to roll the bones and turn one so that he had a set of matched suns, she used the Force to roll it back to its proper position.

The Barabel scowled up at her, while the Bothan bared his fangs in that predatory smile males often got when they realized they were being invited to make an advance.

"For a bent girl like you, maybe we can find some time," he said. "What do you need?"

Alema returned his smile with one just as predatory. "Just an answer," she said. "And maybe a map to your place."

The human stood and stepped a little too close, considering how he smelled. "I've got answers, too."

Alema cocked her brow. "We'll bet you do."

The Barabel hissed and slapped the knucklebones aside, then sank onto his haunches to wait for the game to resume.

Alema ignored him and asked, "So where do we find the Sith?"

The change in the Bothan's expression was so subtle that Alema barely noticed, and the human did a credible job of looking confused. Their Force presences were another matter, becoming drawn and so frightened that Alema thought they might attack.

"You *don't*." The Bothan stood and motioned to the others. "Come on, you two. We've got work to—"

"What about our answer?" Alema's tone was flirtatious, but the strength with which she Force-grabbed him was not. "We just *hate* being disappointed."

The human crashed into his taskmaster's back and appeared confused for a moment—then he heard the Bothan wheezing for breath and looked back to Alema in dread.

"The S-sith are d-dead. Have been for c-centuries."

"Come now." Alema put her hand under the man's chin and drew his face close to hers. "You can't *lie* to a Jedi."

She crushed his jaw with a Force squeeze and sent him stumbling back into the port-master's office, then returned her attention to the Bothan.

"We will ask nicely one more time. Where are the Sith?"

"Don't make a difference *how* you ask," the Bothan answered—rather bravely, Alema thought. "Whatever you do to us—"

"Usss?" the Barabel hissed. "Rak'k is not going to hide them. If OneTail wantz to die, it is fine with him."

Alema turned to the Barabel. "*Thank* you. Where do I find the Sith?"

"Rak'k is risking a living death by telling you," the Barabel replied. "He should be rewarded."

Alema shook her head. "Sorry. We find scales so . . . disgusting."

"Who cares about scales?" Rak'k asked, looking confused. "Rak'k is talking about your ship. When you don't come back—"

"*If*," Alema corrected. "Why do people always underestimate us?"

The Barabel lowered his brow ridge. "How would Rak'k know? He just met you."

"So you did." Alema glanced back at Ship, trying to guess what it would do to any non-Force-user who tried to command it. "Do you think you can handle our ship?"

Rak'k nodded confidently. "The ship has not been built that Rak'k cannot pilot."

Alema wasn't entirely sure that Ship *had* been built, but Rak'k clearly thought he was sending her to *her* death, so it would probably serve the Balance to make the bargain. Besides, about two minutes after she left, her slippery Force presence was going to cause him and his companions to forget all about her—and the bargain. That would not stop them from trying to steal Ship, of course, but at least they would deserve whatever happened to them.

"Done," Alema said. "Where do we find the Sith?"

The Bothan managed to crane his neck around to stare at the Barabel. "Rak'k, you can't tell—"

"The Valley of the Dark Lordz," Rak'k said.

Alema released her Force grasp on the Bothan and grabbed Rak'k instead, pulling him close. "We mean *living* Sith, Bonebrow."

"So does Rak'k," the Barabel said.

"Rak'k!" the Bothan snapped.

Rak'k ignored him and continued, "Go to the valley mouth. You will find their cloister."

The Bothan groaned miserably. "Rak'k, if you didn't just get us *all* killed, you're fired."

Rak'k shrugged. "He did not have good hunting here, anyway." He turned back to Alema. "What are the access codes?"

"There aren't any," Alema said. "Just go to the door and let yourself in. After that, it flies itself."

The Barabel glanced toward Ship, who was throbbing crimson with rage, and looked doubtful. "You are not lying?"

"Of course not." Alema started to pat his cheek, but saw the curling scales again and drew back her hand. "Haven't we always been honest with each other?"

The Barabel considered this a moment, then nodded. "You are going to need transport." He glanced at the Bothan, then added, "Yas'tua has a working swoop."

The Bothan's eyes grew narrow and cold. "No need to fire you now," he said. "If *they* don't kill you, I will."

Rak'k shrugged. "Rak'k does not think so." He looked toward Ship and bared his fangs. "He will be leaving soon on his new starship."

Alema forced Yas'tua to give her his swoop, and ten minutes later she was streaking toward a notched mountain that Rak'k had pointed to as her destination. The more she saw of Korriban's parched terrain, the more she doubted that she had found the right place. Could *this* really be the source of the great Sith conspiracy that Lumiya had hinted at? And yet, the closer Alema drew to her destination, the murkier the light grew, and the harder she found it to continue on.

But continue on she did, for death meant less to her than the fleeting anguish that might accompany it. Her life mattered only if she used it to serve the Balance—to set matters right between her and Leia Solo. Alema could allow nothing to prevent her from getting the help she needed to save Jacen from himself.

At last, she came to a dark canyon cutting deep into the mountain at which Rak'k had pointed her. Until a few minutes earlier, the mountain had looked like nothing more than a high peak. But now she saw that it was an entire massif, a gigantic upthrusting of the planetary crust where the world itself seemed to have quaked with the coming of the Sith.

And standing at the mouth of this grim canyon was the ancient cloister Rak'k had promised, a complex of domed towers enclosed behind a high stone wall. Clinging to the wall exterior were remnants of a blue tile façade, each patch depicting an eye or claw or fang. At its base lay pieces of discarded machinery—portable deflector shields, depleted power core casings, antique laser cannon mountings. All in all, the place looked more like the ramshackle abode of a none-too-tidy hermit than the source of Lumiya's power—but then the Sith *were* masters of concealment.

Alema stopped and dismounted, turning her back to the cloister so she could take the precaution of slipping a defensive dart into the palm of her crippled hand. Then she went to the gate—a four-meter slab of durasteel flaked with red scales of corrosion—and stood for nearly a minute without announcing herself. If there were Sith inside, they already knew she was here. If not, the inhabitants would pay later for making her wait.

Finally, the gate slowly squealed open to reveal a tall Togorian. His face had been shaved naked to display his tattoo striping, which ran along the top his thick snout, then flared into concentric circles around his dark eyes and upright ears. It was impossible to tell whether the rest of his body was shaved as well; it was concealed beneath dark armor and an even darker cloak.

Alema smiled and ran her eyes up and down his imposing, powerfully built form. "At last—just what we were looking for."

The Togorian lashed out so fast that Alema barely realized his hand had moved, but she felt his claws sinking into the back of her good arm. Without speaking, he pulled her inside and dragged her through a murky archway. A dozen steps later, they entered a large courtyard surrounded by dark balconies and gloom-filled doorways, and he threw her down on a floor of black cobblestones.

"Tell how you found us, Jedi, and your death will be swift." He was pinning her down with the Force, his strength so obvious and great that Alema didn't even try to fight. "Hesitate, and your pain will amuse us every day for a year."

"We did not come here for a swift death," Alema said. "And we will amuse you however long you like."

The Togorian's lip curled.

Choosing to ignore the reaction—she had a vial of flesh-eating bacteria from Tenupe that she could use to right the Balance later—Alema smiled back at him. "But we will be happy to explain how we found you."

"Then I will be happy to let you live until you have done so," the Togorian replied. "After that, we shall see."

"Fair enough," Alema said. "We followed the navigation string on a datachip."

"And where did you acquire this datachip?" the Togorian demanded.

"Not so fast," Alema said. "We have questions, too."

The Togorian placed a foot on her ribs and began to step down, squeezing her chest so ferociously that she could no longer breathe. She used the Force to bring up her crippled arm, driving the dart hidden in her hand into the unarmored flesh behind his knee.

The foot came off her chest immediately, and the Togorian leapt back. His lightsaber *snap-hiss*ed to life, but he did not make the mistake of releasing his Force grasp on Alema.

"What was that?" he demanded.

"A warning," Alema replied.

This drew a hissing snicker from the courtyard balcony, and a raspy female voice said, "The skeeto has a bite. I hope you haven't killed poor Morto. He was only following instructions."

Alema glanced over at the Togorian, who—aside from the hateful glare he was casting her way—was showing no sign of the fiery pain that she knew must be burning up his leg.

"He will live," she said. "*Provided* he lets me up."

"Very well." The woman must have nodded to the Togorian—Morto—because Alema found herself able to move. "I see no harm in trading questions, Jedi. You are *never* going to leave here alive."

Alema breathed a sigh of relief and rose, then reached into a pocket and withdrew one of the vials she had brought back from Tenupe. She examined the code she had scratched onto the top to make sure it was the correct one, then tossed it to Morto.

"Rub that onto the wound," she instructed. "*All* of it."

A wave of relief rolled through the Force as Morto caught the vial, then he knelt and began to unbuckle his leg armor. Alema waited until he began to rub in the Tenupian bacteria, then smiled to herself.

Balance.

She turned toward the female voice and was surprised to discover a whole row of cloaked figures standing on the balcony. Save for variations in body size and structure, they all appeared similar to the figure she had seen on Lumiya's datachip, wearing dark cloaks with the hoods pulled forward to conceal their faces.

"Your question?" The voice was low and harsh and masculine, and it came from a figure in the center of the rear balcony, one with pale white eyes barely visible beneath the hood. "And no tricks, Jedi. We Sith have never been known for our patience."

Alema ran her gaze along the balcony railings. "How can you be all Sith?" she asked. "We were taught there are never more than two, a Master and an apprentice."

"You were taught the old ways," the voice said. "We are only *one* Sith now."

Alema had counted more than thirty, but it did not serve her purpose to call the man on his obvious lie. Despite what she had told Morto, her purpose here was not to *learn* about the Sith Order—though that would obviously prove useful. She only needed to win its help for Jacen. She reached inside her cloak for Lumiya's datachip—then lifted her brow when the gesture caused thirty lightsabers to ignite in the blink of an eye.

"Flattering, but we are not that dangerous." She displayed the datachip she had taken from Lumiya's habitat. "This is the datachip we—"

Before she could finish, the chip was torn from her hand and floated up to the Sith with the white eyes. He examined it without bothering to insert it into any sort of datareader, then nodded to the others.

"It's the one." He looked back to Alema. "Where did you find it?"

"The same place I came by my Sith ship," Alema said, confident they already had someone in the spaceport watching Ship—if not actually flying it here. "I inherited it from my . . . master, Lumiya."

The white eyes flared with suspicion. "You are very free with your answers. That is two for one question."

Alema shrugged. "We have no reason to believe you will cheat us," she said. "What would be the point, when you are going to kill us anyway?"

"Indeed," said White Eyes. "*Your* question?"

"We cannot imagine you have a connection to the HoloNet in this hovel," she said. "But we assume you are aware of Mara Skywalker's death."

"We have our avenues of information, yes," White Eyes replied.

"I thought as much," Alema said. "Are you aware that *I* killed her?"

No sound disturbed the courtyard's silence, but the darkness rippled with equal parts surprise and disbelief.

"*You?*" White Eyes finally asked.

Alema nodded. "Us."

She could feel White Eyes and the others examining her Force aura, trying to determine whether she was being truthful. They would not detect a lie, because she was, in fact, responsible for Mara's death. She had worked it all out, using the same logic that had once allowed the Dark Nest to control UnuThul. Since she had been in Hapan space when Mara died, Mara *could* have been following her instead of Lumiya, which meant that Alema *might* be the one truly responsible for Mara stumbling across Jacen, and *of course* that meant Alema was *certainly* the one who had gotten the hag killed. Simple.

It didn't take the Sith long to see that Alema was telling the truth. They deactivated the lightsabers they had ignited when she reached for her datachip, then seemed to regard her with new depths of respect.

"Very well," White Eyes said, "you killed Mara Skywalker. Why did you come here? Are you looking for shelter?"

"*Shelter?*" Alema was insulted by the question. "Do you take us for a coward? Do you think we seek *refuge* while Jacen Solo is out there fighting for the Balance?"

White Eyes shot a puzzled—or perhaps it was chagrined—glance at the Sith to his left, then asked, "If you don't want shelter, then why *did* you come?"

"For help," Alema answered. "And guidance."

The Force rolled with dark confusion, and the raspy-voiced woman asked, "You want . . . *guidance*?"

"From us?" White Eyes added.

"Exactly," Alema replied. "Without Lumiya there to guide him, the truth is that Jacen Solo is stumbling badly. He actually took the academy *hostage*."

"So we have heard," White Eyes said. "What does that have to do with us?"

Alema began to understand—they had no intention of actually risking their lives to support Jacen. They just wanted to hide here while he did all the work and took all the mortal risks—and delivered the galaxy to them on a platter.

"Is *that* how it is?" she demanded. "You create your emperors and just send them out into the galaxy on their own? No wonder all it took to bring Palpatine down was a farmboy and a self-absorbed Princess."

There was dead silence for a moment, and even the Force seemed frozen with shock.

At last, White Eyes asked, "You think *we* trained Jacen Solo?"

"Of course. Lumiya *said* there was a plan." Alema didn't bother to keep the disdain out of her voice. How could these cowards be *Sith*, hiding here in their hovel while one of their own—a single man—conquered the galaxy? "Those were her exact words. *There is a plan—a plan that will be carried out whether or not I survive.*"

At last, the white eyes seemed to glow with comprehension. "*Lumiya's* plan—not ours. Hers and Vergere's."

Now it was Alema's turn to be surprised. "*Vergere* was a Sith?"

"You didn't know that?" asked the raspy-voiced woman. "I thought you were Lumiya's apprentice?"

"Do *you* tell your apprentice everything?" Alema countered.

"Perhaps not," White Eyes allowed. "In any case, Jacen Solo is not our problem. Nor do we want him to be."

"Which is why you won't be allowed to leave here alive," the woman added.

"You keep saying that," Alema said, "but we'd be dead already if you didn't have more questions."

Despite Alema's bravado, she knew her time was running out. The Sith were perilously close to believing they had learned what they needed to know about her, and when they were certain of it, they would attack. She just needed to make certain that Morto was not among those who reached her—the last thing her poor body needed now was a dose of flesh-eating bacteria.

"Whose question is it now?" she asked.

"Let's say it is yours," White Eyes offered. "It's the least we can do."

"How gallant." Alema pointed toward the datachip she had given him, which had vanished somewhere inside his cloak. "That message you sent Lumiya. If you wanted nothing to do with her plan, why did you invite her here?"

"It was sent *before* she developed her plan," White Eyes explained. "Our Master wanted her to join our organization, but she and her escort were ambushed by the Yuuzhan Vong. Lumiya escaped. Lomi Plo and her apprentice did—"

"Lomi Plo was one of you?" Alema gasped. "Truly?"

"How do you know Lomi Plo?" Morto asked, sounding to Alema's experienced ear like a lust-toad lover. He stepped closer, coming up behind her. "What happened to her?"

Alema answered without turning around. "Lomi Plo was our, um, Master." She quickly moved away. "She died at the Battle of Tenupe."

"You're lying." Morto continued to follow her. "Why would she be fighting *Killiks*?"

"She wasn't, silly." Alema turned to face him, but—terrified he would touch her and mar what little remained of her beauty—she continued to back away. "She was fighting *for* Gorog. She was our Queen."

Morto stopped in his tracks. "She was a *bug*?"

"That's no way to talk about her!" If Alema hadn't been afraid to touch him, she would have Force-slapped him so hard his eyes flew from their sockets. "We thought you loved her. Isn't that so?"

"Morto's feelings for his Master are no business of yours," rasped the woman. "And I thought *Lumiya* was your Master."

"Lomi Plo was before Lumiya. We seem to go through Masters like males." Alema eased away from Morto, then turned back to the Sith on the balcony. "You had *nothing* to do with creating Jacen?"

White Eyes shook his head. "Our Master met Vergere while he was a captive of the Yuuzhan Vong. She liked his vision of One Sith."

"But after the first Battle of Bilbringi, she escaped the Yuuzhan Vong and met Lumiya," the woman continued. "And Lumiya convinced her that our Master's plan was too slow; that by the time One Sith were ready to act, Skywalker's Jedi would be too strong to defeat."

"So they decided to create Jacen," White Eyes finished.

"They did the right thing," Alema insisted. "And if you don't help Jacen *now*, the Jedi will destroy him, and the Balance will be ruined."

"The Balance?" White Eyes asked. "Which Balance is that?"

"You don't know the *Balance*?" Alema couldn't believe that a Sith Master would need to ask such a thing. "Between every user and the Force, there is the Balance. Between every Force-user and her enemies, there is the Balance. We serve the Balance by doing to our enemies what they do to us. If we fail, the Force itself will fall—"

"Enough."

White Eyes raised a black-gloved hand, and Alema found herself choking on her words. He cast an inquiring glance along both sides of the balcony above the courtyard. When they all nodded in response, he turned back to the courtyard and looked past Alema to Morto.

"I think our questions have been answered."

Morto's lightsaber sizzled to life. To Alema's surprise, she remained free to act—to reach for her own lightsaber and spin around to defend herself—and she realized the Sith meant her death to be a practice session for Morto. She snatched her weapon off her belt, but instead of igniting it, she backed away and raised it as though asking for permission to speak.

"*Wait.*" Alema had to croak the word, for White Eyes was still using the Force to silence her. "Last . . . question."

The Force hummed with impatience, but the pressure suddenly vanished from Alema's throat.

"Very well," White Eyes said. "One question."

"Thank you." Alema tucked her lightsaber under her arm and rubbed her throat, then said, "Luke Skywalker will soon discover who killed his wife. Do you really want him to track us *here*?"

The impatience in the Force changed first to misgivings and concern, then to disappointment. White Eyes and the others exchanged a long series of glances, then, without saying anything, seemed to reach the consensus Alema had expected.

"Put your lightsaber away, Morto," the woman rasped.

When Morto didn't obey quickly enough, the white eyes flared in his direction and sent him flying. The trip ended with the sharp crack of skull against stone, followed by the sound of crashing armor and a lightsaber snapping off. Alema glanced back and saw the Togorian sitting at the base of a support pillar, one hand pressed to his bloody head.

"Thank you," she said. "But we were thinking of more help than that."

White Eyes' gaze turned to Alema. "You will stay the night," he commanded. "We may have something for Jacen Solo after all."

seventeen

Flying by instruments because visibility was so poor, Jaina dropped out of the smoke and followed the navigation beacon through a gaping hangar mouth into . . . more smoke. Though she had not seen any flames on her approach, it seemed to her all of Rwookrrorro must have been burning to produce such a pall. She hoped it was all rising from below. On the way in, she had picked up some comm chatter suggesting the fires were spreading most ferociously in the forest's midlevels, where they could draw more oxygen from surrounding layers.

A pair of marshaling beacons appeared in the haze, directing her to turn right . . . and *slow down*. Jaina grimaced and obeyed, realizing that in her haste to catch Luke, she had entered the hangar far too quickly. All around her, vague blocky forms materialized into StealthXs, fueling sleds, and armament racks.

No sooner had Jaina set her craft down than a shaggy crew of Wookiees was swarming over it, refueling and checking weapons status. She disengaged her suit connections and extracted herself from the crash webbing, then popped the canopy and sprang out of the cockpit, landing beside a confused-looking Wookiee holding an access ladder.

"Where's Luke Skywalker?" she asked.

The Wookiee pointed through the smoke toward the back of the hangar, where Jaina could barely see a squadron of pilots climbing into their StealthXs. She took off at a run, dodging hoversleds and technicians and coughing on the acrid air. The smoke was less thick inside the hangar than it was outside, but it was clear that the Jedi would be changing bases after their run. She caught up to Luke just as R2—memory-enhanced to help fly StealthXs—was being lowered into the droid socket.

Jaina had not commed or reached out to let Luke know she was coming, but he did not seem surprised as he turned to greet her.

"Hello, Jaina. I hope everything is under control at the academy."

Jaina nodded. "Jag and Zekk are looking after things until we can get some more Jedi Knights there. Most of the GAG troopers were pretty appalled at Serpa's orders, and the rest aren't exactly spoiling for a fight—especially after we returned the lightsabers to the Wampas."

"Good." Luke seemed distracted, as though his mind was anywhere but on the coming fight. "Still, Serpa's battalion isn't all we have to worry about. If Jacen is willing to do *this* . . ."

He let the sentence trail off and waved vaguely around them, the gesture taking in all of Kashyyyk.

"I understand, but there's something you need to know, and I have to tell you in person." Jaina looked around the hangar, trying to pick out a human form that *wasn't* wearing a StealthX flight suit. "Is Ben here? He should hear this, too."

Luke shook his head. "He's supposed to be on his way from Coruscant."

"Supposed to be?" Jaina asked. To her alarm, Luke did not seem at all curious about what she had come to tell him. "Ben is overdue?"

"Not exactly," Luke said. "I sent a message to him . . . after we left Kuat. But I can't tell where he is. Ben is shutting himself off from the Force again."

Jaina *really* didn't like the way Luke was sounding.

"Your parents left last night," Luke added, as though he thought they might have been a substitute for Ben. "They have a plan."

"They always have a plan," Jaina said. "Uncle Luke, are you feeling all right? You seem kind of, well, distracted."

Luke glanced up into the smoke. "We're going after your brother. I don't like doing it."

"He's the one who started this," Jaina said. "But if you're hesitant because he's your nephew—"

"I'm *not*."

R2-D2 whistled down from the droid socket, indicating it was time for their flight check.

"I'll be right there," Luke said. He turned back to Jaina. "What did you need to tell me?"

"Uh, maybe now isn't a good time," Jaina said. "It looks like you've got enough on your mind."

"I'm the Jedi *Grand* Master, Jaina," Luke said. "I know how to keep my concentration."

His tone wasn't exactly sharp, but it *was* commanding, and Jaina knew that trying to hold back now would only distract him even more.

"It's about Alema," she said. "She took out a freighter crew at Roqoo Depot shortly after Mara died."

"That's not surprising," Luke said. "Roqoo Depot is on the way to Terephon, and we know she ended up with Lumiya's ship after we . . . after I killed her."

Jaina shook her head. "This was *before* your fight."

Luke's expression seemed more puzzled than shocked.

"Roqoo Depot is between Kavan and Terephon," Jaina prompted. "Alema was right *there,* the timing was right, and she was in a very nasty mood—she killed half a dozen beings for no reason we could figure out."

Luke's brow shot up. "So you think *she* . . ." He let the sentence trail off, unable—or unwilling—to say it aloud. "How solid is this?"

"Well, we *do* know that Alema likes to use poisons," Jaina said. "That's how she killed two of those people on Roqoo, and Jag said that when he found her cave on Tenupe, it looked like she'd been making them for hunting and self-defense."

Luke closed his eyes, and his Force aura trembled with anger and sorrow. After a few seconds, he nodded and started up the access ladder into his cockpit.

"It certainly seems to implicate her. Thank you, Jaina. I'm sure you'll bring her to justice."

Jaina scowled. "Don't you mean *we*?"

"After my mistake with Lumiya?" Luke shook his head. "It's better for someone else to handle this. Talk to the Council Masters if you need additional resources."

"The *Masters*?" Jaina echoed. Now she felt sure there was something wrong. "What aren't you telling me about this mission?"

Luke dropped into his cockpit. "I haven't told you anything yet, as I recall."

"Then it's time to change that." Jaina grabbed the access ladder and pulled herself up until she was eye-to-eye with Luke. "I'm not letting you go until I know why you're acting this way."

"It's nothing special," Luke said. "A standard assault mission—we're going to soften up the Fifth Fleet so the Wookiees have a fighting chance to stop Jacen's pyromania."

"And?"

Luke sighed. "And I'm going to use the assault as a diversion to make a run at the *Anakin Solo*. Lowie managed to drop a shadow bomb near the bridge, and we might drive it off with another hit. Maybe even take it out."

Jaina dropped off the ladder. "I'm coming."

"Great," Luke said. "Tahiri seems to have disappeared. You can take her place in the Night Blades."

"With *you*."

"Jaina, I don't need—"

"The hell you don't." Jaina turned back toward her own StealthX. "And don't even *think* about trying to lose me. I'll blow out your droid socket faster than you can say *sideslip*."

R2-D2 screeched in protest, but if Luke voiced his consent, Jaina didn't hear it. She was already racing across the hangar toward her own StealthX. The efficient ground crew had refueled the craft and topped off the laser cannon actuating gas. But Jaina had not been carrying heavy weapons when she arrived, and the Wookiees were just now preparing to stock the torpedo compartment.

"Forget it, boys." Jaina jumped onto the cockpit access ladder. "I don't think we're going to have time to load the shadow bombs, and it looks like I'm flying tail cover anyway."

Jaina had barely reattached her suit systems to the cockpit before the order came to launch. She closed her canopy and, once the ground chief had given her the okay, engaged her repulsor drives and spun around. The StealthXs were just launching, a long line of black ghosts gliding out the hangar door, arcing up into the wroshyrs and vanishing into the smoke.

Most of the wing had departed before Jaina felt Luke touch her mind. She opened herself to the Force, expecting to join him in a combat-meld. She felt only his outer presence, reluctant and unwelcoming, and even that quickly drew in on itself until she could barely tell it was there. There would be no emotional joining on this mission; he was not ready to share his pain with anyone. Jaina slid into line behind her uncle, wishing there was some way to comfort him through the Force, but knowing there wasn't. A few minutes later, they were climbing out of the smoke into the blue Kashyyyk sky.

It was almost too early to call the battle a battle. The Wookiee fleet was still on the far side of the planet, just getting itself organized, and the Alliance's Fifth Fleet was hanging back beyond the gravity well to protect the *Anakin Solo*. The only actual hostilities taking place were the blue lines lancing out from the *Anakin Solo*'s long-range batteries, blazing through the Kashyyyk atmosphere to burn what no one had ever thought it necessary to defend.

Jaina found herself alternately hating her brother and mourning his loss, trying to understand what the Yuuzhan Vong could have done to him—or what could have happened to him during his five-year sojourn—to turn him so horribly evil. Could he really believe the efflux he spouted about protecting the Alliance against "terrorist elements"—like their own parents? After all of the torture and loss he had suffered, did he feel so threatened by the ever-changing nature of the galaxy that the only way he could feel secure was by controlling it?

Ultimately, Jaina knew, what had changed her brother didn't matter. He'd become another Emperor, and he simply had to be stopped. It broke her heart, but the only thing that counted now was putting an end to his madness. If Jacen survived, maybe he could be redeemed, as Kyp had been after he destroyed the Carida system. But if not . . . well, there was no need to consider that possibility. It simply wasn't important now.

Jaina felt Luke chiding her through the Force, demanding that she pay attention. Embarrassed by her uncharacteristic lack of focus, she glanced out the canopy and found no reason for the rebuke. The Fifth Fleet was dead ahead, floating between them and the *Anakin Solo*'s flashing turbolasers, a field of white speckles interlaced with the tiny blue filaments of starfighter ion tails.

Then Jaina *felt* it—a pressure building in the Force, a sensation of imminent arrival. Several thousand kilometers to one side of the fleet, crooked snakes of iridescence began to dance between the stars. Immediately a message scrolled across the primary display, reporting the arrival of a large fleet.

"No kidding," Jaina said. "*Whose* fleet?"

UNKNOWN. CLASSIFYING VESSELS NOW.

Jaina's question was answered an instant later when a volley of green dashes erupted from the new arrivals and blossomed against the shields of the Fifth Fleet.

BOTHAN, Sneaker answered. Corvette and light cruiser designator symbols began to populate the edge of the tactical display. SENSOR ANALYSIS CONFIRMS MANUFACTURE.

"*Bothan?*" Jaina was incredulous; the Bothans were the last species she would have expected to come rushing to the Wookiees' aid. "Are you sure?"

NO. CORRELATION IS ONLY 98.76 PERCENT, Sneaker informed her. DAMAGE FROM RECENT ENGAGEMENT PREVENTS CERTITUDE.

Jaina scowled inside her helmet. The damage profile suggested the Bothans had broken away from the Battle of Kuat to come defend Kashyyyk. "It doesn't make sense," she said to herself. "What are they doing here?"

ATTACKING US.

"Not *us*," Jaina told the droid. "You need to realign your friend-or-foe identification files. We've sort of changed sides."

SO THEY ARE FRIENDLIES?

"Maybe," Jaina said. "We'll have to ask Luke later."

NEUTRALS? the droid persisted.

"Close enough."

The Fifth Fleet began to return fire, focusing Alliance attention on the Bothans and making it even more unlikely that the fleet would notice the StealthXs coming. Feelings of guilt and sorrow permeated the Force as the Jedi began to realize how easy their run was going to be—how many of their friends and acquaintances they would soon be killing in cold blood.

Jaina felt her own throat tightening and found herself struggling to blink away tears. For a time, she had flown with the Fifth against the Yuuzhan Vong, and many of the beings she had met then were still serving with it. They were good people—brave, loyal, kind—and it didn't seem right that so many would die today at Jedi hands. But what could the Masters do? Let Jacen burn Kashyyyk to a cinder?

By the time the StealthXs had drawn near enough to worry about being spotted visually, the Fifth Fleet was fully engaged against the Bothans. Both sides were pouring starfighters into the void and hurling turbolaser fire back and forth between them. With her naked eye, Jaina could see tiny balls of orange limning the hulls of many Alliance vessels ahead. On her tactical display, Bothan corvettes were blinking yellow, red, then vanishing almost faster than Sneaker could update the data.

All too soon, the Fifth Fleet started to spread across Jaina's canopy. Its vessels began to assume identifiable shapes—the wedges of Star Destroyers, the fist-headed cylinders of heavy frigates, the sleek curves of Mon Calamari cruisers. The StealthX wing split into six squadrons and angled toward different areas of the fleet. Jaina and Luke fell in with the Night Blades and followed Saba Sebatyne toward the *Vulnerator,* an old *Victory*-class Star Destroyer that had been in service as long as Jaina's parents.

The *Vulnerator* and its two escort frigates swelled rapidly in the forward canopy, their shields glimmering gold with turbolaser energy. When the vessels did not loose so much as a blaster bolt at the approaching Jedi, Jaina began to think it might have been better to have the StealthXs simply sneak through the Fifth Fleet's protective shell and swarm the *Anakin Solo.*

Then a chill raced down her spine, and the Night Blades began to scatter. Space exploded into clouds of fiery brilliance in every direction, and Jaina's StealthX bucked so hard she could not read her displays. Crash webbing bit into her shoulders and damage alarms began to beep, alerting her to a multitude of problems she had no time to register. She sensed Luke diving to one side and jammed the stick over, following, then breathed a sigh of relief when the starfighter actually responded.

"How bad is it, Sneaker?"

The droid sent a report to the primary display. The way the cockpit was bouncing, it was just jumping lights.

"Can't read it," she said. "Are we holding together?"

Sneaker toodled an affirmative answer that sounded vaguely like "for now." Another volley of crimson blossoms opened around them, many laced together by flashing lines of cannon bolts. The *Vulnerator* had anticipated their attack, waiting until the StealthXs had drawn close enough to spot. Then—and this was the smart part, the part that required discipline only the Alliance space navy could instill—the gunners had held their fire until all stations had acquired the target.

Luke was weaving through the storm almost effortlessly, slipping away from turbolaser strikes half a second before they blossomed, ducking cannon bolts as though he had a telepathic connection to the gunner's mind. And maybe he did, for all Jaina knew. She had thought she had a fair understanding of his Force abilities, but if his flying was any example, he hadn't revealed half of what he could do. Maybe not even a quarter.

She concentrated on staying behind him, trying to follow the silhouette of his StealthX as it darted through the fiery curtain surrounding them. Often she could see only the faint glow of his ion engines before their efflux turned dark, and sometimes her only sense of his location came through the Force. It did not take long for her cockpit to stop bucking despite the barrage, and she was finally able to read the damage report Sneaker had put on the display earlier.

THREE.

"Three what?" Jaina asked. It certainly wasn't engines—she would never have been able to keep up with Luke with three engines out.

THREE CASUALTIES, Sneaker reported. YOU WANTED TO KNOW HOW BAD THE FIRST STRIKE WAS.

Jaina gasped into her oxygen mask. Clearly, the *Vulnerator* had developed a very effective technique for dealing with stealth fighters. If a Star Destroyer could take out three Night Blades in an opening salvo, the usefulness of stealth-equipped attack fighters was going to be very limited indeed.

"What about our other squadrons?" Jaina asked. "Were they hit as hard as the Night Blades?"

INSUFFICIENT DATA TO REPLY, Sneaker reported. NIGHT BLADE CASUALTY COUNT IS BASED ON OBSERVED CRAFT DETONATIONS. SINCE STEALTHXS HAVE NO SENSOR SIGNATURE—

"Right," Jaina interrupted. "You have no way of telling."

She glanced at the tactical display and found the rest of the Fifth's Star Destroyers encased in envelopes of short-range turbolaser fire. If the other StealthX squadrons had suffered as many casualties as the Night Blades, the Jedi had just lost a quarter of their fighter wing.

Jaina reached out in the Force, hoping to join the nearest combat-meld and discover that the situation wasn't so bad—and recoiled from the disapproval Luke sent boiling her way. She quickly drew back in on herself and—thinking he was actually having to hold back so she could keep up—concentrated on staying on his tail.

When Luke did not increase the sharpness of his maneuvers and came perilously close to flying them into a fireball, she finally realized that his reason for shunning the combat-meld earlier had nothing to do with concealing his pain.

Luke was hiding from Jacen.

Jacen was the reason the Fifth was so prepared, why they seemed to be expecting the StealthX attack—even with the distraction provided by the arrival of the Bothan fleet. Jacen had been looking for the Jedi combat-meld.

Jaina was still contemplating this when the *Vulnerator* retargeted its batteries and space turned dark again. She checked the tactical display and found the entire Fifth Fleet shifting fire back toward the approaching Bothans. A handful of Star Destroyer symbols were blinking yellow for damaged. But all in all the StealthX attack had been a terrible failure—just how the Masters might plan it if they wanted to minimize Alliance casualties while Luke slipped through to take out Jacen.

That would certainly explain Luke's behavior before launch. If he were planning to try something as reckless as taking out a Star Destroyer alone, it might be reasonable to think someone *else* would have to avenge his wife's death. And he wouldn't want his niece tailing along . . . and if she insisted, rather than risk getting her killed, too, he might try to lose her at the last instant.

"Not going to happen, Uncle."

Jaina tightened up, coming in so close that she could see R2-D2's dome blinking. Luke seemed to sense what she was doing—or what she was worried about—and gave a little wing-waggle. Then he drew in his Force presence so tightly that she could no longer find it. She thought at first he was mocking her, but quickly realized he was showing her what to do. She pulled her own presence so close that Jacen would have to be sitting in the cockpit to sense her.

Luke gave another wing-waggle. They left the Fifth Fleet behind, descending toward the flashing beams of turbolaser light that were all they could see of the *Anakin Solo*. It disgusted Jaina more than ever to have Jacen's flagship named for their younger brother. It was just a name—but it was a name that had stood for something good, and she knew she would feel a pang of regret when they began their attack run. Something else to make Jacen pay for . . . if he survived.

The *Anakin Solo* itself began to appear a moment later, a hand-sized wedge briefly silhouetted whenever a distant turbolaser strike blossomed in the right place. With the dome of a gravity generator bulging beneath its belly and a cloaking cone rising midway down its spine, the profile would have been unmistakable—even had there been another matte-black Star Destroyer running around the galaxy.

The flashes of silhouette grew rapidly larger as Jaina and Luke approached, until it became a fixed stain against the stars. Jaina watched in disbelief as it expanded to the size of a bantha, and still the *Anakin Solo* did not open fire. Unless the visual lookouts were asleep or blind, they *had* to have noticed the StealthXs streaking toward their vessel by now. Even if the two starfighters were not being silhouetted against the crimson fury behind them, they would still be eclipsing and revealing stars at a furious rate, painting a black smear across the blue-speckled void.

Luke must have been thinking the same thing, because he suddenly began to juke and jink so furiously that Jaina could hardly stay on his tail. Sneaker filled the cockpit speakers with screeches and whistles, flashing strain readouts and overload warnings across the primary display too fast to read—even had she dared to look. Still, Luke pushed his StealthX harder, accelerating into a wild series of rolls that made her suspect it was the Force instead of bolts and welds holding his craft together.

Jaina didn't even try to match his maneuvers, contenting herself to remain generally behind him in a covering position. The *Anakin Solo* swelled until all she could see was a mountain of black durasteel, and she began to hope—to *believe,* even—that they had somehow sneaked up on the Star Destroyer. Maybe, just maybe, Luke had been disguising their approach with some Force skill she didn't even know existed. Maybe they'd be able to swing alongside Jacen's abomination of a flagship unopposed, then roll up onto its top hull and launch Luke's shadow bombs without meeting any resistance at all.

And *that* was when the lock-alarms broke out screeching. Jaina's seat slammed into her from behind as a salvo of cannon bolts blew down her rear shields and started chewing through her thin StealthX armor. There was no need to roll out, because she lost control and tumbled toward the *Anakin Solo,* then ricocheted off its particle shields and began to tumble toward a dark cube that—when she caught glimpses of it—looked perilously like an idle turbo-laser turret.

Jaina slammed one control pedal to the floor and released the other, jerking the stick back to her belly and hitting the thrusters. The StealthX accelerated into something that resembled control, and she was relieved to find herself streaking starward instead of into a black expanse of durasteel.

"Damage report!" she snapped. The order came by instinct, then—also by instinct—the question. "What *happened*?"

She looped into a dive and read Sneaker's response. REAR SHIELD GENERATORS OVERLOADED AND DESTROYED, NUMBER THREE ION ENGINE DESTROYED, REAR ACCESSORY MOUNT DESTROYED, DAMAGE CAUSED BY MULTIPLE LASER CANNON STRIKES.

"I figured *that,*" Jaina said. "Where'd they . . ."

She let the question trail off as the dark plain of the *Anakin Solo*'s hull drifted back into view and she saw where the attack had come from.

Luke was attempting to roll onto the top side of the Star Destroyer, still juking and jinking as he tried to position himself for an attack run on the bridge. A few hundred meters behind him and closing fast, a second StealthX was pouring bolts in his direction, angling its fire so Luke could not rise above the *Anakin Solo*'s midline without crossing into a stream of death.

"Jacen!"

INSUFFICIENT DATA TO DETERMINE PILOT IDENTITY, Sneaker informed her.

"He knew!" Jaina ignored the droid's message and pointed her nose after the two StealthXs. There hadn't been enough time since their departure from Kashyyyk for Jacen to suit up and launch. He had to have been waiting for Luke to come after him. "He *knew* the whole plan!"

Jaina's forward canopy erupted into a storm of color as the *Anakin Solo*'s close-defense gunners caught sight of her. She opened the throttles wide and held her own triggers down, relying on her forward shields far more than anyone in a StealthX should, trusting to the Force and her own quick reflexes to keep her shieldless tail in one piece.

As her StealthX sizzled and pinged with cannon hits, Jaina dropped over the hull's edge and slipped in behind her uncle and brother. The enemy fire faded to a trickle of snap shots—with the three StealthXs flying in such close formation, the Alliance gunners were afraid of hitting their commander.

Jaina locked her sights on Jacen and fired. He anticipated and slipped in the opposite direction, and one of her bolts lit up Luke's rear shields.

Jacen dropped back in and added another three hits for good measure, then dodged aside as Jaina fired again. This time, one of her bolts burned through and disappeared into an engine. There was a flash and a puff of smoke. Luke's StealthX seemed to skid and bounce off the *Anakin Solo*'s shields, then—to Jaina's utter astonishment—it rolled over Jacen's fire and disappeared onto the upper hull.

Jaina managed to stitch a line of bolts across Jacen's

upper shields as he pursued, then she followed and found herself struggling to keep up as they streaked past the cloaking cone toward the cratered superstructure of the bridge.

She pressed her triggers. Again, Jacen slipped her fire, and again the bolts only added to Luke's problems. Her brother seemed to anticipate every shot before she took it.

"This'll never work," she growled.

Jaina reached out to Luke, trying to draw him into a combat-meld—and found only Jacen's presence, powerful and dark and mocking. She had no business flying here against *real* pilots, he seemed to be saying; she ought to be back at the academy looking after the young ones.

Jacen's StealthX dropped back into her sights. She felt her fingers depressing the triggers—then sensed a dark chuckle in the back of her mind and realized he was goading her.

Then she heard Luke's voice, clearly, as though it were coming over a comm speaker. *Do it!* She felt him urging her to fire. *Lock 'em down!*

Jaina depressed all four triggers and held them.

Jacen jinked out of the way, taking a wing hit that sent a laser cannon spinning away, and Jaina found herself looking at the stern of Luke's StealthX, watching in relief as it veered away from her line of cannon bolts.

Then Luke's damaged engine erupted in flames. The StealthX seemed to skid, veering back into Jaina's line of fire, and a blast of surprise and panic shot through the Force. She released the triggers instantly, but a quartet of bolts was already leaping from the tips of her cannons.

They caught Luke dead in the stern, chewing through the damaged armor in a flaming eyeblink. The Force boiled with anguish, and then Jaina was flying through a fireball that had once been a starfighter.

She pulled up more by instinct than because she wanted to avoid crashing. Had there been time to think about it, she might well have flown her battered StealthX straight into the looming mass of the *Anakin Solo*'s bridge, because this was one mission from which she truly did not want to return.

Luke Skywalker was dead.

And Jaina had shot him down.

eighteen

Hidden in the smile of an enormous cliff sculpture of a strikingly beautiful Hapan queen, the secret entrance to the Royal Hangar was—like everything associated with the Fountain Palace—a testament to the wealth and power of the Hapan Consortium. It was also designed to accommodate the sleek little skiffs and sport ketches that messengers or secret lovers might fly, not working transports like the *Millennium Falcon*.

As they started down the access tunnel, Han eyed the long line of crystal lumeliers hanging from the ceiling and hoped C-3PO had been right about their clearances. It wouldn't be like Tenel Ka to hold it against him if he hit something—but it wouldn't make it any easier to convince her that Jacen had to be stopped, either.

In the copilot's seat, Leia suddenly gasped, then followed it up with a couple of sharp, short breaths.

Han's eyes dropped to the maneuvering display. "What'd I hit?" As far as he could tell, he still had at least ten centimeters clearance on all sides. "I didn't feel anything."

When Leia did not answer, C-3PO said, "I don't believe you've hit anything *yet*, Captain Solo."

"You don't have to sound so disappointed." Han returned his gaze to the forward viewport and aligned the *Falcon*'s loading mandibles squarely under the last ceiling lumelier. "It's not like you took the bet."

"There would be no purpose in betting against you," C-3PO replied. "I wouldn't have anyplace to accumulate my winnings. Droids aren't permitted to control financial accounts exceeding a million credits."

Han might have retorted that C-3PO had nothing to worry about, but he knew the droid could recall every bet he had ever offered, and he *really* didn't want to listen to the inevitable tallying of accounts.

Once the *Falcon* had finally left the access tunnel and entered the vast opulence of the Queen Mother's Hangar, he glanced over to see why Leia still hadn't answered him.

She was sitting forward in her seat, leaning into her crash webbing, her hand to her mouth. Her eyes were fixed out the forward viewport and focused somewhere, well, *beyond,* and she had The Look. Han's heart dropped— *everything* dropped—and as the *Falcon* swung toward the orange marshaling lights, he was not conscious of moving the yoke in that direction.

"Oh . . . *oh!*" he gasped. "Not again . . . not Jaina!"

"No, Jaina's okay." Leia was shaking her head, but she had the look of someone who had just watched a star explode. "Well, sort of. I don't know."

"You don't *know*?" Han demanded.

He felt like loosing a volley of concussion missiles against the hangar wall, like firing the Sun Crusher into the galaxy core. If something had happened to Jaina, it would be just him and Leia now, because *Jacen* didn't count anymore; they had talked it over on the way to Hapes, nice and calm, and it had taken them about two minutes to decide that *both* their sons were gone now, that Jacen was dead to them. If they were losing Jaina, too, it might be too much for them; Han didn't know if he could be that strong again, if he had it in him to help Leia through this the way he had when Anakin died.

Han managed to guide the *Falcon* into its berth and drop her onto her landing skids, then took a few deep breaths, trying one of those Jedi calming techniques Leia had told him about to keep himself under control.

"Okay," he said. "What do you mean, *sort of*? Either you feel her alive or you don't."

Leia finally seemed to understand the panic she was causing and reached over, clasping his hand. "She's okay—I mean, she will be. I think she's upset because she sensed the same thing I just did—maybe she even saw it."

"Saw *what*?"

Leia squeezed his hand. "Luke . . ."

That was as far as she made it before she broke down croaking and sobbing, and that was all Han needed her to say. Luke was dead. It did not seem fundamentally possible, as though by some natural law the galaxy had to end before Luke did. But he *knew* that was what Leia meant.

"You're kidding." Han couldn't think of anything else to say. "You've got to be kidding."

Leia shook her head. "I felt this surprise, then . . . this *anguish*. And Luke was just gone."

They sat in their seats, Leia letting her tears flow free and Han too stunned to do more than hold her hand, for who knew how long. First Mara, and now Luke. It was more than coincidence. It made him wonder if some dark current in the Force had decided to target the Skywalkers. Or maybe Luke had decided to follow Mara into the Force and tried to take out a Star Destroyer with his lightsaber or something. The one thing Han knew for sure was that Luke could not have gone in the usual way, in a lightsaber duel or a dogfight or just stepping off a pedwalk without looking. It would have taken something big, like a planet exploding . . . or a sudden change in the laws of physics.

After a time, a tentative rap echoed through the hull, coming from the still-closed boarding ramp.

"Perhaps I should answer that," C-3PO offered. "Hangar security masters can be quite unforgiving about suspicious behavior these days."

"Thanks, Threepio," Han said. "Let them know we've just received some bad news. We'll need awhile to put ourselves together."

"No." Leia began to dab her eyes dry. "Tell them we'll be out in a moment."

"Of course, Princess Leia." C-3PO started to turn away, then paused. "And my condolences regarding Master Luke. Could you sense whether Artoo was with him?"

Leia shook her head. "I'm sorry, Threepio. I couldn't tell."

"Yes, well . . . if Master Luke found it necessary to die, I'm sure Artoo would have wanted to be with him."

Another rap echoed through the hull, this one more forceful, and C-3PO started aft. Leia unbuckled her crash webbing and stood, then checked her face in the canopy reflection.

"I'll just have to do this with puffy eyes," she said. "Let's go."

"Are you sure you're up to it?" Han asked. "Tenel Ka's almost family. She'll understand if you need a little time—"

"Thanks, Han, but we don't *have* time." She squeezed his arm. "Not while Kashyyyk burns."

She started aft, pulling Han along. Forty years ago, she had burst into his life like a nova, then continued to burn bright that whole time—his guiding star and beckoning light. So he didn't know why he was so surprised by her strength now, why he hadn't expected her to meet this loss with the same courage with which she met any hardship. Maybe it was because he was having such a hard time accepting Luke's death himself. Not being able to actually *feel* someone die, he still needed to see the body before he could believe it.

When they reached the hatch, they found a small honor guard of Royal Space Marines waiting down on the hangar floor. The captain, a striking woman with narrow green eyes and dark full lips, stepped to the foot of the boarding ramp and bowed formally.

"Welcome, Princess. Her Majesty said to bring you up at once." The captain gestured behind her, where—about twenty meters away—a pair of hammered-aurodium doors guarded an antique mechanical lift. "If you'll follow me, your escort will join us."

Han scowled and joined Leia in *not* descending the ramp. "Our escort?"

The captain shot an annoyed glance in his direction, but reacted as any well-trained Hapan officer would when questioned by a foreign diplomat's male staff. She ignored him. Han clenched his teeth and waited patiently for Leia to take the lead. Bucking four thousand years of Hapan tradition would not convince Tenel Ka of anything.

Leia must have really been off her game, because it took a couple of seconds before she said, "We came alone, Captain. What escort are you referring to?"

The captain scowled and was about to answer when a slender figure in a black flight suit stepped into view. After the long flight from Kashyyyk, the circles under her eyes were even deeper, and her curly blond hair was matted flat with helmet sweat.

"That would be *me*," Tahiri said.

Han frowned, and Leia asked the question, "What are you doing here?"

"I came to see what *you* were doing," Tahiri replied. Han noticed that her hand was hovering near the lightsaber hanging from her belt. "And I don't think I'm going to like the answer."

"Then go away and don't ask." Han had the sinking

feeling he was beginning to understand why Tahiri had followed them—and, just maybe, how Luke had gotten killed. "And I'd do it real fast, before my suspicions start to get the better of me."

The Hapan captain frowned at Tahiri. "You told approach control that you were with the Solos."

"In a way, I am," Tahiri said. "I'm here to detain them."

Han knew better than to reach for his blaster when a Jedi was practically holding her lightsaber, but he had plenty of time to step behind the bulkhead and reach for the door control. Unfortunately, Leia was already starting down the ramp.

"*Detain* us?" Leia demanded. "Don't tell me you're with Jacen?"

"Somebody has to be." Tahiri remained near a landing strut, about three meters to one side of the boarding ramp. "He's only doing what's necessary to save the Alliance."

"You're too smart to buy that." Han caught up to Leia and took her arm, then continued to address Tahiri. "What's he got on you, anyway?"

"On me?" Tahiri looked away, and even Han could read the guilt in her feelings—all he needed was a good pair of eyes and a lot of sabacc experience. "Nothing," Tahiri said. "I'm only doing what's right. Anakin would want me to support Jacen."

This was too much for Leia. "*Anakin?*"

She jerked free of Han's grasp, then stepped onto the hangar floor sputtering something about Anakin never approving of torture and coups. Tahiri reached for her lightsaber, and Han realized the young woman was about to learn a very hard lesson about bad timing.

And so was the honor guard captain, whose eyes widened with alarm as Leia snapped her own lightsaber off her belt. "Put those weapons away *now*!"

The captain reached for her blaster pistol and started to

step between Leia and Tahiri—until Han jumped down and pulled her back by the collar.

"Lady, you *really* don't want to . . ."

Han let the warning trail off as the captain spun on him, holding her blaster pistol under his nose.

"Okay . . . maybe you do." He raised his hands and backed away. "Be my guest."

A pair of lightsabers sizzled to life behind the woman, and sparks flew as Leia and Tahiri brought their weapons together. By the time the captain spun back around, the two Jedi were locked in a furious battle of flashing blades and flying feet.

"Stop!" the captain ordered. She motioned to her squad, who instantly flipped their blaster rifle power settings to stun and leveled the barrels at the combatants. "You *will* stop, or we'll open fire."

Leia landed a jaw-cracking elbow under Tahiri's chin, and Tahiri slammed a knee into Leia's ribs. The captain cursed under her breath, then turned to her marines.

"Hold on!" Han said. "That's a really bad—"

"Fire at will," the captain ordered.

Han dropped, barely reaching the floor before a flurry of stun bolts flashed toward the fight—then reversed directions as the two Jedi batted the attacks back toward their sources. The marines collapsed in moans and spasms, the redheaded captain cracking skulls with Han as she landed atop him.

He rolled out from beneath her, cursing and rubbing his head. The hangar was ringing with security alarms, and royal guards were pouring from hidden crannies and secret passages, but the two Jedi remained oblivious. Leia connected with a vicious thrust kick that bent Tahiri backward over a landing strut crossbar.

Tahiri grunted and pointed at a loose blaster rifle, bringing it tumbling into Leia from behind, catching her between the shoulder blades and knocking her to the floor.

Leia flipped onto her back and brought her legs up over her head, landing on one foot and pirouetting straight into the attack, her blade level with Tahiri's neck.

"Wait!" Han cried. "Not my strut!"

Leia accelerated her pirouette, trying to land the attack before Tahiri had time to block, and that was when Han began to realize his wife was really serious about this—she wasn't in it just to teach the younger woman a lesson.

"Leia, *no*!"

The plea made Leia hesitate just long enough for Tahiri to block, then Leia was on her feet again, keeping Tahiri pinned against the strut, beating down her guard, slipping in knee and elbow strikes with a speed and ferocity that only a Barabel-trained fighter could achieve.

"Leia, *stop*!" Han yelled. "You want to kill her?"

Leia continued to press the attack, and Han realized that was *exactly* what she wanted to do. She had found a handy target for all her rage, just as *he* had when he'd blamed Anakin for Chewbacca's death, and she was determined to make Tahiri pay for what had happened to Luke . . . and for what Jacen had become.

Han snatched the blaster pistol from the captain's hand and, hoping to startle his wife back to her senses, sent a bolt zinging past her. It glanced off the *Falcon* and left a black, smoking furrow in the hull—apparently, the captain had not set *her* blaster to stun. Leia glanced away just long enough for Tahiri to land a spinning back-kick that sent her staggering away.

Han sprang up to grab her. He was taking his life in his hands, but he knew Leia would never forgive herself if she killed Tahiri over a stupid comment and a couple of bad choices. He wrapped his arms around Leia's shoulders and pulled her back—then felt the air leave his chest and his feet leave the floor as she instinctively slammed an elbow into his ribs and started to throw him.

"Whoa . . . Leia!" he groaned. "It's me."

He felt the tension leave her body and his feet return to the floor, then *Tahiri* started to advance, her haggard eyes filled with malice and anger.

"Don't do it!" Han ordered. He pulled Leia aside and, when she deactivated her lightsaber, stepped between her and Tahiri. "Don't you *dare*."

Tahiri stopped two paces away, her lightsaber still ignited, glancing from Leia to Han and looking like a sabacc player trying to decide whether to fold or raise.

"You think *this* is what Anakin would want?" Han prompted. "His mother and his girlfriend trying to kill each other?"

"*I* certainly don't," a female voice said, coming up behind Han—and speaking over the drone of her own lightsaber. "And I won't have it in my hangar."

The anger in Tahiri's face quickly changed to embarrassment. She deactivated her blade and bowed, holding herself parallel to the floor. "I apologize, Your Majesty. I didn't believe they would resist."

"Resist *what*?" Tenel Ka demanded.

"Tahiri was trying to arrest us," Han explained. He turned to find Tenel Ka behind him, dressed in a casual-but-elegant tunic and cloak that managed to make her look both regal and approachable—a stark contrast with the company of scowling guards behind her. "And her timing was *really* bad."

Tenel Ka deactivated her own lightsaber, then motioned Han up as though he had actually remembered to bow. She glanced at Leia's puffy eyes and frowned, then looked back to Han.

"You may explain, Captain Solo."

"Sure," Han said, realizing Tenel Ka must not have felt Luke's death. He wasn't sure how that stuff worked, but since she hadn't been related to Luke, it didn't seem that surprising. Unless she had been close to them, Leia didn't usually feel it when other Jedi died, either. "We think Luke just died. Leia felt it in the Force."

Tenel Ka's face fell, her expression morphing from shock to disbelief to sympathy in about a second and a half. She turned to Leia.

"We are terribly sorry, Princess." Tenel Ka didn't ask how it had happened, probably because she realized her question would only bring more grief—and Leia wouldn't know anyway. "The palace and its staff are entirely at your disposal. Please feel free to ask for anything you need."

Leia nodded, but failed to get out her words of thanks and reached for Han's arm.

"Thanks, Your Majesty," he said. "We appreciate that."

"Of course, you mean while they're under arrest here," Tahiri said, boldly coming up behind Han and Leia. "There *is* still an Alliance detention warrant out for them."

"And *I* have already informed Colonel Solo that in recognition of their heroic service during our recent troubles, his parents have sanctuary everywhere within the Consortium—especially within the Royal Hangar."

"I apologize, Your Majesty," Tahiri said. Still determined to prevent them from pleading their case to Tenel Ka—at least that's why Han *assumed* Tahiri had followed them—she continued to stand behind the Solos. "I can't permit—"

"You cannot *permit*?" Tenel Ka stepped past Han to confront Tahiri directly, followed by enough royal guards to overpower ten Jedi. "This is the Hapan Consortium, Jedi Veila. *I* govern here—not Jacen, not the Alliance, and certainly not *you*."

"Of course," Tahiri said. "I only meant the Alliance would disapprove—"

"At the moment, Hapes provides nearly a fifth of the Alliance's combat capacity," Tenel Ka said. "The Alliance is in no position to *disapprove* of anything I do. Is that clear?"

"Of . . . of course," Tahiri said. "But—"

"There are no buts," Tenel Ka interrupted. "Now tell me, were you injured when you attacked Princess Leia?"

Tahiri's jaw dropped. "*I'm* the one who was attacked!"

"I'll take that as a no." Tenel Ka turned to a black-haired officer at her back. "In that case, Jedi Veila is ready to travel. Return her to her StealthX and have her escorted out of Hapan space, Major Espara."

Espara inclined her head. "As you wish, Majesty. And if I may make a suggestion?"

"Suggestions are always welcome, Major," Tenel Ka said. "You know that."

"Thank you, Majesty," Espara said. "It might be wise to keep the StealthX cloaking unit here on Hapes—just to be certain Jedi Veila doesn't slip away from our escort."

"You can't!" Tahiri objected. "That technology is Jedi property. Colonel Solo would look very unfavorably on that."

Espara was ready with a smooth response. "And yet, the Jedi deserted the Alliance at Kuat, while Colonel Solo is attacking them at Kashyyyk. And *you* are here, attempting to arrest the Solos on behalf of the Alliance." She turned to Tenel Ka. "The war has grown so very confusing. It's difficult to tell *whose* side we're on at the moment."

Tenel Ka's brow rose, then, after thinking for a moment, she nodded. "An excellent point, Major Espara—but I want Jedi Veila gone *now*. Keep the entire StealthX and supply her with a messenger skiff instead."

"Jacen won't put up with this," Tahiri warned. "You're stealing an Alliance starfighter."

Tenel Ka shook her head. "No, Jedi Veila—we are capturing an enemy starfighter. And since *you* were flying it, that must mean you are now an Alliance prisoner of war." She turned to Major Espara. "Have her presented to Colonel Solo with our apologies for any misunderstanding. As you say, the war has grown so very confusing."

Espara smiled. "As you wish, Majesty."

The major waved her company forward and cautiously disarmed Tahiri.

Han pulled Leia to his side. "How are you doing?"

Leia nodded. "Better. Thanks for . . ." She looked away, watching Espara's guards lead Tahiri off, then finished. " . . . for stopping me."

"Yes," Tenel Ka said, joining them. "It was very courageous to step between two angry Jedi as you did."

"Thanks," Han said, feeling a little embarrassed. "It was nothing."

"Nonetheless, please don't ever do it again. We are quite fond of you with *all* your limbs." Tenel Ka smiled and waved them toward the antique lift. "Now perhaps you would tell me why Tahiri is so eager to keep you from speaking to me."

"Because she's been spying on the Jedi for Jacen, I think," Leia said. "And she doesn't want you to hear what he's doing now."

To Han's surprise, Tenel Ka merely nodded. "This is what I was afraid of." She stepped into the lift compartment and waved the Solos in after her, but held out her hand to stop Espara and the rest of her bodyguards. "You may join us in the anteroom, Major. The Solos pose no danger to me."

Espara nodded and closed the doors. As the lift began to rise, Tenel Ka's eyes grew wet, and her lip began to quiver.

"So the intelligence reports I have been getting from Kashyyyk are true?" she asked.

"I'm afraid so," Leia said. "I wish there was a better way to put this, but there isn't. Jacen is burning the planet to the dirt."

A single tear ran down Tenel Ka's cheek. "Why?"

"Who knows?" Han couldn't figure out why Tenel Ka was taking this so hard; she was acting like Jacen was *her* kid or something. "Because he's Jacen, and he doesn't like it when people say no to him."

This was too much for Tenel Ka. The tears started to flow more freely, and she touched a button on the wall. The lift stopped immediately, trapping them all inside the small compartment.

"Forgive me," Tenel Ka said, shaking her head in despair. "I don't know what to make of so much sad news."

Leia scowled at Han behind Tenel Ka's back, silently scolding him for being so callous—even if he *couldn't* figure out what he'd said wrong—then nodded at Tenel Ka, signaling him to fix the mess he'd made.

Han laid a tentative hand on Tenel Ka's shoulder, and suddenly she had her head buried in his chest, sobbing as the tough little girl he remembered from the Jedi academy probably never had. Forgetting for the moment that she was the sovereign of the largest independent realm in the galaxy, he wrapped his arms tight around her and stroked her red hair.

"It's okay, kid." Han looked over her shoulder at Leia, searching for some hint about what to do next. But Leia was only staring at Tenel Ka's back, struggling to hold back her own tears. "We should have found a better way to break it to you. I didn't think losing Luke would hit you so hard."

Tenel Ka muttered something unintelligible into Han's tunic, then pushed herself away shaking her head.

"It's not Luke." She cast a quick glance at Leia, then added quickly, "I'm very sad to lose him, but it's more than that—it's Jacen, too. The galaxy is coming apart around us, and he used to be the one person who seemed strong enough to hold it together."

"His methods are a little too brutal," Leia said gently.

Tenel Ka nodded. "He promised to make peace with the Jedi. Instead, he tries to arrest you at Mara's funeral and takes over the academy on Ossus. Then he sends Ben to assassinate Cal Omas, and now he *burns* Kashyyyk." She shook her head with what seemed equal parts sorrow and disgust. "He took my *last* fleet, Han. He left Allana and me vulnerable—*us*."

Given the other promises Jacen had broken, Han saw no reason Tenel Ka should have been surprised to be left hanging with no planetary defenses. But this hardly seemed like the time to rub her nose in past mistakes. Instead, he merely nodded sagely.

"You can't trust him, Tenel Ka," he said. "It took us a long time to figure that out, too."

"Yes, he has been fooling us all for far too long." Tenel Ka pulled a small hand mirror from her pocket and began to examine her tear-streaked face. "I think the time has come for someone to do the same to him, don't you?"

Han lifted his brow. "Does that mean what I think it means?"

"That *is* why you came here, is it not?" Tenel Ka continued to study herself in her mirror, using the Force to reduce the puffiness around her eyes and balance her skin tone. "To convince me to change sides?"

"At least to withdraw your support," Leia clarified. "Given Corellia's recent interference in Hapan internal affairs, I'm not certain it's fair to ask you to support the Confederation actively."

"Come now, Princess." Tenel Ka lowered the mirror, her face now perfectly composed, with no hint of the tears she had been shedding just a minute earlier. She pressed a button on the wall, and the antique lift began to rise again. "We both know that if you aren't *for* Jacen, you're against him."

nineteen

In a bubble of white agony sat a being fighting to hold on to itself, to remember that it was human, the child of two Jedi, a young man who had hoped to become a Jedi Knight himself. The pain was trying to rob him of this, tearing at his resolve with a thousand forms of anguish—acid that licked nerves raw, poison that raised boiling blisters, needles that turned joints into kilns of throbbing inflammation. The only way to end the pain was to surrender to it, to let it melt him down and forge him into something stronger and sturdier and more enduring.

Ben understood this. Each moment would bring a new and exquisite agony, as fierce and startling as the last, and the pain would never let him die, or grow numb, or escape into catatonic oblivion. He understood all this, and *still* he clung to the knowledge that he was Ben Skywalker, son of Luke and Mara Jade Skywalker, cousin and onetime apprentice to Colonel Jacen Solo, *who is the murderer of my mother.*

That last part, Ben repeated twice. It was the only way to keep his hate—and he was going to need his hate. Hate would help him escape, and when he escaped, hate would give him the power to kill Jacen Solo.

The chair—if a pulsing mass of white tendrils tipped

with black barbs could be called a chair—tightened its grasp, and a cocoon of yellow energy danced up around Ben. The breath left his lungs in a long staccato scream, and he felt his muscles spasm and heard his teeth grinding, then everything went white, and he sank into the timeless anguish of convulsion.

Later, when Ben's nerves had become desensitized and required a new torment, the darkness returned to the dark again, and he grew aware of someone standing in front of his chair. How exactly he did this in the unlit cell, he did not know. He could see nothing, and the Force had been lost to him since the pain began. Perhaps he had smelled something foul, or heard a boot click in a familiar way.

But Ben *knew*. He lifted his chin, as much as his thorny restraints would allow, and said, "Hello, Jacen."

"I *asked* you to call me Colonel."

Ben gathered a mouthful of coppery blood and spat it in the direction of the voice. He did not hear it hit anything.

"Good." Jacen's voice had shifted, and now it came from somewhere near Ben's ear. "Hang on to your hate. It will help you endure." The voice drew closer. "I *couldn't* hate, and it nearly destroyed me."

"*My* hate will destroy you," Ben said.

"Perhaps, given time," Jacen allowed. "But it will take decades to develop the power to confront me openly. And I hope you understand the futility of trying to take me by surprise. Surely, your circumstances have made that painfully clear."

A soft chittering sounded near where Jacen's hand was, and the tendrils holding Ben captive sprouted tiny bristles and injected droplets of venom under his skin. His flesh immediately began to swell and nettle and—as the tendrils constricted—to split and weep ichor.

The darkness dissolved into a fiery curtain of pain, and Jacen asked, "Do you want to die yet, Ben? All you have to do is ask."

"More . . . lies," Ben gasped. "You enjoy . . . this."

"*Enjoy* it?" Jacen sounded genuinely hurt. "You know that's not true. I don't *enjoy* any of this."

An illumination panel flickered to life in the ceiling. Ben's eyes ached as they struggled to adjust, and he began to make out the shapes of a thorn-coated bed on the adjacent wall, and a tendril-draped rack in the far corner. The chamber was larger than he had imagined, at least ten meters across. To one side, a large door opened into a cavernous darkness that could only be one of the clandestine hangars hidden in the substructure of the *Anakin Solo*'s forward weapons turrets.

Jacen moved into Ben's line of sight, dressed in his usual GAG uniform with high boots and black cloak. His eyes were sunken and sad, with purple crescents beneath them and a glassy sheen that made him look as though he were on the brink of weeping—or a demented rage. He reached out and took the tendril binding one of Ben's wrists to the chair.

"How can you believe I *want* to do this?" Jacen pulled the tendril away, not even wincing as it wrapped itself around his forearm and sank its anguish-dripping barbs into his flesh. "I'm *part* of it, Ben. Everything the Embrace of Pain does to you, I feel. We're in this together."

"Fine," Ben said. "How about you take your turn and let me blow things up for a while?"

"Very impressive. I lost *my* sense of humor after the first . . ." Jacen caught himself and smiled, probably because he had nearly violated one of the cardinal rules of torture and given the subject a way to guess how much time had passed. "But that's not important, is it? The point is, I'm doing this to save you."

"*Save* me?" Ben laughed, and aching waves of pain rolled through his chest. "Right. The same way you saved Mom."

Jacen's lips tightened. "I don't know why you insist on

believing something so hurtful," he said. "But very well, let's pretend for the moment you're right. Why would I have done such a thing?"

"You can say *killed her,* Jacen. If you can *do* it, you can say it."

"Perhaps when you start calling me *Colonel,*" Jacen replied. "But however we refer to it, why would I have done such a thing?"

"Because she knew you were working with Lumiya," Ben replied. "You needed to keep her quiet."

Jacen shook his head. "*Think,* Ben. If your mother suspected I was working with Lumiya, wouldn't she have *told* someone? A whole team of Jedi Masters would have come after me, not just your mother."

Ben frowned at this. He knew why his mother had kept her silence: because *he* had been too embarrassed to tell his father about Jacen's dalliance with Lumiya and reveal what a nerf-head he had been, and his mother had been trying to keep his secret. But *Jacen* didn't know that. From his point of view, if Ben's mother had known about Lumiya, then *of course* she would have told his father—and every other Jedi Master with a working comlink. So Jacen *wouldn't* have thought that killing her would keep anything quiet.

"I don't know," Ben said. "Maybe you just wanted to get even."

Jacen scowled in disappointment. "You know me better than that. There's only one reason I would ever do anything so . . . difficult: for the good of the galaxy."

An angry fire welled up inside Ben. "Killing Mom *wasn't* good for the galaxy!"

"And *I* didn't kill her," Jacen replied calmly. "But we're talking hypotheticals here. If you could bring peace to the galaxy by sacrificing your own life—to assassinate me, for instance—would you do it?"

"In a heartbeat," Ben retorted. "Even if it didn't save the galaxy."

"Let's limit ourselves to meaningful sacrifices," Jacen said. "Now, if you had to kill someone else instead—someone like your mother—to bring peace to the galaxy, would you do it?"

"That's a stupid question!" Ben yelled. "Killing my mother didn't bring peace to anything. The galaxy's more of a mess now than before you did it."

"That's beside the point," Jacen said. "And I *didn't* kill her. I asked if *you* would—if you would trade your mother's life for galactic peace."

Ben fell silent, afraid that if he answered, he would somehow stop hating Jacen for what he had done, somehow come to accept that his mother's death was . . . *necessary.*

After a moment, Jacen said, "You won't find a trap, Ben. There isn't one."

Ben still found it difficult to answer. The fact was, he *had* made exactly the kind of trade his cousin was talking about. He had done it twice now. First, he had tried to win Jacen's confidence by suggesting that Jacen kill the Solusars and other adults on Ossus instead of wiping out the entire academy. And just a short time ago—at least he *thought* it was a short time ago—he had stood next to Jacen on the bridge and suggested that the *Anakin Solo* target the Wookiee cities. And why had Ben done that? To allay his cousin's suspicions, so he could kill Jacen and end this war.

When Ben remained silent, Jacen pressed on. "You can't answer because it would be selfish to refuse, even evil. How could you *not* trade one life to save billions? Your mother would have begged you to, if the choice were hers."

"That's . . . not . . . what . . . happened!" Ben could feel his hate slipping away—and with it, his identity. He would have liked to think it was because Jacen was using the Force to influence him, but he knew better. He was losing his identity because he was more like Jacen than even Jacen knew. "You didn't have to kill her."

"And I didn't—but I *would* have. That's the difference between us. I'm willing to carry that burden." Jacen paused and reached over to stroke a muscle node on the side of the Embrace. "And that's why this is necessary—to give *you* the strength to make the same choice."

Ben expected the tendrils to tighten again, or at least to ooze some new kind of toxin that would turn his welts into weeping sores and his weeping sores into boiling abscesses. Instead, the tendrils retracted their barbs and slackened until he was comfortable. Jacen laid a hand on Ben's shoulder and gave it a gentle squeeze.

"Now I'm afraid I must hurt you in a way worse than anything the Embrace has done." Jacen continued to clasp Ben's shoulder, infusing his wounds with soothing Force energy. "A short time ago, your father and my sister made a foolhardy attack on the *Anakin Solo*. Jaina appears to have escaped, but your father's StealthX was destroyed."

Ben frowned, not quite able to grasp what Jacen was telling him. "So?"

"So, his craft was vaporized," Jacen explained. "There was no chance to eject."

"You think he's dead?" Ben knew that his head should have been reeling and his heart cracking, but the truth was, the only thing he felt was disbelief . . . and hatred. He still had *that*, even if Jacen was telling the truth. "Boy, are you gullible."

Jacen's hand clamped down, sending hot fingers of pain through Ben's chest and neck. "I was there, Ben. I saw it with my own eyes."

"You think *you* shot him down?" Ben didn't know what he would do if he actually succeeded in making Jacen lose control of his anger—only that he had to make *something* happen. "That's a laugh."

But Jacen wasn't taking the bait. He removed his hand and said, "Actually, it wasn't me. It was an accident— friendly fire. Jaina got him."

That did shake Ben. It seemed unlikely that Jaina Solo would make such a mistake, and even more unlikely that his father would be caught by it. But freak accidents did happen, and his dad had been very distracted since his mother's death. Was it really so impossible that a grieving Luke Skywalker had made a fatal mistake?

"No—you're making it up." Ben's objection sounded desperate, even to him. It felt like a cold hand had grabbed his heart and started to squeeze. "I would have felt him die—just like I did when you killed Mom."

Jacen shook his head solemnly. "How, Ben? Have you felt *anything* through the Force since you've been here?" He took his vibrodagger from its sheath and activated it, then tossed it onto the floor about two meters away. "Go on, then. Summon that blade and free yourself."

Ben reached for the vibrodagger . . . and couldn't find it. He opened himself wide, and sensed nothing.

"What's wrong?" he gasped. "I can't . . . *feel*."

"Of course not," Jacen replied. "How long could the Embrace have held you, had I let you keep the Force?"

"You can *do* that? You can separate me from the Force?"

Jacen gestured at Ben's helpless form. "Apparently so."

"And now I can't reach out for help," Ben said, beginning to see how Jacen was trying to fool him. "So when you tell me Dad is dead, I can't find him in the Force. I have to take your word for it."

"That's not the reason," Jacen said. "But I see how you might come to that conclusion."

Jacen laid his hand on Ben's shoulder again, and the Force came flooding back in a shocking, painful torrent. He sensed a dozen things at once—his aunt Leia searching for him in the Force, filled with pain and shock and sympathy; his cousin Jaina, down on Kashyyyk, full of sorrow and apology and—now that she sensed him aboard the *Anakin Solo*—confusion; Saba Sebatyne and the other

Masters relieved by his sudden return to the Force. And they were all reeling, bewildered and concerned because he was aboard Jacen's ship.

But mostly, Ben sensed his father—a small, tight presence a deck or two above. He was skulking through the substructures below one of the long-range turbolaser turrets, and he seemed as surprised as everyone else by where Ben had turned up. But there was also a note of reassurance, a promise that he would soon be there to help.

At first, Ben couldn't understand why Leia and Jaina and everyone else still seemed so sad—then it hit him: They couldn't feel his father's presence. Ben was the only one whom his dad was allowing to sense him through the Force. Not even Jacen had that kind of control.

"Neat trick."

Ben didn't realize he'd said this aloud until Jacen scowled.

"It's no trick, Ben. Even *I'm* not good enough to project emotions into other Force-users," Jacen said. "You're sensing the same thing I am. Everyone knows what happened."

"And that's why you think Dad is dead?" Ben asked cautiously. "Just because everyone thinks so?"

"I know because I felt him die," Jacen said. "I'm glad I was able to spare you *that* particular anguish. It would have done nothing to make you stronger."

"Yeah, thanks," Ben said flatly. Now that he was alert to it, he could sense how tightly his father was holding his presence. Even Ben felt only half connected to him, as if he were holding hands with a ghost or something. "How long ago did all this happen?"

Jacen smiled. "You know I'm not going to tell you that."

Ben cocked his head in acknowledgment. "It was worth a shot." He was trying to figure out why his father had sneaked aboard the *Anakin Solo*—it had to involve more than just taking out the long-range turbolasers. With Jaina along, they could have destroyed all four in a single pass and still had two shadow bombs left. "It's been about a day. Everybody's still in shock, but they've had time to start worrying about me."

"It appears their concerns are misplaced. Your thinking is remarkably clear." Jacen glanced at the Embrace, then added, "All things considered, of course."

The smirk in Jacen's voice made Ben want to kill him, and he finally realized his father had probably sneaked aboard to do the same thing. It didn't seem right. The responsibility was Ben's alone. He had gotten his mother killed by telling only her about Lumiya. If he had owned up to his mistake publicly—if he'd had the courage to tell his father and the rest of the Council Masters what he had seen—then his mother would never have gone after Jacen alone. The Masters wouldn't have *let* her, and she would be alive right now and Jacen would be dead, and the galaxy would probably be at peace.

"It's okay to hate me," Jacen said, apparently sensing the drift of Ben's thoughts. "But you mustn't be controlled by it. You must make your hate serve you."

Ben summoned a laugh, managing to sound bitter if not natural. "I don't hate you, Jacen. I *pity* you."

Jacen scowled. "I don't appear to be the one in need of pity, Ben."

"You will be," Ben said. "Dad's not dead. He's coming for you."

Jacen's scowl vanished. "You're not holding up as well as I thought." He patted Ben's arm. "Stop fighting it, and the hallucinations will pass."

A sudden rumble shook the cabin, and the muffled squeal of twisting metal began to weep down from many decks above. An alarm siren blared to life out in the hangar; then a series of muted *thud*s sounded somewhere overhead as a chain of bulkhead doors slammed down.

Jacen was on his comlink instantly, demanding an explanation from his aide Orlopp. Ben caught a snippet of the

Jenet's reply, something about cooling coils and a cata-strophic failure of the number two long-range turbolaser.

"Stop the barrage and inspect the cooling coils of the other batteries," Jacen ordered into the comlink. "Keep me informed."

Ben waited until Jacen had closed the channel, then asked, "Still think I'm having hallucinations?"

Jacen glanced up at the ceiling, and Ben could feel him reaching out in the Force, actively searching for Luke—or any other saboteur. Finally, he shook his head and returned his attention to his captive.

"I'm afraid so," he said. "I don't feel any Jedi presence at all, and if *I* don't, then neither do you—nothing real, any-way."

"That's because he doesn't want you to feel him," Ben said. He sensed his father very near now, on the same deck and moving fast. "But he's here."

"And I suppose you'll help me find him if I let you go?" Jacen scoffed. "Nice try."

Ben glimpsed a dark figure stepping into the doorway. "I don't think you'll need any help finding him, Jacen. Dad's right behind you."

It had to be a bad dream, Ben sitting there in that over-grown bramble, swaddled in thorn-studded vines, his skin flaking away in purple scales, his eyes burning with a pain-mad gleam. Luke had to be imagining this. Not even Jacen would use the Embrace on his own cousin.

"You'll have to do better than that, Ben." Still facing Ben, Jacen laughed and threw his hands up in mock terror. " *'Look! Behind you!'* That ruse was old when the stars were young."

Ben shrugged. "It's your funeral."

"It might be, if I were naïve enough to let you summon *that*."

Jacen pointed at a vibrodagger lying on the deck, about

two meters in front of Ben. Luke didn't know what it was doing there—whether Ben had attacked Jacen with it, or whether Jacen had been using it on Ben—but he started to accept that the horrible scene was real. He was, in fact, standing in the doorway of a secret cabin filled with Yuuzhan Vong torture devices, watching his twisted nephew taunt his captive son.

Luke didn't give Jacen a chance to surrender. He just sprang.

Ben's jaw dropped, and Jacen started to spin, snatching his lightsaber from his belt and igniting it in the same motion, bringing the emerald blade around high to protect his heart and head.

But Luke was attacking low, striking for the kidney to disable in the most painful way possible. Jacen's eyes widened. He flipped his lightsaber down in the same moment Luke's met flesh.

The tip sank a few centimeters, drawing a pained hiss as it touched a kidney, then Jacen's blade made contact and knocked it aside. Even that small wound would have left most humans paralyzed with agony. But Jacen thrived on pain, fed on it to make himself stronger and faster. He simply completed his pivot and landed a rib-crunching roundhouse.

Luke stumbled back, his chest filled with fire. Jacen had caught him on the barely healed scar from his first fight with Lumiya, and now his breath was coming in short painful gasps.

Good, Luke thought. This was *supposed* to hurt.

Jacen followed the kick with a high slash. Luke blocked and spun inside, landing an elbow smash to the temple that dropped Jacen to his knees. He brought his own knee up under Jacen's chin, hearing teeth crack—and relishing it. He parried a weak slash at his thighs, then drew his blade up diagonally where his nephew's chest should have been.

Except Jacen was sliding backward, one hand extended

behind him, using the Force to pull himself toward a tendril-draped rack in the far corner of the torture chamber. Luke leapt after him, bringing his lightsaber around in a low, clearing sweep.

Jacen stopped pulling and started to swing his free hand around. Luke was ready, had been expecting this since the fight started. Still flying through the air, he raised his own hand, palm outward, and pushed the Force out through his arm to form a protective shield.

The lightning never came. Instead, Luke was blindsided by something heavy and spiky, and his body exploded into pain as he slammed into a durasteel wall. He found himself pinned in place, trapped by a bed of thorns Jacen had hurled across the cabin. He felt the hot sting of the thorns pumping their venom into him. His hearing faded and his head began to spin, and he saw Jacen, one hand still raised to keep Luke pinned, sneering and taking his time rising.

Bad mistake.

Luke raised his lightsaber, slashing through the thorn bed as he sprang. Jacen scrambled to his feet, barely bringing his weapon up in time to block a vicious downstroke. Luke landed a snap-kick to the stomach that lifted Jacen a meter off the deck, then followed it with a slash to the neck—

—which Jacen ducked. He came up under Luke's guard, holding his weapon with one hand and driving a Force-enhanced punch into Luke's ribs with the other, striking for the same place he had kicked earlier. Luke's chest exploded into pain, and he found himself croaking instead of breathing.

Luke struck again with his lightsaber, using both hands and putting all his strength into the attack, beating his nephew's guard down so far that Jacen's emerald blade bit into his own shoulder. Jacen kicked at Luke's legs, catching the side of a knee. Something popped and Luke felt himself going down. On the way, he swept his blade horizontally.

Jacen screamed, and the smell of scorched bone and singed hair filled the air. Knowing Jacen would strike despite the wound, Luke rolled over his throbbing knee and spun back to his feet with a clearing sweep.

His blade met Jacen's in a shower of brilliant sparks. Luke freed one hand and drove a finger-strike at Jacen's eyes.

Jacen turned his head, but Luke's little finger scratched across something soft and bulbous. Jacen roared and stumbled away, shaking his head. Luke feinted a dash toward his nephew's blind side, then—as Jacen pivoted to protect his injured eye—Luke hit him with a Force wave.

Jacen went flying, and it required only a soft nudge to steer him into a tendril-draped rack in the far corner. He hit with so much cracking and crashing that Luke worried the rack had broken, but the thin tendrils quickly entwined Jacen in a net of pulsing green.

Luke started forward, his injured knee buckling each time he put weight on it. The rack's slender tendrils were tightening around Jacen, cutting into his flesh and oozing a yellowish irritant that made skin puff up and split. Jacen began to slash his lightsaber up and down, cutting the vines away two and three at a time. If Luke wanted to finish this—and it seemed like a good idea, given how battered he was himself—he had only a few seconds.

Luke closed to within two meters without saying a word. What point would there have been? Jacen wasn't going to surrender, and Luke wouldn't have believed him if he offered. It was better to attack quickly, while he still had the advantage. He brought his lightsaber up to strike.

"Wait!" Ben cried from behind him. "Let me do it!"

Astonished and appalled, Luke put a little too much weight on his injured knee—and fell as it buckled. He rolled beyond the reach of Jacen's lightsaber and looked back across the chamber. Ben was still strapped in the Embrace, but he had summoned the vibrodagger off the floor and was battling to cut himself free of the chair's lashing tentacles.

Luke shook his head. "I don't think so, Ben."

"You have to!" Ben insisted. "I deserve it!"

"*Deserve* it?" Luke returned to his feet, far angrier with Jacen than he had been just a moment earlier. "To kill someone?"

"You don't understand," Ben insisted. "It was my fault. If I don't do this—"

"I said *no*," Luke interrupted. How could Ben believe that he had a *right* to kill someone? "You're very confused, Ben. We'll talk about this later."

Giving his son no further chance to argue, Luke turned back to Jacen, who by now was almost free. Only one leg remained caught, though it was still entwined in a half a dozen places. Luke limped forward, circling toward Jacen's trapped side.

Jacen stopped cutting at the tendrils and flung a hand toward the ceiling.

"Dad, look—"

Luke was already throwing himself to the deck. A tremendous crash sounded from the illumination panel, and the chamber fell instantly dark. He rolled opposite the direction he had just been moving, but wasn't quick enough. The fixture smashed into his head and shoulders, slamming his face into the deck. He heard something crunch in his nose and was instantly choking on his own thick blood.

Jacen's lightsaber droned twice, filling that corner of the torture chamber with flickering green light. Luke Force-hurled the light fixture off his back, then hobbled to his feet.

Jacen launched himself over Luke in a high Force flip. They exchanged perfunctory attacks as he tumbled past, then Luke was alone in the corner, watching the green column of his nephew's lightsaber move toward the door.

Jacen was *running*.

Luke spat out a mouthful of blood and Force-leapt after his nephew, at the same time reaching out to drag him back. They came together in a blinding flurry of sparks, their blades colliding faster than the eye could follow, filling the dark chamber with flashing fans of color. Blows came out of nowhere. Luke caught another kick in his knee and found himself calling on the Force to keep his balance. He landed an elbow and felt a bone in Jacen's face shatter.

Jacen stumbled back, groaning, the green light of his lightsaber briefly illuminating Ben's face as the boy struggled to cut himself free. Luke pressed forward, angling toward the Embrace to keep Jacen away from Ben. Jacen fought his way over anyway, placing himself squarely between Luke and the chair, then gave ground and vanished behind the green ribbons his lightsaber was weaving through the darkness.

Luke Force-leapt after him, knowing that this Jacen—the Jacen he had caught torturing his son—would not hesitate to take Ben hostage . . . or to kill him. Luke landed half a meter in front of Jacen's lightsaber and quickly beat down his nephew's guard—*too* quickly. When he did not glimpse a face in the light of his own blade, Luke knew something was wrong and stopped.

Which was exactly what Jacen was waiting for, of course.

Luke had barely started to turn before a loop of thin tendril slipped over his head and tightened around his throat, oozing toxin and cutting deep into the flesh. The wound swelled and burned as if it were on fire. Luke whipped his lightsaber around, trying to cut Jacen off his back, but Jacen was already spinning away, tightening his garrote and placing Luke's body between himself and the deadly blade.

"Should have let me go when you had the chance," Jacen snarled. "Now you're done."

Luke slammed an elbow into Jacen's ribs, but it was like hitting a permacrete wall. Instead of continuing to fight, he accelerated into the spin, using the Force to hurl them *both* into the nearest wall.

Jacen hit first, his skull clunking hard into the durasteel. The garrote loosened a little. Luke dropped his lightsaber, bracing one hand against the other so he could use the strength of both arms to hammer his elbow up under Jacen's chin.

The garrote went completely slack. Luke followed up with a palm-heel to the same target, using the impact to drive himself away from his attacker and buy some maneuvering room.

Then Jacen let out a bloodcurdling scream and stumbled away, a black silhouette vanishing into the darkness of the torture chamber.

Luke stepped back in shock and confusion, summoning his lightsaber to hand, but knowing by the surprise in Jacen's scream that this was not another trick.

"It's okay, Dad," Ben said from beside him. "It's just me."

Ben took the glow rod from Luke's belt and activated it. Jacen was crawling across the torture chamber, the hilt of a vibrodagger protruding from between his shoulder blades. His face was inflamed and misshapen, his clothes were smoking and tattered, a hand-sized rectangle of scorched skull showed through his scalp, and *still* he was stretching a hand toward his lightsaber.

Luke re-ignited his own lightsaber, then pointed out the door. "Artoo is in the hangar prepping a skiff for launch," he said. "Go help him while I finish up here."

"No way." Ben extended his free hand and summoned Jacen's still-ignited lightsaber. "This kill is *mine*."

Ben's words chilled Luke to the core—chilled him and frightened him. He could hear the hatred burning inside his son, feel the darkness swirling in his Force aura.

"I said *no*." Luke limped after his son and grabbed him by the shoulder. "You can't surrender to your rage, Ben. I did that with Lumiya, and all it did was make me weak. But if *you* do now, you'll be lost to the dark side. I feel it in you already."

"I don't *care* about the dark side." Ben was still holding Jacen's lightsaber, waving it around in careless anger. "Jacen killed Mom, and it was my—"

"Is *that* what you think?" Luke interrupted. He was pained by his son's confusion, but at least he finally understood the hatred and the rage, the thirst for vengeance. "*Jacen* didn't kill Mara. It was Alema—at least that's the way it looks now."

Ben frowned. "Alema?"

"Jaina and Zekk uncovered some evidence putting her near the scene." Luke started Ben toward the door. "I'll explain on the way back to Kashyyyk. We've got to get out of here before the rest of those turbolasers blow."

Ben allowed himself to be pushed across the threshold into the hangar. "The *rest* of the turbolasers, Dad? How many did you sabotage?"

"Four," Luke said. "Just the long-range batteries."

"Then I've got news for you," Ben said. "They've already blown—while you and Jacen were fighting."

Luke glanced at the ceiling, not all that surprised to learn that he had missed the detonations. "We'd better hurry." He tapped a control pad on the wall, and a heavy door clanged down to seal Jacen inside his torture chamber. "Security is going to be all over this part of the ship looking for saboteurs."

"No kidding." But instead of starting across the hangar, Ben shined the glow rod back toward the torture chamber, as though he could somehow see Jacen behind the durasteel door plotting his defense against an attack that was not going to come—at least not today. "Being at the scene doesn't mean Alema is Mom's killer, you know. Jacen was close, too."

"Everyone knows that." Luke did not try to draw Ben away; this decision, Ben had to make on his own. "But if I can't be sure it was Alema, can you be sure it was Jacen?"

Ben exhaled in exasperation, and Luke was relieved to feel the hatred in his son's aura softening to uncertainty.

Luke held his hand out. "Give me the lightsaber, Ben. It isn't time to finish things with Jacen—not this way."

Ben deactivated the lightsaber, but did not pass it over. "So we're just going to let Jacen get away with it?" he asked. "With burning Kashyyyk and torturing me and everything else?"

"Of course not," Luke said. "But we'll come for him when the time is right—for *us*."

Ben thought for a moment, then asked, "You promise?"

Luke nodded. "We have to stop this madness," he said. "And we will—when our judgment isn't clouded by pain and rage."

Ben let out a heavy sigh, then passed the lightsaber over. "In that case, we really need to get out of here." He started across the hangar at a run. "Jacen still has his comlink."

twenty

The air in the forward infirmary reeked of bacta salve and scorched flesh, and casualties were jammed three and four to a bay. Yet Caedus had an entire corner to himself—and not because his injuries warranted it. He had only a few broken bones and some damaged organs. There were patients here who had lost half their limbs to the explosions Luke had caused, and others with third-degree burns over half their bodies.

But the triage droid was skillfully directing new patients to every treatment hub except Caedus's—perhaps because its compassion module could read in their averted glances and angry grimaces the same thing Caedus felt in their Force auras: hostility, anger, and fear. They blamed *him* for the sabotage, as though he should have foreseen the detonation of all four long-range turbolaser batteries—as though he had caused it by attacking Kashyyyk in the first place.

They were right, of course. Had the *Anakin Solo* not been setting fire to the wroshyrs, Luke would never have tried anything so foolhardy. Nor would the Bothans have come to the Wookiees' aid—along with the Corellians and much of the rest of the enemy's fleets, if infirmary rumors were to be believed. Caedus had sacrificed the lives and well-being of a couple of thousand crew members to draw the Confederation away from the Battle of Kuat.

And he would do it again. Now that he had moved the battle away from the Core, Coruscant was no longer at risk, and he had bought the Alliance time to regroup. Now all that remained was to withdraw and let the traitors believe they had driven him back. Caedus sat up—savoring the fiery bolts of pain that shot through him with the effort—and swung his legs over the side of the gurney.

His uniform and cloak, now completely shredded after being cut off his body, were draped half in and half out of a disposal bin in the corner, and his equipment belt was hanging over the back of an empty chair. He felt uncharacteristically vulnerable—partly because he was wearing only infirmary-issue underclothes, but mostly because he couldn't help looking at the empty lightsaber hook on his belt.

Luke had *beaten* him. Luke had just kept coming despite his injuries. He had inflicted more damage on Caedus than he had suffered himself, and he had even escaped the garrote before Ben struck. In fact, it was probably that attack that had saved Caedus's life. Nothing else could have shocked Luke out of his battle rage—only the sight of Ben slipping so far to the dark side.

It was a memory that both frightened Caedus and burned his pride, but it was one that he would have to contemplate at length. Now he knew what to expect when Luke discovered who really killed Mara—and when Luke came after him next time, Caedus would be ready.

Provided, of course, he escaped *this* battle first.

"Where's Orlopp?" Caedus demanded of no one—and everyone—in particular. "I asked for my aide ten minutes ago."

The Bith surgeon and his Codru-Ji assistant exchanged glances over Caedus's shoulder, but it was the skull-faced MD droid who answered.

"You're in no condition for duty, Colonel Solo." The

droid gently tried to push Caedus back down. "If you continue to ignore Dr. Qilqu's advice about sitting up, we may have to sedate you."

"Try it." Caedus turned to Qilqu. "I'm tired of hearing that squawking. Can't you override him?"

Qilqu's cheek folds flattened in alarm, and he looked to the droid. "The colonel has an extraordinary constitution, EmDee. If he feels strong enough to sit up, it will be better to let him."

"Very well." The droid raised its hand, extruding a hypo from the tip of its index finger. "Then perhaps an injection of painkillers will make him less irritable."

"No painkillers—I need a clear head." Actually, Caedus was feeding on the pain, burning it like fuel to keep his hormone levels high and his mind alert. "And I *need* my aide!"

Qilqu glanced outside the bay and nodded. Orlopp stepped around the partition, one of Caedus's spare uniforms tucked under his arm and the ever-present datapad in hand.

"There's no need to be cross, Colonel." Orlopp's long Jenet snout twitched in disgust—no doubt at the smell of Caedus's wounds. "Perhaps painkillers *would* be a good idea."

"Be my guest," Caedus retorted. He pointed at the datapad. "What's the tactical situation?"

"You're going to wish you were still unconscious." Orlopp tapped a few keys on the datapad and passed it over. "The good news is that your plan worked beyond all expectations."

Orlopp wasn't exaggerating. The tactical feed showed the Fifth Fleet—with the *Anakin Solo* at its center—surrounded by the enemy. The Wookiee fleet was shielding Kashyyyk from any further bombardment, while the Bothans, Corellians, and the remnants of the Commenorian and Hutt fleets attacked from the rear.

"What happened to Bwua'tu and Darklighter?" Caedus demanded. "They should be relieving us by now."

"Admiral Bwua'tu sent his regrets," Orlopp replied. "Apparently, he and Admiral Darklighter were ordered to hold their forces inside the Core."

"Of course." Caedus didn't need to ask who had issued the order: Cha Niathal was too good a tactician to overlook an opportunity to have the enemy eliminate her rival—even if it *did* mean sacrificing a little thing like the Fifth Fleet. "I was expecting this betrayal."

"You *were*?" Orlopp sounded genuinely relieved. "In that case, you may want to brief Admiral Atoko on your plan. He's given the order to prepare all vessels for scuttle and abandonment."

"Without consulting *me*?"

"You were . . . unavailable," Orlopp explained.

"I'm available *now*."

Jacen slipped off the gurney—then groaned in shock as the small impact of landing on the deck sent halos of pain radiating out from his two back wounds. His knees buckled, and he would have fallen if the MD droid's hand hadn't shot out to hold him up.

"In your condition, standing is out of the question," the droid informed him. "Even if the swelling in your brain doesn't destroy your balance, you have burn damage to your kidney and a perforation in your lung. You're simply too weak."

"I'm a master of the Force, EmDee." Caedus jerked his arm free of the droid's grasp, then thrust the datapad back into Orlopp's hands. "I'm *never* weak."

Using the Force to hold himself upright, Caedus limped over to the wall comm and opened a channel to the bridge. When the familiar voice of his communications officer answered a moment later, he asked her to connect him to Atoko. While he waited, he took his uniform from Orlopp and slowly—painfully—dressed.

Finally, the admiral's surprised voice sounded over the comm speaker. "Colonel Solo? How are you feeling?"

"Well enough to retain command." Caedus allowed enough anger into his voice to let Atoko know he did not appreciate having his authority usurped. "And I don't recall giving orders to scuttle the fleet."

"And neither have I, yet." Atoko didn't seem fazed by Caedus's displeasure—perhaps because he suspected that soon neither of them was going to be in command of anything. "But the Wookiees are starting to launch boarding craft. Rather than allow our assets to fall into enemy hands—"

"Why aren't you attempting to fight free, Admiral?" Caedus demanded. "If the Fifth is going to be vaped, at least it can take a few Bothans along."

The speaker fell silent, and—were it not for the steady crackle of turbolaser interference—Caedus would have assumed the channel had been closed. As he waited for Atoko to acknowledge the order—or at least to respond—he slowly began to realize that the admiral wasn't the only one who had been shocked by the command. Qilqu and his assistant were both oozing dismay and disbelief into the Force, and even the normally unflappable Orlopp was shaking his head in amazement.

"Admiral Atoko, I seem to be sensing a problem with my order," Caedus said. "Is something unclear?"

"No, sir," Atoko said. "It's very clear. All *too* clear."

"Then there must be a flaw in it," Caedus said. "What is it?"

"The, well, the *crews*," Atoko replied. "There are over seventy thousand beings in the Fifth. We can't just order them to their deaths."

"Ah." Caedus had planned to escape in a StealthX if Niathal betrayed him, so it had not occurred to him that the crew members of the Fifth might be reluctant to give their lives for the Alliance. "You think the vessel commanders will refuse?"

"With no chance of survival or escape, it's . . . a possibility," Atoko said carefully. "Destroying a few enemy ships isn't going to seem like a worthwhile sacrifice when the alternative is an honorable surrender."

"I suppose not," Caedus admitted. "So when the time comes, we should remind them that those are *Wookiee* boarding parties . . . and the Fifth has been shielding the *Anakin Solo* while we burned Kashyyyk."

Again, the speaker fell silent—but only for a moment. "I think that will persuade them, Colonel."

"I thought it might," Caedus said. "Cancel the scuttle preparations and ready the fleet for a penetration attack. I'll give you the coordinates once I've studied—"

"Excuse me, Colonel." Orlopp shoved the datapad at Caedus again. "But I believe you will find the coordinates fairly obvious."

Caedus took the datapad. His vision was still a little blurry, and all he could see was a tight cluster of unreadable designator codes popping onto the top edge of the screen. For a moment, he didn't understand what Orlopp was suggesting . . . then the Corellian fleet began to move aside, creating room for the new arrivals to join in the encirclement of the Fifth.

"Very good, Orlopp," he said. "Admiral Atoko, we'll make for the seam between the Corellians and the newcomers. If we time this right, we should be able to battle through and save at least a third of our strength."

There was a moment of uncomfortable silence, then Atoko's voice asked, "Battle through, Colonel?"

"Of course," Caedus said. "You don't expect them to let us pass without a fight, do you?"

"Well . . . yes, that's exactly what I expect," Atoko said.

Caedus scowled at the datapad. On the little display, the cluster of new arrivals was growing denser by the second, rendering the designator codes more unreadable than ever. Now that he studied it more carefully, the Corellian fleet was moving too abruptly—and too far—to simply be making room. They were worried about crossfire.

Caedus tapped a key, enlarging the image so much that the new arrivals vanished from the display, and he found himself looking at a detailed schematic of the Fifth's battle deployment.

Orlopp quietly took the datapad from his hands. "It's our side," he said quietly. "Those are Novas and Battle Dragons arriving."

"The Hapans?" Caedus gasped.

"Colonel Solo still seems rather confused," the MD droid said to Qilqu. "It's imperative that we declare him unfit for duty."

Caedus was so relieved he did not even flip the droid's circuit breaker. He simply spoke into the wall comm again.

"My apologies, Admiral. You're quite right. Let's make for the Hapans. I'll be in contact again as soon as I return to the bridge and have access to proper battle intelligence."

Caedus picked up his utility belt, then motioned for Orlopp to follow and left the infirmary feeling more cheerful inside than he had in ages. His parents had turned the Wookiees against him, his classmate Lowbacca had hurled a shadow bomb at him, his uncle had nearly killed him, and his cousin had planted a vibrodagger so near his heart that the handle had twitched in time to his pulse.

But Tenel Ka had come to his rescue. She had proven once again that he could always count on her; that no matter what he asked of her, she was willing to do more. Because she *believed*. She understood what he was trying to do for the galaxy . . . for her and Allana . . . and she knew it could not be done without risk and sacrifice. Perhaps one day, after he had won this war and brought a just peace to the galaxy, perhaps then they would no longer need to hide their relationship—perhaps they would even be able to perform their duties from the same world and live together like a normal family.

Caedus opened himself to the Force long enough to reach out to her in thanks—and was astonished to find her not far away on Hapes, but nearby with her fleet. She had come to his aid personally. He was not certain that he approved of her taking part in battles. Who would protect Allana if something happened to her? But he *was* touched, and he flooded his gratitude into the Force.

Tenel Ka's presence turned sad and lonely underneath. At the same time, she seemed to be urging patience, reaching out in invitation, and he realized she wanted to talk. Afraid that something had happened to their daughter, he reached out and found Allana where she should be—far, far away, happy and presumably safe.

Caedus replied to Tenel Ka by filling his presence with curiosity, then snapped his comlink off his utility belt and opened a channel to his communications officer, Lieutenant Krova.

"Queen Mother Tenel Ka needs to talk to me," he said. "Prepare a secure channel to the *Dragon Queen* and contact me when you have her."

"Right away, Colonel," Krova said. "But it will take a short time to match our scrambling protocols. The Hapans have not been very forthcoming—"

"I'm aware of the difficulties," Caedus said. "I won't hold you responsible for the delay."

"Thank you, Colonel. I'll ping you when we have Her Majesty on the channel."

By then, they were leaving the infirmary. The corridor outside was packed with two very different kinds of casualties: those who were going to die no matter how quickly they reached a bacta tank, and those who would most likely survive until they were transported to one of the *Anakin Solo*'s other infirmaries. There were few beings with only minor injuries.

As Caedus squeezed through the crowded corridor, with a battered face and bandaged head, he could feel the admiration of the *Anakin Solo*'s crew for his courage and dedication. But he also sensed their fear of his brutality, and their resentment of the callous way he was spending their lives. They did not love him as did the Coruscanti public, but they *were* in awe of him, and as long as Caedus remained confident in himself and his mission, he felt certain they would follow him into the Core itself.

It took a full minute before they reached a corridor that wasn't jammed with casualties and medical droids, and another thirty seconds to reach a shooter station. They descended a short ramp, stepped into a crew car, and announced their destination, then allowed the onboard brain to scan their retinas to establish their identity and security clearances. A moment later, the car lurched into motion, dropping down a blue durasteel tunnel into the network of shooter tubes—horizontal repulsors—that whirred and rattled personnel and equipment through the *Anakin Solo*'s immense length.

Caedus settled back in his seat, sinking into his pain, and was surprised at how much he just wanted to sleep. The fight with Luke had drained him, of course, but this exhaustion was emotional and spiritual. He was growing ever more isolated as his friends and family deserted him and his followers began to see him as something more than human. There was no one around him with whom he could share his feelings as he had once done with Jaina, or seek advice from as he had once done with Luke, or turn to for unconditional support as he had once done with his parents.

Now there was only Tenel Ka, who was all those things to him during their brief trysts, and the hope that one day they could be together always. Caedus closed his eyes and let his mind drift into the future, not seeing it through the Force but imagining it with his heart.

That was when his comlink pinged for attention. When he checked the display and saw that Krova already had a channel open to Tenel Ka, his weariness vanished, and even the pain of his injuries began to diminish.

He activated the mike, then said, "Queen Mother, what a pleasant surprise. I knew the Alliance could count on you."

"The Alliance, yes, Jacen," she said, using his name instead of his title to signal that their conversation would be personal. Caedus didn't like the old name—it reminded him of the timidity and indecision that had been his weakness as a younger man—but she wouldn't understand being asked to call him by his Sith name . . . at least not yet. "But I am afraid that is no longer true for you."

"What?" Caedus's heart did not sink, nor did his anger well up inside him, because he simply did not believe what he was hearing. "Our signal must have gotten scrambled. It sounded like you said I can't count on you."

"I'm afraid you heard correctly." Tenel Ka's voice sounded as though it were cracking, though it was difficult to be certain over the tinny tones of a comlink—especially with the air hissing past as the little crew car whirred through the shooter tube. "In fact, I am asking for your surrender."

"My surrender?" Caedus began to worry that the MD droid had been right, that he truly *was* unfit to return to duty. "Can you hold on a second? I've got to check something out."

Without awaiting her reply, Caedus turned to Orlopp. "We *are* in a crew car on the way to the bridge, correct? I *am* speaking to Queen Mother Tenel Ka over the comlink, am I not?"

"We are," Orlopp said, nodding. "I'm sorry, Colonel, but you're *not* hallucinating."

"That's what I was afraid of." Even now, Caedus's heart did not sink. This had to be a misunderstanding; once he explained his strategy to Tenel Ka, she would retract her request and resume full support. He reopened the channel. "Look, Tenel Ka, I can't explain over a comm channel, but I had good reasons for slipping away from the Battle of Kuat."

"I'm sure you did," Tenel Ka replied. "You always have good reasons for breaking your promises."

Caedus's anger began to rise. "I was trying to *save* the Home Fleet—and much, much more. You'll understand when I can explain."

"Perhaps so," Tenel Ka said. "You might even be able to explain why you took control of the academy on Ossus after you promised to make peace with Master Skywalker. But how can you explain sending Ben to assassinate Chief Omas, Jacen? A fourteen-year-old boy?"

"I didn't," Caedus said. "He misinterpreted a report and assumed—"

"I am a Hapan queen," Tenel Ka interrupted. "You won't deceive me with equivocation, Jacen. It is an insult that you even try, and there can be no excuse for what you are doing to Kashyyyk. Setting the wroshyrs ablaze? What are you thinking?"

"I am *thinking* the Wookiees betrayed us," Caedus replied. "I am thinking that they brought this on themselves. Everything else, I can explain only in person."

"Good. I shall be looking forward to that," Tenel Ka said. "You will instruct Admiral Atoko to follow my father's orders, and I'll send a skiff for you. Kindly present yourself unarmed."

"You'll send a *skiff*?" Caedus fumed. "Tenel Ka, you can't believe I'm going to surrender—to you or anyone else."

"I am *hoping* you will." Tenel Ka's voice was sad but firm. "Because it is going to break my heart to open fire on you."

Caedus's rage exploded inside him, and his thoughts

began to whirl in disbelief. He reached out to Tenel Ka in the Force, but found her aura drawn in tight, her presence unavailable to his touch.

"Even *you*?" he gasped. "I thought you were made of stronger stuff, Tenel Ka. I thought you understood what I'm trying to accomplish."

"She's plenty strong, kid," said the familiar voice of Han Solo. "It's killing her to do this—and I don't get it. Personally, I'd just as soon blast you back to atoms and pretend you died in that fight with Onimi."

"Dad." The word felt strange in Caedus's mouth, as though he were using it to address someone else's father. "I should have known you were behind this. I suppose Mom is there, too?"

"Right beside him," Leia confirmed. Her tone was resolute—but also sad. "Listen to Tenel Ka. I don't want to see another son die."

"Don't worry about *that*," Caedus said. "I wouldn't *think* of dying before I make you pay for this—both of you."

"For what, Jacen?" Tenel Ka asked. "What have *they* done?"

"They forced *you* into this." Now Caedus understood. The only way to make Tenel Ka betray him would be some sort of coercion. "What are they doing? Threatening Allana? If they do anything to hurt her—"

"Not our style, kid," Han interrupted. "You did this all on your own. All we had to do was show up."

"Your father is telling the truth, Jacen," Tenel Ka said. "Look into my heart, and you will know that the decision is mine alone."

Caedus felt her reaching out, opening her emotions to him. Her presence was filled with sorrow and anger and—most devastating—disappointment. There was love, too, but the kind of lost love that one carries for someone who has died or passed out of one's life forever.

Now Caedus's heart sank, sank so far that it seemed to vanish into the cold emptiness he felt gathering inside him. The unthinkable had happened. Tenel Ka had deserted him, their love just one more offering to his Sith destiny. He knew the sacrifice would strengthen him eventually, as every sacrifice now strengthened him, but this time it did not feel that way. All Caedus felt *now* was angry, stunned, and abandoned.

After a moment, Tenel Ka said, "I am asking you one last time, Jacen. Please don't make me do this."

"I'm sorry, Your Majesty," Caedus replied. "I have no choice."

He closed the channel and turned to find his aide already speaking into his own comlink.

". . . reinforce shields forward!" Orlopp was saying. "Expect fire from—"

The order came to a crackling end as the Hapans' first salvo hit, overloading the *Anakin Solo*'s shields and flooding the ship's systems with dissipation static. The crew car slowed to a crawl as power was diverted to critical systems. The tunnel switched to emergency illumination, plunging Caedus and his aide into cold red twilight.

Alema Rar had never seen a moon explode, but if she had, she felt sure it would have looked a lot like the Fifth Fleet did at that moment. With the enemy pummeling it from every side, the once-mighty fleet had drawn itself into a tight little bundle of mushrooming fire and flashing sheets of heat. The deaths were still panging through the Force in the dozens rather than the hundreds or the thousands, but that would soon change. The seam toward which the fleet was angling—between the Bothans and the Hapans—was closing fast, and Alema did not need a battle forecast to know it would be a death trap for any vessel that attempted to squeeze through.

This was all the fault of those Darth Wannabes hiding on

Korriban. They had made her wait *three* days so they could train her in the use of the meditation sphere and prepare their gift to Jacen.

And what had their "gift" turned out to be? The Holo-cron of Darth Vectivus, filled with such pearls of wisdom as "Never borrow money from someone powerful enough to make you pay" and "Let your employees know you trust them . . . then *watch* them." Who *was* this guy? Their bookkeeper?

Ship reminded her that there were many forms of domi-nation. Darth Vectivus had been a middle manager in a galactic mining conglomerate. He had controlled the lives of tens of thousands of laborers and accrued a vast per-sonal fortune far in excess of his personal needs—or the ca-pacity of his salary to provide.

"And that will help Jacen conquer the galaxy *how*?" Alema demanded. "Not that it matters. Look at the mess he's gotten himself into. If he doesn't die, he'll be the laughing-stock of Coruscant. He'll be as useful to us as *this*."

Alema hurled the Vectivus Holocron in the general direction of the battle. Ship formed a small pocket in the transparent wall and caught it, then informed her that the situation was hardly hopeless.

"Look, we are very impressed with your plasma streams and antimatter pellets, but they aren't enough to take on four fleets," Alema said. "Are you mad?"

Ship thought it probably was, since it was beginning to take a liking to her, but that was beside the point. The Emperor-to-Be was trying to break free; all they needed to do was open a hole for him.

"Us and what fleet?"

Choose one, Ship suggested. *There are four.*

Alema lifted her brow. "We can take over an enemy fleet?" she gasped. "They didn't tell us you could do *that*!"

Control, not command, Ship clarified. *And only because*

*they have no meditation spheres of their own. They have
no defense.*

Alema smiled. "It's always best that way, isn't it?"

Caedus did not need battle meditation to know he had already lost the Fifth Fleet—and to know that only minutes
remained before the *Anakin Solo* was lost as well. The
turbolaser fire was coming not in blossoms or rolling bar-
rages or even in sheets; it was simply *there*, filling every
square centimeter of his observation bubble with fiery
undying brilliance. The color flashed from red to gold to
blue, depending on the angle of contact and the condition
of the shields. But the intensity never wavered, and he
knew that his own gunners had to be firing blind; even the
Anakin Solo's top-grade sensor filters were no match for
this kind of blast-static.

Still, Caedus felt a nagging hope, something pulling at
him through the Force, urging him not to give up. He
squeezed past his meditation chair—which had been
turned to face outward but not yet repaired—then slipped
over the arm into the seat. He began to concentrate on his
breathing, clearing his mind of all extraneous thoughts so
he could expand his battle awareness.

Orlopp stepped up behind the chair and snuffled for attention.

"Not now," Caedus said. "I need to meditate."

"Of course you do," Orlopp replied. "I just wanted to
report that your StealthX is ready for launch."

"Thank you."

Orlopp did not go away.

"Is there something else?" Caedus asked.

"Admiral Atoko is insisting that you give him permission to scuttle the fleet. He claims he has the authority to
do it without your approval."

"Does he really think the Wookiees are going to board
through *that*?" Caedus waved at the firestorm outside. He

was tempted to grant permission, but he still felt that nagging hope, something pulling at him in the Force. "Tell him to hang on for two minutes. If he hasn't heard from me by then, he's free to do as he wishes."

"Very well," Orlopp said—then continued to hover.

"*What?*"

"Your StealthX has room for only one person, Colonel," he said. "How am *I* to escape?"

"I'm trying to work on that now," Caedus said. "But I need to meditate."

Orlopp retreated quickly and quietly.

Caedus resumed his breathing exercise, expanding his Force-awareness to encompass his own fleet, then all fleets in the battle, and finally—when he still hadn't located the source of his nagging hope—the entire theater of combat.

The hope grew stronger, summoning him in the direction of the Bothan fleet, urging him to come toward it. Caedus's first reaction was not one of doubt or suspicion. It was simply amazement. How could the Bothans think him foolish enough to fall for such a primitive ploy? They had obviously located a Force-user somewhere and assigned him to confuse Caedus's battle meditations, just as Luke had done at Balmorra.

Caedus ended his meditation and rose, turning his thoughts to the problem of Orlopp's escape. The Jenet was a fine aide and one of the few subordinates courageous enough to speak frankly when the situation required. Such an aide would be difficult to replace. Unfortunately, the Jenet was too large to fit into the cramped cargo compartment of a StealthX—especially in a bulky pressure suit—but if the missile compartment were emptied . . .

The hope continued to pull, so hard now that Caedus almost felt as if he were being physically dragged. If the Bothans *had* found a Force-user, they had found a good one. Caedus stopped and followed the feeling to its source—to well beyond the Bothan fleet, where he found a broken, twisted presence that had been inserting itself into his struggles far too often of late.

Alema Rar.

But something was different. Her power seemed greatly magnified, far too ancient and somehow even darker than before.

Alema continued to pull at him, filling her presence with the promise of salvation and victory and, well, some other things in which he had no interest. It would be crazy to rush the Bothan fleet, as she was urging, and the Twi'lek was hardly someone to be trusted with one's life—or destiny. But the maneuver *would* be the last thing the enemy expected . . . and what was there to lose?

Caedus dropped back into his chair. "Orlopp!"

"Yes, Colonel?" Orlopp stopped behind him. "Have you thought of a way for me to escape?"

"We're *all* going to escape," Caedus said. "Have Admiral Atoko turn on the Bothan fleet. He's to confront it head-on, full acceleration. Any vessels too damaged to keep pace will act as our rear guard. Starfighters will jump to Rendezvous Alpha."

"We're *attacking*?"

"*Now,* Orlopp," Caedus replied. "If Admiral Atoko gives that scuttle order, you won't need an escape vessel."

"At once, Colonel." Orlopp scurried away.

As Caedus sank back into his battle meditation, a desperate craving for sleep rose inside him. His body was telling him that it needed to heal. Of course, Caedus had no time for rest. He expanded his Force-awareness again and found himself momentarily lost in the maelstrom of fear and bitterness that was the Fifth Fleet. He began to sift through the emotions, seeking out those who felt most calm, those who seemed to be in command, and started to brush them with his confidence and hope.

Soon small eddies of calm and composure began to swirl through the storm. Caedus turned his attention on the heart of the fleet, where he could feel Admiral Atoko's defiant presence fuming over his orders, no doubt contemplating whether to issue the scuttle order anyway.

Caedus filled his thoughts with the conviction that they *would* escape—that it was his destiny to survive and unite the galaxy—then began to press down on Atoko's presence. The admiral seemed startled at first, then confused, but his resistance quickly yielded to obedience, and Caedus continued to press.

A few moments later, a ripple of astonishment rolled through the Force, then quickly became determination as the fleet changed course. The brilliance outside seemed to slide across the observation bubble for a moment, then gradually broke into individual blossoms of energy as the enemy gunners began to worry about overshots hitting a friendly fleet.

Caedus began to glimpse individual bolts of turbolaser fire fanning out from the Bothan batteries. As the Fifth struck back, tiny blossoms of color erupted against the distant darkness. A shudder raced through Force as the Alliance cruiser *Redma* suddenly lost its shields and came apart, and whorls of panic and anguish enveloped other vessels as they took hits and began to spit beings and equipment into the void. But overall, the crews of the Fifth remained focused on the attack, too absorbed in their duties to fall prey to the fear and fatalism that had crippled them earlier.

Incredibly, the Bothans did not fall back. They simply held their position and continued to exchange fire with the Fifth, which—battered as it was—had them outgunned, outnumbered, and outclassed. Concerned the Bothans were laying a trap, Caedus extended his Force-awareness to their fleet—and was consumed by a rush of fiery pain as his body struggled to remain functional.

He opened himself completely to the Force, drawing it in through the power not of his anger or fear—he was too exhausted and sad to feel either—but through his faith in his destiny, through the love that gave him the strength to serve that destiny . . . through his love not only of Allana but also of Tenel Ka, of Luke and Ben and even Mara, of Jaina and his parents and all the others who had betrayed him, of his allies and enemies and his dead mentors. He drew the Force in through his love of them all, of the entire galaxy he was sacrificing himself to save.

The pain remained, but with it came the strength Caedus needed to remain conscious. When he focused his attention on the Bothan fleet again, he began to sense an odd uncertainty among the commanders—and a dark power behind it. Alema Rar was somehow influencing them, instilling in their minds an atypical indecision.

Caedus suspected they were thinking he was too smart to do this—that surely he knew all they had to do was fall back and let their allies catch the Fifth in a devastating crossfire. He began to press down on them, affirming that belief. *Yes, he knew.*

Caedus's vision darkened around the edges, and he began to feel light-headed. Still, he continued to exert pressure, trying to build on the indecision Alema had instilled in them, hoping they would conclude that he *wanted* them to retreat.

That was all it took. The Bothan presences grew decisive, and the fans of their turbolaser fire started to expand as they accelerated *toward* the Fifth. Then Caedus's vision closed in, and he felt himself sinking even deeper into his battle meditation, completely through it to a time not long in the future when this war would be over, when the galaxy would be safe and calm, when he would once again have his family and friends there beside him, helping him to rule in justice and peace.

epilogue

"That was the dumbest move I've ever seen," Han declared to anyone listening—which, given his volume, was everyone in the Great Parley Chamber of Tenel Ka's flagship, the *Dragon Queen*. "And I've seen some pretty dumb moves. What in the blazes made you *advance* when Jacen turned on you?"

Admiral Babo's yellow eyes flashed gold, but he accepted the indignity with a polite smile that managed to bare only the tips of his Bothan fangs. Even Han realized that was pretty restrained, given present company. Sitting at the conference table with them were a couple of dozen brass hats from the impromptu coalition that had just tried to blast Jacen into a bad memory.

"We believed it was an Alliance feint," Babo explained, far too patiently to be sincere. "It never dawned on us that he would intend to carry through with such a foolhardy attack."

"It couldn't have been *that* foolhardy—it worked." Like nearly everyone else who had watched Jacen's miraculous escape a few hours earlier, Han was still trying to figure out how the Bothans had let it happen. "All you had to do was fall back! We would've had him trapped."

"Which the enemy certainly realized," Babo replied.

"Your son is a master tactician, Captain Solo. We had to account for that in our thinking."

Han winced inside at the word *son* and felt Leia tense beside him, but neither of them corrected the admiral. Both their sons were dead to them now—but that was a private pain, to be acknowledged only in their solitude aboard the *Falcon*.

Leia laid a calming hand on Han's arm, then said, "Jacen was lucky. He took a gamble, assuming you would over-think the situation, and you did exactly that."

"There may also have been some Force pressure involved," Luke added from the end of the table. With a bruised face, two black eyes, and half a dozen casts and bandages not quite hidden beneath his cloak, he looked like he had actually taken the beating that Leia and Jaina had threatened to give him if he ever faked his death again. "The colonel may be using ancient battle meditation techniques to confuse his opponents."

Babo's ears pricked up. "That would explain a lot," he said. "And it would give the Confederation even more reason to invite Kashyyyk, the Hapan Consortium, and the Jedi Order into our coalition."

Tenel Ka roused herself from her poised silence at the head of the table, then said, "I hope Bothawui hasn't misinterpreted the actions of the Hapan Consortium here today." She had used her Force talents to hide all indication of the tears she had shed after firing on Jacen, but the pain still showed in the restrained quality of her gestures. "In no way do we share or condone the Confederation's recent aggression, and the Galactic Alliance retains our full support."

Babo brought his bushy brows together. "But you *attacked* Colonel Solo."

"Colonel Solo is *not* the Alliance," Tenel Ka replied simply.

"Thank you for clarifying that, Your Majesty." Babo

flattened his ears in disappointment, but he wasted no time in turning to Tojjelnoot, who was sitting at Luke's right. "What about Kashyyyk? The Wookiees have good reason to support the Confederation—as the Confederation supported them."

Tojjelnoot nodded in agreement, then rose and launched into a ten-minute groan in which he thanked each of the Confederation members for coming to Kashyyyk's defense, then promised to repay the debt fivefold. Next, he listed an inventory of reservations about the Confederation's defiance of Alliance law, and suggested that Corellia and Bothawui were both partially responsible for the attack on Kashyyyk because they had caused the war in the first place. He spent another five minutes praising the wisdom of Tenel Ka's decision, but noted that Kashyyyk interests were very different from those of the Consortium. He ended with a long ramble about the wisdom of Master Skywalker, then explained that the Wookiees would like to hear all sides of the argument before making a decision.

Of course, Babo understood none of what Tojjelnoot said and looked to C-3PO for a translation.

"Tojjelnoot thanks admirals Babo, Kre'fey, and For'o and their fleet and the entire Bothan navy for their help today," the droid began, reciting the Wookiee's long speech from memory. "He also thanks Queen Mother Tenel Ka and Prince Isolder—"

Han noticed Babo's eyes glazing over and raised a hand to silence the droid. "Here's the short version," he said. "The Wookiees want to hear what Luke says."

All eyes swung toward Tojjelnoot, who gave a single affirming growl.

"Very well," Babo said. "What *is* the Jedi position?"

Luke thought for a moment, then shifted forward in his chair. "Our position is this: As long as Jacen controls the Alliance, there *is* no Alliance."

Babo's grin spread wide across his face. "So we are in agreement."

"About that much, yes." As Luke said this, he met the gazes of both Han and Leia, silently acknowledging the pain his words were causing them all. "But the Jedi can only support the Confederation if it suspends its aggression into the Core. We can bring Jacen down by more subtle means. Once he's no longer in charge of the Alliance, I'm confident all parties will work out their differences in a more amicable manner."

Babo's grin vanished. "So you would allow the Alliance to regroup?" He shook his head vehemently. "That's unacceptable."

Luke nodded politely and rose. "I thought you might feel that way," he said. "If you'll excuse me, I really should be in the infirmary with my son."

Babo's eyes widened. "You're leaving? Without talking?"

"I've made the Jedi position quite clear," Luke said. "What could there possibly be to talk about?"

Babo snapped his snout shut, and Han realized that the meeting was about to come to a pointless end that would add years to the war. He glanced over at Leia and tipped his head in Luke's direction, scowling for her to do something.

She scowled back. "What do you expect *me* to say?" she whispered. "Luke's the Grand Master. I'm just a Jedi Knight."

Across the table, Babo rose, causing a general stir as the rest of the Confederation officers followed his lead.

"Perhaps you're right, Master Skywalker," the Bothan said. "It appears we truly don't have any interests in common."

"Does that have to make us enemies?" Han asked, pointedly not rising from his chair. "I mean, at least right now?"

Babo's gaze slid over to Han. "Do you have a proposal, Captain Solo?"

"Sure," Han said. "Why don't we just, uh, sort of ignore each other for a while?"

"Ignore?" Babo asked. "That's a vague term, Captain Solo. Vagueness leads to misunderstandings—and misunderstandings have a terrible way of fostering tragedy."

"I think what Han is trying to suggest is that we consider each other neutral," Leia said. "We won't interfere with each other's operations, and we won't have to expend resources watching each other—resources that might be better deployed against Jacen."

Babo nodded. "I'm sure the Confederation would approve of that arrangement. But the Alliance would have to agree not to interfere in *any* of our operations, even those that might be considered . . . *extralegal* by the normal standards of warfare."

"*Extra*legal?" Han asked. "What's *that* supposed to mean?"

"It means the Bothans are sending assassins after Jacen," Leia said, keeping her gaze on Babo. "And they want us to sanction it."

"Your son *did* order the murder of thousands of Coruscanti Bothans," Babo reminded them. "If you're sincere about stopping him, you shouldn't have a problem with that."

Luke glanced at Han and Leia again, his eyes filled with apology and despair. "The Jedi will be pursuing our own plans for Jacen, but if you actually think your assassins can eliminate him, we won't interfere."

Leia nodded. "We won't stop you from trying."

Babo turned to Han. "Captain Solo?"

"Yeah, fine. Just make sure nobody gets caught in the crossfire." Han took Leia's hand and rose. It was one thing to consider Jacen already dead, another to give permission to target him. "Knock yourselves out."

It wasn't until later, after they had left the meeting and rushed back to the *Falcon* to shed their tears in private, that Leia stretched her arms across the galley table and took Han's hands, then asked the question that had been on both their minds since the day they had decided to speak against Jacen at the Rock Council, the question that had been growing more troublesome each time a new outrage compelled them to take a stand against what their son had become.

"Han, what have we done?"

Han slid around and took her in his arms. "The same thing we always have, Princess," he said. "What we had to."

ROUND-ROBIN INTERVIEW

Featuring *Star Wars* Legacy of the Force authors: Aaron Allston (*Betrayal, Exile, Fury*); Karen Traviss (*Bloodlines, Sacrifice, Revelation*); and Troy Denning (*Tempest, Inferno, Invincible*).

Random House: Okay, let's cut to the chase: the death of Mara Jade at the hands of Jacen Solo. Who came up with this idea, and how was it received by everyone in the initial story conferences?

Troy Denning: *That's* your first question? You make us sound like a hit squad.

Aaron Allston: The idea came up at our late 2004 meeting at Big Rock Ranch, but I resist saying who brought up the idea first. I'm not going there.

Karen Traviss: I'm afraid it was me who suggested that Jacen had to kill someone he loved. But I'm the Brit, remember. We're always the bad guys.

AA: The idea was, if I recall correctly, met with mixed feelings. Everybody recognized the dramatic possibilities surrounding Mara's death. But not everybody was happy with the thought of seeing her go.

TD: But there were no fistfights, nothing like a deadlocked jury. We knew the storyline demanded a crisis that would shock Ben to the core and really make him think about what he was becoming. Nobody killed Mara just for the heck of it.

KT: I mentioned a test that the German SS (or it might have been the Gestapo) used: trainees were each given a puppy—a German Shepherd, I think—and were encouraged to bond with the dog, compete it against other cadets' dogs, and generally love it. Then, once they were totally devoted to the dog, they were told to strangle it. If they couldn't obey that order, they were out. I said that would be a typical Sith test—to be so loyal to the Sith ideal that you'd obey orders and kill someone you loved to prove you could put the job first. There's even an allusion to that in *Sacrifice*, where Jacen thinks about the nosito pups.

RH: Given fan response to the deaths of Chewbacca and Anakin, did you feel any hesitation about killing off another popular character?

AA: Definitely. For that reason and others, it's the event I've looked forward to least out of the entire series.

KT: Well, nobody lives forever. In fiction, it's often better that they go out in a blaze of glory than incontinent and senile in the Coruscant Old Folks' Home. Readers are sad to see much-loved characters die—we wouldn't be doing our jobs right if those deaths left them unmoved—but very few fans resort to threats and abuse.

TD: Good stories have tragedy as well as triumph. My first concern when writing is always to build a story that's both suspenseful and logical (so I'd never terminate a character arbitrarily). Overall, the reaction I received after I wrote Anakin's death was fine. People were sad (so was I)—and a few *were* angry—but most readers agreed that Anakin's death was the kind of thing that has made the NJO a powerful and engaging story.

KT: Fiction should make us feel strong emotions. It enables us as readers to "rehearse" difficult emotional events in a safe environment, so deaths in fiction have a real function in human psychology. And, frankly, the idea that heroes can never die isn't good storytelling as far as I'm concerned. If the reader knows nothing can ever happen to them, where's the drama, the risk?

RH: One objection I've heard to the deaths of popular characters is that if readers want realism, they'll pick up a book by Updike. How do you respond to this?

AA: A lot of fans have that reaction, and a lot don't. It's not a universal thing. Those who object to the deaths do tend to be more vocal about it.

TD: You wouldn't be trying to stir up some controversy, would you?

AA: I keenly remember, as a kid, reading a novel about Robin Hood in which he dies. I was shocked. "Robin Hood can't *die*. The story can't *end*." But the truth is, putting characters in danger and then never killing any of them, or at least any of the important ones, robs a series of any tension. Oh, dear, Luke is in danger again, ho-hum.

And sure, we could have tension by threatening to make characters unhappy without actually killing them. But note that I said "putting them in danger." Physical danger, danger of imminent death, has been a part of the *Star Wars* series since *A New Hope*. So either we have characters in danger, and make that danger meaningful, or we don't have danger at all, which constitutes a major change to the way the universe is portrayed.

KT: *Star Wars* is a broad church, and there's plenty of escapist material already out there that folks can read if they want that, but there are also many, many readers who want something that resonates with the issues they face in real life. Like Aaron says, there comes a point where the story gets stale if the protagonists face no real threats and risks.

RH: What were your feelings about the online contest to supply Jacen's Sith name?

TD: I thought the contest was a good idea, a fun twist. Of course, we'll have to see how the fans like the winner they picked.

RH: Luke has gone over to the dark side before. Will Mara's death push him in this direction again?

TD: You must know we can't answer that.

RH: Hey, you can't blame a guy for trying! Come to think of it, Han didn't handle Chewbacca's death very well, either. Knowing that his son has turned to the dark side, and is responsible for the murder of his best friend's wife—it's hard to imagine even Leia being able to hold Han back after that . . .

AA: That's a weird perspective, actually. That's the perspective of someone to whom Luke, a canon character originating in the movies, is far more important than Jacen, an Expanded Universe character. But it makes no sense from Han's perspective. Luke's his best friend. Jacen's his *son*. He loves them both and would be devastated to lose either one. Instead of strapping on his blaster holster and rushing off to shoot his boy, he's got to feel horribly conflicted.

RH: Was Jacen's turn to the dark side something that was only decided with this series, or was it a plot development slated for some time? Is there an "über-plot" stretching far into the future?

AA: As I recall, it was settled upon for this series, though that determination was made early enough that Troy was able to foreshadow it in the Dark Nest trilogy.

TD: Yes, the kernel of the idea occurred to me while I was writing that trilogy, trying to think about what Jacen discovered on his journey to learn more about the Force. When I learned that the editors at Lucasfilm and Del Rey were looking for ideas for the next series, I told them what I'd been thinking about, and it became the seed for Legacy of the Force.

AA: I'm not aware of any über-plot, though. We've coordinated a little bit with the Dark Nest and Legacy series to maintain consistency, but we're not setting up their plotlines in our series.

RH: Is there something about the parenting style of Han and Leia that contributed to the dark path Jacen has taken? Do they bear any of the responsibility?

KT: I wonder if *any* of the Skywalker/ Solo kids had a good upbringing? If Coruscant had a decent social services department, they'd have taken them all into care, I think—the risks they were exposed to as little 'uns were shocking. Ben's found his own way—which isn't easy for him. The offspring of the A-list can go nuts pretty easily trying to live up to legendary parents, as we know in real life.

AA: It's the generation gap, plus lightsabers.

TD: Jacen was captured by the Yuuzhan Vong and brainwashed by Vergere, so he's been through a lot that wasn't his parents' doing. Ultimately, though, the only person responsible for what Jacen has become is Jacen himself.

KT: Right. I agree that his experiences of the Vong with Vergere did freak him, and distorted his perspective on his own fallibility. But Jacen is actually just a very smart guy with an excessively high opinion of himself. Like so many of those in power, especially the most able, he edges toward the bad stuff a slice at a time, and it's all too easily done, all too easy to self-justify. He doesn't start out psychiatrically iffy, but power corrupts and also warps, and there's no doubt that power can seriously unhinge people. But there's no inevitability about any of it: many, many people who undergo terrible trauma and nightmarish family lives don't end up being conniving killers, and sometimes, despite their best efforts, the most decent, responsible parents produce appalling brats. In the end, the only person responsible for what we do is ourselves.

RH: How did you decide the order in which you would write the novels of the Legacy sequence?

AA: Our editors, Shelly Shapiro of Del Rey and Sue Rostoni of Lucas Licensing, decided that.

RH: How involved are Sue and Shelly? And how do the roles of these two editors differ?

AA: They're really involved, very aware of everything going on with the series. And their roles do differ. Shelly is a bit more focused on the writing merits of the novels, the coordination between the writers, the internal logic of the storylines outside the context of the Expanded Universe. Sue is a bit more focused on continuity, on the needs of Lucasfilm, on the meeting of fan expectations and fidelity to the characters. But if these different responsibilities ever put them at odds, well, they've never let *me* see it.

KT: It doesn't matter in how much detail you plan (we do forty-page outlines for each book) and how much you talk to your fellow authors, you can't possibly know everything that the other guys are doing. That's why we need Sue and Shelly. Having two people with a more detached overview, and who aren't writing it and so can see the wood for the trees, is crucial.

TD: They're the grease that gets things moving, and the glue that holds things together. They probably work the hardest to make sure that all the minor-but-inevitable differences of interpretation in our initial story notes get ironed out. It would be hard to overemphasize their role in the series.

RH: How often do you three talk? And do you communicate mainly by phone? E-mail?

KT: E-mail. I'm in the UK in a wholly different time zone, so phone calls aren't convenient, and I like things in a retrievable, checkable format anyway. We have spurts of communication and then go silent for weeks. The books have to be written, after all.

RH: What do you do when disagreements come up?

TD: Luckily, we share a brain, so we all agree. But seriously, it hasn't been a problem.

KT: Everyone's focused on what's best for the series, not individual interests.

RH: How has your understanding of the light and dark sides of the Force changed in the course of writing these books?

KT: Not so much the Force as the nature of Force users. It strikes me as more and more sectarian every day. As Boba says, it's a small religious schismatic war within a tiny unelected elite that drags in trillions of folk. The reader obviously sees most of *Star Wars* with a heavy Jedi perspective, but I'd bet that the average galactic citizen knows no more about the Jedi Council and what it gets up to than most folk in the real world know about the World Bank.

TD: I've always felt that when Yoda taught Luke about the light and dark sides, he was talking about the light and dark sides within ourselves, not in the Force itself.

RH: The Jedi of Yoda's day believed that romantic and family relationships between Jedi could only lead to disaster. Hasn't that view been pretty well borne out by the history of Darth Vader and his children and grandchildren?

AA: I think that the Republic-era Jedi belief that *attachment* leads to disaster is on-target, but I hope we're going to show that not all love matches constitute that sort of attachment. My belief is that any number of Jedi could marry and have kids without invoking tragedy. I think part of the problem is that the Skywalker family is as important as, and about as lucky as, the house of Atreus from Greek mythology. That is to say, they're very important . . . but not very lucky.

KT: No, I'm inclined to think Yoda got it right. Jedi shouldn't be allowed to have families. These people are superweapons, and once they lose the ability to detach—however much moral decline that so-called detachment got them into in the late Republic—then their family feuds will end up dragging in the whole galaxy. The Legacy of the Force saga is basically a family spat involving an ex or two that creates galactic war. Do they see the irony? I don't know. But like all people with vast power and a sense of dynastic entitlement, they take their eye off the ball and—whatever they *think* they're doing—make decisions based on what's good for the people they love, not for the majority. They're only human. Trouble is, their powers and their influence aren't . . .

TD: Let's not forget that a lot of good came from Anakin Skywalker's line: Luke, Leia, Anakin Solo, Jaina . . . We'll have to see about Ben, but even Jacen was responsible for ending the Yuuzhan Vong war.

RH: Each of you is known for creating or enhancing a specific character: Allston—Wedge Antilles; Traviss—Boba Fett; Denning—Alema Rar. It must be a blast to be able to weave them all into Legacy's multi-book tapestry! Are they your favorite characters to write?

TD: I enjoy writing most characters. If I can get inside their heads and really understand what they want and what they're willing to do to get it, then I can connect with them on a subconscious level, and they just come alive inside my head. When that happens, whatever character I'm writing at the moment becomes my favorite.

AA: Wedge is my favorite character, true. I've said in other interviews that he interests me because he's an ethical killer. The killer part isn't that interesting—from that perspective, he's a guy who always has a means, a motive, and an opportunity. No, it's the *ethics* that are interesting, his struggle to make each choice to kill a correct one, one that will not lead those he commands or inspires down some slippery slope. Like the one Jacen is following, for example.

But I enjoy writing a lot of the characters, and I find it creepily easy to slip into Jacen's mindset when writing him. We're not so very different, he and I. Except he's better-looking and has superpowers and is even more evil.

KT: I love writing Boba, and expanding his hideously dysfunctional family and his total alienation from his own culture was right up my street. (And inevitable—I find it amazing that the man is even sane, given his upbringing.) He's incredibly complex, and that means there are plenty of stories to tell about him. But I enjoyed crazy Alema and Lumiya too—it was fascinating to write the scene with them together in *Sacrifice*, especially at how differently they handle disfigurement. I like the challenge of getting into characters I don't know all that well. I think the one I really savored writing was Admiral Niathal, though—no idea why, but when a "hawkish" Mon Cal admiral was mentioned in Aaron's outline for *Betrayal*, I was captivated by the idea and she just rolled out onto the page.

And, sick as it sounds, I enjoyed writing Jacen. I feel better knowing that all those years I spent working with politicians actually came in useful.

RH: Lumiya first appeared in the *Star Wars* comic books, then made the jump over into novels. Whose idea was it to bring her back for this series? How closely integrated into the official *Star Wars* universe is all the old comic-book material? My impression is that in those early days, there was a lot less attention paid to timeline continuity and so forth.

AA: Prior to Lumiya being chosen, we had a character role, Jacen's Sith mentor, who was referred to only as "the wizard." At some point, someone had the idea to make Lumiya into the wizard, and she was a really good fit.

KT: I think it was Sue Rostoni's idea, actually.

AA: Lumiya's presence doesn't mean that every event from the comics can be considered a part of the current EU continuity, however. It just won't all fit.

KT: Continuity is always a challenge in a thirty-year-old franchise, but as long as people stay sensible about it, recognize the constraints and that it won't ever be perfect, and treat it as fiction and not a religion, then we can all have fun. When the continuity matters more than the stories and themes, the saga will be over.

RH: I know you can't give away any spoilers, but maybe some hints about what may lie ahead in the remaining books of the Legacy series?

AA: Hints without spoilers? That's tricky. How about this: "There will be pages. Lots and lots of pages. Most of them will have letters on them, and the vast majority of those letters will be in the Roman alphabet."

Aah. Now I feel better.

TD: You'll definitely see some grand space battles and classic lightsaber duels.

KT: Boba doesn't grow a heart of gold. . . . I can tell you that.

RH: In addition to *Star Wars*, each of you also has his or her own projects. How do you keep the balance?

AA: By working all the time!

KT: I split my time 50/50 over the year between tie-in work and my own copyright novels. I'm pretty dull—I'm a business, and I run on spreadsheets.

TD: I tend to work like crazy on one project, then come up for air and dive into the next one. I've heard of writers who work on two—or even three—books at once. I can't imagine how—when I'm in the middle of a project, I have a hard time thinking about anything else. Phones go unanswered, the mail stacks up, my hair gets long . . .

RH: Troy, you look good with long hair! Thanks to all three of you for taking the time to answer my questions with such patience and good humor—may the Force continue to be with you!

Read on for a sneak preview of Aaron Allston's

FURY

The seventh novel in
the epic new *Star Wars* series!

CHIEF OF STATE'S BRIEFING OFFICE
CORUSCANT

The advisor's voice was like the droning of insects, and Darth Caedus knew what to do about insects—ignore them or step on them.

But in this case, he couldn't afford to ignore the drone. The advisor, whatever her failings as a speaker, was providing him with critical data. Nor could he raise a boot to crush the source of the drone, not with Admiral Cha Niathal, his partner in the coalition government running Coruscant and the Galactic Alliance, sitting on the other side of the table, not with aides hovering and holocam recorders running.

To make matters worse, the advisor would soon wrap up, and inevitably she would address him by the name he so disliked, the name he'd been born with, the name he would soon abandon. And then he would once again feel, and have to resist, the urge to crush her.

She did it. The blue-skinned Omwati female, her feathery hair dyed a somber black and her naval uniform freshly pressed, looked up from her datapad. "In conclusion, Colonel Solo—"

Caedus gestured to interrupt her. "In conclusion, the withdrawal of the entire Hapan fleet from Alliance forces removes at least twenty percent of our naval strength and puts us into a game of withdrawal and entrenchment if we are to keep the Confederation from overrunning us. And the treachery of the Jedi in abandoning us at Kuat is further causing a loss of hope among the segments of the population who believe that their involvement means something."

"Yes, sir."

"Thank you. That will be all."

She rose, saluted, and left silently, her posture stiff. Caedus knew she feared him, that she had been struggling to maintain her composure all through the briefing, and he approved. Fear in subordinates meant instant compliance and extra effort on their part.

Usually. Sometimes it meant treachery.

Niathal addressed the other aides present. "We are done here. Thank you."

When the office door *whoosh*ed closed behind the last of them, Caedus turned to Niathal. The Mon Calamari, her white admiral's uniform almost gleaming, sat silently, regarding him. The stare from her bulbous eyes was no more forbidding than usual, but Caedus knew the message that they held: *You could fix this mess by resigning.*

But those were not her words. "You do not look well." Hers was the gravelly voice so common to her species, and in it there was none of the sympathy that Admiral Ackbar could project. Niathal was not expressing concern for his health. She was suggesting he was not fit for duty.

And she was almost right. Caedus hurt everywhere. Mere days before, he had waged the most ferocious, most terrible lightsaber duel of his life. In a secret chamber aboard his Star Destroyer, the *Anakin Solo,* he had been torturing Ben Skywalker to harden the young man's spirit, to better prepare Ben for life as a Sith. But he had been caught by Ben's father, Luke Skywalker.

That fight . . . Caedus wished he had a holorecording of it. It had gone on for what had felt like forever. It had been brutal, with the advantage being held first by Luke, then by Caedus, in what he knew had been brilliant demonstrations of lightsaber technique, of raw power within the Force, of subtle Jedi and Sith skills. For all his pain, Caedus felt a swelling of pride—not just that he had survived that duel, but that he had waged it so well.

At the end, Caedus had lost a position of advantage—Luke had slipped free of the poison-injecting torture vines with which Caedus had been strangling him—when Ben had driven a vibroblade deep into Caedus's back, punching clean through a shoulder blade, nearly reaching his heart.

That had ended the fight. Caedus should have been killed immediately. For reasons he did not understand, Luke and Ben had spared his life and departed. It was a mistake that would cost Luke.

Bearing dozens of minor and major wounds, including the vibroblade puncture, a lightsaber-scored kidney, and a fierce scalp wound, Caedus had been treated and resumed command of the *Anakin Solo,* only to experience more injury—emotional injury, this time. In Kashyyyk space, his Fifth Fleet had been surrounded by Confederation forces. Late-arriving Hapan forces could have rescued him . . . but the Hapan Queen Mother, Tenel Ka, his comrade and lover, had betrayed him. Swayed by the treacherous persuasion of Caedus's own parents, Han and Leia Solo, she had demanded a price for her continued military support of the Alliance, and that price had been his surrender.

Of course he had refused. And, of course, he had battered his way out of the encirclement, leading the remnants of the Fifth Fleet back to the safety of Coruscant.

So when Niathal said he did not look well, she was correct. He keenly felt his worst injury. Not the vibroblade wound, not the scalp tear, not the kidney damage—all three were healing. All three were the kind of pain that strengthened him.

It was the wound to his heart that plagued him. Tenel Ka had turned on him. Tenel Ka, the love of his life, the mother of his daughter Allana, had forsaken him.

Niathal's severe expression stayed on him. *You could fix this mess by resigning.*

He gave her a tight smile. "Thank you for your concern, but I'm recovering quickly. And I have a plan. We'll need to follow the recommended protocol of a fighting retreat for the next few days . . . at which time the Hapans will come back into the war on our side. Our job today is to figure out how best to employ them when they return to the battlefield. Since the Confederation thinks they are staying on the fence, we can utilize the Hapans for one devastating surprise attack. We need to decide where that attack will take place."

"You are sure the Hapans will rejoin us."

"I guarantee it. I have an operation in motion that will ensure it."

"What resources do you need to carry it out?"

"Only those I already have."

"Have I seen details of your operation?"

Caedus shook his head. "If I don't forward a file, no one can intercept it. If I don't speak a word of detail, no one can overhear it. Too much is riding on getting the Hapans back for me to wreck things by divulging details too freely."

Niathal remained silent. A more incendiary personality would have taken offense at Caedus's implied questioning of her ability to handle secret matters. Niathal chose not to recognize it as an insult. She merely turned to the next matter on her agenda. "Speaking of secrets . . . Belindi

Kalenda at Intelligence reports that Doctor Seyah has been pulled off the Centerpoint Station project. Seyah reported that he had come under suspicion of being a GA spy."

"Which, of course, he is. What's his new posting, and can he get us any useful information from there?"

Niathal shook her head in the slow, somber way of the Mon Cals. "Kalenda ordered him out. He is already back on Coruscant."

Caedus resisted the urge to break something. "She's an idiot. And Seyah is an idiot. He could have stayed, weathered whatever investigation they brought against him, and begun feeding us information again."

"Kalenda was certain that he would be arrested, investigated, and executed."

"Then he should have stayed in place until arrested! Who knows what his cowardice has cost us? Even reporting on ship and troop movements could provide us with the critical advantage in a battle." Caedus sighed and pulled out his datapad. Snapping it open, he typed a brief note to himself.

Niathal rose and leaned over so that her bulbous eyes could peer, upside down, at his screen. "What is this?"

"A note to myself to have Seyah arrested. He provided Kalenda with false information that led her to extract him from a danger zone, which is the equivalent of desertion under fire. He will confess. He will be executed."

"Ah." Niathal resumed her seat, but offered no protest.

Caedus appreciated that. Niathal was clearly growing to understand that Caedus's approach was best—it kept subordinates motivated, kept dead wood out of the ranks. "What next?"

"Bimmisaari and some of her allied worlds in the Halla Sector just announced they were defecting to the Confederation."

Caedus shook his head dismissively. "Not a significant loss."

"No, but it's more unsettling as the possible first sign of a trend. Intelligence has detected more communications traffic between Corellia and the Imperial Remnant, and between Corellia and the worlds of the Corporate Sector, which may be nothing more than an increased recruitment effort by the Confederation. Or it may have been initiated by the other parties, a prelude to negotiations and more defections."

"Also irrelevant." Caedus felt a flash of irritation. Yes, these were matters that the co-Chiefs of State needed to address, but they would all be resolved when the Hapes Consortium came back into the fold. "Anything else?"

"No."

"Excellent."

When the meeting was done and Niathal had departed, Caedus remained in the office. He stared at the blank walls. They soothed him. He needed soothing.

Inside, he was ablaze with anger, resentment, a sense of betrayal—all the emotions that fueled a Sith.

In the days since his fight with Luke, he had come to the realization that he was all alone in the universe. It was like the plaintive wail of a five-year-old: "Nobody loves me." He could manage a smile at just how self-pitying it sounded.

But it was true. Everyone who had once known love for him now hated him. His father and mother, his twin Jaina, Tenel Ka, Luke, Ben . . . Intellectually, as he had embraced the Sith path, he had known that it would happen. One by one, those who cared about him would be peeled away like the outer layers of his skin, leaving him a mass of bloody, agonized nerves.

He had known it . . . but experiencing it was another

matter. His body might be healing, but his spirit was in greater pain every day.

Everyone he had loved now hated him . . . except Allana. And he would not allow Tenel Ka to turn his daughter against him. He would cut down anyone who stood between him and his child.

Anyone.

Years earlier, before Jacen Solo had been born—before, in fact, Luke and Leia knew they were siblings, before Leia had confessed even to herself that she was in love with Han—Yoda had told Luke that electrical shocks, applied at different intensities and at irregular but frequent intervals, would prevent a Jedi from concentrating, from channeling the Force. They could render a Jedi helpless.

But Yoda had never told Luke that emotional shocks could do the same thing.

They could. And just as no amount of self-control would allow a Jedi to ignore the effects of electrical shocks on his body, neither could self-control keep Luke safely out of his memories. Every few moments a memory, freshly applied like a current-bearing wire on his skin, would yank him out of the here and now and propel him into the recent past.

Boarding the *Anakin Solo*. Finding Jacen torturing—*torturing*—his son Ben. The duel that followed, Luke against the nephew he'd once loved . . . the nephew who now commanded Master-level abilities in the Force, though he had not been, and never would be, elevated to the rank of Jedi Master.

And no pain Luke suffered in that fight was equal to Ben demanding the right to finish Jacen. That demand had brought Luke to where he was now, sitting cross-legged on the floor of an upper-story room of an abandoned Imperial outpost, staring through a wide transparisteel viewport at a lush Endor forest he was barely aware of, his body healing but his spirit sick and injured even after all these days.

Shocked almost beyond understanding by Ben's blood thirst, Luke had prevented his son from executing a death blow against Jacen. Nor had Luke chosen to finish Jacen himself. He had led Ben in sudden flight from the *Anakin Solo*—a flight to prevent Ben from taking the next, possibly irreversible, step toward the dark side that Jacen had planned for the boy.

But was it the right decision? At that moment, it had seemed like the only possible choice. Ben's future, his decency, had teetered in the balance. Had either Skywalker killed Jacen, Ben would have fallen toward the dark side.

Some people came back from the dark side. Luke had. Others didn't. Ben becoming a lifelong agent of evil had not been a certainty.

What was certain was that Jacen was alive. And now, as Jacen furthered his plans for galactic conquest, more people would die. They would die by the thousands at least, probably by the tens or hundreds of thousands, perhaps by the millions.

And Luke would be responsible.

So had it been the right decision? Ben against thousands of lives?

Logic said no—no, *unless* in falling to the dark side, Ben became as great a force for evil as Jacen Solo was or their mutual grandfather, Anakin Skywalker, Darth Vader, had been.

Emotion said yes—yes, *unless* Ben interpreted Luke's refusal to kill as a sign of weakness, and that decision fostered contempt in him, contempt for Luke and the light side of the Force. That could push him along Jacen's path in spite of Luke's intent.

And either way, those thousands would die.

A translucent white rectangle, tall and very thin, appeared on the viewport ahead of Luke. It rapidly broadened, revealing itself as the reflection of a door opening in the wall behind Luke. Jedi Master Kyp Durron stood in the doorway, his brown robes rumpled, his long graying-brown hair sweaty and unkempt. His expression, normally one of mild amusement over what was usually interpreted as a trace of cockiness, was now more somber—neutrality concealing concern. "Grand Master?"

"Come in." Luke did not turn to face Kyp. The view of Endor's wilderness was soothing.

Kyp moved in and the door shut behind him, eliminating the illuminated rectangle from Luke's field of vision. "The door chimes do not appear to be working on this passageway, and you were not responding to your comlink . . ."

Luke frowned. "I didn't hear it. Maybe the battery is dry." He pulled his comlink from the tunic of his white Tatooine-style work suit. The ready light on the small cylindrical object was still lit. A quick examination showed that the device had been shut off. Puzzled, Luke turned it on again and tucked it away.

"Just a routine report. The StealthXs are spread, by wingpairs, across a broad area, under camouflage netting. Many of the pilots found useful landing spots in areas where debris from the second Death Star came down and created burn zones. The younglings are packed into two large chambers, acting as dormitories, on this outpost, but a reconnaissance team of Knights has found a cavern system not too far away that will provide ample space for a training facility . . . and some defense against orbital sensors. The Knights are clearing out a nest of rearing spiders there. Once they're certain the spiders and their eggs are all gone, we'll begin transferring the younglings."

"Good."

"Otherwise, we seem to be dealing well with the local Ewoks."

"Any we know?"

"No . . . the Wicket family group's territory is still limited to areas south of here. But your idea of bringing in Threepio as an interpreter is paying off. The local clan seems to like him."

"Good."

Kyp did not immediately reply, so Luke turned to give him a look. The younger Master seemed to be pondering his next words. Luke cocked an eyebrow at him. "Anything else?"

"There's been some question about our next action against Jacen."

"Ah, yes." Luke turned to look out the viewport again. "I don't know. Why don't you arrange that?"

There was a long silence, then: "Yes, Grand Master."

The rectangle of light reappeared. Kyp's reflection moved into it and it closed again, leaving Luke in silence and peace.

And confronted by the memory of Jacen, bloodied and battered almost beyond recognition, crawling away from him, Ben's vibroblade lodged in his back. Ben's face appeared before him, mouthing the words, *This kill is mine.*

Luke shivered.

STAR WARS®

LEGACY OF THE FORCE

Read each book in the series

   www.legacyoftheforce.com

A long time ago in a galaxy far, far away. . . .

STAR WARS

HE WILL JOIN
US OR DIE,
MY MASTER.